The Truth Is the Light

Also by Vanessa Davis Griggs

Forever Soul Ties
Redeeming Waters
Ray of Hope

The Blessed Trinity Series

The Other Side of Dare
The Other Side of Goodness
The Truth Is the Light
Goodness and Mercy
Practicing What You Preach
If Memory Serves
Strongholds
Blessed Trinity

Chapter 1

The stone which the builders refused is become
the head stone of the corner.

—Psalm 118:22

"Crown me!" said the ninety-nine-year-old man with dark chocolate skin, who didn't look a day over seventy. He sat back against the flowery-cushioned chair and folded his arms, all while displaying a playful grin.

"Crown you?" said a matched-in-tone thirty-five-year-old, resembling a slimmed-down teddy bear as he shook his head while mirroring the old man's grin. "*Crown* you?"

"That's what I just said, so quit stalling and get to crowning me."

The younger man first started to chuckle before it turned into a refrained laugh. "Gramps, I've told you twice already: We're playing chess, not checkers. The rules are different. There's no crowning a piece when it reaches the other side, not in chess."

"You say that there is my queen, right?" Gramps touched the game piece that represented his queen.

"Yes."

"Well, if there's a queen, then there's *got* to be a king with some real power a lot closer and, frankly, better than this joker here." He touched his king. "So quit bumping your gums and crown me so I can get some real help in protecting my queen." Gramps nodded, proudly flaunting his new set of dentures, as he grinned at his favorite grandson.

Clarence Walker couldn't do anything but smile and shake his head in both amusement and adoration. "I've told you. Because there's already a king on the board"—he pointed to the king—"we don't crown in chess. Just admit it. You don't really want to learn how to play chess, do you? That's why you're acting this way."

"I tried to tell you from the git-go that I'm a checkers man and strictly a checkers man. When you get my age, it's hard for an old dog to learn new tricks. I know how to fetch. I know how to roll over and even play dead. But all this fancy stuff like walking on your hind legs and twirling around . . . Well, you can take that to some young pup eager to learn. Teach the young pups this stuff. With checkers: I move, I jump, and I get crowned when I reach the other side. Just like Heaven." He pointed his index finger and circled it around the board. "I get enough kings, I set you up, trap you, wipe the board with you, and like normal—game over." Gramps stroked his white, trimmed beard.

Gramps was on a roll now. "All this having to re-member pawns, knights, rooks, and bishops, which di-rection each moves in, how many spaces they can move when they move . . . I ain't got time for all of that. Then to have a king that's less powerful than his queen? Check and checkmate? Nope, I can't get with that. You know what your problem is, don't you? You don't like me whuppin' up on you like I normally do. You're trying to find somethin' that'll confuse old Gramps. Now is that check or checkmate?"

"No, Gramps. I'm merely trying to help keep you sharp. That's all. Studies show that when you do something new and different, it exercises your brain. You *do* know that your brain is a muscle, so it needs working out just like the rest of your body does."

"Humph!" Gramps said. "If I was any sharper, merely passing by me too closely would cut you." Gramps sensed his grandson had something on his mind he wanted to talk about other than chess. Gramps leaned forward and placed his elbows on the table as he put his clasped hands underneath his chin. "Okay, so what's going on with you?"

Clarence sat back and became more serious. "Gramps, I'm getting baptized this coming Sunday night. I gave my life to Christ . . . for real this time. It wasn't just going forward to shake a preacher's hand like when I was twelve and my daddy made me do it to get it over with. Do you think you'd care to come and see me be baptized on Sunday?"

A smile crept over the old man's face as he leaned back against his seat. "So you done finally seen the light, huh?"

"Yeah, Gramps. I've finally seen the light. And I'm not running from the Lord anymore. Something happened to me on Sunday. I can't explain everything about it. But I know that the same man that walked into that building is not the same man that walked out. Something changed on the inside of me; it was an inside job. *I* see a difference."

The old man nodded. "Oh, you preaching to the choir now. I understand exactly how you feel. I ran from the Lord for a long time myself, both physically and figuratively." Gramps readjusted his slender body more comfortably. "I know your mama is happy about all of this. My baby girl has been doing some kind of praying for you, yes, she has. And knowing your daddy like I do, I'm sure he acted like the father of the biblical Prodigal Son who finally returned home after wallowing for a time in a pigsty."

"Mom is *too* excited. She kept grabbing my face and pressing it in like she used to when I was a little boy. Like she wanted to be certain that I was really real—that it was actually me she was talking to and not some dream or figment of her imagination. Now, Dad, on the other hand, probably would have been happy had I done this at *his* church."

Gramps leaned in. "Hold up there, whippersnapper. You mean to tell me you were somewhere else when this miraculous conversion occurred? You telling me this didn't take place at your daddy's church?"

"No, Gramps. It didn't happen at my daddy's church."

"Well, look out below! I'm sure *that* went over like a boulder falling off a tall building in New York City during lunchtime."

"You know my daddy."

"Yeah. Me, of all people, knows your daddy. Not one of my favorite folks in the world, that's for sure. No need in me trying to pretend he and I are bosom buddies, especially not after the way he treated my daughter. But Clarence, your father did give us you and your older brother, Knowledge. So I don't count him being in her life *all* bad."

Clarence tried to force a smile. "I told him about me being saved and about my scheduled baptism for Sunday. I asked him to come."

Gramps scratched his head. "You don't even have to

tell how *that* conversation went. To him, you getting saved—and in another preacher's house at that—had to be the ultimate openhanded slap to his face. In his super-religious eyes, you are officially and publicly humiliating him. And everybody who's anybody knows your father loves the spotlight and equally detests being disgraced—intentional, accidental, or otherwise."

"That's the part of this that I don't understand. The greater point should be that I've repented of my sins and that I'm changing my ways. What difference does it make where it happened and with whom, as long as it happened? Daddy took it like I was deliberately trying to make him look bad . . . like I was purposely trying to embarrass him by getting saved under another pastor's leadership instead of his. But I heard God speak to my heart just as clearly. And in that moment, I knew I had to move right then and there. I realized where I end up spending my eternity depended on my receiving Jesus."

Gramps picked up his bishop off the chessboard and held it up. He began to make air circles with it. "Are you following what God is telling you to do?" he asked.

"Yes, sir."

"Then Clarence Eugene Walker, in the end, that's all that really matters." Gramps set the bishop back in the same spot he'd picked it up from with a deliberate thud. "Marshall Walker ain't got no Heaven nor a Hell to put nobody in. 'Cause the Lord knows, if he had, I'da been in need of an eternal air conditioner ages ago. In fact, on more than a few occasions Marshall has flat out told me which of the two places I could go, and believe me, it wasn't Heaven. But"—Gramps smiled—"as you can clearly see, I ignored both him and his hearty request. That's what *you* gonna have to do if your father is bothering you about this. Don't let him get you off track, you hear." Gramps struggled somewhat as he made his way to his feet with a slight assistance from his grandson.

"I'm all right," Gramps said, asserting his independence to get up without help. "I've told you I can stand up fine. It just takes me a little longer to get my motor started, that's all. Eventually, I get it going, then watch out." He looked at Clarence, now shaking his head and grinning. Gramps nodded. "You can come pick me up Sunday evening," Gramps said as they left the activity room of the nursing home that he had called home for the past year. "If the Lord be willing and the creek don't rise, I'll be here waiting on you. There's nothing I'd love more than to see you be baptized." Gramps beamed.

They walked to Gramps's room. Inside, Gramps started grinning like a Cheshire cat as he looked down at Clarence's attaché case. "So, did you bring my stuff? I don't want you conveniently leaving here without giving it to me. I might be old, but as I just told you, my mind is still sharp. I ain't forgot, in case you're counting on me forgetting."

"Gramps, you and I both know I shouldn't be doing this."

"Boy, what did I tell you? I'm grown . . . past grown, in case you've failed to notice. Now, did you bring my stuff in that fancy case of yours or not?" Gramps gingerly sat in the tan leather recliner with a built-in massager his daughter, Zenobia, had given him Father's Day. He reached over and turned on the blue retro-styled radio, a modern-day replica of a 1950s automobile engine, that sat on his dresser. "Stand by Me" by Ben E. King was playing. Gramps closed his washed-out, brown eyes and began to sway as he softly sang—his voice as strong as when he was twenty and just as smooth and calming as milk chocolate. There was no question where Clarence had inherited his singing voice.

"Now, that's some real singing right there," Gramps said as the song trailed off. "Ben E. King, Nat King Cole, Otis Redding, Sam Cooke, Mahalia Jackson, Bessie Smith, Josephine Baker, Billie Holiday, Sarah Vaughan, Marvin Gaye, Aretha Franklin, Frankie, Ella, and Lena. And those are just a fraction of some of the greats of my time." Gramps held out a hand to let Clarence know he was still waiting on his "stuff."

Clarence opened his black case. "Gramps, we have some great singers in our time, too. Stevie Wonder, Michael Jackson, Patti LaBelle, Janet Jackson, Beyoncé, Mariah Carey, Alicia Keys, Vickie Winans, Ms. Tramaine Hawkins, goodness! Smokie, Donnie, Kirk, Yolanda, Babyface, Raheem, Whitney, Celine . . . don't get me started." Clarence pulled out a blue insulated lunch box. "Then there are groups like Earth, Wind and Fire and En Vogue, who I hear are back." Clarence handed the lunch box to Gramps. "Here. But I want to go on record that I don't feel right about this. I just want you to know."

Gramps unzipped the lunch box, looked inside, and began to grin as he pulled out its content as though the wrong move might cause it to explode. "Ah," he said, placing the still warm, wax-paper-wrapped item up to his nose. He inhaled slowly and deeply, then exhaled with a sound of delight. The smoky aroma escaped into the room. "Just the way I like it, wax paper and all."

Clarence nodded. "Yeah, three rib bones with extra barbecue sauce, the sweet not vinegar kind, between two slices of white bread, wrapped in your favorite

BBQ Joint's signature paper." Clarence shook his head. "You *know* you're not supposed to have that."

"Yeah, well, you just make sure you keep your mouth closed about this. Don't tell your mother and we'll be fine. She's the only one trying to keep me from my barbecue rib sandwiches. Like I got these teeth, which incidentally cost a pretty penny, merely for show. Waste not, want not—I'm putting these bad boys to work." He clacked his teeth together. "You're a good grandson, Clarence. You really are. Now sing that song I love."

"You mean the one by Douglas Miller? 'My Soul Has Been Anchored'?"

"Yeah, that's the one." Gramps placed the sandwich on the dresser and handed the now-empty lunch box back to Clarence.

Clarence put the lunch box back in his attaché case, then began to sing—holding back his full voice so as not to disturb any neighboring or passing residents of the home.

Gramps closed his eyes briefly as he seemed to take in every note and every word with a metronome-like tick-tock of his head. When Clarence sang the final note, Gramps opened his teary eyes and nodded. "Yes," he said, pumping an open hand upward, "*my* soul's been anchored"—he swung a fisted hand while smiling—"in the Lord!"

Clarence nodded, hugged his grandfather, told him that he loved him, then left.

Chapter 2

If thieves came to thee, if robbers by night, (how art thou cut off!) would they not have stolen till they had enough? if the grape gatherers came to thee, would they not leave some grapes?

—Obadiah 5

Monday night, twenty-seven-year-old Gabrielle Mercedes and thirty-year-old Zachary Wayne Morgan were in Gabrielle's kitchen cooking fajitas. They'd gone to a highly acclaimed play Sunday night and had a wonderful time. Few Broadway plays made their way to Birmingham, Alabama, whenever those plays happened to travel outside of New York. Afterward, Zachary surprised Gabrielle with tickets to The Color Purple scheduled for the BJCC Concert Hall in October. Gabrielle couldn't believe that after all these years of wanting to, she was finally going to see this Broadway hit.

The doorbell rang. Gabrielle glanced at the digital clock on the stove. "I wonder who that could be." She cut the heat on the gas burner to simmer and rinsed her hands at the sink, drying them on the large dish towel she kept draped across the oven door handle for just that purpose.

"I got this," Zachary said, turning the heat back to medium as he took over stirring the rectangular strips of marinated steak in the large cast-iron skillet with plans to add fresh sliced red, yellow, and orange sweet peppers and red onions at the very end to maintain the vegetables' firmness. The doorbell rang again, this time repeatedly.

When Gabrielle saw who was standing there pressing the doorbell, she practically yanked her front door open.

"Well, it took you long enough," Aunt Cee-Cee said as she fanned her face with her right hand and stepped inside. "You must have been in the bathroom or something."

Cecelia Murphy was Gabrielle's aunt on her father's side. She'd taken Gabrielle in—raised her since she was three (close to four) years old after her mother was killed and her father convicted of her murder and sentenced to twenty-five years in prison.

"No. But I *was* busy. I have company in case you didn't notice the car parked outside when you pulled up," Gabrielle said, trying hard not to show her frustration.

"You mean that black two-thousand-and-something Lincoln Town Car? I just thought you'd bought yourself another vehicle." Aunt Cee-Cee tilted her head back, nose up. "What's that I smell? Smells like it's coming from the kitchen?" She started walking in the direction of the scent. "It smells like someone's sautéing onions and peppers."

"We're making fajitas," Gabrielle said, still holding the opened door, since she hadn't asked her aunt to come in. She was now hurriedly trying to figure out what she needed to do to lure her aunt back toward her and out of the door.

"Well, it smells to me like I have fantastic timing," Aunt Cee-Cee said as she continued, undeterred, toward the kitchen. Gabrielle closed the front door and hurried to catch up with her uninvited, unwelcome, and undeniably unpredictable guest.

"Seriously, Aunt Cee-Cee, this really isn't a good time right now—"

Aunt Cee-Cee stepped into the kitchen and saw Zachary just as he was turning off the burner and lifting up the large, cast-iron skillet. He raked a little of the steak, onions, and colored peppers mixture onto a flat flour tortilla.

"Well, hello there," Aunt Cee-Cee said as she walked toward Zachary. "Well, well, aren't you something? You must be the Handsome Chef." She let out a slight chuckle. "There's the Iron Chef. So I can only conclude you *have to be* the Handsome Chef who makes house calls." She scanned him from his head to his chest as she smiled.

Zachary looked at Gabrielle, who now stood next to the frumpy-looking visitor.

Zachary set the skillet back down on the stove. "No, but I thank you for the compliment. I'm Gabrielle's friend, Zachary Morgan."

"I'm Cecelia Murphy"—she extended a hand—"Gabrielle's aunt. But everybody calls me Cee-Cee."

Zachary quickly wiped his hand on the towel and shook Aunt Cee-Cee's outstretched hand. "All right then, Cee-Cee. It's a pleasure to meet you."

"Ah, that's what you say now. Give it some time." Aunt Cee-Cee laughed, then hopped up on a bar stool at the kitchen counter. "That sure does look good. I'm *starving.* Gabrielle, why don't you fix me one of those things Zachary's making. Oh, and can you get me something cold to drink? I need to wet my throat." She fanned her face again with her hand. "You wouldn't happen to have a beer or wine cooler around here, would you?"

"No, I wouldn't." Gabrielle's response was stern and cold.

"I would be glad to go and get you something," Zachary said, obviously wanting to make a good first impression. "There's a Quik Mart about five miles from here—"

"You don't have to do that," Gabrielle said before Zachary could finish his sentence. "I have something to drink in the refrigerator. She can drink one of those." Gabrielle turned and looked squarely at Aunt Cee-Cee. "Besides, she'll not be staying long enough for you to go get anything and make it back."

Aunt Cee-Cee glared at Gabrielle only briefly before she broke her stare with a warm (though obviously phony) smile. "Gabrielle's right. I won't be here that long. So"—Aunt Cee-Cee turned her attention back to Zachary—"are the two of you dating?"

Neither Gabrielle nor Zachary answered.

"I said, are you two dating?"

"Yes," Zachary said when he realized Gabrielle wasn't planning on answering the question. "But we're actually calling it courting." He couldn't hold back his own blush.

"Courting? Oh, how cute! You don't hear that word much these days. I suppose it's better than wham, bam, thank you, ma'am." Aunt Cee-Cee slid down off the bar stool and sat in a chair at the glass-top kitchen table. She looked at Gabrielle, her way of letting her niece know that she was still waiting on both her food and drink.

"Gabrielle is a special woman. We want to do things right," Zachary said. He looked at Gabrielle once more, who still hadn't moved to get her aunt a plate or beverage.

"So, Mister Handsome Chef, what do you do for a living?"

"I'm a d—"

"Aunt Cee-Cee, why don't I fix your fajita to go?" Gabrielle promptly went and picked up the plate with the fajita Zachary had already begun making.

Aunt Cee-Cee fastened her gaze on Gabrielle like a laser. "Because I'm not going yet. And honestly, the quicker I get something to eat, the quicker I'll get out of here. I'm hungry, and I don't care to eat while I drive. Like texting, it's dangerous to drive and eat. In fact, there should be a law against both." Aunt Cee-Cee softened her face with a smile.

After rinsing her hands, Gabrielle hurried to finish rolling the fajita for her aunt.

"Now," Aunt Cee-Cee said, turning her full attention once more toward Zachary. "You were saying. What is it you do for a living? Because I hope you know I wouldn't want my niece, who's like a daughter to me . . . raised her myself, hanging out with no scrub. That's what they call a guy without a job who lives off others, right? A scrub."

Zachary laughed a little. "Well, you know, you might call me a scrub."

Aunt Cee-Cee pulled her body back and placed her right hand over her heart.

"Hold up," Zachary said with a chuckle. "Before you conclude that I'm not good enough for your niece, allow me to clarify. I'm a doctor. In my line of work, I wash my hands a lot, a whole lot. So technically speaking that makes me somewhat of a scrub."

"A doctor." Aunt Cee-Cee's words were flirty and sweet. "Oh, my goodness. Mercy me. My Gabrielle is courting a *doctor*, a real doctor. Well, isn't that something." She smiled at Gabrielle before turning back to Zachary. "What type of doctor are you?"

"A burn specialist. I specialize mainly in burn victims, although lately I've been spending my time equally in the emergency room when I've been needed."

"A multitasker," Aunt Cee-Cee said. "Gabrielle, why haven't you called and told any of us that you're courting a *doctor?*"

Gabrielle set down the plate with the fajita and a can of Pepsi in front of her aunt. "The last few times I've phoned, you haven't taken or returned my calls," Gabrielle said.

Aunt Cee-Cee eyed the can. "You got Coca-Cola instead of Pepsi? I prefer Coke."

"All I have is Pepsi. But I can give you water if you'd prefer that. Water is wet." Gabrielle smiled, knowing full well her aunt never drank water, not even with medicine.

"Oh, no. Pepsi is fine. I was just asking. I think somewhere in the Bible it says we don't have because we don't ask." Aunt Cee-Cee picked up her fajita and took a cautious bite. "This is really good," she said. "Handsome Chef, you're a great cook. The meat is so tender and moist and has such a marvelous flavor." She took a bigger bite.

"Actually, Gabrielle did all the work. The tender and taste is from the marinade. Lime juice breaks down the meat to make it tender and give it that flavor. She marinated it overnight. I merely stirred and added the vegetables when she went to open the door."

"I'm sure you're giving Gabrielle way too much credit. I'm willing to bet you did a lot more than you're letting on. The peppers and onions are perfect." She took another bite, then opened her can of soda. A hissing sound escaped when the top popped. "Aren't you two going to eat before it gets cold? It's really delicious." She smacked as she spoke.

Gabrielle was about to say something when Zachary moved over to her, put his arm around her shoulders, and pulled her in close. "We *like* ours cold," he said.

"Suit yourself," Aunt Cee-Cee said. When she finished that one, she asked for another. She chatted on about how terrible things were at their house financially and her not knowing what they were going to do as she woofed down a third fajita. She then asked for yet another one. "Oh, but could you wrap that one up for me as a to-go?" she said. "Those are *so* good." She licked her fingers, then wiped her mouth with a napkin.

Both Gabrielle and Zachary looked at what remained in the skillet. Originally, there had been enough for them to have at least two full fajitas each. Aunt Cee-Cee had eaten three and was asking for one more. If they made her the one she was asking for now, there would only be enough left for one fajita. Gabrielle made the last two fajitas and gave them both to her aunt.

"Oh, aren't you the sweetest thing!" Aunt Cee-Cee said when Gabrielle handed her the wrapped fajitas. "Would you mind putting them in a bag for me? And if it's not too much to ask, would you put two cans of soda in the bag as well? Your uncle Bubba will need something to wash his fajita down with." Aunt Cee-Cee stood up as she waited on Gabrielle to finish.

Gabrielle put the fajitas and drinks in a grocery bag and walked her to the door.

"I'll call you later tonight," Aunt Cee-Cee said. Then she whispered, "Is the doctor spending the night tonight?"

"No, Aunt Cee-Cee. We won't be doing things like that. There'll be none of that."

"You mean he's not spending the night right now. But you don't mean you're not planning on doing *anything* with that man until or unless you get married, now, do you?"

"You mean sex before marriage . . . fornicating?"

"Well, you don't have to be so graphic about it. But, yes, that's exactly what I mean. Listen, honey, you don't need to let a man like him get away. That's a real catch you have in there." She tilted her head in the direction of the kitchen.

"Aunt Cee-Cee, I'm a Christian now. I told you that. I gave my life to the Lord. God frowns on fornication. Zachary and I agreed we want to do things God's way, and only His way. And that means keeping ourselves pure until we're married to whomever."

Aunt Cee-Cee started laughing. It sounded more like an animal in severe pain than human. "Yeah, well, trust me. I know plenty of Christians, and being a Christian doesn't seem to be stopping most of them from fornicating or committing adultery. I'll tell you this: You'd better take care of that man and his needs or he'll find someone who will. Take it from Aunt Cee-Cee; I know how men can be. Sure, in the beginning they'll tell you they're in total agreement about something like being chaste. But men are wired totally different from women. Men don't need as much emotional bonding as we do to move to the next level. That man is tall, light-skinned enough, handsome, can cook, or at least will pick up a spoon and help out, he has a job, *and* he's a doctor to boot. Oh, you'd *better* at least let him sample the cake batter and not have to wait for the baked cake."

"Good night, Aunt Cee-Cee." Gabrielle opened the front door.

"I'm going to call you either later tonight or tomorrow. Better yet, why don't you just call me when you're free so I won't interrupt anything. You'd best heed what I just said. Call me, now. I have something I *desperately* need to talk to you about. It's important, so don't take long in getting back with me. It can't wait any longer than a day."

Gabrielle mustered up one more smile. "Good night," she said.

After Aunt Cee-Cee left, Gabrielle closed the door. She stood there for a few minutes, her forehead resting softly on the door as she quietly listened for her aunt's car to crank. Hearing the car drive away, she exhaled slowly.

"Wow, what a character," Zachary said.

Jarred slightly by Zachary's presence, Gabrielle turned around and forced herself to smile yet again. "Oh, you don't *even* know the half of it."

"Just from those thirty-five minutes, I believe I received a pretty good introduction," Zachary said. "So . . . where would you like to go eat?"

Gabrielle put her hands up to her face to compose herself, then took them down. "I'm so sorry. I can't believe she did that. Wait a minute—yes, I can. That's classic Aunt Cee-Cee. And the funny part is, she has no idea that what she just did was totally wrong or completely selfish. No idea at all."

"Oh, she knows," Zachary said. "I get the distinct feeling Aunt Cee-Cee knows *exactly* what she's doing. *Exactly*."

Chapter 3

*Go from the presence of a foolish man, when
thou perceivest not in him the lips of knowledge.*

—Proverbs 14:7

"Marshall, your son is being baptized Sunday night at six. Are you planning on being there or not?" fifty-four-year-old Zenobia Walker said as she waited, not so patiently, on the phone for her ex-husband to respond. When it came to their two sons, there wasn't anything she wouldn't do to keep them from being hurt.

Sixty-four-year-old Reverend Marshall Walker took his time in answering his second ex-wife, ten years his junior. He'd married her straight out of high school, and he still knew how to put a little starch under her collar. "Zenobia, I've already had this discussion with Clarence. He called me Sunday night after going to that Followers of Jesus Faith Worship Center and rededicating his life—"

"He says it's not rededicating, Marshall. Clarence

says this is his first time honestly giving his life to Christ. I know that's hard for you to appreciate since you're the last one on earth who'll admit you don't perform miracles. But this is an important event for your son, and I would think you'd want to be there to support him in this," Zenobia said.

"Our son is not a little boy anymore. He's a grown man now. That means he's used to disappointments in life. I already have something scheduled. It was scheduled long before Clarence decided to get baptized . . . *again*. Frankly, I still don't understand the logic behind a person choosing to go into the water twice. It's not the water that saves us anyway. It's our faith in Jesus Christ. I baptized him with water when he was twelve. Believe me, he's not going to get any cleaner just because he wants to go down into the water again. But if that makes him feel better, then more power to him."

"Okay, Marshall. It's obvious you haven't changed one bit. That's one of the reasons you and I didn't make it as husband and wife. Can't nobody tell you nothing! You think you know everything and everything has to go your way. You don't care about anybody but yourself. Well, I'm going to pray for you because you're wrong about this. You're *so* wrong. Your son has been out there in the world for decades now doing God knows what. Then one fateful day, he goes to a church. He hears the Word. Okay, I'm sorry if it wasn't your church. But the point is, he heard the Word. And God's Word caused him to see that he needed to make a change in his life . . . that he needed to hook up with Jesus. He saw that it was time he got right with the Lord." Zenobia let out a sigh.

"So, whatever it is that you have to do," she continued, "I don't see how anything could be more important than your being there to support your son during this, if it's at all possible. Clarence is finally doing what you've always wanted him to do," Zenobia said. "He's doing what you and I have been praying to God to happen. Clarence has given his life to the Lord."

Reverend Walker released his own loud and audible sigh. "Zenobia, I told you: I have a commitment already. Otherwise, I'd be there. You know that my life is not my own anymore. I have responsibilities and obligations. As I said to Clarence on Tuesday when I spoke to him again, if I didn't already have something scheduled, I would be there. But I do. And I'm not one who breaks one commitment for another commitment later. That's just not how I conduct my business. You'll be there for him. I'm sure Knowledge will come if he's available. Clarence knows how happy I am that he's made the decision to change his lifestyle. And if he needs me, you and he both know I'll be right there for him. As I stated to you earlier: I've seen him go down in the water before. Just because he decided *that* particular water baptism at age twelve didn't count doesn't mean it didn't happen. Nor does it mean that I must rearrange my entire life and schedule to accommodate what *they,* over *there,* decided to schedule, on short notice, I might add."

Zenobia nodded her head, her medium-length, feather-cut hair moving as though it were trying desperately to stay with each of her nods. "Fine, Marshall. I'm going to pray for you."

Reverend Walker laughed. "Oh, you don't have to pray for *me.* God and I are straight. Everything is wonderful in my life. But if you want to pray just to be doing something, then by all means, pray away."

"See." Zenobia slowly shook her head as she primped her mouth. "I don't know why I even bother trying to be civil to you. Listen, you have a wonderful time Sunday night doing whatever it is you're going to be doing. All right?"

"Same to you," Reverend Walker said evenly and calmly. He hung up the phone.

"Ugh! That man!" Zenobia said, raising her fist to the ceiling. "I can't believe I was actually married to him once upon a time. Talk about being blind but now I see! Ugh!"

"Calm down, Mama," thirty-seven-year-old Knowledge Walker said as he walked into the den popping a black grape into his mouth. "I still don't see why you let Daddy get to you like you do." He brushed his two hands quickly together to dispel any remaining moisture from his hand.

Zenobia rolled her eyes as she shook her head once more. "I can't believe he's not going to come to your brother's baptism on Sunday night."

"Clarence is getting baptized again?"

Zenobia squinted her eyes at Knowledge as she glared at his six-foot-two frame. "Don't you start with me," she said. "I'm not in the mood to play with you today, and especially not after your father just got my blood pressure up."

Knowledge hugged his mother. "Mama, you must learn to let things go, specifically when it comes to Daddy. He's not going to change. You know that. Clarence likely knows Daddy's not coming. He's okay with it. I know *I* knew it. Daddy's always *too* busy."

"So, I'm the only one holding out hope against hope that he'll finally see the light and start treating you both the way he ought to?"

"Mama, Daddy is . . . Daddy," Knowledge said. He spun her around and began massaging her tensed shoulders. "And I can assure you, the last place Daddy probably wants to be on Sunday night is watching his wayward son, who has now seen the way, being baptized at a church other than his own, by a minister other than himself. Unless of course that minister happens to be one of his little minions he's instructed to do so as he oversees everything from his high, golden perch." Knowledge spoke the last of his sentence with an overly proper accent.

Zenobia turned around and swatted her son softly. "Knowledge, that's not nice. You still have to respect your father. I don't care how angry and frustrated he makes us."

"Oh, I respect him as my father. I just refuse to lie, even when it comes to him."

"Why don't you give your daddy a call and see if you can't talk him into seeing how wrong he is for not coming? I checked the church's Web site. He's not preaching anywhere Sunday evening or that night. So whatever his plans are, they don't involve him having to cancel a speaking engagement or church service."

Knowledge shook his head. "No, ma'am, Mama. We both know once Daddy has decided something, nothing and no one can change his mind."

"Yeah, but—"

"Yeah, but nothing," Knowledge said. "I love you, Mama. But you need to drop this and move on. Capiche?"

"Yes, I get it," Zenobia said. "I really do understand. And I really *am* trying."

Knowledge kissed his mother on the cheek and grinned at her.

"Stop that," Zenobia said with a laugh.

"Stop what?"

"Stop making things light with your pragmatism when things start to get heavy."

"Ah, Mama. Admit it: you love the way I use my skills as a negotiator. It's just the art of negotiation in practice. This is why the finance world pays me the big bucks."

Zenobia tilted her head slightly and looked sternly up at him. "Oh, so is that why the FBI is so interested in you lately?"

"Mama, I told you. The FBI is interested in me and my skills in finance and accounting. That's what happens when you're good at your job and word gets back to the Big House." Knowledge plucked his white silk shirt twice with both his thumbs and index fingers like a bird pecking at the ground trying to snatch up a worm. It was his way of emphasizing his pride in himself.

"People in high places begin to search you out for positions in their organization. The government is stepping things up within the financial world. There's too much corruption too high up. People aren't sticking up banks with guns and a note the way they used to. Things are high tech now, sophisticated. And the government is looking for the best of the best to put a halt to a lot of these things, or at least slow them down. I know you've seen the movie *Men in Black*. Well, the government really is looking for the best of the best now."

"Yeah, okay. That's what you keep telling me. You'd just better be sure that's the only reason the government is interested in you. I mean that, Knowledge."

Knowledge kissed his mother again on the cheek.

"Mama, you raised me better than that. I won't embarrass you or our good name. I'm the good son, remember?"

"Knowledge . . ."

"I'm just kidding, Mama. Well, I'm out of here. It's Thursday and I have to pick up Dominique and Jasmine from ballet and Deon from karate. I'm just glad Isis found a place with both activities next door to each other. At least I don't have to run all over town dropping them off and picking them up for this. After I get them, I'll go by the daycare and pick up Dante before they close at six and end up charging me a late fee."

"Poor Dante . . . having to be the last one picked up," Zenobia said of the six-month-old. "You should have stopped by and gotten him before you came here. I'm sure he would have loved to see his granny. And how is Isis these days?" Zenobia asked of her daughter-in-law. "We don't see very much of her hardly ever."

"Oh, she's good. The law firm is keeping her busy. But as she tells me often when I try to get her to slow down: this is what she was born to do. And I must admit, when you see her in action, grilling a witness on the stand, connecting the dots, that wife of mine *is* good. I believe they're thinking of making her a junior partner soon."

"Well, I hope to see all six of you Sunday night. In fact, I think it would be great if we all got together for dinner after church. I could cook a nice, big meal, check Gramps out. Clarence could come over and maybe bring his two children. It would be fun."

"We could do that. I need to check with Isis to be sure she's available. But me and the children could be here. As for Clarence getting his two daughters . . . you know Tameka and Clarence are like a Mac and a PC: they both work well respectively, but they use totally different operating software to function. With Clarence's previous line of work, he didn't always get the children on his weekend. If it's not his weekend this week, Tameka may not cooperate just to get back at him for all the times he *didn't* get them when he could have."

"But this is a special weekend. Their father is being baptized. I'm sure Tameka will be fine with us having a family gathering here at my house," Zenobia said. "You just see about Isis and I'll handle Tameka."

"Yeah, Tameka still loves you. You two are sort of like Ruth and Naomi in the book of Ruth in the Bible. 'Where thou goest, I'll go. Thou God will be my god.'" Knowledge quoted Ruth's words to her mother-in-law, Naomi.

"You know what would really be great? If we all went to church together this Sunday . . . as a family. Then afterward, we could come here for dinner. We might even consider visiting Clarence's new church. You know, show our solidarity as a family unit."

"Okay, Mama. It's time for me to go now. Because you know that's not going to fly. There's no way I can tell Daddy I won't be at church Sunday because I'm going to the church that stole his other son away from him. No way."

"Knowledge, don't even play saying things like that." Zenobia's tone was serious. "Nobody has stolen anyone from anywhere. You sounded just like your father then."

"Well, Mama, I know you don't want to hear this. But Daddy isn't always wrong." Knowledge headed toward the door. "I do know from comments Daddy has made, just recently, that he doesn't care much for Pastor Landris, not much at all. I'll call you later tonight and let you know for sure whether we're coming to dinner Sunday. But if we don't, I'll definitely be there for my brother Sunday night."

Knowledge opened the door and left as Zenobia stood there unconsciously trimming and tidying up a few of her hangnails with her teeth.

Chapter 4

*Curse not the king, no not in thy thought; and
curse not the rich in thy bedchamber: for a bird
of the air shall carry the voice, and that which
hath wings shall tell the matter.*

—Ecclesiastes 10:20

"Hey there, Miss Countess," Gramps said. "Where
you headed so bright and early this morning?"

"Morning, Ranny," Countess Gates said to the ninety-
nine-year-old, Tootsie Pop–looking bald-headed man
most folks, with the exception of her, generally called
Gramps. "I was on my way out to the garden for a
morning walk."

"Would you mind having some company?"

"No," she said with a smile. "You're welcome to
come if you like."

Gramps walked alongside Countess. She looked up
and her eyes followed a red robin that flew right past
them as soon as they reached the gazebo. She smiled at
Gramps. "For an old man, you sure do get around well.
You do better than some of the people who work here."

He grinned. "Who you calling old? You know age ain't nothing but a number and a state of mind. That's all it is. A person can be twenty and think and move like they're fifty. I've seen them; see them now. You ever meet a young person that complains about everything? Every time you turn around, something on their body is ailing them."

"Hypochondriacs," Countess said.

Gramps stopped and tilted his head. "Look at you. Using all them big, fancy words on this old country fellow. I just call them kind of folks constant complainers."

Gramps could tell Countess was having a good day today. With her diagnosed Alzheimer's, you never knew from one day to the next what to expect from her. Recently, it was from one minute to the next. Whenever she went back in time in her mind and he tried to strike up a conversation with her, she would react to him as though he were some dirty old man trying to pick up some young girl. He would merely play along with her whenever she went to that place—apologizing if he'd offended her in any way.

He was thankful that, so far, the disease hadn't attached itself to his mind. Sure, he had plenty of his own forgetful moments. But his was a natural progression of life. He couldn't imagine what it must feel like to look at your own children, grandchildren, or great-grandchildren and not know them. Being in a home filled with senior citizens, he had witnessed all too often the hurt registered on various family members' faces when their loved ones didn't have a clue who they were. And then there were the ones who were forever walking, trying to go "home." But home for them was a place in time, a place that no longer existed in the present world.

Gramps and Countess sat out in the gazebo for a

while, neither one of them having more than casual things to say. They talked about the plants, specifically the beautiful, velvet-looking, multicolored shades of red, yellow, blue, and purple pansies the gardener had just put out. They discussed the trees that were beginning to shed their leaves as they tried to guess how old some were. And the sky that was a perfect indigo blue with not a cloud marring it. Countess sneezed. She sneezed again, and then again.

Having said "Bless you" following three of her sneezes, Gramps pulled out a handkerchief and handed it to her. A habit that began with his mother when he was a teenager going to church; she always gave him a fresh handkerchief to put in his pocket. When he was old enough for her not to insist, he did it because there was always some need to have one, even if only to hand over to a woman spilling tears in church or on a date.

"Thank you," Countess said, sneezing again as she used it now to wipe her nose.

When they got back inside the building, Countess went to her room and Gramps went to his. After minutes of dozing in his recliner, he looked over at the old black trunk he kept in the corner of his room. Stuff was stacked up on top of it. He got up and started removing those things. Opening the trunk, he began to pull out this and that until he finally found what he was looking for. He smiled as he touched the wooden, hand-carved box. He couldn't help but admire the workmanship of the seventy-something-year-old box. It was indeed impressive. Carefully, he took it out of the trunk, closed the trunk's lid, then carried the box over to his bed.

His grandson was going to be baptized Sunday. Clarence had finally heard the voice of Jesus and chosen to give his life to Him. Inside of that now-antique-looking wooden box was an antique pocket watch

Gramps wanted to give to Clarence. It would be his way of letting Clarence know that time still has a way of catching up with you. He of all people could testify to that. But one could also use time to his or her advantage. Here he was less than two months from turning one hundred. *Who would have ever believed he would have made it this far and still be clothed in his right mind? If anybody, he, of all people, should have lost his mind a long time ago. But for the grace of God . . .*

Just as he was about to put the special key he'd kept in a secret place into the keyhole to unlock the box, there was a knock on his door. Before he could even respond, the door cracked open.

"Ranny, it's me . . . Countess. Is it okay for me to come in?"

He quickly set the box down and pushed it to the side. "Sure, Miss Countess. Come on in."

Countess pushed the door open and sauntered in. "I washed your handkerchief and ironed it," she said, holding out the pressed, white, square-folded poly/cotton to him.

"Oh, Miss Countess, you didn't have to go and do that. You could have kept that thang." He took the handkerchief and laid it on the bed. "I have a drawer full of handkerchiefs. In fact, when folks ask what I want for any occasion, I generally tell them handkerchiefs and socks. You know, you can never have enough handkerchiefs or socks."

"I know. I just don't like keeping folks' things, not if I can help it. I now realize with all that's happening with me, sometimes I just can't help it. And socks . . . I have yet to figure out why it is that socks, especially men's socks, have a way of just walking off between the ride from the dirty hamper and coming out of the dryer back into the clothes basket. And it's always just one of them. Two go in but only one comes out," she said.

Gramps laughed. "That's a good one. 'Two go in but only one comes out.' Yeah, I'll have to use that one."

Countess looked at the box on the bed. Her look turned into one of puzzlement. "Wow, where did you get *that* from?"

"What?" He followed where her eyes were fixed. "You mean this here box?"

"Yeah. I haven't seen that in a while."

"No, ma'am, Miss Countess. I don't believe it's possible you've ever seen this before." He tried to smile. It was obvious she was having one of her moments now.

"Yes, I have," she said adamantly. "I've seen that box before. That one right there." She pointed at it so there would be no mistaking what she was referring to.

"Okay, Miss Countess. You've seen this box before," Gramps said, quickly agreeing with her so he wouldn't upset her. He was certain that there was no way she could have ever seen that box. It had been deep in that trunk since he'd arrived at this place, well before her arrival. He'd never taken it out before, so she couldn't have seen it sitting around his room at any time. The box was definitely not something you'd find in a store, since it was hand-carved and homemade. And this particular box had been made more than seven decades ago.

Countess Gates cocked her head to the side. "Listen, Ranny, I'm not having one of my 'moments,' senior or otherwise, as so many fondly whisper behind my back as though what's going on with my mind somehow affects my hearing and my ability to understand spoken English. And I'm telling you that I've seen *that* box *right* there before, and I mean *that* box right *there*." She gave him a stern look. "All right. I'll prove it.

When you open it up, it has wings etched inside of the lid. At least, the one I saw did. It's called a Wings of Grace box."

Gramps was now the one staring back at her as, with great intensity, he studied her face. *How was this possible?* He picked up the special key, and with a slight trembling in his hand, he unlocked the box and opened it up.

And just as Countess had said, wings were etched inside the top of the lid.

Chapter 5

*But it displeased Jonah exceedingly, and he was
very angry.*

—Jonah 4:1

Pastor George Landris picked up the telephone and
pressed the seven numbers listed on the card he
held in his hand. He'd put this call off long enough.
God had been speaking to his heart about calling, but
he had concluded it wasn't really necessary or truthfully really any of his business. Not really.

"Reverend Walker," he said when the voice on the
other end said hello. "This is George Landris."

There were a few moments of silence. "Pastor Landris. How are things with you these days?" Reverend
Walker finally said. "How are things going?"

"Things are going. Of course, I know you already
know there's always something going on in all of our
lives, whether it's something we really want to deal
with or not."

"So . . . what's on your mind?" Reverend Walker said,
not one to disguise his distaste for unnecessary chitchat.

"Your son . . . Clarence. I didn't know until the other day that your son had come forward this past Sunday to be baptized."

"And how did you happen to learn that Clarence was my son? I mean, you have thousands of members. I'm sure you're like me when it comes to knowing everything going on in your church and everybody who happens to grace the church's parking lot," Reverend Walker said.

Pastor Landris thought about how he wanted to answer this question. He was well aware that he wasn't Reverend Walker's favorite person in Birmingham. The last conversation they'd had was when Reverend Walker called him to register his thoughts regarding one of his members, Gabrielle Mercedes, being allowed to minister through dance at the church after it was learned that she'd once been an exotic dancer. That exchange had left no question on just how far he and Marshall Walker would have to go to close the gulf that had only increased each time the two pastors spoke.

Pastor Landris began. "We generally have a New Members' orientation class on Wednesday nights. During that time, prospective new members turn in certain papers that list family information."

"A smooth move, Pastor," Reverend Walker said. "What a way to mine potential members." He jotted a note to himself as he spoke. "Find out who the family members are, then go after the entire family. A brilliant move. I've pondered how you've managed to grow so expeditiously over there at Followers of Jesus Faith Worship Center."

"That's not what we do here, Reverend Walker. We use that information in case of emergencies or to carry out something that may be a blessing for our members."

"Oh, okay. Sure," Reverend Walker said with deliberate skepticism in his voice. "So you happened to see my name in Clarence's information. Well, I'm amazed you even have time to look at every single congregant's sheet. That's true dedication to growing the Kingdom right there. True dedication. Then again, you are much younger than I am, so you have the energy to do that kind of stuff."

Pastor Landris pressed his lips together to keep them from parting to speak on their own. This conversation was not going in the direction he had planned at all. "Reverend Walker, I don't look over the information. We gather it to put it in a database, a secure database. That way if anyone on staff has a need to pull it up, we have access to it. When Clarence's information was being entered into the system, the person entering it happened to recognize your name and thought I might like to know. I was sent a note, and I must say that I'm glad this fact was pointed out to me."

"Oh, so let me guess," Reverend Walker said. "You're calling because you want to let me know that you're sorry for stealing my son away from me and my church. That you never intended for something like this to happen. That you have no control over who comes to your church or over those who choose to join with you."

Pastor Landris frowned. "No, that's not why I called at all. In fact, none of that ever even crossed my mind. But apparently it has crossed yours. Actually, I was calling to ask if you'd like to come and be a part of the Sunday night service. Maybe do a special prayer, or if you'd like to assist with the baptism of your son. I just thought that would be special and wanted to personally extend the invitation."

"Well, Pastor Landris, and I hope you don't take this

the wrong way, but I baptized Clarence once already. Twenty-three years ago, to be exact. I took him to the water and baptized him myself. Personally, I see no reason to go through these theatrics again. But hey, it's like you told me in no uncertain terms the last time we talked. You remember . . . when I tried giving you some sound advice regarding that woman dancing in your church after she'd been dancing for the devil. You will do things the way you believe God is leading you to do it. Therefore, if God is telling you that one baptism is not always sufficient and that some people need to do it again, then knock yourself out. That's between you and God."

"Reverend Walker, I don't know the specifics with your son. All I know is that I'm preaching the Word the way God is giving it to me to do. Matthew 9:37 lets us know that the harvest truly is plenteous, but the laborers are few. I'm just out here trying to help bring in the harvest for the Kingdom of God. I don't want God holding anything against me because of things I didn't do that were assigned to me to do. The Spirit of the Lord has anointed me to preach the gospel to the poor, to heal the brokenhearted, to preach deliverance to the captives, to recover the sight to the blind, which is not merely addressing physical blindness, to set at liberty those that are bruised, and to preach the acceptable year of the Lord. That's what I've been called to do."

"Oh, look at you. Over there quoting Luke 4:18–19 as Jesus read it from the Old Testament scrolls of Isaiah 49:8–9. You never fail to impress with your knowledge of the scriptures. And you are right. You're doing what you say God has given you to do. It's evident something is happening over there the way everybody is flocking to be a part of the ministry you're heading. I just pray it's godly and correct."

"This is God's work. I'm just an assigned overseer. The earth is the Lord's and the fullness thereof; the world and they that dwell therein," Pastor Landris said.

"Okay," Reverend Walker said, looking to find a way out. "I appreciate your thinking of me. Thank you for calling and making such a wonderful appeal for me to come and be a part of your Sunday night service. But I already have plans. And as I've previously told my son, I won't make it to see this blessed event, but my prayers will be with you all."

"Reverend Walker, let me ask you something. Have I done something to you that I'm not aware of? Have I offended you in some way that I don't know about? Because if I have, whether it was a case of commission or omission, I want to make it right. We're on the same team here. At least, I have been led to believe that we are."

"Well, I'm on the Lord's side. So, if you're on the side of the Lord, then we're on the same team."

"But we also know that, being on the same team, people have different positions they are assigned to play. On a football team somebody is the quarterback and someone else may be the kicker. In basketball, you have a point guard and maybe a rebounder. We may not all play the same position or have the same style, but the object of the game is to do our part to contribute to the team and, in the end, for our team to score and ultimately win the game."

"Great analogy, Pastor. But we also need to be sure we're playing from the same playbook."

"Absolutely," Pastor Landris said. "And I'm using the Holy Bible, the Word of God."

"As am I."

"Then we're playing for the same team. It just may be our interpretation of the plays doesn't always line up, but the ultimate results should be to win those to Christ who don't know Him. And to be certain that we're applying the two greatest commandments as so wonderfully outlined by Jesus: to love God with all our heart, mind, and soul, and to love one another."

Reverend Walker let out a quiet sigh that Pastor Landris managed to still hear. "Pastor Landris, I thank you for calling. I appreciate your extending a personal invitation to me to come Sunday night. It is short notice. I do already have a commitment. But please know that my prayers will be with you."

"Okay, Reverend Walker. But who knows what God is doing. I am just being obedient here. God instructed me to call and extend this time to you. I've done that. If you see that you're able to make it, please know that the offer for you to come and be a part is open. I think it's wonderful that your son has repented of his sins and turned toward the Lord. That's something to celebrate, and I know the angels in Heaven are rejoicing. I'm sure you're rejoicing about this as well. I don't advocate that people go in the water just to go in the water. There is a symbolism in water baptism. As you know, Jesus Himself was baptized by John the Baptist. For whatever reason, your son came forward to be saved. For whatever reason, he did not believe he was truly saved from the time you're referencing. That's something he is working out between him and God. He came forward to be saved and to be baptized. I'm merely doing my part. I preach the Word, give people the opportunity to receive Jesus Christ as their Savior, baptize them when I can, and feed them with even more of the Word of God after that. That's it."

"Of course," Reverend Walker said. "Of course."

Pastor Landris hung up after they each said goodbye. "Lord, touch Reverend Walker. Touch his heart.

Bless him. Only You know what's going on with him. I'm merely doing what You've told me to do. Bless his son along with all those who are scheduled to be baptized on Sunday. Bless them in their quest to know You better and to grow more and more in Your grace. In Jesus' name I pray. Amen."

Chapter 6

Behold, the Lord's hand is not shortened, that it cannot save; neither his ear heavy, that it cannot hear.

—Isaiah 59:1

Aunt Cee-Cee had called Gabrielle the next day after her surprise visit, just as she said she would if Gabrielle didn't call her. Gabrielle was at Dance Ministry Tuesday night when the call came, and Bible study was Wednesday night. So she returned her aunt's call on Thursday night, and an all-too-familiar recorded voice informed her that the number had been temporarily disconnected.

Gabrielle and Zachary had been doing quite a few church-related things together, so they decided to go to the baptism on Sunday night. And since Zachary had his own practice and he wasn't on call to deliver babies, who often had their own schedules, Zachary was more available for nighttime activities. Gabrielle had always believed that people married to doctors didn't get to see them much because they were always on call.

So far, Zachary's profession hadn't interfered with their budding relationship. He'd been called to the ER only twice. Things seemed to be working out just fine for them.

"Clarence!" Gabrielle called out to her friend when she saw him walking toward her after the baptism. She hurried to him and hugged him. "I am so happy for you!" she said, her feet now dangling in the air from his lifting her off the floor with excitement and enthusiasm.

"Thank you," Clarence said with a grin on his face. "It was so great. I've been in the water before for baptism, but this time was different. This time for me was truly symbolic of a death, burial, and a resurrection."

"I know what you mean," Gabrielle said. "But truly, how do you feel?"

"Like a new creature. Seriously. I'm not just trying to be cliché here. I feel like I have grown wings and I could take off and fly right here and now. And on top of everything, my family came to support me: my mother, Gramps, my brother, his whole family including his wife, who is superbusy these days, my two beautiful girls, and even their mother. I couldn't believe they were all here. It's been so long since we've done anything like this. This night has been amazing. And then to look up just as I was about to step into the pool and see my father standing there, I was almost in shock. He'd told me he had a previous commitment and that he wouldn't be able to make it. So when I first saw him, I thought my eyes were merely playing tricks on me. But it was really him, standing right there as Pastor Landris and the others were about to lay me in the water."

"That was your father?" Gabrielle asked. "That tall, slim man that came up there?"

"Yes. And I can't express to you how much it means to me to see him here for this," Clarence said. "I didn't realize how much it would mean until I saw him. This has truly been a blessed night for me. And then you, both of you here . . . cheering me on."

Just then, Clarence's family came up behind Gabrielle and Zachary.

"Daddy!" said eight-year-old La-la, short for LaClarence, as she ran into her father's arms.

Clarence picked her up with a smile. "Hi, sweetheart."

"You got baptized," La-la said. "We saw you go down in the water, then come back up."

"Yep, I was baptized and I'm what they call saved now." Clarence looked at his ten-year-old daughter, who merely stood and stared aloofly at him. "Valencia, aren't you going to come give Daddy a hug?"

Valencia walked over slowly to Clarence. He set La-la down and hugged Valencia, who was making it more than clear that she was not into hugging him. Clarence smiled as he rubbed both his daughters' hair, which had been curled instead of their normal style of pigtails or ponytails.

Zenobia came over and hugged Clarence. "That was so special. I can't tell you how proud I am about what you've done. God is so good! I don't care what anybody says: God still hears and answers prayers. If we just don't become weary in well-doing."

"Amen to that," Gramps said, slowly making his way toward Clarence. "I told you a long time ago that your arms are too short to box with God. Didn't I tell you?"

Clarence hurried to his grandfather and hugged him. "Gramps," was all he said. He waved as Gabrielle and Zachary waved good-bye to him and strolled away.

"Boy, don't go getting all sentimental on me, now. You'll have me over here crying, and it just don't look right for an old man to be crying." Gramps patted his grandson on his back. "Your mama was right. That was a right mighty special service we just witnessed in there. I see even your daddy made it. That's great. That *is* great."

"Yeah, that was something, wasn't it?" Clarence turned and gave his older brother a quick hug. "Knowledge, you wouldn't by chance happen to know anything about what may have caused Daddy to change his mind, now, would you?"

"Who me?" Knowledge said. "I spoke with him, but the last I heard, he was busy already and wasn't going to make it. I was just as surprised as everyone else here when he stepped up there."

"I'm sorry I didn't make it to dinner today," Isis said as she hugged Clarence. "I wanted to be here for your baptism, so I took care of some business earlier today in order for me to be able to come tonight."

At five foot four, thirty-three-year-old Isis was a sheer knockout. She worked out, without fail, at least an hour each and every day, which was evident by her toned body. No one would guess just six months ago she'd delivered a seven pound, six ounce baby boy, Dante. She'd worked right up until the moment she'd gone into labor. Then she returned to work a mere three weeks following his birth, despite both her mother's and her mother-in-law's thunderous objections.

"You young women are going to pay for the way you don't heed to old folks' tried and true advice when it comes to things like this," her mother, Dionne, had said. "Trying to do too much too fast. Both my grandmother and mother told me that a woman needs to stay in the house for six weeks after giving birth. Now, I admit I didn't believe it to that extent because I definitely went out of the house after about two weeks. But I wouldn't have dared thought about going back to work after only three weeks. No way."

"Your body needs time to fully heal," Zenobia had argued.

Neither of the two mothers' words had dissuaded her from returning to work quickly. Isis loved being a lawyer. She loved being victorious in her cases, not just for her clients but for the feeling of accomplishment it brought to her. Of course, the side benefits for all of her hard work, besides what she could give and do for her family, were luxury items like the pewter pindot leather, front-pocket Versace purse she was carrying and brand-named shoes such as the peach peep-toe Christian Louboutin presently gracing her feet.

Isis was happy to see that Clarence was turning his life around. Isis and Clarence had known each other for a long time, since Clarence was twenty-three and Isis was twenty-one. In fact, the two of them had met first. She and Clarence had talked for a few months, as friends. They'd hung out together, even gone out a couple of times, not officially calling it dating, just a movie and getting a bite to eat here and there. They even went dancing at a few clubs. But she appeared more interested in Clarence than Clarence seemed interested in her. Then one night, she happened to be at Clarence's apartment when his older brother, Knowledge, stopped by.

Knowledge was smitten from the moment he laid eyes on her. That was the word he'd used when he'd talked to Clarence about her—smitten. Clarence had laughed at his brother and teased him about his possibly being sprung from jump street. Isis was about to start law school when she and Knowledge met. Knowledge couldn't believe the beautiful, light-skinned woman standing regally before him, with a killer smile and a warm, enchanting laugh, was also smart and hopelessly engrafted with an abundance of pure, raw drive and ambition.

Clarence had assured his brother that he and Isis weren't in a *relationship* relationship—that they were only good friends. So when Knowledge let it be known he wanted to date her, Clarence hadn't *verbally* objected.

Knowledge convinced Isis to marry him before she graduated law school. He supported her career path one hundred percent. Upon learning she'd passed the bar exam, she also learned she was pregnant with twin girls. When daughters Jasmine and Dominique were only two weeks old, she'd received a call from a firm she'd interviewed with eight months earlier and desperately wanted to work for. They'd asked her if she could possibly start the following week. Without telling them she'd just delivered twin babies, she'd enthusiastically said she could. That action eight years ago had been the beginning of her pattern of returning to work after her babies turned three weeks. Of course, at the time, she didn't realize it would become a pattern.

Despite her efforts not to, she'd gotten pregnant again with their now-five-year-old son, Deon (named in a phonetic way after her mother). Because she'd asked for and been granted a particularly high-profile case, when she learned she was pregnant with Deon, she knew she couldn't use her pregnancy as an excuse. The case was set for trial a month after Deon was born. She more than proved to her superiors that a woman could still be a mother and be counted on to do the job she was hired to do at the same time. She'd gone back to work when Deon was three weeks old, went to trial that following week, and won the case hands down, bringing to the firm a lot of income in legal fees with that judgment.

Isis was truly a powerhouse, and anyone who met her instantly knew it. So, knowing just how dedicated his sister-in-law was to her work, Clarence was beyond touched when she showed up for this occasion. He knew she'd deemed this night highly special when she'd made such a tremendous effort and sacrifice to be present for it.

As for what changed with his father that either allowed or forced him to come, Clarence didn't have a clue. But he decided to heed one of his grandfather's old and wise sayings and not "look a gift horse in the mouth."

Chapter 7

And Elijah came unto all the people, and said,
How long halt ye between two opinions? if the
Lord be God, follow him: but if Baal, then follow
him. And the people answered him not a word.

—1 Kings 18:21

"Daddy, I just want to thank you for coming," Clarence said to his father in the church's vestibule when the two of them met up after the rest of his family had gone home. His mother had volunteered to take Gramps back to the nursing home.

"Sure. I'm glad I was able to make it," Reverend Walker said.

"So what happened to your other engagement?"

Reverend Walker hesitated a few seconds. "It was something I was able to do at another time. So, that's what I decided to do."

Clarence was quiet for a half a minute, hoping his father would go into more details. He quickly realized that was all he was going to get on what had caused his father to change his mind. "Well, I'm happy you came.

It was really special seeing you here for something as important as my baptism."

Reverend Walker visibly sighed heavily. "Well, I just wanted to come and speak to you before I left. I need to get on back home now."

"So, the rest of your family didn't come with you?"

"No. I came by myself. I didn't realize everybody was going to be here like this. Of course, I knew your mother and Knowledge would be here. But there was Gramps, your two children, Knowledge's entire family, including Isis. Isis hardly comes to church anymore. At least, she doesn't come to Divine Conquerors. Seems to me she's putting that job of hers above everything and everybody, including God, which can be danger-ous. So, I admit I was surprised to see her here tonight. And you even managed to get your ex-girlfriend slash drama queen to the second power to come—ol' Miss Tameka Washington. When I saw her a little while ago standing here talking to you, I literally stopped in mid-stride."

"Daddy, you're not being fair to Tameka. She's not a drama queen. Mama got Tameka and the girls here. You know how much Mama cares about us. She talked Tameka into bringing Valencia and La-la to dinner ear-lier today at her house, and then they all came here. Everyone seemed to enjoy the service tonight."

Reverend Walker nodded his affirmation, then placed a hand on Clarence's shoulder. "Now, you know that giving your life to Christ in a particular church doesn't necessarily mean you have to become a *member* of that church. There's a difference in being saved, which is to come into the body of Christ, and congregational membership."

"Yes, I know."

"And you know there's nothing that would make me

happier or prouder than to have you come back and
hook up with me and your brother over at Divine Conquerors Church. Wouldn't that be something . . . the
three of us working together again for the Lord?"

Clarence didn't want to ruin this time with his father. "That would be something, Daddy."

"Well." Reverend Walker smiled as he nodded. "You
pray about what God would have you do. You know the
right thing that you *ought* to do. But pray about it, and
you'll see that God is telling you to come on home
where you belong. Now, if you want to really talk
about some rejoicing, there will be a great celebration
when you come back home to *us*. Yes, I can promise
you that. I promise that." Reverend Walker hugged
Clarence.

"We'll talk some more later. This is just the beginning of things with us, Clarence, just the beginning. I
know God has a calling on your life. You know it, too.
Just don't let the devil mess you up. People can do a
good thing without it being the *right* thing. You always
want to do the right thing when it's at all possible." He
slapped his son's back.

"Bye, Dad. And thanks again for coming." Clarence
watched his father walk out the door. He looked around
the now practically empty place and saw Pastor Landris
looking his way.

Pastor Landris smiled and waved. Clarence smiled
and waved back.

Chapter 8

Take away the dross from the silver, and there shall come forth a vessel for the finer.

—Proverbs 25:4

Johnnie Mae Landris visited her mother at the nursing home. Since her oldest sister, Rachel, put their mother in that place almost three months ago—in accordance with her mother's wishes before the Alzheimer's had progressed to the stage where she was presently—Johnnie Mae had made it her business to visit once a week, sometimes twice.

Johnnie Mae had heard far too many tales about the awful things that can take place in a nursing home. And even though this nursing home's staff appeared to be both caring and professional, she still wanted them to know that someone was attentive and that they were being monitored, at least to the best of her ability. No one on staff would want to deal with her if her mother was ever abused, neglected, or mistreated. She wasn't going to stand for that even a little bit.

"Hi, Mama. What are you doing?" Johnnie Mae said when she found her mother in the activity room on Tuesday afternoon. Johnnie Mae liked to come on Thursdays, but she often changed up her routine so the staff wouldn't get comfortable with when to anticipate her visits.

Countess Gates looked up. "Hi, baby."

"So, you're playing checkers, I see."

"Yes. This is my friend, Ranny. He claims he's a checkers man, but I've beat him two out of three times already."

Having made his next move, Gramps looked up. "Hi. You must be Johnnie Mae."

"Yes, I am," she said, impressed more with the fact that her mother must have said something about her for him to know who she might be.

"You can just call me Gramps. Everybody else does." He extended his right hand.

Johnnie Mae shook his hand. "All right, Gramps."

"Everybody but me," Countess said, concentrating on her next move. "He's not my gramps. I just call him Ranny."

As Johnnie Mae sat in the vacant seat at the table, she thought about her own younger years. Back when people would tell her what they preferred being called, and she would persist in ignoring their wishes and insist on calling them by their real names. She was thankful she'd been delivered from doing things like that. It had been disrespectful and inconsiderate of her. If this man preferred she call him Gramps, then Gramps it would be.

"A triple jump, and now you need to crown me!" Countess said, satisfied.

Gramps smiled and sat back in his chair as he shook his head. "How did you just do that?" He studied the board that now gave Countess four kings with his two lonely checkers. "Well, this game is all over but the shouting."

"I'm sorry," Johnnie Mae said, directing her comment to Gramps. "Maybe I distracted you."

Countess waved her daughter off. "Ah, you didn't distract him nothing. I've set this play up on him so many times he should have seen it coming a mile away. He never does, which is why . . ." She watched him, with nowhere to go, move one of his checkers. "I . . ." She jumped both his checkers. "Keep winning." She removed his two checkers from the board.

Gramps grinned. "That's okay. I'll get you next time."

"Next time, smext time," Countess said. "He's been trying to get me to play chess with him. That's what folks do when they can't beat you in checkers."

Gramps chuckled.

"You know how to play chess?" Johnnie Mae asked Gramps.

"A little. One of my grandsons has been trying to teach me." Gramps stood. "Well, I'm going to go to my room now."

"You don't have to leave on my account," Johnnie Mae said.

"Oh, I'm not," he lied.

"He seems to be a nice man," Johnnie Mae said after he was gone.

"For an old man," Countess said. "I think he lets me win, though."

"Is that right?"

"Yeah. He likes to flirt with me. Letting me win is one of his ways of flirting."

"Well, Mama. He's a nice-looking man."

"Do you know how old that man is?"

"Seventy maybe," Johnnie Mae said with a hunch. "Eighty at the most."

"The man is close to a hundred," Countess said with a slight chuckle.

Johnnie Mae laughed, more at how her mother said it than what she'd said. "Mama, I don't think he's close to one hundred. Do you see how he gets around?"

"It's because of what he eats and drinks. And he says he's never smoked, not even when he was younger. He's some kind of expert on the body. Like one of the nurses here liked to eat ice. He told her she needed more iron and that's why her body was craving ice. She laughed at him, but when she started taking iron supplements, she stopped eating ice. We were glad about that because she was getting on our last nerves. I mean, the woman was an ice addict. Every time you saw her, she had ice crunching on it. Ranny can even look at a person's fingernails and determine things going on in their body."

"Okay, Mama."

"No, seriously. Most of the folks he tells stuff to here are the younger folks. 'Cause you know the older folks here have their share of ailments. The receptionist that works here, Karen is her name."

"Carolyn," Johnnie Mae said, correcting her mother.

"Yeah, Carolyn. Anyway, she was handing somebody something one day and complaining about how tired she was. He asked her if he could look at her fingernails. He said her nails were flat and thin. He then asked if she had problems with her thumbnails splitting oddly. She said both her thumbnails tended to split across in the middle of her thumb and it could be painful because it wasn't where she could take it off until it grew out. You know what he told Karen?"

Johnnie Mae started to correct her mother again on Carolyn's name, then decided it really didn't matter. "What?"

"That she had a vitamin and mineral deficiency. He asked her if she was tired a lot, then told her she needed multivitamins with zinc and B something or other."

"B6?"

"No."

"B12?"

"Yeah, that's it. He told her he thought she had a B12 deficiency. Well, she didn't believe him. You could tell it by the way she was trying to humor him. But about a week later, she came and told him she'd gone to her doctor again and specifically asked them to check her B12 levels, and it turns out that was her problem. Ranny had told her she needed to eat more meat since that's a source of B12. He may be old, but he's a smart old man, that's for sure."

"Interesting," Johnnie Mae said.

"Yep. He has this beautiful wooden box in his room. I saw it last week. It's one of those Wings of Grace boxes."

Johnnie Mae smiled. "Oh, so you remember the Wings of Grace box from some years back? He has a box that reminds you of that box?"

"No. He has one."

"You mean he has one that's similar to it. . . . It reminds you of it."

"No. I mean he *has* one. Now you're starting to act just like he did. Like I don't know what I'm talking about. I told him I'd seen that box before . . . that it had wings on the inside of the lid."

"So you're telling me that he has a box, a wooden box, and when you open it up, there are wings etched on the inside of the lid?"

"That's exactly what I'm telling you. It's just like the one you had that time. You remember. Well, he has it now."

"Mama, look at me. Do you know who I am?"

Countess looked at her. "You're so beautiful," she said with a smile. "I know how much you love me. Of course I know who you are. You're my Johnnie Mae." She smiled.

"Mama, can you take me to Gramps's room?"

"Who?"

"Ranny. Can you take me to see Ranny? I need to talk to him."

"Why?"

"I want to see that box. I want to ask him about the box."

Countess shrugged. "It's just a box, an old box at that. You had one. He has one. It must be a pretty common box. Who knows, maybe the one he has is the one you used to have. Looked the same to me."

"Mama, you're right. It may be the same box I had. It could be that he bought it from someone. That's why I want to talk to him. So can you show me which room is his room?"

"Sure, baby. But I'm warning you right now: he seems to like younger women. That's why I believe he keeps flirting with me every chance he gets. You watch yourself around him. Don't let his sweet talking fool you, 'cause he's a smooth talker."

Johnnie Mae smiled as she walked with her mother out of the activity room into the corridor.

"Where are we going now?" Countess asked. "You're

such a beautiful, nice lady. Can you help me? I've been trying to go home, but these folks won't let me go. What was your name again?"

And just like that . . . Johnnie Mae's mother had slipped back.

THE TRUTH IS WILDLIGHT · 59

such a beautiful, nice lady. Can you help me? I've been
trying to go home, but these folks won't let me go.
What will you do now again?"
And just like that, Johnnie Mae's mother had
slipped back.

Chapter 9

Let not then your good be evil spoken of.
—Romans 14:16

Johnnie Mae helped her mother to her room. She
didn't press her any more about "Ranny," as her
mother called him. She visited with her mother for
about an hour, her mother asking her a question, she
answering it, then not five minutes later, her mother
asking the exact same question again as though she'd
never asked it or had it answered. When Johnnie Mae
left her mother's room, she went to the nurses' station.

"Hi, Mrs. Landris," one of the nurses said. "Is everything all right?"

"Oh, Gina. I almost didn't recognize you with that
red hair," Johnnie Mae said.

"I dyed it. What do you think?" Gina primped and
patted her hair.

"That color looks good on you," Johnnie Mae said.

"My husband doesn't like it. He says he prefers it
blond. But that was the same way he reacted when I
dyed it from brown to blond. I wanted to change things

up a bit. You know, it's hard for a black woman to find an interesting color that goes with her skin tone."

"Well, if you like it, I think that's all that counts," Bernadine said when she walked up, a chart in her hand. "Hi, Mrs. Landris. Did you have a good visit with Ms. Gates today?"

"Yeah, I did. She seemed to be doing fine, then she went back to another time. But listen, she was sitting with a gentleman when I came in, an older gentleman. They were in the activity room playing checkers."

"Oh, that's got to be Gramps. Isn't he the nicest man?" Gina said. "He loves a good game of checkers. Now, you talk about somebody with a mind on him—"

Bernadine bumped Gina softly. "What Gina meant was . . ."

"It's okay," Johnnie Mae said. "I'm not sensitive about my mother. I know what's going on with her. There's no need in us pretending. Yes, it's hard on us as a family, but we just have to do what we have to do. My mother gets confused about things, and we know that's part of this illness that's stealing so much from not just her, but us. She even thinks Gramps is a lot older than he is." Johnnie Mae started laughing. "She thinks he's close to one hundred."

"But he is," Gina said.

"He is?" Johnnie Mae said.

"Yeah. In fact, his family is planning a big birthday bash for his centennial in November."

"Wow, he looks great!" Johnnie Mae said. "And he gets around so well."

"That he does. But he's so respectful of everyone," Bernadine said. "I wouldn't be concerned too much about him with your mother. He's such a sweet guy. He makes it his business to help take care of the people around here, always trying to brighten someone's day."

"Your mother gets a little confused and thinks he's an old man trying to hit on a twenty-year-old woman," Gina said. "Gramps is so sensitive to when she and some of the others are not in the present that he just goes along with them and fixes things to make them feel better."

"He appears to be a very nice man," Johnnie Mae said. "Would it be okay if I went to visit with him for a few minutes? You know, stop by and let him know how much I appreciate the way he is with my mother."

"I can call his room and see if it's okay," Bernadine said. She checked. "He said he would love to have you come by." She told Johnnie Mae his room number. "He's not too far from your mother's room."

Johnnie Mae thanked them and left. After a short walk, she knocked on his door.

"Come in," Gramps said.

Johnnie Mae opened the door and walked in with a smile.

"Well, hello again. Come on in. Have a seat." He nodded toward the one other chair in the room. "To what do I owe this pleasure?"

"My mother."

"Oh. So she told you I've been hitting on her, has she?" Gramps smiled to ease any tension. "Said I was trying to talk to her even though she's got a boyfriend. His name's Jericho. Countess believes that her folks conspired to put her in this place to keep her from marrying him. But she's determined she's going to marry him regardless of what her mother is trying to do."

"Jericho is my father's name. He died in 1998. But that's not why I came by to see you."

"As long as you know I've *never* nor would I *ever* do anything to hurt your mother. Miss Countess is a fine woman, yes, she is. She's something special. I like walking and talking with her out in the garden, near the gazebo. She loves the outside, loves flowers and plants. When I see her heading that way by herself, though, I make it my business not to let her go out there alone. They watch folks pretty well around here, but I don't want any surprises. Especially not when it comes to Miss Countess."

Johnnie Mae nodded. "I appreciate that." She swallowed hard. It was becoming abundantly apparent that Gramps truly cared for her mother. She hadn't thought about something like this happening. People their ages still looking for companionship, maybe even love, from someone other than family. "My mother mentioned you had a box."

He smiled. "Oh, she did, did she?"

"Yes. She said it had wings on the inside of the lid."

Gramps leaned forward. "Yeah. That was the strangest thing. I still don't know how she did what she did."

"What's that?"

"How she knew about it. All I can figure is that she must have gone through my trunk and seen it somehow, although I can't for the life of me see how."

"Excuse me," Johnnie Mae said with a frown.

"Oh, it's okay. I'm not upset or anything if that's what she did. I know how things can be with folks, around this place especially," Gramps said. "They wander around these halls. Get confused. End up in the wrong room. Think maybe it's their room. They wonder what's happened to all of their things since nothing in the room is familiar. Your mother may have seen that old trunk over there." He made a sideways motion with his head toward the trunk. "She likely opened it to see if any of her things were in there. Saw the old wooden box. Only one other thing I can't figure out, and that's how she managed to open it without the key. You see, you need a special key to unlock it."

Having followed his nod toward the trunk with her eyes, Johnnie Mae said, "Gramps, would you mind if *I* saw that box?"

He shrugged. "That's no problem." He went to the trunk and took out the box, which was not buried down as far now as it had been before. "I had it out when I was looking for something to give to my grandson. He got baptized this past Sunday night—"

Johnnie Mae stood up almost in a daze and met him. "My goodness," she said. "My mother was right. It *is* the Wings of Grace box. You really *do* have one."

"Are you saying you've seen this box before, too?"

"Yes. It has wings on the inside of the lid . . . beautifully etched wings." She touched the box gently as though she were approaching a scared puppy.

"Wait a minute, now. What are you and your mother up to? You couldn't have possibly seen this box before. This is handmade." He shook his head. "Not possible. I know the person who made this here box. And I know that this box has never left his possession. I know this for a fact. So you couldn't have possibly ever seen *this* box before."

"Gramps, if you don't mind me asking, where did you get this box? Did you buy it from the man who made it? How long ago was it when you got it?" Johnnie Mae suddenly put a hand up to her mouth. "Oh, my goodness." She started shaking her head slowly. "Ranny . . . Ranny. My mother calls you Ranny. Oh . . . my . . . goodness. Ranny is short for Ransom. You're Ransom Perdue!"

Chapter 10

The fining pot is for silver, and the furnace for gold: but the Lord trieth the hearts.

—Proverbs 17:3

Johnnie Mae called Angela Gabriel Underwood. "Angel, I'm telling you, no one was more shocked than I was. It really is Ransom Perdue."

"My great-grandmother's friend, Ransom Perdue?" Angela asked. "The one Great-granny mentioned in her journal more than once?"

"Yes. The same one Pearl mentioned when I met her and she was telling me the story behind Sarah Fleming and Memory Patterson."

"Wow, that's something."

"When I told him how I happened to know who he was, his face literally beamed as soon as I mentioned Pearl Black's name."

"Oh, I would love to meet him," Angela said. "What about Memory Patterson? That's his daughter. Did you tell him about her?"

Johnnie Mae smiled. "I told him a little. I don't want

to overstep my boundary. I'm trying to get in touch with Lena Jordan or Theresa Greene now. I left a message for both of them. I haven't spoken with either of them in years."

Angela started laughing.

"What's so funny?" Johnnie Mae asked, thinking maybe she'd missed something.

"Have you ever thought about starting your own PI business or something?"

"Now what would make you say something like that?"

"I'm starting to detect a pattern with you," Angela said.

Now it was Johnnie Mae's turn to laugh. "You know, I hadn't thought about that. But you're right. Let's see: I met Sarah Fleming when she was hidden away at a nursing home in Selma, Alabama. She believed her daughter hadn't died when she was born. I admit I *did* think she was merely an old woman living in a stage of a senior's confusion."

"But you soon learned, when you came to Asheville, North Carolina, she was not only in her right mind but telling the truth," Angela said.

"Thanks to Pearl and that Wings of Grace box, which incidentally is the reason I also figured this out about Ransom Perdue."

"The Wings of Grace box? What does it have to do with anything?"

"My mother, bless her sweet heart, was telling me that her friend, Ranny as she calls him, had a Wings of Grace box. Well, of course I thought she was having one of her moments again. But I went to see Ranny, who prefers being called Gramps. And there in his possession, just as my mother had said, was the box."

"The same box?" Angela asked.

"Not the exact same box. After Gramps got over the shock that my mother had been right when she'd told him she'd seen that box before, and my going to see him and acknowledging the same thing, we talked. I learned he'd made five of those boxes."

"Five?" Angela said. "Five is the Hebrew number for grace."

"Yeah," Johnnie Mae said. "The first box was practice. He told me it was severely flawed so he trashed it. The second box was much better, but he believed he could still improve upon the etched wings. He did, and ended up making three boxes for Sarah and her mother. He decided to keep that first good box and put his odds and ends in it, not realizing the sentimental value the box would take on later in his aging years."

"So what happened to him? Where has he been, did he tell you? My great-grandmother thought a lot of him. I could see that much in the bits and pieces she penned about him in that journal she wrote. They were really close friends at one time for sure."

"Yes, he did tell me. Tears streamed down his face after I mentioned Pearl's name. Then I told him Pearl's great-granddaughter was also living here in Birmingham. I really believe it would mean a lot to him if he could see and talk to you."

"Mean the world to him? It would mean the world to me. To meet someone who knew Great-granny when she was young, absolutely it would. How old is he now?"

"He's ninety-nine. But let me tell you, he doesn't look it *at all*. He looks a lot younger than someone turning one hundred in a few weeks. I don't know what he does, but whatever he's doing, he needs to package it and sell it. He would be rich! Ransom Perdue gets around very well. His mind is sharp." Johnnie Mae's call-waiting feature beeped. She looked at the phone display. "Angel, this is Lena. Let me call you back."

"Okay," Angela said, then clicked off.

"Hello," Johnnie Mae said. She didn't want to assume it was Lena, just in case it was someone other than she who was calling from that number.

"Johnnie Mae?"

"Yes, this is Johnnie Mae."

"This is Lena Jordan. I just got your message. It's so good to hear from you. Richard and I were just talking about you all the other day, wondering how y'all were doing. It's been ages since last we talked. Although we have been getting those beautiful Christmas cards y'all send every year. You have such a beautiful family."

"Thank you. Yes, it has been about three or four years since the last time we saw each other. I wasn't sure if this number was still the right number to reach you."

"Oh, yes. It might take a while for me to get back to you, but we're still kicking, although not as high here in Atlanta. Look at me," Lena said with a detectable smile in her voice, "just taking over the conversation. I know you must have called for a reason."

"Lena, something happened today that I need to tell you about. I was at the nursing home visiting with my mother. And while I was there, I met another one of the residents there. A man. He says his name is Ransom Perdue."

"Ransom Perdue? Are you sure about that?"

"Yes."

"Our Ransom Perdue? Maybe it's just someone with the exact same name."

"I can't be one hundred percent certain, but I will say that everything fits. He's ninety-nine years old, so the age lines up. He says he's from Asheville, North

Carolina. And he remembers both Pearl Black and your grandmother, Sarah," Johnnie Mae said.

"I don't believe it. I don't believe it's him." Lena's voice was shaking somewhat now. "Is it possible someone may have stolen Ransom Perdue's identity? You know, it's also possible this is all just a setup."

"Lena, in this day and age, anything is possible." Johnnie Mae was silent as she thought a second, mulling over a few things. "I will admit: he looks much younger than the age he proclaims. Honestly, I wouldn't have put him to be a day over seventy."

"See." Lena's voice seemed to have gotten stronger. "How much would you like to bet it's someone who merely stole Ransom Perdue's name and identity?"

"But what about what he knows about Sarah . . . about Pearl . . . and about Memory?"

Lena allowed a short pause before she said anything more. "He mentioned Memory?" Lena asked, referring to her mother, Memory Elaine Patterson Robertson.

"Yes. When I told him who I was and the things I knew, he asked me if by chance I might happen to know anything about Memory. And if so, did I happen to know where he could find her."

Lena made a loud grunt. "Humph. Okay, that proves he's an imposter. Ransom Perdue left before Memory was ever born. I happen to know *that* for a fact. And he never came back. My grandmother, Sarah, believed her half-brother, Heath, or possibly even her father had Ransom run out of town, or worse, killed. He never knew about Memory, so how would this guy, who is claiming to be Ransom, know to even ask about her by name?"

"I don't know."

"I'll tell you how. This guy didn't know about the real Ransom being tricked away from his family before

Memory's birth. He may have stolen Ransom's identity, got enough information after the fact to know about Sarah, Pearl, and even Memory since anyone trying to get information later in life could have access to that information."

"Lena," Johnnie Mae said, "I can see where you're coming from. But there are things about what you're saying that don't make sense. Memory only learned the truth about Sarah being her real mother a few years ago herself. How would this man know about Memory *and* Sarah unless he was the real Ransom?"

"You see, that's what I'm trying to tell *you*. Because Sarah was hidden away in those homes for almost seventy years of her life, and Memory didn't meet Sarah until a few years ago, the real Ransom wouldn't have known any of this. Maybe this con artist just recently took on Ransom's identity. Or maybe he met Ransom earlier in life, then after Ransom died, he knew he could become Ransom and it wouldn't matter to anyone."

"Lena, why go to all of this trouble to fool someone? Especially now?" Johnnie Mae asked, a frown registering on her face. "When I met him today, he could have easily said he wasn't the same Ransom Perdue I was referring to and that would have been the end of it." Johnnie Mae became quiet. "Except . . . there was the Wings of Grace box."

"What Wings of Grace box?"

"This Ransom Perdue has one of those boxes in his possession," Johnnie Mae said. "One like the real Ransom used to make. He would have had to go to a whole lot of trouble if this is merely a scam."

"Yeah, but a lot of things aren't adding up for me," Lena said. "Aren't you the least bit suspicious about how all of this is playing out?"

Johnnie Mae pondered that thought. An elderly man named Ransom Perdue just happened to be at the same nursing home as her mother. And from what her mother and the nurses had indicated, he spent quite a lot of time with her mother. Then her mother just *happens* to see the Wings of Grace box and conveniently somehow remembers to tell her about it. When Johnnie Mae goes to check it out, it turns out to be true. That's when she learns Gramps is actually Ransom Perdue.

"But why would anyone go to this much trouble to make us think *this* Ransom Perdue is Sarah's Ransom Perdue?" Johnnie Mae asked out loud, still trying to work through this puzzle. "It doesn't make sense."

"If you ask me, I'd say it looks like it has Montgomery Powell the Second's handprint all over it." Lena was referring to Sarah's grandnephew who had earlier worked hard to keep Sarah locked away and from returning to her rightful position in the Fleming family hierarchy, and thereby taking back her house he'd illegally confiscated. A home that—to Montgomery's dismay since Sarah's death—Memory now legally lived in.

Johnnie Mae thought about it for a minute. She, of all people, knew how conniving and hateful Sarah's grandnephew could be. A scenario like this *would* fit right in line with something he might do.

"Well," Lena said, "let me call Theresa and Memory and tell them what's going on. It looks like we'll be heading to Birmingham shortly. That's a sure way for us to get to the bottom of this, once and for all. True silver and true gold will still be silver and gold after the heat and after the fire. Tell Ransom Perdue to guess who's coming to dinner."

Chapter 11

It is good that a man should both hope and quietly wait for the salvation of the Lord.

—Lamentations 3:26

"Zachary, you're bringing who here, when?" Leslie Morgan said to her son.

"My friend Gabrielle Mercedes in two weeks," Zachary said.

"It will be good to see you, but why are you bringing a woman with you? She's not pregnant, is she? Oh, my goodness, please tell me you haven't gotten someone pregnant. I told you some women will do whatever they can to get their hooks into a good-looking, successful man like yourself. Zachary, baby, I told you—"

"Mom, Gabrielle is not pregnant. Gracious, you need to stop that. You just start flying all over the place with your thoughts."

"Well, what kind of a name is Gabrielle Mercedes anyway? It sounds like a stripper name to me. Please tell me you're not bringing a stripper to my house."

Zachary paused for a moment. Gabrielle wasn't a

stripper, at least not anymore. And this was definitely not a conversation he wanted to have with his mother over the phone. The fact was that Gabrielle *used* to be an exotic dancer. But she'd given her life to Christ now, and that dancer life had become part of her past that had been pardoned by God and cast into the sea of forgetfulness. That's how Pastor Landris had explained past sins of those who had given their lives to the Lord and had become new creatures in Him.

"Mom, weren't you the one who used to tell us not to judge or make fun of other people's names? That was you, wasn't it? It looked like you . . . sounded like you . . ."

"Yeah, okay," Leslie said. "But you call me out of the blue to tell me and your father about some young woman who used to know your aunt Esther. That was fine. Great news. But now the two of you are dating and you want to bring her here to meet us. Are you sure something's not going on? Because you know how I am, Zachary. I don't like to be sandbagged. If she's pregnant or if there's something I need to know about her, you need to tell me now . . . before she comes here. I hope you know that the truth is the light."

Zachary thought about the words his mother was saying. And he knew from more than a few personal experiences, his mother didn't have a problem with embarrassing him in front of others.

"Mama, I want Gabrielle to see Aunt Esther again. It's like I just told Dad: it's possible that seeing Gabrielle might help Aunt Esther in her recovery that's been slow when it shouldn't be. Aunt Esther taught Gabrielle how to dance. And Gabrielle is good, too. The two of them haven't seen each other since before the accident some ten years ago." Just saying the word *accident* in context with his aunt caused Zachary to want to change the subject. He didn't want to talk or even think about it.

Seeming to sense that Zachary might be beating himself up again, Leslie said, "Zachary, I've told you to let it go. Your aunt's accident wasn't your fault. It's something that happened. No one but God knew it was going to happen. It could just as well have happened anywhere and at any time, so let it go. Okay?"

"But if I hadn't—"

"Zach, sweetheart, it does no one any good to go back and try to relive what's already done. No amount of 'what if's or 'if only's will change what *did* happen. Your aunt is doing the best she can to get better. Sure, it's been a slow process. But she's doing much better . . . better than when she first began. And you've made us all *so* proud with what you've done with your life—my son, the doctor."

"You're right, Mom. But I want to do what I can. I owe Aunt Esther that much. And I know her heart is going to flip when she sees Gabrielle again. I told Gabrielle I also wanted her to come to Chicago to meet all of you. She's excited about it."

"Just as long as you know there will be no sleeping together, in sin, under my roof. Not when you're not married to each other," Leslie said. "No shacking here. No."

"No problem," Zachary said. "We'll just get married before we get to your house and that will solve *that* problem."

"Boy, don't play with me." Her voice was stern. "You are nowhere near ready to get married. And you sure will not be marrying just anybody and bringing her here talking about being my daughter-in-law, the mother of my darling little grandchildren to come. That's not going to happen. Not if I can help it. So, what does this woman . . . this Gabrielle Mercedes do for a living?"

"Mom, will you please give it a rest? Gabrielle and I are in a relationship. I'm bringing her to see Aunt Esther and to meet all of you. That's all. That's the end of everything you really need to know right now."

"See, that's the part you keep saying that I don't get. Why do you keep emphasizing you're bringing her to meet us? The only time you should be saying something like that is when you're really, truly serious about a woman, and maybe /. . maybe you want us to meet your future bride. Otherwise, e-mail me pictures. I have an e-mail address now. And exactly how long have you known this woman?"

"Gabrielle, Mom. Her name is Gabrielle."

"Okay. Gabrielle. How long have you known Gabrielle Mercedes?"

"You mean from the first time we met?" Zachary said.

"Okay, I can see already that you're trying to set me up. Okay, Mister Smart Guy. Let's try it this way. When did you first meet her? Then when did the two of you start dating?"

"I met her this year at a church-sponsored Inaugural Ball here in Birmingham on January twentieth. And we're not calling it dating, we're calling it courting, and that seriously started back earlier this month."

"Early September. So, you two have been dating for what? About a month now? That's definitely not enough time for you to be bringing her here to meet us." Leslie stopped for a brief moment and sighed hard. "Well, at least she goes to church."

Zachary was thinking that they hadn't been courting quite a full month yet. But he wouldn't dare correct her now. It would be more than a month by the time they arrived in a couple weeks. "Yes, she goes to church," he said, choosing to stick with the safe topic. "In fact, she's a faithful member of Followers of Jesus Faith Worship Center, and she's on the dance team. And just this past week, she was hired to the staff of the church as head of the Dance Ministry. She'll officially start the Tuesday after we get back from Chicago."

"Okay. So is that all she does for a living? Work at the church? What is she doing right *now* to feed, clothe, and house herself?"

Zachary wasn't ready to tell his mother that she worked as a maid. That would be all that his mother would need to start throwing around her favorite description when it came to him and the women who wanted to date him: gold digger.

"Look, Mom, I have to go. We'll see you in about two weeks. Oh, and you know that Queen is flying in with us as well."

"Queen needs to go back home to her husband," Leslie said with a bite to her words. "I'm not in agreement with this separating stuff, not like this, while you're supposed to be working things out. I don't know how she expects to work out anything miles apart. And she's pregnant. She doesn't need to be traveling this way. She knows she's miscarried in the past. Queen needs to sit down until this baby gets here. And you need to stop enabling her and tell her to go home and work things out with her husband."

"Mom, I'm just going to be a good brother and support my sister. That's it. She's grown. If she wants to stay here with me while she and Greg work out things, then I don't have a problem with that. Greg needs to get it together. He's too much of a mama's boy."

"And Queen can be high maintenance herself. She has to learn that marriage is both give and take. They both need to learn that. It's about compromising for the betterment of the relationship. How else do you think I've managed to stay married to your father this long?"

"I thought it was because he was such a great catch and you were lucky to hook him. Weren't you the one I heard telling one of your friends what a hunk he used to be, and how all the other girls were after him, but then you turned on your charm and—"

"Okay, Zachary. Now you're trying to be cute. I told you about eavesdropping and gossiping. I'm getting off the phone. I'll see you in two weeks. You just remember what I told you: there will be no shacking up in this house, so you make sure you let your little friend know the deal prior to you arriving. I don't want to hurt anybody's feelings, but I will. You know I'll do it."

Zachary smiled as he hung up. If only his mother knew. Gabrielle was barely letting him kiss her. And as they had already discovered, the fire between them was way too hot to even play around with *that* sometimes. So they were doing their best to limit the number of times any matches were ever struck.

But he and his mother had always maintained their relationship on a need-to-know basis. And this was one more thing he didn't think his mother needed to know. She would only turn it against him as merely a calculated ploy for her to get him to marry her quickly. Another trick his mother had warned him about that he needed to look out for.

But Gabrielle was worth the wait. Even if this was only a ploy, and he didn't question her spiritual commitment and sincerity, Gabrielle Mercedes was absolutely worth the wait.

Chapter 12

The heads thereof judge for reward, and the priests thereof teach for hire, and the prophets thereof divine for money: yet will they lean upon the Lord, and say, Is not the Lord among us? none evil can come upon us.

—Micah 3:11

Reverend Walker smiled as Raquel Winston walked over to his table. He quickly stood to his feet.

"Thank you, Raquel, so much for coming, especially on such short notice." Reverend Walker leaned down and gave the thirty-year-old bombshell beauty a quick and respectable peck on the cheek.

"Better be careful, Reverend. You, of all people, know how folks talk," Raquel said. She looked around the restaurant and smiled at a few gawking men. She was used to the staring—stares followed her wherever she went. She didn't even fight it anymore. "So what's up?" she said as she sat down and Reverend Walker pushed her seat in for her.

He sat down across from her. "Would you care for anything to drink?"

"I would, but since it's lunchtime, and I'm still on duty, I suppose I must pass." She picked up the glass of water on the table and took a sip. "I suppose I'll just have to settle for tea."

"Then maybe you should have accepted my dinner invitation instead of insisting on meeting for lunch," Reverend Walker said.

"Oh, no." She shook her head and frowned as she scanned the menu. "Been there, done that. We both know how that all went. Lunch works fine. I'm on the clock, so if you're going to tell me what this is all about, now would be a good time."

Reverend Walker smiled, and then licked and popped his lips. "Sure. And since this *is* technically work re-lated—" Just then the waiter came and interrupted them to take their orders. Reverend Walker and Raquel were regulars, so they ended up ordering their usual items.

"Now, where were we?" Reverend Walker said, after the waiter left. He scanned Raquel from her head down to where the table stopped him from going any farther.

"Excuse me. I thought you said this was work re-lated."

He smiled as he stared into her naturally green eyes, then shook his head as though to clear it, and contin-ued. "Pastor George Landris—"

"Not him again," Raquel said, now drumming the fingers of her right hand on the table.

"Yes, him, again. You really need to check into the goings-on over there at that church. I'm telling you, there are some shady things happening at Followers of

Jesus Faith Worship Center. And the IRS really needs to investigate them *and* Pastor Landris."

Raquel sat back against her chair. "So are you registering a formal complaint?"

"I am."

"Well, then we need to fill out the appropriate paperwork. You're more than welcome to come to my office—"

"I don't want my name associated with this."

She shrugged. "If you believe something is going on over there, then why wouldn't you want to do the right thing and report it . . . put your name on record?"

"Because he and I are supposed to be brothers in the Lord, that's why. Although I'm not so sure we have the same Father. I'm serving the Lord, the Father of Light. I believe his father may very well be the father of deception," Reverend Walker said.

"That's a pretty strong accusation there, Reverend. I've never known you to be scared to speak your mind." Raquel stopped talking as the waiter brought a large bowl and placed it in front of her, and then served Reverend Walker's plate.

After the waiter left, Reverend Walker bowed his head and said a quick prayer. Raquel merely watched him as he did it.

Reverend Walker looked at her as he began to eat the slaw he'd received along with his fried snapper and pilaf rice. "If I wasn't sure you'd find something there, I wouldn't have come to you. Look, write up the complaint. List it as anonymous. I know you can do that. Check him out, and if everything checks out, no harm, no foul. If it doesn't, you could end up famous as the woman who cleaned up religious corruption."

Raquel smiled and shook her head as she ate some

of her onion soup. "Wow, what a sales pitch. You must really hate this guy. What did he ever do to you?"

"It's not about me. It's about the Kingdom of God. And I'm tired of preachers thinking they're above the law." He cut a piece of his fish and ate it. "Clergy twisting rules and regulations to accomplish personal needs and desires. People are flocking over to that church like sugar ants to syrup. You'll be doing the Christian community a great service. It's not like the IRS doesn't randomly audit. And should you get a tip—"

"A credible tip," Raquel said, correcting him.

"Should you receive a credible tip, then it's your job to investigate it. If he has nothing to hide or has done nothing wrong, then he'll be vindicated and at least people can feel secure about their giving to him and that church."

"It sounds to me like you might be a bit envious." Raquel took a sip of her tea. "Maybe the green-eyed monster has found its way to good old Marshall Walker." She smirked.

"Listen, green eyes, this could be your big break. You go back to the office, put in a report or whatever you do to get things rolling. Pastor George Landris is nothing to play with. If you find out he's not on the up-and-up, everybody will be praising your name."

"I don't need praise. In case you haven't noticed, I get it walking down a street or into a room." She turned and flashed a smile at a man sitting nearby who was about to fall out of his chair trying to look at her. "Well," she said, finishing her meal. To maintain her ideal weight of 115 pounds, she rarely ate more than soup or salad for lunch. "I'll see what I can do. But if I see there's no merit to this, I'm dropping it."

"Fair enough. And frankly, it's what I would not only

expect but want you to do. I'm not trying to go after this guy. I've just heard so much, especially recently, and I think someone needs to investigate him and put the rumors to bed one way or the other."

Finished eating, they left together. Raquel walked past a waiter holding up a plate of spaghetti. Gawking at her, the waiter dropped the plate into a customer's lap.

"Why don't you watch what you're doing!" the customer, who now wore the spaghetti, yelled at the waiter as the waiter profusely apologized while trying to help clean up.

Raquel looked at Reverend Walker and laughed as she stepped outside and waited on the valet to retrieve her car.

Chapter 13

This poor man cried, and the Lord heard him, and saved him out of all his troubles.

—Psalm 34:6

"Daddy." Zenobia leaned down and kissed her father when she raced into his room at the nursing home. "What's wrong?"

Gramps continued to wipe his eyes with his handkerchief. "I can't tell you. Not now, not here. Can we go somewhere more private? Can we go to your house?"

"But I need to know what's going on. Did something happen here? Did one of the nurses do something to you? One of the doctors? Did something happen with one of the other residents? What has gotten you so upset?"

Gramps put his black square-rimmed glasses back on. "I don't know quite how to tell you. I thought I could go through with this at first, but I don't know." He shook his head.

"Go through with what, Gramps?" Knowledge asked.

Gramps looked from Zenobia to Knowledge. "Where's

Clarence? I asked all of y'all to come. Where's Clarence?"

"He's on his way," Zenobia said. "But you need to tell me what's going on. If you don't, and you continue to be so upset, I'm going to go talk to the nurses and find out from one of them what's going on. And somebody's going to tell me something!"

"The truth, that's what's going on," Gramps said. "The truth is about to come to light. It always does. I don't care how long it takes, just like a moth to a flame, the truth will always find its way to the light."

"What truth, Daddy?"

"Let's just wait 'til Clarence gets here, and then I'll tell you."

Knowledge looked at his watch. "He should have been here by now." He took out his cell phone and tried calling Clarence. His call went straight to voice mail.

Zenobia took her father's hand and held it as she sat down next to him on his bed. Clarence came rushing in fifteen minutes later.

"It's about time," Knowledge said, not hiding his annoyance. "Where were you? I tried to call you on your cell phone but it went straight to your voice mail."

"I was on my way to Bible study when Mom called and said it was an emergency. I turned around and came right over. I suppose when you called, I must have been in a dead spot because I haven't been on the phone," Clarence said. "So, what's the emergency? Gramps, are you all right?"

"I'm fine. I just need to tell y'all something. But I've changed my mind. I don't want to do it here. It's going to take a little spell to tell it, and I don't want to do it here."

"Okay, Daddy. We'll go to my house. You can tell us there."

"I don't mean to be so much trouble, but things are about to change, and y'all need to know what's about to come down the pipe." Gramps stood and grabbed his hat.

"I'll go sign Gramps out," Knowledge said, opening the door and walking out. He met them at the front door with a signed paper in hand. "I told them I wasn't sure he would be back tonight . . . just in case."

When they reached Zenobia's house, Gramps was a bit more settled. They were all in the great room. Gramps sat in the wingback chair while everyone else sat, lined up on the couch, facing him.

"Okay, Gramps, what's up?" Clarence said after no one else said anything.

"I was born November 4, 1909, in Asheville, North Carolina."

"Yes, Daddy, we already know that," Zenobia said. Then feeling she might have been a bit harsh, she softened it with, "Remember?" She now wore a worried look.

"Zenobia, please . . . just let me talk, all right," Gramps said. "In the past, you children, specifically you, have asked me about my earlier life—"

"And you've always avoided talking about it with any of us," Zenobia said. "You said there was nothing much worth telling."

"Well, it's time I share some things with you. I didn't have a heap, material-wise, growing up. There were times when I felt like I didn't quite fit in. My folks liked working the land; I preferred working with wood and my hands. But my ma gave me love, and my pa worked his fingers to the bone as a sharecropper, trying to make sure there was enough on the table to eat. It was a hard life, but we colored folks were used to it."

"It's African-American now, Gramps," Knowledge

said. "The proper term is African-American. We don't call ourselves colored, Negro, Afro-American, black, or any of those *other* terms anymore."

Gramps cut him a sharp look, then continued to speak. "I met a woman named Sarah Fleming. She and her family were very well-off. They lived in this big fancy home. Mister Fleming hired me to do some woodwork around his house. When I saw Sarah, his lovely eighteen-year-old daughter, we hit it off right away. It was love at first sight."

"Black folks with that kind of money? That must have been inspiring," Zenobia said. Knowledge looked at his mother and shook his head, opting not to bother correcting her. She'd already told him she was born black and she would die black, even if her birth certificate did say Colored.

"They weren't colored . . . umm, black . . . African-American," Gramps said, "whatever y'all want to call it. They were white folk."

"You fell in love with a white woman?" Clarence said, joining in.

"*We* fell in love with each other. It was a mutual thing."

"Well, I can just about tell you where this story is heading," Knowledge said. "A white woman and an African-American man during that time, it's amazing they didn't string you up or shoot you right out."

"Came close enough," Gramps said. "Sarah and I were planning to be married. Her father acted all right with it when Sarah told him. But he wasn't; didn't think races should mix. Which weren't nothing but the pot calling the kettle black, since he was in love with Mamie Patterson—a dark-skinned woman just like me. Everybody knew Mister V, Victor Fleming Senior, had his nose wide open for Mamie. Yet, there he was trying to 'reason' with me to not pursue anything with his daughter. Said he wasn't the one with the color problem, but that society wasn't near 'bout there yet. He didn't want nothing to happen to his Sarah just 'cause she might happen to be with me." Gramps nodded as though someone had asked him a question. "Could somebody get me a drank of water?"

Zenobia jumped up and quickly went and came back. "Here you go, Daddy."

He took several sips before setting the glass on the table next to him. He continued. "Well, Sarah was a little spitfire of a woman, and she weren't about to let anybody keep her from what she was bent on doing. And she was dead set on being with me. We started sneaking around after that. I ended up being her first. After Mister V learned we were still seeing each other and weren't planning on abandoning our love affair, he started acting like he was warming up a bit toward me, like he was okay with us."

"Yeah, I bet he *did,*" Knowledge said.

Zenobia cut her eyes at her eldest son. "Knowledge, will you just let Daddy talk."

"I was just making a comment. We all know where this is going. We know the history when it comes to stuff like this." Knowledge crossed his legs and folded his arms as he sat back against the couch.

"Well, I know it firsthand," Gramps said. "Mister V came and told me about a job in Richmond, Virginia, he'd lined up for me. They were paying good money, good money. He said I could go, make some money, and be in a position to take care of Sarah and a family. He seemed sincere enough. Assured me he would take care of Sarah 'til I came back for her. Course on my way to this great job, things changed quickly. I can't say for sure whether it was Mister V's doing or not. But

I got stopped before I cleared North Carolina's state line good. You two boys don't know *real* fear until you've been stopped by hooded men you know mean you no good." He drank more of his water.

"Well," Gramps continued, "they were talking about stringing me up then and there. You talking about somebody doing some kind of praying, I cried out to the Lord, you hear me. Then one of the men said I fit the description of someone that had robbed some folks in the community. He said he was a policeman, and they needed to do things by the book. He took me to jail. They tried and convicted me, even though I was nowhere near that town and there was no evidence proving I was. They sentenced me to ten years on a chain gang. But you know: that policeman actually saved my life. I didn't know it at the time, but he kept them from dangling me from a tree." Gramps shed his glasses and wiped his eyes with his handkerchief.

Gramps shook his head. "On the chain gang, them folks weren't no joke. When I was close to finishing my ten-year sentence, they said there had been a mistake. I wasn't the one who'd done that crime after all. So they was letting me go early. Six months before my ten years was up, and they come telling me that. No apology, no compensation for time lost. Nothing, but 'We made an error. You now free to go.' That was it."

Zenobia got up, went to her father, and put her arm around him. "I'm so sorry, Daddy. I never knew any of this." Now she was crying.

"Oh, that was a normal thing back in my day. We learned to call on the Lord early. When things start riding your back, you fall on your knees and tell the Lord about it." Gramps sat back in his chair and motioned for Zenobia to go sit back down. He had more to tell. "I'm just thankful that my fate wasn't like so many other innocent men gone now. So when I tell folks that the Lord saved me, He saved me in more ways than one."

"What happened after you returned to Asheville?" Clarence asked. "Did you go back and find Sarah?"

"I was going to go look for her," Gramps said. "But as soon as I got back to Asheville, and my old friend, Pearl Black, heard I was in town, she quickly came to see me and told me I needed to lay low in a hurry. We pretended that I left town just as quick as I'd come. Pearl sneaked me back to her place and hid me out for about a month. She and I grew up together. When we were kids, we were closer than white on rice. Pearl was a tad bit older than I was, but we were like peas in a pod. She was like a big sister. Course, I'd been gone all that time, and both Pearl and I were a lot older by the time I returned. But minds don't seem to age like our bodies do. With us, it was just like it was when we were younger. That was around the beginning of April in 1943. She was thirty-nine; I was thirty-three."

"And you actually remember how old she was?" Zenobia asked with a mischievous grin. "Most men I know have a hard time remembering their own age, let alone recalling someone else's. And that was a little over sixty-five years ago."

Gramps remembered because he and Pearl discussed their ages at that time. "You remember dates like that when you have markers, like when you were released from hard labor. Where we were in life was so different from where we thought we would be. Pearl thought she would be married with a houseful of children. And I never thought I'd leave that prison alive." With his hand shaking, he picked up his glass and sipped his water.

"Pearl had been there with the Flemings," Gramps

said, continuing the tale. "Pearl was a midwife, as was her mother before her. Pearl happened to be there when Sarah delivered her baby. Pearl was the one who helped bring my daughter into the world."

"Your *daughter?*" Zenobia practically screeched the words as she sprung up.

"Yes, *my* daughter. You see, Sarah was pregnant when I left. At first, Sarah's daddy believed the baby was this other fella's that lived down the road from them. But when the real truth came out and her daddy saw Sarah was more determined than ever to keep her baby and still be with me, that's when he seemed to come around and try to help us. That was the only reason I left her to go take that job. Sarah was having our child, and I wanted to do right by my family."

"So, I have a sister?" Zenobia asked, sitting down as though she was in shock.

"No . . . yes," Gramps said, sounding confused. "Okay, you see, the baby *was* born. When I got back to Asheville, the first person I saw was my friend Samuel L. Williams. Sam told me he'd heard Pearl had delivered a baby girl for Sarah, but the baby had died right after she was born. More like, they just let the baby die. It was a mere rumor he'd heard circulating throughout the community, mind you, but he felt it was pretty credible. He said Pearl had been the one to deliver the baby. If I wanted to know the truth, she would know and could tell me. That's when I went looking for Pearl, but she was already looking for me. She said it wasn't safe for me to be there. She got me to make a big show of leaving so anybody who'd possibly heard I'd come to town would think I'd just as quickly left. Pearl then hid me out at her place. She told me the whole story of what happened that day and the little bit she knew about the time afterward."

"Okay," Knowledge said, "hold up for one minute, Gramps. I think *I* need something to drink." Knowledge started for the kitchen. "Does anybody else need anything?" Both Zenobia and Clarence shook their heads. Knowledge came back with the strongest beverage his mother had in her house—a can of soda—and sat down. "Okay, Gramps. By all means, please . . . continue."

Chapter 14

*I called upon the Lord in distress: the Lord an-
swered me, and set me in a large place.*

—Psalm 118:5

Gramps continued on with the story. "Pearl told me
Heath, that was Sarah's half-brother, instructed
her to let my baby die. I can't tell you how my heart
sank when I heard Pearl's words. A poor, innocent
child and that monster wanted Pearl to kill her."

"So Pearl let the baby die?" Zenobia asked in a quiet
resolve.

"Pearl said Sarah was out of it. She didn't know
what was going on. Pearl didn't know what she was
going to do to save my baby, but she told me she was
prepared to do something. As it were, Pearl told me
that Grace, Sarah's mother, stepped up to the plate. She
said Grace took my baby"—Gramps wiped his eyes
again—"and carried her to this other woman, a colored
maid, who just happened to be in the house when she
went in labor and had also just delivered her baby ear-

lier. Grace told this woman—her name was Mamie . . . Mamie Patterson—that instead of one baby, she'd delivered two."

"That doesn't even sound plausible," Knowledge said.

"Why not, Knowledge?" Clarence asked. "Back then it would have been easy to pull something like that off."

"Well, did they?" Zenobia asked. "Did they pull it off?"

"Yes. Pearl said she recorded Mamie's delivery as a twin birth. The plan was to protect the baby from folks like Heath until it was safe to disclose the truth, the truth that Sarah wasn't told but instead tragically made to believe that her baby had died. But then soon after that, Victor Senior took sick and died. And Heath and his brother, Victor Junior, were in charge of running things. And the first thing them two did was send Sarah away. Claimed she'd lost her mind and needed to be institutionalized."

"So why didn't her mother do something to stop it?" Zenobia asked.

"Because she didn't have any power," Gramps said. "According to Pearl, she didn't even know where Sarah had been sent. That's how they kept Grace in line. But she did what she could. And that little evil devil Heath . . ." Gramps stopped as he shook his head. "I just shouldn't have left. If I'da stayed instead of leaving, things might have . . ."

"Daddy, you can't go back and change things. That's what you used to tell me all the time: Whatever is . . . is. We deal with what is," Zenobia said.

"I know. But every time I think about all the bad things that happened, I just find it hard to forgive myself. I feel like it's all my fault because I wasn't there to protect them." Gramps wiped his eyes again with his handkerchief. "I should have been there."

"Did you ever find"—Zenobia swallowed hard—"your daughter? My sister?"

"No. I left on the twenty-ninth of April intending on locating Sarah. She deserved to know our daughter had lived. Our daughter was with this other family now. They had moved and no one knew or could tell me where they were. After about a year of trying, I headed for Detroit, Michigan. Went to work for the Ford Motor Company, who were hiring coloreds as janitors and for other type of jobs that weren't great but paid better than most. I met your mama. We married, had your two brothers and you, Zenobia. Course later on things did open up more for colored people at Ford. I moved into a better position. But by then, it was close time for me to retire." He shook his head. "Who would have ever thought or believed that even with me retiring at the age of seventy, I would still be around some thirty years later? God has been good to me. He's been so good."

"Daddy, do you know my . . . sister's name? Did Pearl happen to know or tell you her name?"

"Memory." Gramps nodded.

"I know you have a good memory, Daddy. But did Pearl happen to know your daughter's name?"

Gramps grinned. "Memory. That's actually her name: Memory Elaine."

Chapter 15

The memory of the just is blessed: but the name of the wicked shall rot.

—Proverbs 10:7

"Why are you telling us this now, Gramps?" Knowledge asked when he saw how the words his grandfather was speaking were affecting his mother.

Gramps got to his feet. "I'm telling y'all this now because of a wooden box I made with wings on the inside of its lid that has somehow set off a chain of events."

"A box you made?" Knowledge asked.

"Yes. As I said, when I was young, I loved working with my hands. I loved creating things from wood; I had a special relationship with wood. I crafted this wooden carved box for Sarah. Her mother liked it so much, she asked me to make two more. I gave them those three boxes with wings etched on the inside of the lids, but I kept one because it wasn't as perfect as I wanted, but wasn't bad enough to throw away. I've had that box now for seventy-something years. I packed it and took it with me after I came back from that prison camp. And it's been with me ever since."

"Gramps, you just said it set off a chain of events," Clarence said. "What chain?"

Gramps sat back down. "Yeah. I pulled out that old box from the trunk in my room. You know the one that sits over in the corner?"

"Yeah," Zenobia said.

"Well, I pulled out the wooden box to get an old watch out of it."

"The one you gave to me when I was baptized last Sunday," Clarence said.

"Yeah." Gramps nodded. "That one. I pulled out the box to get the watch, and just when I was about to unlock it, Miss Countess knocked on my door and came in." Gramps then recounted everything that happened with Countess.

Zenobia forced a smile. "Well, Daddy, I'm sure there's a good explanation as to how Miss Countess knew about the wings on the inside of the lid."

"I'm not finished yet. Her daughter, Johnnie Mae is her name, came to my room because her mother had told *her* about the box. She didn't believe I actually had a box as her mother had reported to her. She thought her mother was probably experiencing one of her moments as she's known to do a lot, especially lately."

"Countess is that woman in a more advanced stage of Alzheimer's that you walk with outside from time to time," Zenobia said, attempting to clarify who Countess was.

"Yeah," Gramps said. "Well, it turns out Miss Countess wasn't having one of her moments at all. Johnnie Mae couldn't believe her eyes when I pulled out the box for her to see. And that's when she began to put everything together."

"Everything like what?" Knowledge asked, frowning.

"Everything, like her mother calling me Ranny."

"Okay, so she calls you Ranny. That's short and cute for Ransom," Clarence said.

"Yeah, and that's exactly what Johnnie Mae figured out. That Ranny was her mother's name for Ransom. Turns out Johnnie Mae met both Sarah and Pearl at one point in her life. So she was more than familiar with the name Ransom Perdue," Gramps said.

"Daddy." Zenobia clamped her hand over her mouth and went to her father. "Is she sure about this?"

"Yeah, she'd met Sarah first, then Pearl. That's how she came to know about the box. They call it the Wings of Grace box on account of the wings and the fact that Grace most likely dubbed the boxes with her first name."

"Is Sarah still alive?" Zenobia asked. "Is that what this is all about? Is that why you wanted to leave the nursing home? So you could tell us something about Sarah."

"No. Johnnie Mae says Sarah died four years ago." He shook his head as he dabbed at his eyes with his handkerchief. "I can't believe Sarah was still living and I never found her in all this time. I should have kept looking. I shouldn't have given up so easily. Now they got all these newfangled gadgets. There's that Internet thing. If I'd only told one of you about my past, maybe we could have checked on it ourselves to see if we could have found out something."

"Now, Daddy, don't go getting worked up about this." Zenobia rubbed his back with a caring touch. "Sarah could have just as easily looked for you when she was in a position to do it. It's not like you were hiding out or anything," Zenobia said.

"You don't understand. Sarah thought I was dead. When I didn't come back like I said I would, what else could she believe? She didn't know I'd been arrested and locked away. As sheltered as she was about life, she still knew the times we lived in. I'd either gotten cold feet and run off, was seriously injured, but most likely dead, since death was the only thing I promised her when I left that would keep me from coming back for her."

Zenobia hugged her father as she rocked him. "But I'm so thankful that you weren't killed. And as selfish as this might sound, if things hadn't happened the way they did, I wouldn't be here and neither would my children." She looked over at Knowledge and Clarence. "If you had been with Sarah, you never would have met Mother and you never would have had me. So even though it was bad, all things did work out."

Gramps patted Zenobia's arms draped around him. "Sit, sit. There's something more I need to tell."

"What else?" Zenobia said. "What more can there be? This is already a lot to process."

"Johnnie Mae told me yesterday that my daughter is still alive." Gramps looked in Zenobia's eyes. "Memory is alive! And Johnnie Mae knows how to get in touch with her."

"Memory is alive?" Zenobia said, kneeling down in front of her father. "Are you sure?"

"She's alive and living in old man Fleming's home in Asheville, North Carolina." Gramps began to chuckle. "Can you believe my daughter, who I ain't never laid eyes on a day in my life in all her seventy-four years of being on this earth, is still alive and living in the place where all of this began?" He began to wipe his eyes again. "That's what I needed to tell y'all. Johnnie Mae has contacted her. She called me earlier today and told me Memory's whole family is making arrangements to be here tomorrow. And I'd like all of us to be together . . . to do this as a family."

"I have a sister?" Zenobia said, still processing all of it. She went and sat back down on the couch. "A sister. And she's alive? After all these years, she's still alive?" Zenobia broke down and began to cry as both of her sons comforted her.

Chapter 16

*And of some have compassion, making a differ-
ence.*

—Jude 22

Gabrielle was excited. She was finally going to see
Miss Crowe. Zachary teased her after he'd spoken
with his mother.

"My mother says there will be no sleeping in the
same room in her house," Zachary said.

"Did you tell her we wouldn't dare think of doing
anything like that?" Gabrielle said.

"Nope."

"Nope?"

"Nah. I like to irritate my mother from time to time.
It keeps her on her toes."

"Zachary, you should have told her. I don't want her
thinking badly of me."

Zachary walked closer to her. "My mother's going
to love you. I did tell her you were a churchgoing
woman. She happens to like that . . . a lot." Zachary
grinned. "So, what would you like to do tonight?"

Gabrielle shrugged. "Let's watch that movie you brought over the other day."

"*Fireproof.* Yeah, that's right. I brought it over, but we didn't get to watch it," Zachary said, smiling mischievously.

"Quit acting like we were doing something wrong and that's why we didn't watch it."

"What? I didn't say anything," Zachary said.

"It's not what you said. It's the way you're acting. You know, I'm starting to think you might be a little bad."

"Ooh, now you sound like my mother. I believe you and my mother are going to get along splendidly." He tapped her on her nose. "I know my daddy's going to love you."

"Yeah, well. It's the mothers that generally have problems with their sweet little sons and the women they bring home to meet them." Gabrielle put a hand on one hip. "But you are bad."

"I am not," Zachary said with a deliberate whine.

The telephone rang. Gabrielle went and looked at the caller ID. She made a face. "Hmmm, I wonder who this is." She clicked on the talk button. "Hello."

"Hi, may I please speak with Gabrielle Booker," a woman's soft voice said from the other end.

Just that one word gave Gabrielle pause. She hadn't been called Booker in eight years. Not since she'd legally dropped that surname and opted for her middle name to become her last. Her first reaction was to tell her that she had the wrong number. She felt if this woman was *that* behind the times that she was asking for her by her old name, it couldn't be anyone she cared to talk to.

"This is Gabrielle," she decided to say instead of

merely hanging up. At least she would find out who this was and what she wanted.

"I'm sorry to bother you, but I'm calling in association with the Red Cross. You gave blood once—"

"That was ages ago," Gabrielle said with a sincere frown as she tried to remember how far back that had to be. "I was eighteen, and I only did it that one time."

"Yes, but the reason we're calling is that we have someone who is in desperate need of a donor. Actually, it's a bone marrow transplant," the woman said.

"Whoa. Hey, look, I'm not interested in being a donor of anything, let alone something that has to do with transplants."

"Ms. Booker, it's not what you think. The procedure doesn't require you to lose anything. Well, not anything that won't regenerate completely in a few weeks. But this is a child we're talking about. And it's very possible you may be a perfect match. All we're asking is that you go in and let them do a blood workup on you to see. If you're not a good match, then that will be the end of it. But if you are, and you agree to, you would then check into the hospital—"

"Hospital?" Gabrielle looked over at Zachary and widened her eyes.

"It would be an outpatient procedure. I promise you, it's not bad. You can't die or anything like that from the procedure. But this is only if you happen to be a match and if you agree to do it. Ms. Booker, this child is going to die if she doesn't get a donor soon. Her mother is heartbroken and, as you can probably imagine, desperate to save her child's life. I'm sure you must understand how she feels seeing that's it's a child . . . her daughter."

"I'm sure this must be hard for her, but I'm not interested in doing anything like this."

"But Ms. Booker—"

"Listen, Miss or Mrs. . . . what did you say your name was?"

"My name is Mrs. Wendy Watts."

"Listen, Mrs. Watts. First of all, you are looking at very old records. My name is not Booker anymore, it's Mercedes."

"I'm sorry. Please accept my apology. I'm updating my information now."

"Well, you really don't need to bother updating your records with any of my information. I'm not interested in giving blood again, and I sure don't care to have anyone calling my house about being a donor of any kind."

"But Ms. Mercedes, this child—"

Gabrielle hated the tactic this woman was using. Telling someone it was a child made it harder for anyone to say no. But she also couldn't be sure if it really was for a child or just this woman's way of manipulating her heart and conscience.

"Would you please take me off your list? I asked the last person who called me about donating blood years ago to take me off the list. I don't know how I managed to get back on it. And quite frankly, I don't know how anyone got this phone number since I didn't have this number when I originally gave blood."

"Ms. Mercedes, I apologize if I've upset you. It was not my intention to do that. All we try to do here is to help others. For me, this is not just a job, it's my mission. Will you at least think about this and get back to me? I can give you my number and you can call me back to let me know. Do you have a pen and paper handy?" The woman waited.

Gabrielle really didn't want to pretend she was interested in considering this or in calling her back. Still, she got pen and paper and took down the phone number. "If I change my mind, I'll call you. But I'm going to be honest with you, Mrs. Watts, because I don't want you sitting around thinking you've found someone when you clearly haven't. I'm most likely not going to call you back. I'm pretty certain this is not something I'm interested in doing."

"I do pray you reconsider. It's a little girl, and she's only eight. I'm going to do all I can to help her. All I ask is that you think about it. Just think about it, that's all I ask right now."

Gabrielle swallowed hard as she placed the phone back into its base. *An eight-year-old little girl.* She couldn't help but think about the child she'd given up some eight years ago.

Zachary went over and held her as he began to rock her. And it was only then that she realized the loud sobbing and wailing sounds she was hearing were actually coming from her.

Chapter 17

The rich and poor meet together: the Lord is the maker of them all.

—Proverbs 22:2

"**I**nstead of watching a movie," Zachary said, leading Gabrielle away from the telephone to sit on the couch in the den, "why don't we just sit and talk."

"I'm okay," Gabrielle said as she wiped away her tears. She tried to put on a good-front smile. "See." She bounced on the balls of her feet. "I'm fine."

Zachary pulled her down as he continued to hold a wrapped arm around her. "Okay. Talk to me," he said.

She tried to maintain the smile, but the tears continued to make a trail down her face. She wiped harder as though the strength of the wipe would somehow scare any other tears from trying to make the trek from her eyes.

"Talk to me," Zachary said once more.

"I'm always the one talking. You know pretty much most of the things in my life," Gabrielle said. "Why don't you talk? Tell me how things went at work today."

"That phone call upset you. I could tell from what I heard on your end of the conversation, it had something to do with you being a donor."

Gabrielle looked up into his eyes. His eyes had such a calming effect. She saw how much he really cared. "You must think I'm awfully selfish and heartless."

"No. I don't think any such thing."

"Yeah, but that was someone calling about me possibly being a donor for someone who's obviously in need of a bone marrow transplant. According to her, the person might die if she doesn't get it." Gabrielle started crying again. Zachary held her even tighter.

"Listen. There are people who are in need of donors all the time. Why is it upsetting you like this?" Zachary asked.

"It's a little girl. That woman says she just might die."

"A little girl is in need of a bone marrow transplant?"

"Yes. And Mrs. Watts told me it won't kill me or cause me any problems if I were to do it. Of course, they aren't sure I'm a good match. But for whatever reason, they believe there's a strong possibility I might be."

Zachary sat back with her still in his arms. "Truthfully, there really aren't enough African-Americans in the donor pool. But I can understand you not wanting to do it. A lot of people don't. But what I don't understand is why you're reacting to it this way."

Gabrielle pulled away and looked at him. "She's an eight-year-old girl. I suppose I started thinking about the baby I gave away. She's eight now, the same age as this little girl. I can't help but feel for this family. What if this was my child? I feel bad saying no. And what if this child dies and I could have done something to help save her and I didn't? But I really don't want to do this. I don't. And I feel bad that I'm apparently so selfish."

Zachary pulled her back into his arms. "You're not being selfish. If it's something you wanted to do, that would be fine. But if you don't want to, you shouldn't be guilted into doing it. I'm sure the woman who called wasn't trying to make you feel guilty. She was merely trying to make you think about what it could mean if you decided to do it."

After a few minutes, Gabrielle pulled herself together and scooted over out of Zachary's soothing arm. "Why am I thinking about my daughter so much?" she asked, mostly to herself. "I was fine when I gave her up for adoption. I've been going on with my life without stopping to think about her. But since I've been saved, all I seem to do lately is think about her. I wonder what she looks like." Gabrielle smiled.

"Does she have any of my features, any of my mannerisms? I wonder if she's happy. Are they treating her right? Does she know she's adopted, and if so, how is she dealing with me having given her up? Does she think I didn't love her or want her? Does she like to dance?" Gabrielle laughed. "I need to get it together. My emotions seem to be all over the place these days." She briefly pressed her hands hard against her face.

"If I might ask, did you set things up where your daughter is able to find you when she's of age?" Zachary asked.

"Yes. I did do that, although I don't know what I'll do if she ever *does* decide to contact me. What if she hates me? How do I explain to her why I did what I did?"

"You be honest with her. You tell her what you told me: that *because* you loved her so much you wanted her to have the best in life. Something you didn't feel

you could give her at the time. That when we love . . .
we do things that may not make sense to others, but our
hearts are in the right place at the time. We never *mean*
to cause harm."

"Like you?"

Zachary looked at her. "What do you mean?"

"We've touched on this somewhat, but we've never
really talked about it. Miss Crowe. Tell me what happened with her. Why did she go to Chicago the way she
did, and why do you feel that what happened to her . . .
her accident . . . was your fault?"

Zachary sat forward, lacing his fingers into each
other. He blew hard into his now-fisted hands. He re-
laxed his hands and sat back against the couch, rapidly
pressing the thighs of his pants with his hands. "I suppose now is as good a time to talk about this as any."

"Well, you've probably heard that the truth is the
light."

"Yeah, I've heard that. The truth is the light." He
blew out hard again. "The truth is the light."

Chapter 18

Say not thou, I will recompense evil; but wait on the Lord, and he shall save thee.

—Proverbs 20:22

Gabrielle sat back and turned more toward Zachary as he began.

"There were four of us. You've met Queen. She's the baby of the family. I'm the knee-baby. We have an older brother named Yancey. The oldest was my sister Xenia."

Gabrielle let out a slight giggle. "It looks like your parents liked using the most difficult letters when naming their children: X, Y, Z, and Q."

He let out a slight chuckle in response. "Yeah. I'd never thought of it quite like that. I suppose maybe that's why we like to tease one another by using our initials instead of our actual names from time to time."

"I'm sorry. Forgive me. I didn't mean to interrupt," Gabrielle said. "Please continue."

"It's okay. You pointed out something I hadn't really

thought of. Those really are some of the most difficult letters to use for names, and yet my mother and father managed to do just that. I'll have to ask my mother if she did that on purpose."

"Just don't tell her I was the one who brought it up. The last thing I need is to get on your mother's bad side: me questioning her reasoning behind the naming of her children."

"Well, in truth, there is some logic behind the names. I'm named more after my father, whose name is Zechariah. My father didn't care for his name too much when he was growing up, so he decided it would be cruel to do the same thing to me. Still, my mother wanted one of her boys to carry his name, although I suspect it was as much my father's doing as my mother's. They decided even though legally my father's name wasn't Zachary, he still went by it, so it would be fine to name me that officially."

"So, you could have been a junior?"

"I'm sure they thought about that. But honestly, I love the name Zachary."

"Well, not that I get a vote, but I love Zachary as well."

"You mean you love the name Zachary or that you love Zachary?"

She hit him playfully on his arm. "Don't start that. I've told you, we don't need to play over there in that sandbox. I don't want either one of us to end up getting sand in our eyes."

He laughed. "You have the funniest way of putting things. Playing in the sandbox. Sand in our eyes. . . ." He tilted his head down and smiled as he looked softly into her eyes. "You still didn't answer the question." When she didn't immediately respond, he said, "Do I need to ask the question again?"

"No, I heard you the first time." Gabrielle tried hard to keep him from seeing that she was now blushing.

"And the answer is?" He said it like a game show host.

"The answer is: you need to finish your story and stop trying to be sneaky and call yourself changing the subject. We're talking about you and your family and what happened. Remember? Not me and you. So, go ahead."

"Yeah, okay. But don't think we won't be coming back to this subject later. Because I can tell you how I feel about you, Gabrielle."

"The logic behind the names," Gabrielle said. "You were telling me how your folks came to the names Xenia and Yancey. You've already told me about Queen being named after your aunt Esther and your mother compromising by being able to add Queen before Esther, which also happens to reference to the biblical Queen Esther."

"Yeah, that explained Queen's name. As for Xenia, my mother was an English teacher. She loves English and loves reading the classics. She happened to have been heavy into Greek epic poems at that time, and of course, there was Homer's *Odyssey*. She named Xenia after the idea of xenia, which is one of the themes in that poem."

"I suppose then you should be glad she didn't name you Zeus."

He put his hand up to his face and did a peek-a-boo gesture. "Oh, please. You don't know how glad I am about that. But my daddy wouldn't have ever gone for a name like Hercules or Zeus. He's too into the Lord to have his child named after something that references a god. That's why he didn't catch Xenia. It was an *idea* and not a goddess."

"Zeus, the god of the sky and thunder. Aphrodite, the goddess of love, lust, and beauty. Apollo, the god of music, medicine, and health, and also said to be the god of light and truth." Gabrielle shook her head. "So many little *g* gods. And to think that there really is only one true God, big *G*. The blessed trinity: God the Father, God the Son, and God the Holy Spirit."

"You sure do know a lot about Greek mythology," Zachary said. "I know you and my mother are going to hit it off wonderfully."

"Yeah, well, reading that stuff was okay when I was growing up. But there's nothing like Jesus: the true Truth and the Light."

"Amen to that!" Zachary said. "Let the church say amen!"

She shoved him playfully. "Okay, Zachary. So far we've talked about names and Greek myths."

"Yeah, and I've learned I should have known you back when that course in Greek mythology was kicking my behind."

"Tell me more about Xenia," Gabrielle said with a warm smile.

"Xenia. Did you know that *xenia* is the term for hospitality? Well, that's what my sister Xenia was about. She was the kindest, most generous person you could have ever met. She cared about people and those that needed help. I remember when we were children, there was this girl who wore these raggedy clothes to school. The kids in school picked on her and teased her mercilessly. Not only did my sister befriend this girl, but she came home, went through her clothes, and took enough for her to have a week of nice things, including a brand-new pair of tennis shoes." He began to chuckle.

"My mother went through the roof when she found out that Xenia had given away her new clothes, including the pair of brand-new tennis shoes she'd just bought her. And do you know what Xenia did after that?" Zachary said.

"No. What?"

"She invited the girl to our house for dinner along with her parents. My mother didn't know she'd done that. But one thing you could always count on at our house with my mother was plenty of food, whether she was expecting guests or not. My mother only found out what Xenia had done when the family of five showed up at our doorstep. But it turns out Xenia was right in what she'd done." With an ankle resting on his knee, he began to play with the hem of his pants leg.

"They were good people who had fallen on hard times," Zachary continued. "The father had MS but he was still trying to go to work every day. He told how difficult it was for him to get ready for work. How he had to start getting ready hours in advance just to be sure he made it to work on time. They didn't have insurance, and one visit to the hospital had devastated them financially. The family was doing well if they had food to eat, let alone buy clothes. They made do. But education for their three children was important to them. After they left, my mother gathered up bags of clothes, some of mine, some of hers and Dad's, some from friends who she knew had family members that fit their sizes, and she took them over. They are still friends to this day."

"That was nice."

"Yeah. Xenia had that kind of effect on people. I remember one time she found this bird that had somehow broken its neck. Everybody told her the bird didn't have a chance of making it with a broken neck. But she bandaged its little neck up and kept that bird in her room, feeding it with an eyedropper."

"Did the bird recover?"

"No. The bird died, and you would have thought a family member had passed away. But that was Xenia. She was four years older than me, but unlike our older brother, Yancey, who was named after my mother's father, Xenia never made me or Queen feel as though we were a bother to her when we were around." Zachary began to fidget. He placed his foot back down on the floor and readjusted his body.

"What happened to her, Zachary? What happened to Xenia?"

He sat back against the couch and the muscles on his face stood out as he clenched his teeth. "Her boyfriend killed her. He was an abusive jerk. They had been dating for about two years. He was a jealous, controlling freak. She was twenty-three, working as a nurse, doing what she loved to do best. Something happened where she had to stay at work longer than she was originally scheduled. When she got home, he was waiting for her. He thought she was with another man and trying to cover by using her job as an excuse." Zachary wiped at both of his eyes before any threatening tears had time to fully emerge.

Gabrielle placed a hand on one of his and squeezed it. She could feel the tenseness in his hand. "Zachary, I'm so sorry."

"That animal went into her apartment with her. Beat her up. While she was attending to her wounds, he left and came back, burst down the door, and threw gasoline on her. He lit . . . a . . . match and threw . . . the match on her while telling her if he couldn't have her, he would make sure no one else would ever want her."

"Oh, Zachary," Gabrielle said as she flinched at the thought. And before she could stop herself, she began to cry.

"My sister became a ball of fire right there as that monster first looked on at her, engulfed in flames. Then he claims he came back to his senses and helped put her out with the bedspread he took off her bed. He called for help. Of course, we only heard *this* version of the story *after* the first lie he'd told that he'd found her like that. I suppose he had to amend his story since Xenia didn't die, and she was able to tell what happened. He confessed to what he'd done but would be pleading temporary insanity. A few weeks later, Xenia succumbed to her painful injuries, and she died. With a plea deal, they were going to give him a year in prison with ten years' probation and mandatory psychiatric counseling. That's it. He killed my sister, and he was going to get to walk away without really paying for what he'd done. They were talking about suspending the year in prison."

"So, is that why Miss Crowe went to Chicago like she did? Because of what was going on with your sister?" Gabrielle asked, still holding on, now with both hands, to Zachary's hand.

"No. My daddy found out the plan I'd made with two of my friends. I was in college at the time, but I was determined to avenge my sister's death using the Old Testament law of an eye for an eye. Vengeance—that's what was going on that caused my aunt to jump in her car and drive frantically to Chicago. My father discovered my plans of vengeance. I believe one of my friends who had agreed to help me told him what I was plotting. My father had immediately tried to talk some sense into me. But I was so blinded with rage, hurt, and anger, I wasn't hearing any of what he had to say.

"My father told Aunt Esther, thinking she could talk me down. Aunt Esther was my heart. She was always the one person able to reason with me. She tried talking to me about it over the phone. When she could tell I wasn't listening, no matter what she or anyone else had to say, she instinctively got in her car and headed to Chicago, despite the icy conditions my father had warned her about." Zachary loudly blew out a heavy sigh and began shaking one of his legs.

"Aunt Esther was trying to stop me from ruining my life. She was trying to save me from myself," Zachary said. "She was on that road that night because she knew I was planning to make my sister's killer pay. That I was planning on taking someone else's life." His jaw tightened.

Gabrielle released his hand. "Zachary," she whispered. "You wouldn't have gone through with it, would you? You were just upset. That's how people talk when they're upset. They want people to pay. They claim they want to hurt that person. But they don't really mean it."

"My plan was already in motion. Two friends and I were going to kill him. It was all planned out. It would have looked like an accident, but we were going to take him out. And honestly, if my aunt hadn't been in that accident that night, I'm pretty sure I would have gone through with it. I was just that mad and hurt. God forgive me," Zachary began to cry, "but I was going to do it."

He looked in Gabrielle's eyes. "But God has changed me. I don't feel that way anymore. But I did have hate in my heart then. And I was angry enough to want to do someone else bodily harm. How much better was I than him? Nevertheless, I felt justified in what I was going to do to him. But in truth, I was just as wrong as he had been. They say anger is one letter short of danger. And anger really can be dangerous. It took my aunt almost losing her life, trying to save me from me, before I was able to see that and just how wrong I'd been."

Gabrielle held him as he released what she believed had to have been years of pent-up feelings and words locked away inside of him. "It's okay. It's okay. Jesus is a healer. He's forgiven you, and look at you now. Look what you're doing with your life now, Zachary. You're saving others' lives. Look at how God has turned things around in your life. It's okay, Zachary. It's okay." She gently rocked him, and just allowed him to let it all out.

Chapter 19

*But there is a spirit in man: and the inspiration of
the Almighty giveth them understanding.*

—Job 32:8

"I heard back from Lena," Johnnie Mae said to her
husband as she chopped up cabbage for supper.
"She's spoken with everyone. They'll all be in Birmingham tomorrow."

"Everybody?" Pastor Landris said, wrapping his
arms around her waist and kissing her on the cheek. He
picked up a piece of raw cabbage and put it in his
mouth.

"Yeah. Lena said they were waiting for Memory to
fly in to Atlanta. Theresa and Maurice have rented a
van. That way they can all come together," Johnnie
Mae said, referring to Lena's daughter and son-in-law.

"Is Bishop Jordan coming as well?" Pastor Landris
asked, inquiring about Lena's husband, Richard.

"Lena said it would be her and Bishop Jordan, Theresa, Maurice, and their two children, and Memory. I
suppose they can all fit in a seven-passenger van."

"Did they say how long they would be staying? Are they just coming down to meet with Ransom and then going right back?"

"She didn't say," Johnnie Mae said. "But it will be good to see them again after all this time. They've been through a lot." She primped her mouth. "And just when it looks like things are normal, something like this pops up. Life is truly hidden with surprises."

"I'm just starting to wonder about *you*," Pastor Landris said. "How is it that you seem to manage to end up in the middle of people finding each other?"

"It *is* becoming a pattern. Maybe I need to seek the Lord out about this. Ask Him what's going on." Johnnie Mae was slightly teasing about asking God about it. She shook her head as she rinsed the cabbage in the stainless-steel colander. She dumped the washed cabbage into a heated boiler. "This discovery really could be attributed more to my mother than to me. I just happened to pursue what she'd said about that box. And here we are again. I'm starting to think there's something to those Wings of Grace boxes."

"Do you think *this* Ransom Perdue is really legit?"

Johnnie Mae shrugged. She turned the eye on the stove down and placed a top on the boiler. Everything else was ready. The cabbage was the last thing she was cooking, that and rolls already in the toaster oven. They were having Salisbury steak, mashed potatoes, corn on the cob, candied yams, cabbage, and buttered rolls for supper.

Johnnie Mae sat down at the kitchen table. "Honestly, he appears very credible to me. But Lena is not convinced this isn't some cooked-up scam. I mean, what if this really was a well-planned setup like Lena and Theresa think it could be?"

"Well, I can see why both Lena and Theresa would

feel that way." Pastor Landris sat with Johnnie Mae. "Montgomery Powell the Second was not exactly pleased about losing everything after Sarah returned to her rightful position and regained power. Kicking him out of that mansion like she did was hard on him. Then Sarah leaving the house to Memory, especially after Montgomery, and his father before him, went to such great lengths to make sure Sarah would never get anything, ever."

Johnnie Mae sat forward. Pastor Landris took his hand and moved a strand of hair from her face and pushed it behind her ear. He smiled as he looked in her eyes. Johnnie Mae took his hand and kissed it.

"I think Sarah actually left the house in a trust for Theresa's children. When I talked to Memory a little after Sarah died, she told me how Montgomery had tricked her into signing for him to purchase the house after Sarah's death. But the women were smart enough to tell each other what was going on, and Sarah was able to outwit Montgomery on that. Memory lives in the house, but it's set to be there for Theresa's children."

"So, do you think Montgomery hired this guy to pretend to be Ransom Perdue? Told him what to say to convince folks he was the real deal? Even planted him here with plans for you or someone to find out so he could have access to Memory."

Johnnie Mae shook her head. "No, I don't think so. If Montgomery was going to do something like that, then why not plant him to run into Memory in Asheville, North Carolina, or Lena or Theresa in Atlanta. Besides, my mother just went into that nursing home. I believe Ransom was already there when she got there." She shook her head fast. "No. In spite of Lena and Theresa's skepticism, I believe this really is Memory's father, Ransom Perdue.

After they get here tomorrow and get settled in, I'm going to their hotel and take them to the nursing home to meet him."

Pastor Landris took one of Johnnie Mae's hands and began to caress it. "So, you've already told Ransom all about of them coming tomorrow?"

"Yeah. He knows. After I discovered who he was and told him about Memory, he couldn't wait to meet her. He wants to hurry, almost as though he's afraid after all this time he'll not live to see her. It should be something to see them all meet for the first time. Ransom says he's planning to have his whole family there, at least the ones that live here in Birmingham."

The phone rang. Pastor Landris got up and picked it up to see the caller ID. "It's a Z. Walker," he said. Johnnie Mae gestured with a shrug, puzzled as to who it might be. Pastor Landris pressed the talk button. After the initial hello, he gave the phone to Johnnie Mae.

"Hello," Johnnie Mae said, trying to read her husband's face as he gave no further clue as to who it was.

"Mrs. Landris, my name is Zenobia Walker. I think you met my father, Ransom Perdue, the other day at the nursing home where your mother also resides."

"Yes. Everybody except my mother calls him Gramps. She calls him Ranny."

Zenobia gave a slight and short laugh. "Yes. Gramps. Mrs. Landris, I have my father here with me. He told me about your mother and the wooden box. He just finished telling us about Sarah Fleming and her daughter, Memory. And if we're to believe all of this, then that would make Memory my sister. Honestly, I'm having a difficult time wrapping my head around all of this."

"I'm sure it's a shock and is something that would be hard for anyone to grasp."

"Are you sure this isn't some scam or something? I

mean, my father doesn't have anything for anyone to be trying to get their hands on. Nothing except maybe some land in North Carolina that he shares with a few other relatives. Daddy's not interested in claiming any of it, and none of us are, either. But other than that, my father doesn't have that much of anything."

"Ms. Walker—"

"Please, call me Zenobia."

"Okay, Zenobia. Ironically, I've been in this story from a long way back. And believe it or not, the other side of the family is just as skeptical about this as you are. They're not sure your daddy is the real Ransom Perdue or at least *their* Ransom Perdue."

"When Daddy gave me the note with your name and phone number after he told us everything . . . Whew!" She made a blowing sound. "I still can't believe all of what he told us. I never suspected any of this. My daddy was just my daddy: a rather boring father, who lived in Detroit, went to work every day to provide us with our needs and some of our wants, and a man who grew to be a boring old man who equally loves his children, grandchildren, and great-grandchildren alike. Now I learn about a whole other life I never knew existed. A woman he almost married named Sarah Fleming: a rich white woman back during a time when they hanged a black man for just looking as if he wanted to look at a white woman. And then to learn she was pregnant with his child. That he was tricked away, to never return, because of a setup to lynch him. But he ended up imprisoned instead just so they could keep him from his family."

"So, that's what happened to him," Johnnie Mae said. "I'm sorry. You see, I know most of the story, but that part about your father almost being lynched and being in prison I didn't know. I just knew he left and no one ever heard from him again."

"Except his friend Pearl Black. She saw him after he came back to Asheville looking for Sarah and his child ten years later."

"Yes, I met Pearl. She was the person who gave me the Wings of Grace box. Sarah had given it to her, then gave me the special key needed to open it and told me where I could find Pearl. That's how I happen to know her. But you say your father came back to Asheville *after* all of this and he saw Pearl?"

"That's what Daddy said. He said it was around April of 1943."

"Hmmm," Johnnie Mae said, mostly to herself. "I didn't know that. Pearl never mentioned that. But then again, I don't suppose she would have a reason to mention something like that to me."

"Daddy said you told his other family about him."

"I did, and I've talked with Lena; that's Memory's only child. They're coming here tomorrow. I got one of the nurses to let me talk to him and I told him."

"That's when he called me and said it was an emergency. He summoned all of us, me and my two sons, to the nursing home. He nearly scared me to death. I thought something awful had happened. Then he didn't want to talk about it there, so naturally I assumed maybe someone had done something to him at the home. You can never feel too comfortable and let down your guard. He's still here at my house. Memory is planning on visiting him at the nursing home, and he thought you were going to come with them."

"Yes. I've agreed to bring them, unless that's a problem with you."

"Well, I'd prefer we do it at my house instead of the

nursing home. I'll give you my address, and you can bring them over here—that's if you don't mind."

"Zenobia, I have a thought. And you can tell me if you don't like it or don't want to do it. But why don't all of you come here to my home. That way it would be in a bigger, more private place than the nursing home but a more neutral ground for all."

Zenobia paused a second. "I think that's a great idea. But I wouldn't want to put you out or cause you to go to any trouble."

"It's no trouble. Look, Zenobia, I told you earlier: I've been in this from the beginning. With this new development, I would be honored to do whatever I can to help. It's the least I can do . . . for Sarah. I helped in bringing her back together with her daughter. It's only fitting that I would do the same with Memory's father."

"I don't know what God is up to, but I must admit: He never ceases to amaze me."

Johnnie Mae laughed. "For sure, there's definitely never a dull moment with the Lord. Like you said, we never know what He's up to. We just need to be obedient. And I really don't mind everyone meeting over here. I really don't."

"Then, yes. Give me your address, tell me what time, and we'll be there."

"Let me check with the others to make sure this works for them as well. I'm sure they're going to agree. I'll see what time they're looking at, especially since they're the ones driving in."

"That's fine. I understand. We'll just keep our evening free. I just want to be sure my sons are able to be there. My oldest son doesn't usually get off work until four-thirty, plus he has four children. Though if he needs to, I'm sure he can work it all out."

"I'll tell you what. Why don't we set a time of six PM? And if we need to change it, we can."

"Six is fine with me. Just let me know for sure." Zenobia gave her both her home and cell phone numbers, then wrote down Johnnie Mae's home address.

Chapter 20

Abstain from all appearance of evil.
                                        —1 Thessalonians 5:22

Pastor Landris opened the certified letter he'd received from the IRS. He couldn't believe what he
was reading. It was a formal accusation of him not reporting income and assets and of possibly abusing his
powers in his ministerial position. The letter had been
delivered to the church. He was officially being asked
to come into the IRS office and address several issues
he was being accused of. The listed items almost
floored him, as there was no way he was guilty of any
of the things included.

He had called his personal accountant as well as the
church's accountant. They assured him what had been
filed was fine and that it was likely just some routine
audit. But after he faxed the letter to both accountants,
his personal accountant, Stanley, called him back and
told him this was more than a random audit.

"Pastor, I hate to tell you this, but this doesn't look

good. It's saying that you didn't report certain income as income. This is one of those whistle-blowing-type letters. I reported everything that you gave me. Is it possible you forgot to give me something?"

"No, Stanley. I don't play about things like this. You know how you were saying I was including things as income that were considered love offerings and not necessarily reportable, and I told you that I didn't even want the appearance of evil. If someone gave me a love gift, I kept a record and gave that record to you. I don't play when it comes to the Lord's business."

"Well, given the number of high-profile ministers who've been under the microscope here recently, I'm a little concerned. This letter appears to be an inquiry to address some person who has filed a formal complaint against you," Stanley said.

"So what you're telling me is that anybody could have called the IRS and said I did something inappropriate without producing any hard evidence to support their claim?" Pastor Landris asked.

"Yeah. Especially when it comes to someone in your position. You're in a position of authority where you *could* be doing something wrong, and someone does need to watch out for that. Citizens who either give to the ministry or are watching out for crooks who prey on people in this area have every right to bring to the government's attention people who might possibly be abusing or gaming the system."

"Okay, so what do we do now?"

"I'll call and set up a meeting with this agent, and we'll see what's really going on. Unless you have things that you've hidden from me and thus hidden from the government, this should be pretty easy to put to rest." Stanley paused for a few seconds. "Are you sure you gave me everything? You don't have any off-shore accounts? Any money you received under the table from someone who can prove that you did?"

Pastor Landris thought back to his eldest brother, Thomas. Thomas had messed him up some years ago by selling his millions' worth of Microsoft stock without telling him he'd sold it, then proceeded to reinvest the money in some unsavory business practices, trying to make some extra money for himself. It had been a nightmare of a mess, but all of that had been straightened out with the IRS. Pastor Landris had paid the owed back taxes and penalties, which also happened to be in the millions, on the money, despite much of it having been lost and swindled, thanks to his brother. Pastor Landris had learned a valuable lesson during that period at a great expense: No matter what, *you* are ultimately responsible, so handle your own business, and handle it well. At least know everything that's going on. Following that debacle, Thomas hadn't been allowed anywhere near his finances.

Of course, Pastor Landris later learned that his brother suffered from a mental illness called bipolar disorder, which might have contributed to his impulses to recklessly throw money away. It had been rough in the beginning trying to get him help. Thomas had been doing well, seeing a doctor who started him on medication to help control the disorder. Then Thomas had gone through that period when he'd taken himself off his medication. With much prayer and love, along with a doctor's help, Thomas was still on his medication and was even dating a nice woman who was spiritually strong in the Lord and didn't take any lip when it came to Thomas doing right. Pastor Landris could see they were headed for the altar soon, although both Pastor Landris and Johnnie Mae had secretly wished Thomas and Sapphire Drummond would have made another go of it.

But after that meltdown Thomas had with Faith, a.k.a. Trinity, and Sapphire doing all she could to help Thomas to get better through mental health support, Sapphire and Thomas went in totally different directions. Then the dreadlock-wearing Sapphire cut off her dreads even before Pastor Landris cut off his, and she began sporting a small, natural Afro. Four years ago she'd met and, a year later, married a wonderful widower with three teenage children. To Sapphire's surprise, at age forty-one, she became pregnant, and the couple had a beautiful little boy. But because of her age and this being her first child and the possibility the child could be born with Down syndrome, it was touch and go there for a while.

So Pastor Landris could see no way anyone could have done something that he didn't know about when it came to his finances. In fact, wisdom had led him to hire Stanley because of his stellar reputation as a great accountant and his work ethics, integrity, and honesty.

"Stanley, unless someone gave me money and I didn't know it had been given to me, I have given you something on everything that I've ever received. You know how much money I get from the church. You know about my speaking engagement money. As I've said, even when people give me money and call it a love offering, I've given you that total and instructed you to include it in my income count. I haven't ordered any lavish items at the church or for the church. No platinum toilets in my house. I don't have my own personal jet or a church plane at my disposal. When people bring me in to preach or speak and pay for my flight, I give that to you so you can count it as income. Everything I do, to the best of my ability, is on the up-and-up."

"All right then, we have nothing to worry about. I'll call and see if we can't get this straightened out. Get Ms. . . . ." He paused to look for the name of the IRS agent on the letter.

"Winston," Pastor Landris said quickly. "Raquel Winston."

"She has a nice name," Stanley said.

"Well, get back to me and let me know what we need to do to take care of this."

"Will do," Stanley said.

Chapter 21

And having food and raiment let us be therewith content.

—1 Timothy 6:8

Angela rang the doorbell of Johnnie Mae's house. Johnnie Mae answered the door almost out of breath, wearing purple fuzzy slippers.

"Angel," Johnnie Mae said. "What are you doing here?"

"Your page proofs from your publisher came to the church today. Since you took off today and tomorrow, I thought I'd bring them to you."

Johnnie Mae frowned. "You could have given them to Pastor Landris. You didn't have to drive all the way over here to bring them to me."

"There were a few other things you really needed to handle." Angela held up her briefcase. "Gabrielle's paperwork came back for the department head of the Dance Ministry appointment. You need to sign them so she'll get her paycheck on time. Plus, you need to approve the final budget for the Dance Ministry before Gabrielle takes it over."

"Come in, come in. I'm sorry. I just have you standing out there. I'm trying to get things ready for this evening, and I'm running around like a chicken with its head cut off."

Angela laughed. "My great-granny used to say stuff like that all the time." Angela stepped inside. "I didn't want to just send it by Pastor in case you have some questions. Plus, I didn't know if you wanted to sign them now and have me take them on back."

"You're always looking out for me. Have I told you lately how much I appreciate you?" Johnnie Mae said. "Unfortunately, I don't have time to look at those papers now. If you had called first, I could have saved you a trip and just told you to send them by Landris."

"Well, since I'm here, is there anything I can help you do?" Angela set down her briefcase and purse next to the large vase of flowers on the glass, round table in the peach-colored, marbled-floor foyer.

"Normally, I would say no out of politeness. But honestly, I could use some help. I'm having guests over tonight. You remember I told you about Ransom Perdue."

"Yeah, Great-granny's old friend. The man your mother led you to at the nursing home."

"Can we go in the kitchen while we talk? You can help me finish up in there."

"Sure." Angela followed Johnnie Mae to the kitchen. She washed her hands at the sink. "What do you need me to do?"

"Put the petite quiches on a tray and put them in the oven. I thought I'd fix a little something, you know, for them to snack on."

"Who them?"

Johnnie Mae laughed. "I'm sorry. I'm acting like you know everything that's going on since we talked the other day." Johnnie Mae scooped the honeydew melon with the melon baller. She glanced at the digital clock on the oven. "I have thirty minutes before they're due here," she said, scooping faster and putting the melon balls in the bowl with the already-scooped watermelon and cantaloupe.

Angela lined the quiche on the tray as quickly as she could. "Who?"

"Ransom Perdue, his daughter Zenobia, her two sons—I don't know their names—and the rest of her family, which, according to her, includes six grandchildren and a daughter-in-law."

"Ransom is coming here. Wow, I didn't know that. Somebody from Great-granny's past is going to be right here, someone who knew her when she was a little girl." Angela put the baking sheet in the oven and set the temperature appropriately. "What else do you need me to do?"

"Yeah, it will be Ransom and his family and Memory Patterson Robertson, Lena and Bishop Jordan, Theresa Jordan Greene, her husband, and their two children." She stopped a second. "What else can you do? I made some crabmeat appetizers. If you could put the bowl in the middle of that crystal platter and place those Town House crackers around the platter, that would be a big help. The other things are ready except for putting the potato chips in a bowl. I have the coffee ready to brew at six on the dot so it will be fresh. Chicken wings are already on the dining room table. Would you like to stay and meet them? I know you said you'd like to meet Ransom. Today would be a good time."

"No. I wouldn't want to meet him on a day like this.

I'd just like to sit and talk to him about Great-granny. So, no, I'll wait until another time to meet him. This sounds like a family affair." Angela took out the crab-meat appetizer and, after opening the crackers, took a fork and placed some crabmeat on one of the crackers. "Mmmm, this is great," she said. She went to the sink and washed her hands again, realizing that she wasn't at home where sampling was acceptable. "Sorry," she said as she dried her hands on a paper towel.

"That's quite all right," Johnnie Mae said. "You're helping me out. The least I can do is feed you while you work." Rinsing and drying her hands, she then picked up the now-mixed bowl of fruit that included black seedless grapes, kiwi, strawberries, cantaloupe, honeydew, and watermelon.

"That looks *good,*" Angela said, singing the word *good* as Johnnie Mae whisked past her.

When Angela took the platter with the crackers and crabmeat appetizer into the dining room, she jerked her head back slightly. "Wow, I thought you said you were doing a *little* something. This looks like a full spread to me. Buffalo wings, honey chicken wings, croissant sandwiches with ham, turkey, and is that one with roast beef also?"

"Yep."

"Yeah. Brent and I get that tray all the time. We love those sandwiches." She set the crystal platter down. "Triple-layer fudge chocolate cake." She walked over to it. "Ah! I absolutely *love* this cake! The only thing is, it's so rich."

"Tell me about it. That's why I only eat a little piece. I have to watch these hips. And I don't plan on watching them expand outward any more than they have already," Johnnie Mae said with a laugh. She and Angela headed back to the kitchen to load up again.

"And you still have *more* things," Angela said as Johnnie Mae took out a turtle cheesecake along with a plain cheesecake with strawberry sauce on the side.

"I think the quiches are ready," Johnnie Mae said.

Angela found a large red pot holder. "I was just about to take them out."

"My goodness, where does the time go?" Johnnie Mae said as she glanced at the clock. "I don't care how early you start, time still seems to get away from you."

"Why don't you go and change your shoes," Angela said. "I'll finish putting the other things on the table. In fact, Brent is picking up the children from daycare," Angela said, referring to their two cute, energetic little boys. Brent the Second was three years old and Shaun was a little over a year old.

"I'm thankful I had the foresight to take Princess Rose and Isaiah over to Marie's house," Johnnie Mae said, referencing her second oldest sister. "Landris is picking them up on his way home. I'm sure had they been here, I would have really been strung out trying to get this all done."

"It's because you tried to do too much," Angela said.

"Maybe so, but I want this to be special." Johnnie Mae looked around the kitchen. "The chips and the punch . . . I need to put the punch in the punch bowl—"

"Point me to the location of your chip and punch bowls and I'll take care of them. You need to change out of those shoes and maybe tidy up a bit, especially your hair."

"My hair is *that* bad?"

"You'll see. But nothing a little tightening up won't take care of," Angela said.

"Well, tonight isn't about me, anyway. It's definitely going to be interesting." Johnnie Mae left the kitchen and trotted up the stairs to her bedroom.

Chapter 22

*Who gave himself a ransom for all, to be testified
in due time.*

—1 Timothy 2:6

The doorbell rang. Johnnie Mae glanced at her watch. Five minutes before six. *Someone is early*. Usually, she would have been ready. Maybe she *had* tried doing too much.

"I'll get it!" Angela yelled up the stairs to Johnnie Mae.

"Thank you!" Johnnie Mae yelled back. "I'll be down in a few minutes."

Angela opened the door. "Hello," she said, holding the door open as the guests began to stream in.

"Angel?" Lena said. She leaned in to hug her. "It's been years. How are you?"

"I know. The last time we saw each other was eight years ago." She patted Lena's back as she pulled away. "I'm great."

"Well, you look good," Lena said.

"I've put on a *little* weight," Angela said.

Lena shooed her. "Please. I should be so blessed to be your size."

Bishop Jordan walked in and gave her a courtesy hug. He didn't know Angela.

"Hi, Angel," Theresa said, her daughter and son walking close to her legs as she moved. "Go on in, Mauricia and M-double-G." M-double-G was the nickname for Maurice Greene the Second.

"Oh, my goodness! Look how they've grown." Angela stooped down and hugged both children. "Mauricia, how old are you now?"

"I just turned eight," Mauricia said, looking in Angela's eyes without a hint of shyness. "My birthday was September eleventh. I lost a tooth the night before my birthday."

Angela stroked Mauricia's hair that was braided and strung with lots of white beads. "You did? Let me see." She looked as Mauricia pointed to the empty space at the top.

"Well, hello there, little man," Angela said to M-double-G. "And how old are you now?"

M-double-G held up his hand with all five fingers spread wide. "Five," he said, then he stepped in and ran over to his grandfather.

Maurice nodded to Angela as he stepped past her. "How are you?" he said.

She smiled. "Great."

Memory stepped up. She smiled as she nodded. "Angela, or Angel, is it?"

"Yes, ma'am," Angela said. "Either one. Most folks call me Angel."

"Well, it's very nice to meet you after all I've heard about you. I'm Memory."

"Please, all of you come on in and make yourself at home," Angela said.

"Hi, everybody," Johnnie Mae said as she waltzed down the stairs. She hugged each one when she reached them. "It's so good to see you! Man, it's been a long time."

"Yeah," Memory said, embracing Johnnie Mae with a warm hug. "I was telling Lena and Theresa on our way over here that we're going to have to stop meeting like this."

"So far, it's turned out well in the end." Johnnie Mae patted Memory's back.

"Yes, it has. Let's hope the trend continues to hold."

Angela was about to head for the door with her briefcase and purse in hand. "Johnnie Mae, unless you need me, I'm out of here." She held out a large folder with the contract and budget and an envelope with Johnnie Mae's next novel's page proofs.

"Would it be too much trouble to ask you to take those and put them in my bedroom on my coffee table?" Johnnie Mae asked Angela.

"No, I'll be happy to do that. I'll let myself out when I'm finished."

Johnnie Mae gave Angela a hug. "Thank you for everything. I really appreciate you. You are such an . . . angel." Johnnie Mae smiled at her own play with Angela's name.

"God always knows what we need, even before we know we need it. And just think: I thought I was coming over here to bring you something, when God really had me coming to help you out," she whispered.

Angela took the information, as requested, up to Johnnie Mae's bedroom. Johnnie Mae showed everyone to the living room, which adjoined the dining room (when the French doors were completely opened), and its table and buffet server full of food.

Angela went downstairs and opened the front door just as a young man was about to press the doorbell.

"Great timing," the man said. "I'm Knowledge Walker. You must be Johnnie Mae." He held out his hand to shake hers.

Angela switched her briefcase from her right hand to her left to shake his hand. "Hi. Actually, no. I'm Angela Underwood. I'm a friend of Johnnie Mae's."

"Oh, I'm sorry," Knowledge said.

"No problem. I was just leaving."

"But this is the Landrises' house, isn't it?" an older woman said, carrying a baby in a carrier.

"Oh, yes. Johnnie Mae is inside. She's expecting you. Why don't I show you in," Angela said, holding the door and opening it wider.

"Gramps is coming. Clarence is bringing him," Knowledge said to Angela.

"Yeah, Great-gramps doesn't move so fast," a little boy said.

"Deon, that's not nice," one of twin girls said.

"I'm Zenobia Walker. This is my son, Knowledge, and his three children. Dante," she said, raising the carrier up. "That's Deon—"

"I'm five!" Deon said, holding up his fingers to prove it.

Angela laughed. "Well, hello, Deon." She shook his hand. "There's another little boy in there, and he's also five."

Zenobia nodded toward the twins. "That's Jasmine and Dominique."

"Yeah, and we're eight," Dominique and Jasmine said in unison.

Angela laughed again. "Wow, would you believe there's a little girl in there, and she's also eight. Wow . . .

what are the chances of something like this happening?"

Angela led them to the living room once the group was inside and handed them off to Johnnie Mae. She hurried back to the door to welcome Gramps and Clarence, excited that she would finally get the opportunity to meet the infamous Ransom Perdue. They were already approaching the door when she returned. Angela looked at the man called Ransom Perdue, and that's when her briefcase fell from her hand to the floor.

Clarence rushed to pick up her briefcase for her. "I got it." When he held it out to her, he saw her just standing there, staring intensely at Gramps. "Have you two met before?"

Angela shook her head slowly, unable to take her eyes off Gramps. "No," she said, finally realizing she was visibly staring.

"I'll be. If you're not Pearl Black's kin, then fish can't swim. Have mercy." He held out his hand. "My name is Ransom Perdue. Now little lady, exactly who are you?"

"I-I-I'm Angel Gabriel, I mean Angela Gabriel," she said, stammering. "Actually"—she took in and then slowly released a deep breath—"I'm Angela Gabriel Underwood. Most people call me Angel. Pearl Black was my great-grandmother." Angela continued to stare at him.

"Gramps!" Johnnie Mae said. "Come on in. We're all here waiting for you." Johnnie Mae looked at Angela. "Are you okay? Now, I told you, if you want to, you're more than welcome to stay."

"No. I-I-I really need to get home," Angela said, continuing to stammer. "I'll talk to you later." She hurried away. Johnnie Mae closed the door after Clarence cleared the doorway. Angela stopped, turned around, and then just stood there. She couldn't believe what she'd just seen. But there's no way what she was thinking right then could be true.

No way.

Chapter 23

Whosoever therefore shall humble himself as this little child, the same is greatest in the kingdom of heaven.

—Matthew 17:4

Pastor Landris was in the game room with the children while Johnnie Mae continued to host the Perdue family upstairs. He and his two children had spoken to everyone when they first arrived. He was surprised when Clarence Walker came up to him and gave him a manly hug. Pastor Landris remembered Clarence from his baptism almost two Sundays ago.

"Hi, man," Pastor Landris said, slapping him on his back. "Good to see you. I certainly didn't expect to see you here," he said.

"Now, talk about a small world," Clarence said. "That's my mother right there"—he pointed—"Zenobia Walker. And that's Gramps, Ransom Perdue, my grandfather."

"Mister Perdue," Pastor Landris said, shaking his

hand and speaking a little louder than he normally would.

Gramps stood up. "Hey, there. You don't have to yell. I hear just fine. I remember you from my grandson's baptism. That was a great speaking you did at that service. I said I'm gonna have to come visit your church whenever I can get somebody to bring me."

"Well, you just let us know and we'll be glad to come and get you. We have Wednesday night Bible study at seven and two Sunday morning services. Of course, I don't want Clarence's father getting upset with me about stealing you away to our church," Pastor Landris said. "As long as we don't get in trouble, we'll certainly be happy to have you."

Gramps nodded. "All right, now. I'm gonna hold you to that. Maybe Miss Countess and I can come together one of these Sundays. I'd love to hear you preach, although you don't look to be the whooping kind of preacher. Of course, looks can be deceiving."

"No, Gramps. He doesn't whoop. But he absolutely preaches the unadulterated Word of God," Clarence said.

"I'ma have to check you out one of these days," Gramps said to Pastor Landris. "And I certainly appreciate you and your lovely bride here"—he nodded at Johnnie Mae—"opening up your home like this for all of us." He wiped at one eye. "She's been an absolute jewel. She had chocolate cake and everything. Oh, Sarah would have loved this. Sarah used to say, 'I've always been partial to chocolate,'" he said, slightly imitating her. "Just like that. She loved her some chocolate, that's for sure. I still can't believe all of this is happening. Finding my child after all these years. Who would have ever thought it? Thank You, Jesus. It's somethin', ain't it? My daughter, Memory; her daughter, Lena; Theresa, and all of her family; my daughter, Zenobia, and most of her family. The Lord is good. And I'm a living witness that His mercy endures forever." Gramps started to cry.

"'Oh, that my head were waters, and mine eyes a fountain of tears,'" Gramps said, quoting the first part of Jeremiah 9:1. "I seem to be worse than Jeremiah, the weeping prophet, these days. I can't seem to stop these tears from flowing here lately."

Memory stood and put her arm around her father. She rubbed his shoulders with her hand as though she were trying to start a fire with flint and a stick. "It's okay, Dad. It's the quality that counts now. God fixed it where we found each other. We'll just need to spend as much time as we can now. That's what I learned when I finally found out about my mother." Memory started wiping her eyes as well. Zenobia came over and hugged the both of them.

"When my mother said we were going to the house of a woman named Johnnie Mae, she didn't call her last name," Clarence said. "Imagine my surprise when I learned Johnnie Mae was Johnnie Mae Landris, my new pastor's wife, no less. I'd like to second Gramps's emotion . . . about you and Mrs. Landris having this here for us like this. It was perfect. I admit feeling a little strange at first . . . meeting people you didn't know even existed and learning that you're kin. Then feeling like you've known each other forever. It's strange."

Knowledge walked over and extended his hand to Pastor Landris. "Pastor Landris. I'm Knowledge Walker, Clarence's older brother."

"Good to meet you, Knowledge. That's a different name, for sure."

"Yeah. You'd have to ask my mother what she was

thinking." He chuckled. "The kids were relentless when I was growing up, although I love my name now."

"Hey, I've always heard that the name doesn't make you, you make the name," Johnnie Mae said. "Take it from someone who struggled with her own name. Imagine being a girl named Johnnie, albeit Johnnie Mae. People are shocked when they meet me."

"Well, we're glad to have you all here," Pastor Landris said to Knowledge.

Knowledge nodded. "Those are my children over there playing with their new cousins. My baby son, Dante, is asleep. Come here for a minute, Jasmine, Dominique, and Deon." The children got up and came over. Knowledge introduced them to Pastor Landris. Pastor Landris in turn introduced Princess Rose and Isaiah to them.

"Unfortunately my wife couldn't be here," Knowledge said as the children went back over to play with the others. "She's a lawyer, and she's working hard on a case that's coming up soon."

Pastor Landris spoke to Memory, Lena, Bishop Jordan, Theresa, Maurice, and their children. No one would have been able to tell from the casual way Pastor Landris and Theresa spoke to each other that they'd once been engaged, and were almost married.

"Well, I didn't mean to interrupt this fellowship," Pastor Landris said. "The children and I wanted to speak to everyone. I'm taking Princess Rose and Isaiah down to the game room for a little while."

"We want to go play," Jasmine said.

"Yeah," Mauricia said. "Can we go, Mom?"

"I'm sure Pastor Landris doesn't want to babysit a bunch of children," Lena said.

"No, actually it's fine with me," Pastor Landris said.

"Yeah, 'cause y'all are super boring," Deon said.

"Deon," Knowledge said with a fatherly tone to his voice. "That's not very nice. Now apologize for saying that."

"He doesn't have to apologize," Gramps said. "The boy is right. All we've been doing is talking grown folk talk and you women been here crying like somebody turned on a faucet and left it dripping. If Pastor Landris is brave enough to think he can take on a bunch of youngbloods, then I say let the children go have a little fun. That way, we can talk a little more about some other super-boring stuff we ain't touched on yet."

Everybody laughed.

"Gramps, you're a mess," Theresa said. "Well, you children mind Pastor Landris. And if they give you any trouble, especially my two, you just send them right on back up here."

"That goes for my three as well," Knowledge said, giving his three "the eye."

Pastor Landris took the children down to the game room, thankful he'd stopped and gotten Princess Rose and Isaiah something to eat before coming home. Although there was some food left, there wasn't much. He had his eye on that chocolate cake that was almost gone. Johnnie Mae smiled and blew him a kiss on the sly. He knew that besides her letting him know how much she loved him, that kiss was telling him she'd already put him up a slice.

The children were in the game room playing their preferences of various games. The phone rang. Pastor Landris looked at the caller ID to see who was calling so he could determine whether to answer it or just let it go to the answering machine.

"Pastor Landris," Reverend Walker said after Pastor Landris said hello. "Marshall Walker here. I promise I won't hold you long. I'm sure you, like I, have had a long day today."

"Reverend Walker," Pastor Landris said, acknowledging him. "What can I do for you?"

The noise level in the room was quickly getting louder.

"Daddy Landris is on the phone," Princess Rose said to the others. "We need to be quieter until he gets off."

Pastor Landris smiled and winked at her. She smiled and winked back.

"It sounds like you have company," Reverend Walker said. "If you like, you can call me later."

"We're fine. I merely volunteered to sit with the children for a little while. They're fine."

"Well, you're certainly a better man than me," Reverend Walker said. "My three girls are more than enough for me. Sometimes my five older sons' children end up here on an occasional visit. But I don't keep them any longer than to say hello, how are you, I give them a big Grandpa hug, and say good-bye. When they're here, I let my wife do all the work. That's women's work anyway."

Pastor Landris didn't bother wasting his time commenting on that statement.

"The reason for my call," Reverend Walker said, "is I'd like to have you come speak at our church one afternoon. I was thinking it would be great if our congregations could fellowship together. I apologize for not having done something like this already."

"Reverend Walker, you don't have to do this. You and I had a discussion about my preaching style, and I'm well aware of what you think about it. When Poppa Knight died, you made it abundantly clear you didn't feel I was the right person to preach his funeral because I didn't bring enough 'fire' with my messages."

"If you're bringing that up for me to take back what I said, then I can't do that. For Poppa Knight's funeral, he deserved for it to be preached the way he preached during his lifetime. He preached with fire, and I knew I could do his home-going justice," Reverend Walker said. "I owed him that much."

"I wasn't asking for you to take anything back. I was merely pointing out what you and I both know to be true."

"Pastor Landris, I'd like to press a reset button between us. I know I've possibly come off a little blunt at times with my thoughts and opinions."

"You mean like when you called a few months ago to tell me I shouldn't allow someone to dance in our Dance Ministry because of her past life. A past, by the way, she'd asked to be forgiven of. A past, I informed you, that we all have, including you, regardless of what that past may contain. A past some folks may even believe is known only between them and God." Pastor Landris was thinking of the envelope he possessed that was given to him by Poppa Knight that Reverend Walker had no knowledge he had. "I told you then, Reverend Walker, and I say it now: none of us are perfect. None."

"Well, Pastor Landris, there are some sins I do believe are worse than others. And I stand by that statement."

"Reverend Walker, there are no big sins and little sins. A sin is a sin is a sin."

"Okay, Pastor Landris. Just to keep us out of the weeds of a debate, let's just agree to disagree on some things. You believe what you believe, and I believe what I believe. There's nothing you can say that's going to convince me that I'm wrong about my feelings concerning some things that people want to act like never happened. Well, Pastor Landris, in my eyes, there are no spiritual statutes of limitations."

"Reverend Walker, unless there is nothing in your past that you've ever done wrong, I don't think you should even go there."

Reverend Walker chuckled. "Look at how the devil is in operation. I call you to do the right thing, and just look at where we are. Pastor Landris, I'd love it if you'd check your calendar and see if you're available any Sunday in the next few weeks. I'd like to do this soon. I'd like for us to be friends and brothers the way God wants us to be. I'm trying my best to do my part. I leave where this goes from here on you."

"I'll check my calendar and get back with you," Pastor Landris said. The children started getting loud again.

Pastor Landris smiled as he saw how the children were getting along so well. The sound of their laughter and joy was like music to his ears. *Except we come as little children.* He thought of the scripture where Jesus spoke of people coming to Him as little children, and smiled again.

Chapter 24

And it shall come to pass in that day, that the light shall not be clear, nor dark.

—Zechariah 14:6

Angela went home. Brent followed her upstairs after she barely spoke to him and their two sons. He picked up both children and followed his wife to their bedroom. He found her sitting in the middle of the bed with the cigar box her great-granny had given to Johnnie Mae, who in turn had given to her.

"What's wrong?" Brent said, putting Brent the Second and Shaun on the floor. Shaun promptly found something on the floor he wanted to put in his mouth to see what it tasted like. Brent took it out of his hand, shook his head no, and stuck it in his pocket.

Angela was pulling pictures out of the box and looking at them.

"Angela . . . Angel, what's wrong?" Brent said again.

"I'm fine," Angela said, glancing up for a second, then back to her mission.

"Why do you have that box out?"

"I'm looking for a picture I saw in here. I know I saw a cute picture of a man . . ."

"Should I be worried?" Brent joked.

She flashed him a look that told him she wasn't in the mood to play.

"Okay, from that look, maybe my joke should have been a serious question to you. Should I be worried about whatever has you going right now?"

"Here it is," she said, holding up the picture. She shook her head as she covered her mouth with her hand. She slid off the bed and handed the photo to Brent. "Who does that man remind you of? When you look at him, who do you see?"

"Honestly, it looks like a younger male version of your grandmother, Arletha."

"That," she said, pointing her finger at the man, "is Ransom Perdue."

"Are you sure? He's a nice-looking man. So I take it you must have finally met him."

"Yes. I met the older version of that picture, which is strikingly canny to the older version of Arletha. But, Brent, how is that possible?"

"Maybe this isn't really Ransom. Maybe you're mistaken. Yes, he looks like a young male version of Arletha. In fact, the resemblance is almost scary. But maybe this photo is a picture of Arletha's father and not Ransom Perdue." He turned the photo over. "There's no name on the back."

"Brent, listen to what I'm saying. I met the older Ransom Perdue. For a man who is about to celebrate his one hundredth birthday, he looks closer to someone in his seventies, at the most, eighties, which means he looks close to Arletha's age now. And when I looked into that man's face, I literally dropped my briefcase." She put her hands to her face and rubbed it.

"This makes no sense," Angela said. "Great-granny was married to Samuel L. Williams, my great-grandfather. I'd never seen a picture of him, and honestly, when I first saw this picture in this box, I thought it was a photo of him with Great-granny." She shook her head. "The man in *that* photo standing next to Great-granny is *not* Samuel Williams. That's a picture of Ransom Perdue."

"What about the fact you discovered that Arletha was born a Black and not a Williams?" Brent asked. "That's why it was hard to find out the true identity of Arletha, besides the fact that she changed her name from Black to Brown and she was born using a midwife during a time when records weren't always filed as they should?"

"I thought it just meant Great-granny got pregnant by Samuel Williams and they married after Arletha was born. They did marry. Great-granny and my great-grandfather had three other children, a daughter named May, then a year and a half later, a daughter named Frances, and a year after that, a son named Leon, after Samuel's middle name, since he already had a Samuel Junior from a previous union. But what if the truth is different from that? What if Great-granny was pregnant by Ransom Perdue?"

"That makes no sense. When would that have happened?"

"It would have happened . . ." Angela went and got a pencil and a paper. She began jotting down numbers and months. "Arletha was born January 28, 1944. To figure out approximately when Arletha would have been conceived, we need to go back nine months prior to that date. Nine months before Arletha's birth date would be . . ."—she began using her fingers to count back the number of months she needed—"April 28,

1943. She would have been conceived around that date, give or take a few weeks."

"Okay," Brent said. "So before you go sharing this theory of yours with anyone else, especially Arletha or Ransom Perdue, you need proof that he was even *with* your great-grandmother in April or May of 1943."

"Oh, the thought of *thinking* about Great-granny . . ." Angela said. "You're right."

"Mommy, I want some juice," Brent the Second said.

"Deuce, deuce," Shaun said, trying to say "juice." He bumped his fingers together.

"Okay, sweetheart. I'll get you both some juice." She put back in the box the other things she'd pulled out, closed up the box, and placed the photo on top of it. "Give Mommy one minute, and I'll go get you some juice." She picked up the phone and called Arletha.

"Hello," Arletha said.

"Hi, Grand. How are you?" Angela said. They had gotten a lot closer than when Angela first got Arletha to finally confess that she was really her grandmother. Arletha had consented to Angela calling her Grand instead of Grandmother a year after she admitted the truth.

"Hi, darling. I'm fine. Old Arthur has been acting up again," she said, her nickname for her arthritis. "But I'm about to slap something on him and see if I can't straighten that joker out *real* quick. I done told him to quit messing with me."

"Listen, Grand, I need to get back that journal from you. You know, the one I let you see when you were in the hospital. The one your mother, Great-granny, wrote."

"My goodness," Arletha said. "How long ago was that?"

"Please tell me you have it," Angela said, praying silently as she spoke. "Please tell me you still have it."

"I'm sure I still have it somewhere. It's just a matter of me remembering where I might have put it when I called myself putting it up in a safe place. That's the problem with getting old: you start forgetting stuff that you shouldn't be forgetting."

Angela tried to calm herself. She took in deep breaths. "Will you please see if you can find it?"

"Sure. I'll go look for it as soon as I hang up this phone."

"And will you let me know the moment you find it? I'd like to come and get it."

"Okay," Arletha said. "But what's this all about? Why the sudden urgency to get the journal? I mean, you haven't asked about it in almost three years. Now you're hot and heavy to get it."

"I just need to . . . I want to read some things. That's all. Just please, let me know as soon as you find it," Angela said.

"Mommy, I want some juice," Brent the Second said, this time more forcefully.

Brent picked up Shaun and grabbed Brent the Second by his hand. "Come on. Daddy will get you some juice."

"But I want Mommy to get it," Brent the Second said, pulling back as his father tried to keep him moving forward. "Mommy said she was going to get it."

"Mommy's busy right now," Brent said. "Daddy's going to get it." Brent stopped and made his oldest son look at him. "Don't you want Daddy to get it?"

"No," Brent said. "I want Mommy to do it. Mommy said she was, and I want her to get it."

"Well, I hear my great-grandson in the background,"

Arletha said. "You go get his juice. I'll call you when I locate the journal."

"Thanks. I really appreciate this." She hoped Arletha heard the desire in her voice.

"And then you're going to tell me why this became so urgent," Arletha said.

"I told you, I just want to read it. That's all."

"Okay. But you do know that lying is a sin. And lying to your grandmother is a double sin." Arletha chuckled. "Kiss the babies for me. Tell my handsome grandson-in-law that I said hello." She hung up.

Chapter 25

And when ye come into a house, salute it.

—Matthew 10:12

Gabrielle, Zachary, and Queen arrived in Chicago on time. Zachary's mother and father offered to pick them up from the airport, but Zachary wanted to be sure he had his own car to get around in, so he told them not to come because he was renting a car. Zachary was going to rent a midsize car, but Queen argued he should get a luxury vehicle.

"What's it going to look like with us driving up in a midsize car and you're a doctor? You know people are going to think you're not doing well," Queen said.

"Queen, I told you to go and sit down so your feet won't swell. You didn't need to be traveling, but since you insisted, then at least will you take care of yourself."

"You sound just like Mama," Queen said. "I certainly hope you're taking note of this, Gabrielle. You might want to run while you still can. Next thing you know, he'll be hovering over you like he does over me."

"I think it's cute. I wish I'd had a brother who cared about me the way Zachary cares about you."

"Now, please, Queen, go sit down and let me do this my way," Zachary said. "In fact, you can sit over there until I get the car. I'll pick you both up at the curb."

"You heard him," Gabrielle said to Queen. "Let's go over here and sit down."

"Two against one. Okay. I know when I'm outnumbered." She and Gabrielle went and sat down.

Zachary got the car and came and picked them up. Queen's suitcase was the largest. She'd also brought a garment bag. Gabrielle's suitcase was medium-sized, but that's because Zachary told her they would only be there for four days counting this traveling day.

Leslie Morgan met them at the front door.

"Oh, my goodness," Leslie said. "Queen, look at you." She put a hand on Queen's stomach. The baby kicked. "Look at that. My granddaughter is brilliant. She already knows her grandmother. I can't believe I'm finally going to be a grandmother!" She stood up straight. "Zechariah, they're here!" Leslie yelled toward the back of the house.

"Zachary," Leslie said as she turned and hugged her son, "the doctor."

"Mama," Zachary said, bending down to hug her back. When he straightened up, he turned toward Gabrielle. "Mama, I'd like to introduce you to Gabrielle Mercedes."

"Hello, there," Leslie said, managing a smile on her face. "Welcome to our humble abode. I've heard a lot about you. I can't wait to get to know you better for myself."

"It's a pleasure to meet you as well, Mrs. Morgan." Gabrielle shook her hand.

"Oh, you can call me Leslie." She touched Gabrielle's elbow. "Daddy, they're here." Leslie called Zechariah again.

Zechariah came into the area before they reached the den. "I was coming," he said. "I dozed off for a minute. The TV was watching me." He hugged his daughter and son, then shook Gabrielle's hand once he'd been formally introduced to her.

"Well, dinner's already ready. I know you all are tired from your trip," Leslie said.

"It wasn't that bad," Queen said as she sat down on the couch in the den and placed her feet up on the coffee table. "I'll just be glad when they stop making us take off our shoes to go through checkpoints. I hate that. It's even worse when you're pregnant and can barely see your feet much anymore."

"How did you enjoy the trip up?" Leslie asked Gabrielle.

"It was interesting. This is the first time I've ever flown before," Gabrielle said.

"You mean ever?" Leslie asked.

"Yeah. Ever. That's why I was excited but a little nervous. I got to sit by the window, and it was something being all up in the clouds like that. I felt so close to God, I can't explain it. Looking at everything from above and seeing how small things look when you're higher up. It really put things in perspective from God's vantage point."

"So, when you travel to other cities, how do you usually get there?" Leslie asked.

"Leslie, give the girl a break," Zechariah said. "You're acting like this is a game of twenty questions or bust or something."

"I'm sure Gabrielle doesn't mind me asking her things like this? Do you?"

"No, ma'am. But to answer your question, I've

never gone anywhere too far outside of Birmingham and the surrounding area."

"You haven't?" Leslie said, pulling her head back in amazement. "Not even to Six Flags Over Georgia or Disney World? Every child has gone to one of those places."

"No. I've never gone."

"Not even after you grew up?" Leslie asked, tilting her head and frowning now.

"After I grew up, I mostly worked all the time."

"See, Leslie," Zechariah said. "The girl was a responsible adult who held down a job. She didn't have time to be lollygagging around. I think that says a lot about her."

"I agree, Zechariah," Leslie said to her husband; then she asked Gabrielle, "So why didn't your folks take you anywhere as a child?"

"Mom, you are not going to believe how helpful Queen has been," Zachary said.

"Z., haven't I told you it's rude to interrupt people when they're talking?" Leslie gave him a stern look. "Now, Gabrielle, you were saying?"

"I was raised by my aunt. We didn't have a lot of money to do a lot of things. We never visited any relatives, and we never went anywhere fun like Disney World or even the state fair."

"I'm sorry to hear that." Leslie pressed her lips together. "And what did you do after you graduated from high school? Did you attend college?"

"Mom—"

"Zachary," Leslie said in a controlling tone while giving him another solid look. Smiling, she turned back to Gabrielle. "Go on, dear. Zachary won't be interrupting us anymore."

Zachary laughed. *My mother is something else*, he thought.

"I didn't go to college, although I really wanted to. I did a few odd jobs. Just recently I was hired to work in ministry at the church where I'm presently a member."

"You'd best be careful of church-related jobs," Zechariah said. "You get fired from one of them and you have to find yourself another church home. Because it's hard to worship when you're mad at your ex-boss and your ex-boss is your place of worship."

"The odd jobs you mentioned," Leslie said, her attention still on Gabrielle, "after you graduated high school and before you got this one. What exactly were they?"

"Mom, I'm really hungry," Queen said. "Your granddaughter needs to eat. I'm sure we're not the only two. Who else is hungry?" To Z., "You're hungry, aren't you?"

"Well, it's ready," Leslie said.

"Great," Queen said, struggling to get up.

"Sit, sit, sit," Leslie said, jumping to her feet. "I'll get you something and bring it in here to you."

"Mommy, you're the best," Queen said, smiling and getting comfortable again.

"Yeah . . . well. I didn't think you should be traveling at this stage in your pregnancy," Leslie said.

"Oh, Mom, you *always* wait on Queen," Zachary said. "She wouldn't know how to fix anything to eat in your house if she had to. She probably doesn't even know where the plates are. Now at *my* house, she at least has to order the food in if she wants to eat."

Queen rolled her eyes at her brother. "Now, you're wrong for that," she said.

"Gabrielle, would you care to come and help me in the kitchen?" Leslie said.

Zachary's eyes widened. He wanted to shake his head, to tell Gabrielle to say no.

"Sure," Gabrielle said. "I'd love to."

"I'll go help you, too," Zachary said as he got up.

"No," Leslie said, "you won't. We women can handle this just fine by ourselves." She looked at Gabrielle and smiled. "Can't we, Gabrielle?"

Realizing what just happened, Gabrielle nervously returned the smile. "Of course."

Chapter 26

It is better to dwell in the corner of the housetop,
than with a brawling woman and in a wide house.
—Proverbs 25:24

"The problem with most folks is they want to change you into who they want you to be instead of appreciating who you already are," Leslie Morgan said as she handed Gabrielle an empty plate and she began to fix Queen's plate.

"I totally agree. I'm who I am, and that's what I appreciate so much about Zachary. He seems to accept me as I am," Gabrielle said.

"But he really doesn't know *everything* about you, wouldn't you agree?"

"I've not tried to hide anything from him." Gabrielle put a spoonful of collard greens on her plate. "I've told him things up-front. I've been transparent with him."

"I believe that. You seem to be an honest young woman. You're very beautiful as well. I can see why my son would be intrigued with you." Leslie put two large spoonfuls of macaroni and cheese on the plate. "Queen loves my macaroni and cheese."

"It does look good," Gabrielle said as she put a large spoonful on her plate.

"Is that your plate or Zachary's?" Leslie asked.

"It's mine," she said. "Zachary prefers fixing his own plate."

"Well, I'll fix his plate. That way he won't have to come in here to get it."

"I can do it. It's just he and I have had this discussion, and he in no uncertain terms told me his hands were not broken and he was more than capable of fixing his own food and his own plate."

"That's what men may say. But a man likes to be pampered every now and then, even when he says otherwise," Leslie said.

"Well, I'll be happy to fix it for you. You already have Queen's plate, your husband's, and your own. It's no problem for me to fix Zachary's." Gabrielle took the empty plate Leslie was now handing to her.

"Do you love Zachary?"

Gabrielle stopped and looked at her. She didn't quite know how to answer that.

"What?" Leslie said. "That's not a hard question. Either you do or you don't. And since according to Zachary the two of you have only been dating since September, what's that, six weeks . . . a month. I can appreciate you not being in love just yet if you're not."

But therein was the problem. Gabrielle had fallen in love with Zachary early on.

"Let me make it easier on you," Leslie said. "Zachary loves you."

A slight laugh escaped Gabrielle's mouth. "I'm sorry, but I doubt that."

Leslie put a baked chicken wing on Queen's plate. She then held up another piece of chicken. "This one's for Zachary. He likes the breast."

Gabrielle held up Zachary's plate to receive the chicken Leslie was placing on it.

"Which piece do you prefer?" Leslie asked, the tongs hovering over the pan of golden-brown, baked chicken.

"The drumstick," Gabrielle said.

"Good choice," Leslie said, placing a drumstick on the plate Gabrielle now held up. "A lot of people want the breast, and there are usually only two breasts. Zachary and his father like that part. Xenia used to like that piece as well. It was always a problem when they were growing up. That's why I used to buy two chickens. I didn't want anyone not having the piece of chicken that they wanted, not if I could help it."

Gabrielle smiled. "Zachary told me about Xenia. I'm sorry about what happened."

"Yes. That whole period was rough on our family. Did Zachary tell you what he was about to do after that happened?"

"Yeah, he told me."

"See. He loves you."

"I don't know if I would go that far just yet. I believe he cares deeply about me and for me." Gabrielle put creamed corn on both plates. "But love?"

"Trust me. He told you about Xenia. He told you about his own dark past. He brought you here to see us, to meet us. Zachary loves you. And he wants us to love you, too. That's why he was trying so hard to keep me from asking you any questions in there. A true Morgan to the core, he was trying to protect you."

"Mrs. Morgan . . . Leslie, with all due respect: he

asked me to come so I could see Miss Crowe. He told you about me and Miss Crowe."

"Yes, he told me. But Gabrielle Mercedes, you wouldn't be here right now today if my Zachary didn't have strong feelings for you, and I dare say, loves you." She smiled as she put a square of cornbread on each plate. "Now, the cornbread is nice and warm, just the way everybody likes it. I'm going to ask you a question again. And I do hope you'll either answer it or tell me you're not going to. That way Queen and Zachary's plates won't get cold." Leslie held out the real utensils already wrapped in white cloth napkins.

"Okay," Gabrielle said, taking the two sets of the napkin-wrapped utensils.

"What various jobs did you do early on in life that Zachary was working so hard to keep me from hearing about?"

Gabrielle took a deep breath and released it slowly. "I used to be a waitress."

"Nothing wrong with that," Leslie said.

"Then I became an exotic dancer."

Leslie nodded as though she knew that was coming.

"I did that for about eight years. This year, January fourth, to be exact, I went to church, heard the Word, went and gave my life to Jesus, and I've never been the same since. Jesus is Lord of my life. I immediately gave up that line of work, got a job as a maid. I lost that job shortly afterward due to downsizing. I took a job as a personal home housekeeper where I ended up, ironically, working for your son."

"Okay. The dancer part I believe. But *you*, somehow, working as a housekeeper for my son, then him deciding to date you, rings fiction to me."

"Mom," Queen said as she came into the kitchen.

"What's taking so long? Did you have to go out and kill the chicken yourself?" Queen teased her mother.

"All done," Leslie said, handing the now-filled plate to Queen. "In fact, Gabrielle is finished as well. Aren't you, Gabrielle?" She smiled and held the swinging door open for Gabrielle, who was successfully carrying her two plates. "Bon appétit, all!" Leslie said.

Chapter 27

*Produce your cause, saith the Lord; bring forth
your strong reasons, saith the King of Jacob.*

—Isaiah 41:21

"Clarence, I want to invite you to come and sing at
a program we're having here at church in two
weeks. It's October eighteen, three pm to be exact,"
Reverend Walker said. "Since it's in the afternoon, it
won't interfere with your church. I've asked Pastor
Landris, and he's agreed, to come and share with us. I
thought it would be a special treat if you'd bless us all
with a song."

"Sure, Dad. I'm not busy that day. I can do that,"
Clarence said.

"That's great. That's great."

"You sound like you weren't expecting me to agree
so quickly."

"I was praying that you would. I suppose I'm just
surprised you didn't give me a harder time about it,"
Reverend Walker said. "It's been a long time since
you've been there."

"Dad, I don't purposely try to give you a hard time. There are just some things you and I don't, and probably never will, agree on," Clarence said.

"You never know. Look how God has already changed things. A few years ago when I was talking to you about coming back to the Lord, you blew me off without a second thought. Now look at you. You've given your heart to the Lord. Got baptized again."

Clarence started to correct his father, but technically his father could be considered correct. He had gone in the water twice. It wasn't that big of a deal to start an argument about it. And that's what he believed his father would have done had he pressed the subject.

"You've walked away from your old business. Now you're back in church, working for the Lord. I want the people at Divine Conquerors Church to be encouraged by what you've done in your life. So . . . what are you doing to make a living now?"

"I have a business degree, remember? Mama made sure both Knowledge and I got our college degrees. Knowledge put his degree to work in the business world his way; I put mine to work in another. My way was not the right way, but I have lots of hands-on experience as a small business owner. I've been working on turning that building now sitting idle into a restaurant or something like that. I'd like to combine maybe a restaurant with a stage. Bring in various events and acts for Christians to attend. You know, be entertained while getting some good, down-home soul food cooking. Soul food with *soul food*. Get it? Soul food, as in the Word of God, and soul food as in down-home cooking."

"Yep. You've always had a fondness for good food."

"Yep, that's me. I've always had a fondness for good food." Clarence shook his head. How his father was able to serve him a backhanded slap no matter what the subject was never ceased to amaze him.

"Clarence, I believe in you. And if you're looking for someone to invest in a venture such as that, let me know. I have some dollars put aside I'd like to put to work. I can't think of any better place to do that than in something like what you're talking about. But you need to run it by Knowledge first. You know your brother is a genius when it comes to business. The government has just recruited him to help crack down on business corruption. And of course, Isis is the perfect person to look over any contracts before you sign anything."

"Yeah, I know all of this, Dad."

"Well, I need to get off this phone. Now, you know you're welcome to visit the church without some special program. Divine Conquerors Church *is* and always *will be* your home church; I don't care where you say your membership is. We've lost a lot of members, but if you were to come back and take over being the Minister of Music, we could build things back up again in a hurry. I know we could," Reverend Walker said. "You still know how to play the organ and the piano, don't you?"

"Yes, Dad. But it's been a while. And people don't play organs much anymore. I have a keyboard. That's what musicians are using more these days. But I've kept up my playing skills pretty much on the side, mainly for pleasure, of course."

"A keyboard? That's even better. You just let me know, and I can have you working at my church making a really good salary before the week is out."

Clarence grinned. "The more things change, the more they remain the same."

"Well, you know my philosophy: if it ain't broke,

why mess with it? All I've been doing for all of these years I've done for my children, all of them. My sons by my first wife are clearly not interested in having much to do with me. I hate that, but there's nothing much I can do about it other than pray for them, the same way I prayed for you. You're getting there. God is still working on you yet. You came back to the Lord. If I can just get you back to Divine Conquerors, I'll be a happy father. I'd like you, along with Knowledge, to be in position to take over for me when I'm ready to retire. That's why I've worked so hard all of these years. It's all about my legacy and what I'll leave my heirs."

"I thought you were doing it for the Lord," Clarence said.

"That goes without saying. See, that's why you and I have so much trouble communicating."

"Dad, I really don't want to do this with you, okay. Everything I do now is for the glory of God. So, let's just leave it that I'll be at the Sunday afternoon program you've asked me to come to. And I will sing praises unto our Lord."

"Thanks, Clarence. That works for me," Reverend Walker said. "I'll see you on the eighteenth . . . unless you decide to bless us with your presence and come even before then."

Clarence chuckled a little. "Okay, Dad. For sure, nobody can ever accuse you of giving up too easily."

Chapter 28

And when I looked, behold, a hand was sent
unto me; and, lo, a roll of a book was therein.

—Ezekiel 2:9

"Angela, I finally found it," Arletha said, speaking about the journal Angela had asked her about. It has been a week now since Angela had asked her grandmother for the journal her great-grandmother had written.

Angela finally breathed a sigh of relief. "I thought it was lost for good," Angela said.

"I told you it was here somewhere. I just wasn't sure where I'd put it. I was doing some kind of praying to hurry up and find it. I have so much junk. I guess I really need to get rid of some of this stuff. I found some things I hadn't seen in twenty years."

"So, why was it so hard to find?" Angela said.

"Because I called myself putting it up. The only problem is, I put it up so well, I'd forgotten exactly where I put it. I should have given it back to you after I looked through it. I'm going to learn. I'm so glad you asked me about it though. I just flipped through it, and it made me appreciate how my mother had taken the time to write some of this stuff down specifically for our benefit. I don't think I appreciated it as much the first time I read it as I did this time around," Arletha said.

"Well, I'm coming to get it right now," Angela said.

"Child, do you know what time it is? It's almost nine PM. This can certainly wait until tomorrow. If you've waited this long, then you can wait another few hours. I just wanted to let you know that I'd finally located it. Especially since you've called me practically every single day asking if I had. Whatever you're up to, it must be good."

"Grand, I'm not up to anything."

"Uh-huh. Well, I'm getting ready to go to bed. So you can come by tomorrow and it will still be here."

"I could be there in twenty minutes. Surely you can wait up twenty more minutes. I'd like to read through it tonight. You know, having children, this is a good time for me to get some real things accomplished," Angela said.

"Okay, Angela. You come on and get this. But you're going to tell me what this was all about at some point. I mean that."

"If there's anything to tell, I promise you I will definitely let you know."

"Well, come on. I'll be waiting for you."

"Thank you." Angela hung up, then looked upward. "Thank You, Lord," she said. "Thank You."

Chapter 29

That which hath been is now; and that which is to be hath already been; and God requireth that which is past.

—Ecclesiastes 3:15

Ransom Perdue had been blessed over the past few weeks. He had gone to see his grandson being baptized. He had somehow, God only knows how, been reconnected with a daughter he knew had been born but he'd never gotten to see or even known whether she still lived. His family had instantaneously increased when he met Memory; her daughter, Lena; Lena's husband, Bishop Richard Jordan; Lena's daughter, Theresa Greene; Theresa's husband, Maurice; and their two children, the shy and beautiful Mauricia and the rambunctious and handsome M-double-G.

Originally, they'd only planned to stay a couple of days. Lena, especially, had been skeptical that Ransom was even the real deal. She confessed to him later how she'd first believed him to be merely a ploy used by

Montgomery Powell the Second. When Ransom heard the full details of what had happened to Sarah, he was just as upset about it as they were. He understood why the thought of a nearly one-hundred-year-old man showing up like he seemed to, so conveniently near Johnnie Mae—the one person this family would likely trust—would have spooked them. To Ransom, Montgomery sounded just as ruthless and despicable as his evil father, Heath.

And Ransom knew how foul Heath was. The two had bumped against each other in their young years. For Heath to have a son and have passed on his hatred and bigotry coupled with the power and money Heath had illegitimately obtained, in Ransom's eyes, as well as Memory's and Lena's, was a bad combination. Neither Sarah nor her mother ever stood a chance against them. He only wished he knew whether Victor Senior had been the one who had set him up to be permanently taken away.

Ransom had known Sarah's mother, Grace. He was able to share with his newfound family things they didn't know about the Flemings. But there wasn't enough time in the day to make up for almost a century of history Ransom carried within him.

Memory wanted to know her father better. She'd grown up with more than one lie in her life. For decades, she'd been led to believe that Mamie Patterson was her mother and Willie B. Patterson was her father. When she learned, at the age of seventy, that in fact Mamie was *not* her biological mother but instead a woman named Sarah Fleming was, she couldn't believe something like this could happen in America. But it did, and it had. When she looked back, she knew it was more than probable, and was indeed a fact of life—secrets and lies merely facts of her own life. How many countless other people had lived and died a lie without ever knowing *their* real truth? At least she now knew hers.

Memory had known her skin tone was like that of a white woman. And it had given her both advantages and disadvantages throughout her lifetime. She fit and didn't fit at times. But she'd always been a free spirit, a rebellious person, a survivor. She owed Mamie Patterson a lot, even before learning the truth. When she heard the whole story, she realized how many others she owed for her life. Grace Fleming, who had stepped up at the last minute and ensured that instructions from Heath, her mother's half-brother (who she later learned may not have even been that much, but possibly merely a stepbrother), were not carried out by the midwife in attendance. A midwife named Pearl Black.

Pearl had been the daughter of a midwife. And Pearl had had no intentions of letting the little baby die. Pearl Black wasn't sure how she would manage it, but she wasn't about to carry out Heath's directive. She would somehow find a way to sneak that baby out of there, making it appear she'd died. But she wasn't going to allow the baby to die. Pearl would have come up with something. But she didn't have to. Grace had quickly and immediately stepped in within the first breath of life that baby (later named Memory Elaine) had drawn.

It had been Grace who had scooped up Sarah's baby while Sarah lay unconscious from something Pearl had given her prior to the baby's birth. It was Grace who had saved the baby by carrying her into the room where their maid, Mamie Patterson, had earlier delivered a son. It was Grace who told Mamie she had delivered twins instead of the one birth. Twins that were like salt and pepper, night and day, light and darkness, vanilla and chocolate. Grace was the one who told Pearl to record it as such in her midwife book. How they would fix things later on was not on any of the three women's minds at the time—that could be straightened out at a safer time. But for now, the goal was to save the baby. And they were determined to do just that, by whatever means were necessary.

Grace, the last person Ransom would have expected to hear had gone out of her way, totally out on a limb, to save *his* mixed child. Grace, whom Ransom had known to hate colored folk, almost with a passion, had been the one to put everything on the line to save the child that carried his blood, hers, and her daughter's through her veins.

Grace had given one of the boxes he'd made to Mamie for his daughter to have someday—a father believed to be long gone or dead. Inside that Wings of Grace box (as everyone called the boxes he'd never known would become legends) she'd given to Mamie for Memory was a necklace. An alexandrite necklace with history, which was worth millions. A necklace that would later bring Memory, Lena, and Theresa together. It was hard and hurtful at times, but bring them together was—in the end—precisely what that necklace had done.

They'd talked about a little of this while they were at Johnnie Mae's house. But the real discussion of this happened the following day. Memory and her family had a suite at the hotel where they were staying. Zenobia decided to take off from work Friday after their meeting that Thursday night. She'd called the nursing home and informed them she would be keeping her father a few days more. There was a discussion about whether she could or should do that. Isis, Zenobia's daughter-in-law, put in a call to inform the nursing home director that her mother-in-law and grandfather had every right to do this if they so chose. The nursing home was there to render a service, not to act as his jailer. The director quickly backed off any further objections she may have had.

Ransom even stayed at the hotel with Memory and her family on Saturday night. Memory and Lena told him all about the videotape Grace recorded. The other Wings of Grace box Grace left for them with things that helped them with Sarah. The surprise information relating to his birth: that he was born to Adele Powell, a black woman who had passed for white. A woman who could not tell her white racist husband that the child they had produced together was dark-skinned, not because she'd been with a black man, but because her life-sustaining veins contained the blood of her African heritage.

So she'd done the only thing she knew to do to save herself and most likely her child. She sought out a black midwife in another town, pretended she was just going into labor so this woman would deliver her baby, found out if there was any possible way the baby had the whiteness of her skin color along with the whiteness of her husband's. When the midwife told her the baby was not a white child, she'd asked the midwife to take the baby and find him a good home. After all, it was the way of their people. To take care of children that weren't theirs by birth but, because of their color, were theirs. It turns out she'd been wise to give up the child, who very quickly turned from light to dark. And that midwife had turned out to be Pearl Black's mother.

The baby had been given to a good family—the midwife claimed he had been named Ransom when the mother had asked for the Bible and pointed to a word, thus naming her son. That part had been the tale Pearl's mother had spun as to how she came to have this baby who now needed a good home. This motherless child whose father couldn't bear to raise him alone. So much of Ransom's life's story was also not true. And most of this truth hadn't come to light until almost all of the key players had passed on.

Adele Powell was the same woman, they'd later learned from the tape and information Grace left, who had given birth to Heath Powell while she was still married. It was revealed later that she was having an affair with Victor Fleming Senior. That's how Heath ended up with the last name Powell instead of Fleming—his full name being Montgomery Heath Powell. Adele had convinced Victor that, in spite of her being married, this child was his. That's how Heath came into so much of Victor Fleming's power and wealth. He believed Heath was his son. Shortly after Heath was born, Adele's husband suddenly and mysteriously died. A month later, Adele married Victor and became pregnant with their second son, Victor Junior. Adele died giving birth to him. Victor Senior then married Grace. Grace gave birth to Sarah, the child who would grow up to become her father's heart.

But Sarah Elaine Fleming fell in love with a dark-skinned, black man named Ransom Perdue. A man Sarah would not learn, until close to her own time to depart this world, was technically her stepbrother, as Adele Powell was Ransom's biological mother and Adele had been married to Sarah's biological father.

Zenobia had become concerned. Maybe there were some things her father really didn't need to know or hear. After all, he *was* an elderly man. And although he didn't appear to be frail, she couldn't say how much his heart truly could take.

But Ransom had wanted to know everything that they knew. And that's what he'd done with his new-found family. He'd listened to as much as they were able to tell him, not just about the past that was part of his old world, but about their individual pasts—the good, the bad, *and* the ugly.

Chapter 30

*And Simon answering said unto him, Master, we
have toiled all the night, and have taken nothing:
nevertheless at thy word I will let down the net.*

—Luke 5:5

That Sunday morning when it was their normal cus-
tom to be in somebody's church, the Jordans,
Greenes, and Memory (who didn't regularly attend
church now) decided to visit Followers of Jesus Faith
Worship Center with Pastor George Landris. Bishop
Jordan was excited about hearing Pastor Landris preach
once again. It had been such a long time. And Ransom
would be able to visit, thus fulfilling a type of promise
he'd made to the preacher who had allowed his home to
be the meeting place for him and his family. Zenobia
decided she would go to church with them as well.

As usual, Pastor Landris spoke on a subject that
blessed those in attendance. His sermon topic was
"Nevertheless, with God, Is Always More Than Enough."
He took it from Luke, the fifth chapter, verses one
through eleven.

Pastor Landris began by saying, "Luke 5:5 reads, 'And Simon answering said unto him, Master, we have toiled all the night, and have taken nothing: nevertheless at thy word I will let down the net.' How many of you are doing something today that you know God told you to do? How many of you look at what you've been told to do and wonder if you're crazy to either do it or keep doing it when it doesn't look like it's working out the way you envisioned when you began it? Don't look at me like I'm speaking a foreign language. Many of you know *exactly* what I'm talking about. I want you to look at the word *nevertheless*. If you were to break that word down, you will see three words: *never the less*." Pastor Landris put emphasis on each word. "But *never the less* with God is always *more than enough*." Pastor Landris paused as the congregation first got it, then erupted with sporadic moments of praise.

"Yes, God told you to do something. You were excited because He showed you the end at the beginning. You saw where God was going with it. You put your hand to the plow. You set out on your God-ordained journey. You stepped out on faith. And the next thing you know—nothing seems to be working out quite the way you envisioned it would. Those folks you thought would be excited about what God called you to do don't show up or support you when you're doing what you were instructed to do. Then there are the obstacles that seem to pop up on every corner, one thing after another. Obstacles, honestly, you thought God would have cleared from your path before you ever got there, or at least *when* you got there. But they're there, rearing their ugly heads, sticking their tongue out at you." Pastor Landris rubbed his chin, then released a curt laugh.

"Listen, people of God, nobody said that your road

was going to be easy. But sometimes you can't help but to look up toward Heaven and say, 'Come on, God. Can I get a break down here right about now?' Oh, somebody here knows exactly what I'm talking about. You've worked hard at this thing. You've been faithful. You learned your craft. You've toiled at it. You're tired now. You're ready to put away your net. But *nevertheless,* God *still* has use for what you have." Pastor Landris nodded as some stood to their feet, clapping and shouting, while others merely nodded.

"As in this passage of scripture in Luke 5, Simon, whom we know as Peter, was a fisherman. Simon knew his craft. He and his crew had worked all night long. They knew the best time to fish. They knew the places where you would more likely catch fish. Jesus asked Simon if He could use his boat to teach the people from. After Jesus finished speaking to the people, He said to Simon, 'Launch out into the deep, and let down your nets for a draught.' Can't you just see Simon Peter, who knew what he was doing . . . Simon, who knew that the best time to fish was at night as they'd already done? It definitely wasn't in the heat of the day. And definitely not at that particular place Jesus was telling him—not if he wanted to catch anything. He'd tried it already and had come up empty-handed. And now to be told by someone who wasn't even a fisherman by trade how to do his job." Pastor Landris nodded and bit down on his bottom lip as he grinned.

"But we have to take note that this was Jesus telling him to do something. Simon explained to Jesus that they had toiled all night and had nothing to show for their efforts. But then Simon said something that would prove to be to his benefit. He said, 'Nevertheless at thy word I will let down the net.' Right where Simon was, he decided to be obedient to the Word. And Luke 5:6–7 says, 'And when they had this done, they enclosed a great multitude of fishes: that their net brake. And they beckoned unto their partners, which were in the other ship, that they should come and help them. And they came, and filled both the ships, so that they began to sink.' When it comes to God, *nevertheless* is always, always, *more than enough!*" Pastor Landris swung his fist upward.

"God has told you things to do. It looks like you have less to work with. You have less help, less resources, and had less results in the past. But you need to continue to be obedient to the Word even though it may look like you're losing. Do what God is telling you to do merely because God is telling you to do it. That's all you need to know: that God is telling you to do it. Nevertheless, with God, is always more than enough."

Pastor Landris began to point to his Bible. "It's here in the scriptures. Simon was obedient to what Jesus told him to do. And there was so much, it filled two ships to the point where they both began to sink. That sounds like abundance to me. That doesn't sound like never the less; that sounds like more than enough! When you're obedient to God and His Word, church, I'm telling you, there won't be room enough for you to receive all that God has in store for you! Continue to be faithful. Don't stop. Continue."

The congregation was on its feet now. Ransom was sitting between Memory and Zenobia. They all stood to praise God. Later, he put his arms around his daughters and hugged them. "Nevertheless, with God, is always more than enough," he said. "Yes, Lord. I'm a living witness. You are a God of More Than Enough."

"God's Word is truth," Pastor Landris said. "And the Truth is the Light. Jesus is the Truth, and He is the Light.

Therefore, the Truth, that's a capital T, is the Light, a capital L."

Ransom wiped his eyes and looked up as he lifted both of his hands. "Thank You, Jesus," he said. "Thank You, Jesus. The Truth is the Light."

Chapter 31

Then Peter opened his mouth, and said, Of a truth I perceive that God is no respecter of persons.

—Acts 10:34

"Zachary, I'm going to be honest with you," Leslie said as they sat on his bed in his old bedroom. "I think Gabrielle is a nice young lady. She's probably going to be great for someone and even possibly a great wife and mother. But, honey, she's not the right woman for you."

"Why are we having this discussion?" Zachary asked.

"Because you brought her here, which means that she means more to you than you're leading on. You can't fool me, Z. You know I can read you like a Toni Morrison novel or a Shakespearean play. I'm your mother. I knew you before you stepped foot on this earth."

He laughed. "You really should look into writing a book. You certainly have a flare for words," Zachary said.

"Don't be getting smart with me." She primped her mouth. "I love you. No matter what you do or have done, I've always loved you. That time you used up all the sugar when I told you not to make any Kool-Aid because I needed the sugar. Then you decided to fix your disobedience by replacing the sugar with salt. Who was the one who taught you not to do anything like that ever again? Me."

"Yeah, by making me eat one of those horrible cookies you'd made," Zachary said.

"They wouldn't have been horrible if you hadn't caused me to put a cup of salt in the mix instead of the cup of sugar it called for." She shook her head slowly as she grinned at him and playfully hit him.

"Mom, you have to admit. That *was* funny, and a bit of genius working there."

"Yeah, okay. I'll admit it . . . now, anyway. It was funny, okay. But what wasn't funny was when you almost ruined your life when you were plotting revenge against Xenia's murdering boyfriend." She stood up. "I hated him as much, if not more, than you did. That was my baby he killed." She spun back around toward him. "But you were wrong to even think about what you wanted to do. Wrong."

"I know, Mom. And I thank God that I didn't go through with it," Zachary said.

"But at what expense? If your aunt hadn't come and ended up almost dead from that horrific accident, would you have gone through with your plans?" She sat back down. "Can you even imagine how difficult a time that was already for me? I had lost my child . . . my baby, and here you were putting yourself practically on a silver platter for me to lose you, too. It wasn't enough that that reprobate took one of my children.

You were actually plotting to assist him in being responsible for taking yet another one."

"Mama, we've had this discussion. I told you I was wrong and that I was sorry. I turned my life around. I decided to become a doctor because of all that. I'm a specialist in burn victims now, so maybe I can help save people the way the doctors were unable to save my sister." Zachary put his arm around his now-crying mother and hugged her.

"*Now* you seem to be on the right track. And I am proud of you, Zachary. I'm proud of how hard you've worked to make something of yourself. We're all proud of you. You sacrificed a great deal. Your aunt Esther has said you've more than made up for what you did. And that monster didn't get away with what he did to my baby." She rolled her tongue against the inside of the top of her lip. "Vengeance is the Lord's. And someone ended up taking *him* out. We can only pray that he repented and gave his life to Christ before he died. You can't do people the way he did my child and think you're not going to pay before you leave this earth. Not if you don't repent. No matter how bad a person believes himself to be, there's always someone else out there who's badder."

"Yeah, I know. I'm older now. And with age, comes wisdom. I was nineteen and stupid back then. Dad was trying to talk to me. You were crying and being hysterical. And Aunt Esther was going to come up here and stomp some sense into my foolish self. I get that I made some mistakes. But that's what life's all about. You remember what you did when you helped us as we learned how to walk."

"Like you remember what I did," Leslie said, pulling back and gazing at him.

"I remember watching you with some of your younger nieces and nephews. How you would tell their mothers to let them fall. That it wasn't going to hurt them, and they would eventually get it. Well, that's how real life is. When we try things in life, sometimes we fall. But just like you and the others encouraged those babies who fell to get back up and keep at it, that's how we have to do in life." Zachary pulled his mother closer and hugged her some more. "We get back up, and we keep at it."

Leslie pulled away after a few moments. "I don't think you should continue with Gabrielle." She stood up, refusing to look at Zachary now. "She told me what she used to do. She strip-danced for other men, which I know is not a crime. And there *are* worse things she could have been doing for a living, although that's pretty close to down there in my book." Leslie turned back and looked him straight in his eye. "I'm not a prude or anything, but I don't know why a woman would subject herself to something like that. There's something morally lacking, in my opinion, with a person who chooses to do things like that. Maybe it's just me." She tried to force a smile at Zachary.

"Now, she did tell me of her conversion to Christ this year," Leslie continued, "which I admit is admirable. I rejoice with her and the angels about that. And contrary to what I know you're thinking right now, I'm not holding her past against her. I'm not. She's a sister in the Lord, and I acknowledge that. I promise you; I'm not judging her."

Zachary pulled back, a puzzled look on his face.

"Well, I'm not," she said with inflection. "I don't have a problem with her being in my house. I don't have a problem with her being around your father . . . alone, which is what they're doing right now while we're in here talking. Queen is taking a nap, so it's just him and her. That doesn't concern me, just so you can see I'm sincere in what I'm saying. Gabrielle also told me she worked as a maid, and that she was your house-keeper at one point." Leslie looked at him for confirmation, and if true, then an explanation.

Zachary nodded and rocked his upper body to keep up with his nod. "Gabrielle told you the truth. Everything . . . it's the truth."

She stared at him hard. "You hired her as your house-keeper? Was this before or after you decided to start dating her?"

Zachary chuckled. "Technically, it was before."

"Zachary!" she said with disgust.

"Let me explain, since apparently you and Gabrielle didn't cover everything when you grilled her," Zachary said. He pulled his right ankle on top of his left knee and began picking at the hem of his pants leg, as he had a habit of doing.

"I'm listening."

"Queen hired her through an agency. I knew Gabrielle. She and I had gone out to dinner, in fact. But since Queen was handling everything, I didn't know she had hired Gabrielle until after Gabrielle asked to be reassigned because she thought I was cheating on my pregnant wife."

Leslie's eyes widened. "Your pregnant wife?! What pregnant wife? What *wife*?"

He chuckled. "Queen. Gabrielle thought that Queen was my wife."

"How on earth could she possibly manage to come to that conclusion? Your last name is Morgan and hers is Mabry. What did she think? That the two of you had some kind of marriage where she didn't even believe in a hyphenated last name?"

"She thought when she arrived at the house that the woman she met was married and pregnant. She later thought that the woman she met named Queen was the wife of the doctor who owned the house she was assigned to work for. So when she learned I was, first of all, a doctor and, second, the doctor whose house she was cleaning, she wanted nothing more to do with me. Personally, I think that speaks volumes about her character."

"I agree. But Zachary, that's my point. You *are* a doctor. And you're respected now because of your position. I know you have a good heart and you're a good person, but people judge folks by the people around them. What happens should it get out that your wife, if you continue on the path I see you're headed on, used to be a stripper or that she used to be a maid? Forget about how it would look if it got out that she used to clean your house and now the two of you are married. People will wonder if they can trust you, if they can trust your judgment."

"Mom, you really do need to write books so you can channel your imagination into something worthwhile. You could be rich with the tales that spin out of that head of yours." He tapped her on the forehead.

"I don't think you should continue with Gabrielle. I think you need to walk away while you can and before you get in too deep."

"Mama, it's already too late, and I'm already in too deep," Zachary said. "Gabrielle is a wonderful person, and I love her. She's full of life; she's honest, caring, and giving. She is loyal . . . someone I can trust. And most important of all, Gabrielle *loves* the Lord."

"So, have you two . . . you know?"

He grinned and put his foot down on the floor. "I

could mess with you for daring to go there, but I don't want to play with you on this or mislead you in any way. Gabrielle and I have agreed to keep ourselves until we get married. And that's whether it's married to each other or married to someone else."

"Easy for her to say. I don't think it's as easy for you male species."

"Why not?"

"Because you men have a men thing going where it's not cool to keep yourselves until marriage. You get more kudos for the number of women you conquer than for how long you can keep yourself."

"You know, I don't think that ration flies with our Father in Heaven. There are no separate rules for women than for men when it comes to doing what's right in the Lord's sight. God is an equal opportunity God. When the Bible says to abstain from fornication, it isn't just speaking to women. We men are going to have to answer for a lot of things the world tells us is cool."

"So, I can't talk you into dropping Gabrielle?"

He shook his head. "No. And I hope you'll really give her a chance."

"I told you. I like her just fine. I mean, she even fixed your plate when I suggested I thought she should."

"You were merely testing her to see if she would go militant on you, weren't you?"

"You know me like a book," Leslie said. "One more question. Are you planning on asking her to marry you anytime soon? I'm just asking because if the rule is that you two are planning to keep yourselves until marriage, I can see this is going to be a really short courtship. You and that woman have love sparks flying all over the place. Some of your sparks have been so strong that when I took your father his plate earlier today, he rubbed my hand and grinned. Dirty old man." She burst into a smile.

"Mom, TMI. TMI."

"TMI?" she said. "What's that supposed to mean?"

"Too much information. I'm still your child. That's entirely *too much information*."

They both laughed.

Chapter 32

*That I might make thee know the certainty of the
words of truth; that thou mightest answer the
words of truth to them that send unto thee?*

—Proverbs 22:21

Angela couldn't wait to get home and go through
the words in the journal her great-grandmother
had written and left. Angela's children were down for
the night.

Brent was watching some television show that made
no sense to her. She'd told him she was going over to
Arletha's house after Arletha called.

Brent, at first, questioned why she didn't just wait
and go the next day. But he quickly nodded as soon as
the words left his mouth. He knew his wife well. It had
been a week of waiting and Angela didn't want to wait
any longer to find answers to at least a few of her questions. That's if there were any answers to be found in
that journal. Otherwise, she would have to try a different approach that could very well involve DNA testing,

although she would have to get each party's consent to do something like that.

In her bedroom, Angela began reading, more like scanning, the pages. She was looking for something specific . . . something that would point her to Ransom Perdue. She had seen his name in the journal the first time she'd gone through it. But it didn't mean anything then. This time, she was determined to pay closer attention . . . to look for code writing, which was what she believed her great-grandmother would have done if she wanted to tell something without coming right out and telling it.

Then she saw something written in the journal.

Ransom returned the first of April. Like an April fool's joke. The year of my dreams was 1943. Dreams can seem real. Ransom and I grew up together. There will always be a special bond between us. He's always known that he could count on me to be there for him. He could count on me being in his corner. Always.

Angela turned the page and read some more.

Only God knows the real truth. God alone. On the last day of April of that same year, I knew that Ransom was truly gone for good. It was all merely a beautiful dream, but it was my dream. And I would forever have a piece of him with me. Now, until the end.

There were other things penned.

Samuel L. Williams was Ransom's closest friend. He said I needed to stop dreaming and start living my life the way God intended for me to do. I know he loves me. He has always loved me. Even when my first husband

*and I married when I was twenty-two, Samuel loved
me. My love for Samuel was genuine, but it was a different kind of love. I didn't think I could ever have children after Ray beat the first one out of me all those
years ago. And that was the last time I let Ray put his
hands on me, too. But glory be to God! God made that
doctor who said I would never be able to get pregnant
again into a lie. And on January 28, 1944, I gave birth
to my miracle child: Arletha Jane Black. Samuel and I
married shortly after her arrival. I then had three more
children: May, then a year and a half later a daughter
we named Frances, and a year after that, a son I
named Leon after the L in Samuel's middle name, since
he already had a Samuel Junior. Samuel L. Williams
was a good man. He was a good friend. He was a good
husband. And he was a good father. No, he couldn't
walk on water, but he sure knew how to pray over and
bless a little and feed many.*

It was obvious to Angela from the way this journal
was done that Pearl had written all of this after the fact.
Like the Old and parts of the New Testament of the
Bible, things occurred, but at the time it was happening,
no one thought it important enough to write it down.
Then after the significance was known, it was imperative
to recall and record events for generations to come.

April 28, 1943, the date Angela had determined, give
or take a few weeks, Arletha would have been conceived. Now all she needed to establish was that Ransom Perdue actually was there during that time and
not merely as a dream as her great-grandmother was
trying to lead anyone who happened to read this journal to believe.

Angela believed her great-granny wanted someone
to figure this out if already pointed in that direction.

But Great-granny didn't want to put something out there if that person had no idea what to look for. Angela knew what she was looking for. She was beginning to put the pieces together, thanks to her having looked into the eyes of Ransom Perdue.

Now all she needed was to decide who to go to with this information first. Should she tell Arletha? Maybe discuss it with Johnnie Mae? After all, Johnnie Mae *was* the person to whom her great-grandmother had left the entire box of information. Should she pay Ransom Perdue a visit at the nursing home before she took this any further? He would be the best person, wouldn't he? What other living person could answer the questions she posed better than him? Ransom would know if there was something more between him and her great-grandmother. He would know, as her great-granny so often would say, whether she was "barking up the wrong tree."

Ransom Perdue would know if something actually happened that could have *possibly* led to Arletha's— her grandmother's—birth.

Chapter 33

And when Paul had gathered a bundle of sticks,
and laid them on the fire, there came a viper out
of the heat, and fastened on his hand.

—Acts 28:3

Reverend Walker watched as Raquel sashayed into her office and sat down at her desk.

"You wanted to see me?" Reverend Walker said, almost smiling as he awaited the good news he was anticipating after being suddenly summoned by Raquel. "I'm hoping your call means you have some good news for me." He smiled and leaned forward.

"That depends."

"On?"

"On how honest you've been, and how well your financial records have been kept and filed."

"So what are you saying? That phone call my office received to come here was legit and not just your way of getting me into your office on an official pretense to discuss my submitted complaint against Pastor Landris?" Reverend Walker frowned.

Raquel leaned in. "We're still following up on your complaint. Although I must say, from everything we have discovered so far, there's nothing there. Nothing. In fact, the way things look, we actually owe George Landris a refund with interest on monies he was legally entitled to have written off that he didn't, or didn't need to have included that he did. The man is as straight as they come. Frankly, I'm impressed with him."

"I don't believe that."

"What are you implying?" Raquel said.

"I'm not implying anything. But you can't tell me you can't find anything wrong going over there at that church or with the good Pastor Landris. I know a lot of ministers and other high-ranking businesspeople. Everybody tries to game the system some way or another," Reverend Walker said.

"Which is why you're here right now. There are complaints that have been recently filed on *you* that suggest there *are* some real problems. Going back just three years, there's income you received that you didn't list in your tax filings. There were gifts listed, like your church paying off all your credit cards and a few personal loans totaling nearly one hundred thousand dollars. You and your wife each received a Mercedes-Benz, and neither of the values were reported," Raquel said, reading from an opened folder on her desk. "*Two* Mercedes . . . his and hers. Sweet." She looked up.

"Those were love offerings . . . gifts. They don't count as income. They were things our church wanted to do for us. Various church members came together and bought us those cars. They paid the insurance and gave us a gift certificate for services, like oil changes."

"Oh, believe me, all of that is listed in this complaint," Raquel said as she wrote something. "Except for the insurance and oil change gift certificates you just mentioned."

"Who filed that complaint? Because whoever it is must be someone out to get me. People had better be careful. The Bible clearly admonishes folks not to touch God's anointed ones."

"Does that threat include me?" Raquel said.

"Threat?" Reverend Walker said. "I wasn't threatening anyone. I was merely quoting the Bible. This is still America. We still have freedom of speech and freedom of religion. I was merely stating what the Bible has to say." He sat back in his chair. "I would never threaten someone like you. Never."

"Well, I thought since you and I were already working together on the complaint you lodged against Pastor Landris, it was only fair that I tell you about this in person. I wouldn't want you to think there was anything nefarious taking place here. You know, you file a complaint against someone, we decide to look into you. That sort of thing. We don't do that. So I thought it best and fair to have you come in, and I tell you this face-to-face." She closed the folder.

"Can you tell me who filed the complaint against me?"

"Actually, there have been several filed against you—one from a Moses Beam, another from a group of deacons in your church. But to be honest with you, the one that *really* got our attention was filed by Jeanette Means. Ironically, all of these came in right around the time you filed your complaint against George Landris."

"Bunch of venomous snakes. Did these people file anonymously the way I did against Pastor Landris?"

"No. If they had, I wouldn't be disclosing their names to you. They apparently don't feel a need to hide their identity from you or anyone else. They don't care who knows they're filing these complaints on you," Raquel said.

"Moses Beam is just an envious old preacher who wishes he could draw to his failed church the number of people I have just on my Pastor's Aide board."

"I take it the money you receive from the Pastor's Aide has been included in your reported income."

"Why should it?" Reverend Walker frowned and pulled his body back in defiance. "It's a gift. As a preacher, I'm entitled to receive gifts from people. I don't report my birthday presents to the IRS. Who does? Those are gifts, and it's silly we're even having this discussion."

"Not so silly, Reverend Walker. Certainly you are entitled to gifts, but there are rules and regulations that govern those gifts and the amounts received before it must be reported." She wrote something else on a stick-it note and put the note inside the folder.

"And those crooked deacons are just mad because they want to run things, and I've told them God placed me in my position, and I'm in charge, not them. That's the problem with some deacons. That's why a lot of churches have gotten rid of the deacon board altogether. Well, I don't need to have to report everything I'm doing or thinking of doing to them. If God is telling me to do something, they don't need to try to stop me. When will folks learn? They can't stop God's program."

"Okay. And Jeanette Means?"

"Miss Jeanette . . . she was my secretary. She worked for me for years, more than two decades, if we're actually keeping count."

"That's what she stated in her written complaint. She has provided us with some shocking papers and proof. I suppose she must have kept a record of years of *everything*."

"That's illegal, isn't it? I mean, if she was taking things from the church like that without us knowing she was doing it?"

"Reverend Walker, out of appreciation and respect for your son, Knowledge, let me give you some good advice. When you receive your official letter, cooperate fully. Don't try to lie, because you'll only be adding perjury to all of this other stuff. And if I were you, I would start praying right now that this is resolved on the IRS side and not end up as a criminal investigation. Because based on what I've seen so far without the kind of scrutiny this is about to receive, paying back taxes and penalties, which are likely going to be massive, will be a lot better than adding jail time along with it." Raquel stood up to signal to him that their unofficial, official meeting was over.

"You can take that for what it's worth," she said. "But as you like to remind me, Knowledge was good to me and my family. He helped save my mother and father's house and their 150 acres of land years ago. And for that, I will eternally be grateful. You wanted to meet informally to file a report, anonymously, on George Landris. I did that. Your certified letter from the IRS will be arriving in the next couple of weeks. Take care of it as best and as quickly as you can, if you're given that opportunity. Because otherwise, it's not going to be pretty. I see what's coming down the pipes. And from all I see that's merely alleged, you'll be lucky if you still have a church or a congregation when you're finished." She held out her hand to shake his.

He looked at her hand. *How could something like this be happening to me?* he thought. *Bunch of traitors. I hope God strikes them all down!*

He then shook Raquel's hand as though her fingers were limp noodles, and left.

Chapter 34

He revealeth the deep and secret things: he knoweth what is in the darkness, and the light dwelleth with him.

—Daniel 2:22

Pastor Landris spoke at Reverend Walker's church. The congregation was mixed with those from Followers of Jesus Faith Worship Center and Divine Conquerors Church. It was an overflow crowd. Pastor Landris had done very few speaking engagements lately. He was well received. Many of the members of the host church came up to Pastor Landris and told him how much they enjoyed his teaching and how much they had learned in just those few minutes he was up in the pulpit.

Reverend Walker overheard some of his members and lamented that he'd had the wild idea of inviting Pastor Landris in the first place. He had believed his members were going to solidly reject Pastor Landris's style of preaching. Instead, things appeared to have completely and totally backfired. And to top everything off, Clarence had sung "I Trust You" by James Fortune & FIYA and had everybody in that building (except for the ones who were rocking or shouting in their seats) on their feet giving praises.

Nothing seemed to be going the way Marshall Walker had thought. He had hoped by the time Pastor Landris came to preach, news would have leaked out that he was under investigation from the IRS. Instead, he was now the one who was possibly looking to have that information break in the news.

A businessman who had expressed interest in expanding near the area where both Pastor Landris and Reverend Walker's churches were, approached both preachers after the service was over.

"Pastor Landris . . . Reverend Walker. My name is William Threadgill. I was wondering if I might have a moment of your time," Mr. Threadgill said.

Neither preacher said anything one way or the other.

Noting their hesitation, Mr. Threadgill pulled out a business card and handed each man one. He continued. "I have tried making an appointment with each of your secretaries to speak with you privately. For whatever reason, I've not been able to get past them to speak with you directly."

"Okay," Reverend Walker said, reading the information on the business card. "So what is this about?" They were on their way to give Pastor Landris his love offering for speaking so Pastor Landris could leave.

"I'd like to speak to you both about a business proposition from one of our high-level elected officials, who would be interested in possibly partnering with you. I believe it will bring lots of funds to each of you as well as your respective churches. I'm also a businessman, and I'd like to speak with you about a separate proposition I have. I'd love to sit down with both of you and tell you more about it. I'd prefer to not give any prudent information in a setting such as this, though. You understand."

"I believe you've already sent something to us, and we're not interested," Pastor Landris said, handing him his card back.

"Pastor Landris," Mr. Threadgill said, "there will be a substantial payment for both of you regardless of the final outcome. Even bigger if we can make this project work. I believe we can. The elected official I represent can help make some things happen for you. I think you should at least hear his proposal out before you walk away."

"As I've said," Pastor Landris repeated, "we received a hint of your proposal and it's not something our congregation is interested in participating in either now or at a later date."

Mr. Threadgill chuckled. "See, Pastor Landris, I don't think you realize just how much money you're walking away from when you say that. Your church, which I'm sure has some worthy projects you're presently working to accomplish, could probably use some extra funds. I'm talking about six figures available just to you if you can see your way to support this. What would it hurt for you to hear me out?"

Reverend Walker's ears had perked up the first time Mr. Threadgill mentioned something was possibly available to him. And the church certainly could use the money. With the economy still down and the number of people leaving Divine Conquerors Church and taking their money with them, the church's collections had been down massively.

That's why he had let Miss Jeanette go. She had been loyal. She'd always gone above and beyond the call of duty. Whatever was asked of her, she did it, and then some. But it was either cut his own salary some-what or get rid of a few people on staff. There was no way he could live on less money, even if it had been a small cut. He had no choice but to let Miss Jeanette go. But he did take up a special offering for her for all of her years of service at the church. He then encouraged someone with good secretarial skills to come forward and give their talents to the service of the Lord.

Someone did step forward on a volunteer basis. *Why waste money paying someone when you can get the same work for free?* he thought.

Reverend Walker had some things coming down on him. Raquel had forewarned him. He'd extended a hand to Pastor Landris, and now it appeared God was opening a door for him with money and access to a high-level elected official, someone in a position to make things happen, including making some things go away. Contrary to what was being implied, he and Mr. Threadgill had already spoken enough on a previous occasion for him to realize that much. Pastor Landris might not want to walk through this door, but he couldn't afford not to. He stayed and spoke with Mr. Threadgill a few minutes longer.

Reverend Walker hurried to his office, where Pastor Landris had gone to before him and was waiting while he finished talking with Mr. Threadgill.

"Pastor Landris, the congregation really seemed to enjoy the message you preached this afternoon," Rev-erend Walker said cheerily. "Now, I know you said you weren't charging us a specific price to preach here today. So please accept this check as a love offering from us at Divine Conquerors. Let me know if it's not enough." He handed Pastor Landris an envelope with a check for a thousand dollars inside—a total that Ralph, the church treasurer, had balked at when he'd told him to cut it.

Reverend Walker had quietly explained to Ralph that Pastor Landris was no run-of-the-mill, little country preacher who would be happy with the customary two hundred fifty to five hundred dollars they generally paid the other preachers who visited them. Pastor Landris was a man with a following, a minister known throughout the United States. To get someone of his caliber to even step foot in their presence would generally cost them closer to ten thousand. One thousand dollars was cheap. And they would have had to pay the others' travel and hotel expenses in addition to that amount had they flown in a preacher comparable to Pastor Landris's level.

Ralph had agreed. He always went along with Reverend Walker in the end. And after Pastor Landris preached and the collection was taken up, Ralph saw, without a doubt, that Reverend Walker had been more than right. Those in attendance were beyond generous—that measly one thousand dollars had been a mere investment in the church's ultimate financial return that afternoon.

"Thank you," Pastor Landris said as he took the envelope without opening it to see how much the check was.

"Oh, and Pastor—" Reverend Walker pulled out another envelope from inside his Armani suit jacket. "This is a love gift given to me to give to you from someone who was in attendance here and asked me to pass it along, since they were unable to do so themselves."

Pastor Landris accepted the envelope more cautiously. Mostly because the envelope bulged, which indicated to him it contained cash money. And from the size and the weight of it, he could only conclude some-one had put a lot of one-dollar bills inside of it, fifty to seventy-five dollars maybe. But Pastor Landris was used to things like this—people giving him love offer-ings, money, and other gifts, wanting to bless him, sometimes slipping their last few dollars in his hand when they shook it.

That was something he used to fight against. He used to try to give it back to them, until one of the Mothers of the church—Mother Robinson—told him point blank, "Pastor, don't block our blessings. When you won't receive what someone is trying to do or to give you, whether they're being obedient to the Holy Spirit or just wanting to bless you, you block *their* blessings by not receiving it."

Early on, it had still been hard for him to accept money from people he knew were struggling but desir-ing to give him something out of their appreciation or love. But after he started receiving these gifts and of-ferings without telling them no or that they didn't have to do that, he began praying special prayers and bless-ings for them. And the praise reports started pouring in from every one of those givers.

He figured this envelope, filled with some amount of cash, was merely from another person who wanted to bless him the best way they knew how. He would open the envelope later, hope whoever had given it had put a note with their name inside of it. He would then pray for them, just as he'd done for so many others.

Chapter 35

*Thou hast turned for me my mourning into danc-
ing: thou hast put off my sackcloth, and girded
me with gladness.*

—Psalm 30:11

Gabrielle couldn't wait to see Miss Crowe. She felt
fluttering activity in her stomach. Would Miss
Crowe know her? According to the family, Miss Crowe's
mind seemed to be fine. It was the quickness in which
she did things, and getting her words to come out the
way she wanted them, that was the problem. They felt
she would likely remember Gabrielle even if it had been
ten years now since she'd last seen her.

When they arrived at the home where Miss Crowe
was being taken care of, the family felt it best that
Gabrielle not come in with them in the beginning.
They would prepare Aunt Esther, not fully telling her
about Gabrielle, just that someone from her past was
there. Everyone was curious to see whether she would
know Gabrielle when she saw her, and if not, whether

she would remember her when they told her who she was.

Gabrielle stood just outside Miss Crowe's room. When she heard the first sound come from Miss Crowe's voice, she almost lost it. It was indeed her mentor and friend. She began shaking her right hand as though she were trying to flick something off of it.

"Auntie," Zachary said, "we have a surprise for you. It's someone you used to know a long time ago. She's here to see you. Is it okay if we bring her in now?"

"Yeah," Aunt Esther said with no enthusiasm or excitement.

That was Gabrielle's cue to come in. She came through the door and looked at the frail woman in the bed. "Hi, Miss Crowe. Do you remember me?"

Miss Crowe began to squint. "Come," she said, holding up a crooked finger, "closer."

Gabrielle walked over to the bed. Zachary moved over so she could stand in his spot. Gabrielle smiled at the woman she'd known as Miss Crowe.

"Closer," Miss Crowe said.

Gabrielle leaned down, her face only about a foot away from Miss Crowe's face.

"Book her," Miss Crowe said, tears beginning to stream down her face. "Is it really you?" The words were slightly slurred but clear enough. "Is it really my Gab, my Gabrie, my Gabri . . . elle?" she finally managed to say.

Gabrielle started to cry. She nodded. "Yes, Miss Crowe. It's really me. It's really your Gabrielle. Oh, Miss Crowe." Gabrielle broke down and hugged her as she cried even harder. "I'm sorry, I don't mean to cry. But it's so good to see you. Oh, Miss Crowe, I love you so much and I'm so glad to see you. Thank You, Jesus.

Thank You for letting me see her again. Miss Crowe, I love you, and I thank you for so much! So much."

Miss Crowe raised her hand slowly, something her family had not seen her do often. She put her hand on Gabrielle's back and began to first pat, then rub her. "There, there. It's all right," she said, slurred but clearer than her other words. "I luv you, too," she said. "You are even more beautiful than last I saw you."

"Miss Crowe. I didn't know what happened to you. Nobody told me anything. I've thought about you so much, I can't tell you how much."

"There, there. God had us in His hands. God is good," Miss Crowe said.

Gabrielle stood upright and wiped her tears away with her hands. Queen pulled tissue out of the box near the bed and pushed some into Gabrielle's hand.

"You still dan . . . dan . . . dance?" Miss Crowe said, stammering somewhat.

Gabrielle smiled as she nodded. "Yes, Miss Crowe. I still dance. And I dance for the Lord now. I just got hired as the director of the Dance Ministry at our church."

"Oh, that good," Miss Crowe said, having a time getting the *s* to join with the word *that* in her sentence.

Gabrielle took Miss Crowe's hand and held it. Zachary pushed the chair up to the bed and indicated that Gabrielle should sit down. Gabrielle did without taking her eyes off Miss Crowe.

"You in church now?"

"Yes, ma'am. It took a while and some doing, but I made it."

"I pray . . . pray . . . prayed for you," Miss Crowe said. "God has an . . . ans . . . answered my prayers."

"Thank you for praying for me. Thank you for believing in me. Thank you for all that you did that made my life good. I just want you to know that in the end, your labor was not in vain. And I praise God through dance now."

"You still good?"

"She's still good," Zachary chimed in. "I joined that church after I saw her dance for the Lord," he said. "She's real good."

"You two friends? What?" Miss Crowe said, directing her attention and question to Zachary.

"We are . . . together, Aunt Esther." Zachary beamed. "We're seeing each other."

"God is good," Aunt Esther said. She began to cry. "Only God can do."

"Yes, Auntie, God certainly is good. Look how He brought all of us here today."

Aunt Esther closed her eyes. Gabrielle took a clean tissue and wiped Aunt Esther's tears away.

"One day," Aunt Esther said, opening her eyes, "Jesus gon' wipe all our tears away. God is so good."

"Well, Esther," Zechariah said. "We don't want to tire you out. Zachary and Queen brought Gabrielle all the way from Alabama just to see you."

"Dance for me," Aunt Esther said to Gabrielle.

"Miss Crowe, why don't you get some rest, and I'll come back tomorrow. If you still want me to, I'll come and dance for you tomorrow."

"All I do is rest. Years of rest. I tired of rest . . . ing. I want to see you dance. Find some music and Gabrie . . . Gabrielle, I want to see you dance. For me. Dance. Please."

"Okay, Miss Crowe. Whatever you want."

There wasn't a radio in her room. Aunt Esther hadn't really cared much about music or listening to chatter . . . until now.

"I'll go check with the nurses' station and see if I can borrow a CD player, radio, or something from one of them," Zachary said. His father nodded.

"Miss Crowe, while Zachary is going to find some music for me to dance to, would you mind if we pray?"

"Prayer is the key," Aunt Esther said. "Faith unlocks the door. Pray. I'd like that a lot."

Gabrielle and the rest in the room held hands with Aunt Esther as Gabrielle prayed. There was such an anointing in that room as she did. Everybody felt the charge that flowed from hand to hand, and it was all in the atmosphere. Zechariah was crying by the time Gabrielle finished. He patted Gabrielle's hand, hugged her, then hugged his sister.

"Esther, I love you," Zechariah said to her, releasing her from his embrace. "God is doing something miraculous right now. I can feel it. Something is happening right now. Healing is going forth by the power of God, in the name of Jesus! Right now."

"I believe," Esther said, then she smiled.

Zachary came back inside with a radio/CD player. "One of the nurses had this. She said we could use it. I asked her if she had any gospel CDs. She had a few. I got the one with Karen Clark Sheard's 'God Is Here.'"

Gabrielle smiled. That was the song she had danced to for her audition for the Dance Ministry. By the power of the Holy Ghost, she knew they were going to be blessed by the Lord with this song and dance.

Zachary put in the CD. They sat Aunt Esther completely upright so she could see Gabrielle's every move. Zachary turned on the music.

And Gabrielle danced with a joy she had never quite known before. She danced, she leaped, she bowed, and she praised.

And when she finished, there was not a dry eye in that room. In fact, one of the nurses had stopped by, and even she was wiping her eyes and giving God praise.

"God is good," Miss Crowe said. "He so good!"

Chapter 36

*For ye are not as yet come to the rest and to the
inheritance, which the Lord your God giveth you.*

—Deuteronomy 12:9

Melissa Peeples had been hired to put together a
one-hundred-year birthday party on November
seventh by the daughter of the centenarian. Zenobia
had heard nothing but praise for Melissa's skills as an
event planner and was glad she'd secured her early.

A lot had happened in the past few weeks. Zenobia
had just learned that she had a sister she didn't even
know existed. She and her family had met Memory
and her daughter Lena and Lena's husband, Richard,
along with granddaughter Theresa; her husband, Maurice; and great-grandchildren Mauricia and Maurice
the Second, whom they called M-double-G. Just like
that, their family had grown expeditiously, and life as
they'd known it had changed.

Zenobia's other two brothers and their family would
all be here for their father's birthday celebration. Zenobia
had gone online and sent the appropriate e-mail to Willard

Scott to have their father highlighted on his *Today* show segment. Melissa had also sent media releases to the television stations about his birthday, which was officially November fourth. They had decided to hold his party on the seventh so it would be on a weekend and allow more people to be able to come.

They'd put down a deposit on the ballroom, so that was all done. The ballroom contract prohibited outside food from being brought in, so they had already contracted with them to have a full course meal provided at twenty-seven dollars a plate. That was a lot of money, especially when you're preparing for about two hundred guests, but Zenobia felt her father was worth a great birthday celebration.

After hearing about what happened in his earlier life—almost being lynched, falsely imprisoned for ten years on trumped-up charges, especially back during that time when black men really had it hard—she felt his life deserved to be celebrated in the highest form of fashion.

Everything was set and on schedule. Zenobia had called the venue and left a message that she'd need to amend the number of guests, now that their family list had grown. Memory insisted she would help with the cost. After all, this was her father, too.

So getting a callback three weeks out from the event, telling her she would have to find another venue, was not something Zenobia had wanted to hear. The cancellation was due to some mix-up. Apparently, the person who'd taken her reservation had not completed the paperwork properly. It had not been entered into the system, and so when someone else had called for that same day, the ballroom had been rented out to them. It was human error, and unfortunately, there were no other rooms that size available. The woman who called Zenobia to tell her this was devastated. But Zenobia could tell she was more upset about the six thousand dollars they would be losing on just the food she was set to buy from them than for the inconvenience Zenobia would now have to deal with.

The other person who had rented the room was only having a political rally. There would be no food and no table or chairs set up since it was a standing event. She had tried to convince them to take another room, even offered to give them a break on the rate. They would be standing anyway, so it wouldn't matter if they were in a smaller area.

But this was an elected official who was doing a campaign fund drive, and he wasn't hearing it. He made it perfectly clear that it didn't matter to him if this was a celebration for the oldest living person in the world and media from everywhere was coming to document the blessed event. He had a re-election campaign to run and an office to keep, and he wasn't about to give up the best room in the building for nothing or no one, end of discussion. The bigger the room, the more people he would be able to pack in.

So Zenobia was left, at the last hour, to find an available place. And there appeared to be nothing anywhere. She decided to call Clarence.

"Clarence, we need a place to hold Gramps's birthday party," she said.

"I thought you had a place already. In fact, you told me you just got back the invitations, and you were about to mail them out."

"I did, and I did. So now the invitations have the wrong information printed on them as to where it will be held because it's not going to be there now." She jotted herself a note to add that expense to her list of reimbursements from the ballroom's cancellation.

"What happened?"

"Human error. They double booked the ballroom. I booked it back in March, and they just discovered they didn't enter my information into the system. They've booked the room out to someone else." She sighed hard. "So now I need to find somewhere to have Gramps's birthday celebration. And at this late date, there's nothing nice left. If I don't find somewhere soon, we might have to use your place and try to fix it up quickly."

"Mom, you know I wouldn't mind you using the place. And I'm working on having it converted to something that would likely be more perfect for something like this. But if I can be honest with you, I'm not there yet."

"What do you mean you're not there yet? Are you already trying to backslide? You haven't been on this faith walk but about a month and you're already looking back?" Zenobia said.

"That's not what I was talking about, Mother. I meant the building has a lot of work to be done to make it more acceptable to the clientele I hope to have patronizing it. There's still that high stage, the bar, and of course those nasty little poles gracing it. Even if I wanted to let you use it and we just did some temporary cosmetic things, I believe people will notice the bar and the poles."

Zenobia laughed. "Yeah, I suppose you're right. Plus, a lot of people probably won't step foot into the place as it stands now, worrying about what someone will say or think about them." She shrugged. "I don't know what I'm going to do. We need a place, and we need a *nice* place. This is my daddy's one hundredth birthday, and I want it to be one he'll remember and cherish."

"I'll tell you what: let's pray about it, and see where God leads us," Clarence said.

"Oh," she said, fanning her face quickly with her hand. "God is so good! My baby boy just suggested we pray." She looked toward the ceiling. "God, now I *know* You can do all things! Oh, Clarence, I just wish you were here so I could hug you right now."

Clarence laughed at his mother, and then he prayed.

Chapter 37

Honor widows that are widows indeed.
                                    —1 Timothy 5:3

Gabrielle went back and visited with Aunt Esther the following day. They were only going to be in Chicago one more day after this before they would be heading back to Birmingham. Both she and Zachary had to be at work Tuesday morning.

Aunt Esther's face lit up when Gabrielle walked in. Gabrielle returned the smile. Zachary had brought her, but told her he had to go check on something, so he would drop her off and come pick her up later. Gabrielle knew this was his sly way of giving her and her mentor some time alone together. It was things like this that made her love Zachary even more.

"Book-er," Aunt Esther said. "Gabrielle," she further said. She smiled. "See how much that prayer worked. My speech is getting better already. And look." She lifted one leg up off the bed, circled it around, then did the other. "I blew the therapist away when I first did that this morning. She asked what happened. I told her . . . it was God. All God."

"Yes, Miss Crowe. Every good gift and every perfect gift comes from above. It's all God. God brought you back into my life, and I'm so thankful to Him for that."

"Sit," Aunt Esther said, patting her bed.

"Are you sure? I can just pull up the chair close."

"Sit," she said, patting the bed as she pushed herself up straighter. "I want to be close. It been a long time. It's been a long time." She smiled, getting her *s* on the word *it's*. "See, I'm getting better with each moment. I may get well enough to go home."

"Just don't overdo it," Gabrielle said as she sat down next to Aunt Esther.

"You don't believe God can fully heal me?"

"Oh, I believe God can do anything. That I believe. He took me and changed me and my life. There's nothing too hard for our God. If you believe, I believe with you."

"I believe," Aunt Esther said. "Tell me what I missed? Did you go to Juilliard?"

"No, ma'am. I didn't. I didn't get to go anywhere but to work."

"What? I don't understand. You were supposed to go to The Juilliard School to learn dance." Aunt Esther was getting upset.

"Miss Crowe, don't get worked up now. It's all right. Things still worked out for me okay." Gabrielle wasn't telling the whole truth, since she did have a hard time at first. "You know what? I recently danced for this one lady who owned a dance studio. She was so impressed by me that she asked who taught me how to dance. I told her nobody but you. When she heard your name, that's when I learned how famous you were. I didn't know you were that well known."

"But I arranged for you to go to The Juilliard School. I paid for it. I thought you'd gone. I didn't hear from you, and I wondered why you didn't come by to tell me of all your experiences. You didn't go?"

"No." Gabrielle frowned. "I didn't know I was supposed to go."

"I sent a letter. I spoke with folks. That was my surprise to you. Remember I had a surprise? That was my surprise. But you didn't go? You never heard from them at all?"

Gabrielle put her arm around Aunt Esther and hugged her as she brushed her hair down with her hand. "You did that for me? You really were my angel." She began to cry.

"We need to find out what happened. You were set to go. Everything was paid for. You were going to shine, my little floating dandelion. I'll find out what happened."

"Don't you worry yourself about it, okay. You were the best gift God ever gave me, after my mother. Things still worked out. No matter what bad Satan may have been up to, God still used it for good. I've been in a pit, I've been sold away to slavery, I've been a prisoner, I've tried to do right and have had folks to lie on me and to me. But in the end, I'm still standing. And I'm here with you now. I love you for all that you did for me and all that you were to me. And Miss Crowe"—Gabrielle pulled back and looked in her eyes—"God is not through with either of us yet." She smiled. "He's not through. We have much more work to do. There's so much more God requires of us. I believe that."

"You're a gift. Don't let anyone keep you from your dreams. God has you . . . in His hand." Aunt Esther held out her hand, then did a dance move she'd taught Gabrielle early on with her hand. "No one."

Zachary came in and found the two of them sitting on the bed together. He smiled. "Sorry, Auntie, I had to run an errand. Did you two have a good visit?"

"Yes-s-s," Aunt Esther said, holding the *s*.

Zachary bent down and kissed her on her cheek.

Aunt Esther smiled as she looked up at him. "Thank you," she said to Zachary. She then turned to Gabrielle and said, "No one."

Chapter 38

Howbeit when he, the Spirit of truth, is come, he will guide you into all truth: for he shall not speak of himself; but whatsoever he shall hear, that shall he speak: and he will show you things to come.

—John 16:13

Angela had gone back and forth about what she should do. She had convinced herself that it was best she keep this to herself. At least, until she could talk to Ransom Perdue. Therein was her problem. How should she approach him? What should she say? How do you begin a conversation where you ask an elderly man if it's possible he might have slept with your great-grandmother? No, that definitely wasn't the way to approach it.

Just the thought of it was hard—her great-grandmother possibly in love and acting just like young people act who are in love today. That was not the great-granny she knew and loved. Great-granny was grounded. She was deliberate . . . slow to speak and slow to make angry. She always had sage advice. She could knock you down with her words and pick you up in the same sentence. She was honest. But a woman who might have done what this was suggesting and leading her to was incomprehensible for Angela.

She had seen Johnnie Mae the week after Ransom had gotten to meet everyone at her house. Johnnie Mae told how special everything had been. Gramps, as she called him, had such joy meeting and hugging his daughter after all those years of thinking about what may have become of her. Angela could appreciate how that felt.

But Angela had been preoccupied with her own thoughts at the time. She'd met Ransom Perdue. Johnnie Mae had never seen her grandmother. Arletha still didn't care to visit Followers of Jesus Faith Worship Center. There were just some things her traditions would not allow her to accept. She didn't go back to her old church, either. Especially after she learned that when she was in the hospital not one of them cared enough to come see her or to find out how she was. She'd settled at Divine Conquerors Church. And she was one of the few members who didn't care to come to the afternoon program when she learned Pastor Landris would be preaching at Divine Conquerors.

Angela saw the resemblance between Ransom and Arletha instantly. Even Brent confirmed she wasn't just making things seem the way she wanted them to. He thought the photo she'd shown him did remind him a lot of Arletha. If it really was a picture of a young Ransom Perdue and not Samuel L. Williams (which to Brent was still a possibility, since there really wasn't a name anywhere on the picture), that person was more likely than not Arletha's father.

But other than the photo and the few lines she'd

found written in the journal that could possibly be referring to a *real* Ransom and not just a dream, Angela had nothing. If she went to talk to Ransom, should she just tell him what she was thinking? Should she come at it from a different angle in case he was inclined to deny Arletha?

But if he *was* Arletha's father, wouldn't he want to know about it? Would he actually deny his paternity as though he owed child support or even back child support? Surely, if there was a possibility that Arletha was his child, and he didn't know it, he would embrace the news as happily as he'd welcomed his other children. And if she wasn't, Angela could put this nonsense behind her and be thankful she hadn't stirred up anything by sharing her thoughts and findings with Arletha.

She began to pray. "Lord, please guide me. I don't know what I should do. You know everything. You know our risings and our lying down. You know what's around the curve before we ever get there. I don't know what to do. Please direct my path. Guide my feet and my tongue. Please."

Chapter 39

Forbidding to marry, and commanding to abstain
from meats, which God hath created to be re-
ceived with thanksgiving of them which believe
and know the truth.

—1 Timothy 4:3

"Gabrielle, I just want you to know that I think you're a wonderful young woman," Leslie said as the two women sat in the house alone on the white couch in the living room. Zachary had gone to visit one of his friends, as had Queen. Leslie had sent Zechariah to the store to bring back some milk since he had just drunk the last of it and she needed milk to make mashed potatoes.

"Seeing you dancing like that the other day . . . it was anointed and powerful," Leslie said. "That's all I can say."

"Thank you. I appreciate that," Gabrielle said. "But as Mary Mary's latest song says, 'It's the God in me.' God gave me this gift. I'm just glad I'm able to use it in

His service, hopefully to point someone to Jesus by doing it."

Leslie released an exhausted sigh. "Listen, I really do like you. I really do."

"But—" Gabrielle said, supplying the word for her.

"*But* . . . I don't think you're the right woman for Zachary. He needs someone who can challenge him from time to time. Zachary can be strongheaded. Sometimes he wants to do a thing before he thinks the whole thing through. He needs a woman who will let him know when he's about to go over the cliff, then stop him before he can do it."

"And you don't believe I can do that? You don't believe I can love him enough to be that person who complements him . . . who adds to the best of all that he is or can be?"

"I won't lie to you, because God in Heaven knows my heart. I don't believe you can be what my son needs. He's finished with medical school and his internship. He's just begun his own practice. Zachary has a ton of bills in the way of student loans due to his lengthy college education. Becoming a doctor isn't cheap by any stretch of the imagination. People see the amount of money a good doctor can make, but they have no idea what it cost to get there. There's the cost in time, and the cost of money, the cost in sacrifices. Zachary has made great sacrifices to get where he is today."

Gabrielle smiled. "And you think him being with me will hurt him?"

"I think you could be the cause of him losing out on some things and benefits he might otherwise enjoy if you weren't in his life." She shrugged. "I'm not trying to hurt you. I promise you that's neither my personality nor who I am as a person. It's hard for me to say these things to you . . . hard because I *do* like you so much. But I love my son. Dearly. He's not thinking things through. Someone needs to have a level head. Zachary is merely caught up in the moment right now. A moment that I think, given time, will pass. But right now Zachary is in love with you."

"Oh, you think he's in love?" Gabrielle said.

"I know he is. Trust me: he wouldn't have brought you here for us to meet if he wasn't deeply in love with you. My son, the doctor, loves you."

Gabrielle stood up and walked toward the fireplace mantle, away from where Leslie was sitting. "But we haven't known each other long enough for him to be in love with me like that. And he only brought me here to see Miss Crowe again."

"It's never taken Zachary long to know what he wants. That's how he's made. He's a sharp thinker. Impulsive, yes. But sharp, nevertheless. I suppose you can say he gets that from me. And yes, bringing you to see his aunt again was a part of your trip, but it was a double bonus. My son loves you. There's so much of me in him."

"What do you mean?"

"I mean, I knew I loved his father the first moment I laid eyes on him. Fedora hat cocked to the side. Seeing him, as I stood on that next to the last step at that house party that night . . . he practically took my breath away! Sure, we dated for a while. But my love just increased from that first time I saw him. We were merely going through the motions of what other people expected we should do before we could set a date to be together forever. Honestly, now, if you don't date for a certain amount of time, does it really mean you can't possibly be in love?" Leslie shook her head. "Can you learn more things about that person in time? Sure. But then you can also marry someone and still find there are things you didn't know. That's all a part of life."

"Well, I don't think you have to worry about me and Zachary getting married anytime soon. It's like you just said. He has a new practice going. He's trying to unwind from having been in school for so long. He barely knows me."

Leslie stood up and walked over to Gabrielle. "And he loves you anyhow. And I believe he plans to ask you to marry him soon. But if you love him at all, if you have any feelings of him having the best in life, then walk away. Give him a chance to breathe and maybe think about things a little more. I'm sure he's probably also dealing with hormones when it comes to you. Wanting to be with you, but then you having cleverly told him there will be no sex without marriage."

"That wasn't a clever tactic. The Bible tells us not to fornicate. I'm trying to live by that. Zachary said it's what he wanted to do as well. I didn't trick him into this with an ulterior motive."

Leslie took Gabrielle by the hand and pulled her back over to the couch. She sat down, bringing Gabrielle down with her as she held both her hands. "Gabrielle, I might not be saying everything right. And believe me, if Zachary knew I was having this conversation with you, he would be furious with me. But if you love him, if you truly love him, let him go now before either of you get in too deep. Love him enough to let him go."

"What if *I* love him and I'd like to spend the rest of my life with him?" Gabrielle felt a tear make its way down her cheek. She freed one of her hands and brushed it away. "What am I supposed to do with my feelings? What am I supposed to do about a hurting heart?"

Leslie squeezed her hand. "This is hard for you, I know it is. But I also believe you have a lot of love inside of you. I believe you're going to think about what I've said, and you're going to see that I'm right. God may have forgiven your past, but the world will still bring it up when it wants to bring you down. I would hate for all of Zachary's hard work to be brought down from something he didn't even do. And you and I both know there's a good possibility someone is going to bring up your past as a dancer or as a maid, and they'll somehow twist it to make him look bad. How will you feel then?"

Leslie stood and pulled Gabrielle up. "All I'm asking is for you to consider what I'm saying. If you believe I'm out of line or way out there, then dismiss it and keep on going regardless of whom and how much it might hurt later. But if you let someone go, and things happen where that person comes back to you, then it means it was meant to be. That's all I'm trying to say. That's all I'm trying to say here."

"What all are you trying to say?" Zachary said to his mother as he strolled into the living room. "What are my two favorite women in here talking about?"

Leslie looked at Gabrielle and smiled as she hugged Zachary. "You," she said. "We were talking about you. But it was all good. Isn't that right, Gabrielle?" Her eyes seemed to actually twinkle as she winked at Gabrielle.

Chapter 40

But as for you, ye thought evil against me; but God meant it unto good, to bring to pass, as it is this day, to save much people alive.

—Genesis 50:20

Melissa called Zenobia. "I think I've found the perfect place to have your father's birthday party," Melissa said.

"Thank goodness. Because I've called everywhere and I'm not having any success. I was thinking we were going to have to transform my son's old establishment into a more hospitable place and have it there."

"Would you prefer having it at your son's place?" Melissa asked.

"Oh, no. It's not a good place in its present state. But if there was nothing, it would have had to do. So what place did you find?"

"Followers of Jesus Faith Worship Center has a wonderful and large place to hold a banquet. In fact, earlier this year we hosted an Inaugural Ball there. It will seat the number of people you're inviting. It has great ambiance and atmosphere. And I've already spoken with the church and it's available and quite affordable. In fact, this would end up saving you money."

"Wow, it sounds perfect. I've been to the church before."

"You have," Melissa said. "Well, I'm a member there."

"So is one of my sons. Clarence Walker."

"Clarence Walker is your son? Well, it's a small world. He hasn't been a member long. But I happen to know him because he has this amazing voice, and my husband, who is a minister there, says the Minister of Music is turning cartwheels. He's just that good."

"He is good, but then I'm his mother so I'm totally and unapologetically biased."

"So, is the church banquet hall a go for you?" Melissa asked.

"Absolutely," Zenobia said. "I'm just glad you thought of it. I didn't even think about a church with a banquet hall. The church where I attend doesn't have anything large enough to do something like what we're planning. Just tell me what I need to do next."

"I'll call them back and tell them we definitely want to reserve it for Saturday, November seventh. We'll have it for the whole day, so that way we can get all the decorating done," Melissa said. "As for the food, you have two choices now that we're going with the church option. They have a staff that can prepare food just like they were going to with the ballroom you'd already reserved. They use real china and crystal glasses, unless you just want something scaled down. And their prices are less per person than what you were going to pay. And I can attest from my own personal experience that the food is twice as good. Guaranteed to make you want to slap somebody, it's just that good. I promise you." She shook her head as she smiled.

"Wow, talk about God taking a negative and turning it into a positive. What looked like a bad thing is starting to become a true blessing. I never would have thought about doing this. God really will take what Satan intended for bad and turn it into good."

"Oh, yeah. That's something I've learned," Melissa said. "We just have to trust Him as we continue on. We have to trust that God not only *can* but *will* work it out. Now, as for the other option when it comes to the food, you can have food brought in—"

"Oh, no," Zenobia said. "I love this just the way you've already laid it out. We rent the church's banquet hall. We pay the staff to do the catering. You're handling the decorations and everything else. Looks like all I'll have to do is pick my father up and show up ready to have an enjoyable and memorable time."

"That's the plan," Melissa said. "I'll reserve the banquet room. I'll let you know how much everything will be so you can write them a check. I'll get them to fax me menu options so we can get that ordered."

"I hope you know you're getting a huge bonus after this is over."

Melissa laughed. "Well, I just appreciate your choosing my company to handle this big day for you. I'm not happy unless you're happy. But I do have a thought. Tell me what you think about it, and if you don't like it, we'll nix it."

"Okay."

"What would you think about maybe getting your son, Clarence, to sing with the Worship Ensemble, that's our smaller group of singers, doing background singing?"

"I love that idea. More importantly, my father would love it!" Zenobia said. "Can you arrange it? I know Clarence will be glad to do it."

"Sure. I'll talk with our Minister of Music about the ensemble. And if they can't do it on short notice, maybe we can use a track for Clarence to sing to."

"I think that will be so special. My father loves to hear Clarence sing. Now, how awesome will it be for Clarence to sing at his birthday party."

"All right. Then I suppose I have everything I need from you at this time. I'll check back with you later so we can choose the meal you want served. It looks like we're back on track."

"Thank the Lord! Clarence, believe it or not, prayed that God would work things out. Well, God has exceeded anything I was ever expecting."

"That's how God does it. I know. You should see the wonderful man God brought into my life. Please, don't get me started. It would be impolite for me to have to ask you to hold my mule," Melissa said, referencing a popular song back in the day where the person who was telling of the goodness of God told someone to hold his mule so he could shout then and there.

"I know that's right," Zenobia said. "I would be too busy shouting myself to be able to hold your mule."

Chapter 41

But we have this treasure in earthen vessels,
that the excellency of the power may be of God,
and not of us.

—2 Corinthians 4:7

Clarence called Gabrielle as soon as he hung up with his mother. Gabrielle had returned from her visit with Zachary's family. He hadn't spoken with her in a while, not since he was baptized in September.

"Hey, lady. What's going on?" Clarence said.

"Nothing but the rent," Gabrielle said, then she laughed when she thought about the double meaning of those words. "Okay, thanks to you, I'm not renting. I'm still paying for my house just like I was before the economy tanked, again thanks to you. So, what's going on with you? You sound mighty chipper."

"Chipper? Men aren't chipper. At least, not this man. Listen, I'm going to tell you why I called, and then I want you to tell me what all has been going on with you. But before either of these things, I want to congratulate you on being named director of the Dance Ministry. You go, girl!"

"Thank you. I'm still trying to work my job at that house I was assigned to. You know, when I needed a job, they were there for me. I'm able to do what I need with the Dance Ministry and still do that as well. It's a lot of work, a lot more than I thought. I'm not sure how long I'll be able to do both, but for now, the money is definitely coming in handy. As the director, I'm required and credited for attending Bible study and church services. Missing these services was why I never wanted a part-time job in the past. So this is working out perfectly, not that I work at the church to get paid for attending."

"You don't have to explain this to me. This your boy you talking to. I'm the one who watched your life change as you lived for the Lord, and it got my attention. Now I'm right there at Bible study, and I see why you never wanted to miss it. Pastor Landris is off the chain."

"You certainly can tell old people who still think they're hip," Gabrielle said.

"What are you talking about?" Clarence said.

"Who says 'off the chain' anymore?"

"Well, apparently I do, because I just did. Okay, okay. I know I'm crunk."

Gabrielle started laughing. "Yeah, you're crunk, all right. You're off the heezy."

"Okay, now, I might be older than you, but I recognize when someone is making fun of me at my own expense."

"*Moi?* I would never make fun of you, Clarence." She laughed. "Okay, so what did you call to tell me?"

"My mother wants me to sing at my grandfather's

birthday dinner slash party. He'll be one hundred on November fourth, but his celebration is that Saturday, November seventh."

"One hundred years old? Wow, that's great."

"Yes. And he still gets around on his own. He's still in his right mind. We have a lot to be thankful for. So I was touched that my mother asked me to sing at this event. An event, by the way, that is going to be held at our church's banquet hall."

"Our church." She laughed. "That sounds so funny when you say it. It's a good funny, though. So they're having it at *our* church?"

"In the banquet hall."

"That's where they had the Inaugural Ball back in January. It's really nice," Gabrielle said.

"Well, I had this idea and I wanted to see if you'll help me pull it off."

"If I can."

"Dance while I sing at the celebration."

"Dance? You want me to *dance?*"

"Yeah. I've picked out this song I want to do. Don't worry, it's gospel."

"Oh, I wasn't doubting that," Gabrielle said.

"Let's both use the gifts God has given us to-gether—not *of* us, but showing the excellent power of God. We don't have a lot of time, but I know how good you are. My mother said they were thinking about ask-ing the Worship Ensemble to sing background for me, but I think I'd prefer getting a track and doing it with that. That way neither the church band nor the Ensem-ble will have to be worried about practicing on such short notice. You and I can pull this off, I know we can. Besides, I haven't seen you dance since you became saved. I'd love for you to bless us on that day with a praise dance to the Lord in conjunction with my grandfather's birthday celebration."

"Clarence, I know what a perfectionist you are. Everything that you do, you like it to be done with excellence. This *is* kind of short notice for us to make it perfect."

"Please. We don't have to be perfect to do it with excellency. If you won't do it for me, will you at least do it for my poor, old, aging grandfather?"

Gabrielle laughed. "Okay, Clarence. I'll do it because you asked me . . . and for Grandpa."

"Actually, it's Gramps, not Grandpa. He likes being called Gramps."

"Okay, I'll do it for Gramps."

"Great!" Clarence said. "Now, tell me. How is Z. or Z. W. or whatever you call him? How are things going with you and the good doctor?"

Gabrielle put her hand up to her lips and pressed, then took it down. "I think I'm going to break up with him," she said after a few moments of silence.

"What? I thought things were going well for the two of you. So what happened? He wasn't all he was cracked up to be? You figured out he wasn't your type? He was selfish, inconsiderate, stuck on himself . . . he thought he was too good for you? You realized you didn't love him and you probably never will? What?" He paused, and his voice became more concerned. "Wait a minute, he didn't hurt you, did he?"

"No, Clarence. None of those things. I'm thinking about breaking up with him because I love him."

"So, I guess what you're saying is that you love him, but he doesn't love you."

"No, I'm fairly certain that he loves me, too."

"Okay," Clarence said with a touch of sarcasm. "I'm

sure in some parallel universe all of this makes perfect sense. But here on earth . . . I'm sorry. I don't get it."

"I'm thinking maybe I'm really not good for him. And even if I am, would my past come back and hurt him at some point? I don't want to hurt him. Because Clarence, I really do love him. More than anyone I've ever been with before, I really love this man."

"Wow, that's jacked up," was all Clarence could say.

Chapter 42

I know thy works, that thou art neither cold nor hot: I would thou wert cold or hot. So then because thou art lukewarm, and neither hot nor cold, I will spew thee out of my mouth.

—Revelation 3:15–16

Zachary had been really busy at work since he'd come back from Chicago. Queen was talking to her husband, who had finally decided he needed to get his act together. He was coming to visit Queen at Zachary's house to see if they could get their marriage back on track. Queen agreed to see him, but she wanted them to go talk to someone outside of their marriage. She called the church and made an appointment with one of the counselors on staff.

Zachary didn't make it to Bible study on Wednesday night. There was an accident at a plant and several people were severely injured and burned. He and Gabrielle had tickets to see the Broadway show *The Color Purple* on Friday. He knew how much she was looking forward to seeing it.

He called and talked with her Thursday. She'd been different since they'd returned from Chicago. He couldn't figure out what happened between their wonderful time at his parents' and them arriving back in Birmingham. He'd asked her last week when she hardly talked to him if he'd done anything he wasn't aware of. She'd said no. When he asked her what was wrong, she'd said nothing. He didn't want to bug her about it, but it did bother him. He was planning on going over to her house Thursday night, but something came up at the hospital that delayed him.

"I said seven, but is it all right if I come at nine tonight?" he asked Gabrielle when he called. "I have two patients that I need to check on, and I'll be through for the night."

"Sure. That will be fine." Gabrielle hung up. She did need to do something one way or the other. Right now she was more in a limbo state. She wasn't cold or hot; she was being lukewarm. And Jesus said He would spew people like that out of His mouth because they weren't one or the other. She now better understood that scripture. Either be hot or cold. Who likes lukewarm? Her phone rang again.

It was not a familiar number. She answered it, fully expecting to tell someone they'd dialed the wrong number or that she wasn't interested in what they were trying to push, sell, or support through donations.

"Hello," Gabrielle said.

"Gabrielle?" A voice timidly spoke her name, almost as though she knew her.

"Yes."

"Listen, I know I'm not supposed to contact you. But I feel I have no choice. It's a matter of life and death now. With each passing day, we're running out of time. There's no place for rules and regulations."

"Excuse me, but it sounds like you have dialed the wrong number."

"You're Gabrielle Booker, aren't you?"

"Actually, no. And if you're calling for Gabrielle *Booker,* then you can't possibly know me." Gabrielle said it so nasty that it left a bad taste in her own mouth. She realized just how much more work in her walk with the Lord she truly had to do.

"You're right. It was my error. You're Gabrielle Mercedes now. Please forgive me." The woman's voice sounded so weak. "But Gabrielle, we *don't* have a lot of time."

"Why do you continue to act like I know you? I'm sorry, but your voice is not familiar to me."

"My name is Jessica Noble."

"Okay. Well, your name is not familiar to me, either. Ms. Noble, I don't mean to be rude. But you've said twice now that we don't have a lot of time. If you don't mind me saying this, that sounds a bit nuts. And honestly, I don't know if you're for real or just playing around on the phone. Regardless, this isn't a good day or a good time."

"Gabrielle, I apologize. I'm tired from not having gotten much sleep. You're right. I haven't made much sense during this call. I suppose I would be a bit angry if I were in your shoes, as well. Let me begin again. We have *indeed* met. Once before."

"We have? Well, your name doesn't ring a bell to me *at all*. Where exactly did we meet?"

"In a hospital room. A little more than eight years ago."

"Were you a nurse?" Gabrielle asked as she noticed that her breathing was now suddenly becoming somewhat shallow. "You'll have to forgive me if I don't recall you."

"You wouldn't have known my name. You see, I was the one who took the baby out of your arms the last time you held her."

Gabrielle held her breath, then slowly released it.

"I'm the woman who adopted your baby girl. And she desperately needs you right now. *We* need you right now. Gabrielle, that little girl is my heart. I promise you, she is. And she's all I have left now. Please, you have to help us. You have to."

Chapter 43

It shall be health to thy navel, and marrow to thy bones.

—Proverbs 3:8

"Gabrielle?" Jessica said. "Are you still there?"

"Yes. I'm sorry, but you're not supposed to contact me. That was the agreement. I wasn't supposed to know who you are so I couldn't come back later and try to see or take back my baby if I changed my mind. And you weren't supposed to contact *me*."

"But you signed for your daughter to be able to find out about you," Jessica said.

"After she turned, eighteen, yes. But she's not eighteen yet," Gabrielle said.

"No, she's eight. And she's a beautiful, fun-loving little girl who is in desperate need of a bone marrow transplant so that she'll have a chance to even *see* eighteen."

Gabrielle sat down before her wobbly legs abandoned her completely. "Are you sure?"

"Gabrielle, the only thing that could have made me

call you is if there was no other hope, no other way, if all was lost. I'm sure."

"About a month ago, a woman from the Red Cross called me about donating . . ."

"That was at my request. I was hoping you would consent without having to know who it was for. But you wouldn't talk to her about it or agree to it—"

"Why didn't you tell her to let me know what was going on?"

"Because legally, she couldn't do that. She could call and ask you about possibly being a donor, but she couldn't go any further than that. Now things are declining drastically. My daughter is going to die if she doesn't get a match. My husband and I had all the money anyone could ever want or need. And we have loved that little girl since you released her to our hearts. She has been the love and joy of our lives. My husband died in a car accident five months ago. Now I'm facing the possibility of losing her if we don't find a bone marrow match. You're her mother. It's a great possibility your marrow will be a match for her. If she has any siblings, her sibling could also be a match."

"I don't have any children," Gabrielle whispered.

"Maybe her father does if neither of you are a match for her. The doctors say siblings are likely to match even better most times than a parent. My baby has a rare disorder that generally strikes children. I realize this is a lot to ask of you and definitely not what you signed up for when you gave her up for adoption. Ms. Mercedes, you gave her life once. Please help to give her life again if you possibly can. Please."

Gabrielle started to cry. "Yes. Yes. Tell me what to do. Tell me what I need to do."

Jessica started to cry also. "Thank you. Thank you so very much. I have prayed about what to do. I know this is not the norm. But when it's your child, you'll do whatever you have to do to keep her healthy, happy, and safe."

"I don't know whether I'll be a match, but I will certainly do all that I can to help save . . . your daughter's life. Whatever I can."

Jessica told Gabrielle she would call back with the instructions of where she would go to be tested to see whether she was a match. Gabrielle prayed that she would be. And if she wasn't? Well, the alternatives, either of the alternatives left—the child's father, who would be a titanic problem because of who he was now, or one of his children—would not be a good scenario to deal with. Not good at all.

"Lord, please, please, Lord. Let me be a match. Help me to be able to help this child one more time. Please. Please."

No sooner had she hung up than her doorbell rang. She wiped her tears away, put on a happy face, and went to answer it. *Zachary must have finished up earlier than he expected,* she thought. *Thank You, Lord. Because I really need him right now. I really do.*

Chapter 44

The soul of the sluggard desireth, and hath nothing: but the soul of the diligent shall be made fat.

—Proverbs 13:4

Gabrielle opened the door. "Hello," Aunt Cee-Cee said.

"Hey girl," Gabrielle's oldest cousin, Laura, said as she stepped inside. "You've gained weight." Forty pounds overweight, Laura struggled past a size 8 Gabrielle.

"Get in the house and quit dillydallying around," Gabrielle's third oldest cousin, Angie, said to her two children. Angie looked around once she stepped inside the foyer. "Girl, this house is the bomb. How come you haven't invited us here before?" She handed her ten-month-old baby daughter to her mother. "Mama, here. Take Jenice while I check this place out," Angie said. "Y'all know I need my own room because I have these three children, so don't nobody start tripping."

"Hold up," Gabrielle said to no one in particular. "Excuse me, but am I missing something here?"

"Our luggage and things," Angie said. "I need my

stuff. Luke and Jesse are getting them. They are slow as Christmas. But Daddy said we not gonna kill him trying to haul all our junk by himself."

"Nobody move!" Gabrielle yelled out when it was apparent no one was paying her any attention. Gabrielle turned to her aunt. "Aunt Cee-Cee, what is this?"

"It's exactly what it looks like. It's us moving in with you," Aunt Cee-Cee said, placing a hand on her hip.

Gabrielle started shaking her head. "Uh-unh. No. That is not going to happen. You all need to turn right around and head right back to your own house."

"We don't have a house to head back *to*," Jesse said as he strolled past her with two large suitcases in tow.

Gabrielle looked at her aunt. "What is he talking about?"

"Can we please go in the den and talk about this?" Aunt Cee-Cee said.

"No. Nobody's going anywhere until I find out what's going on."

"They foreclosed on our house, we were evicted, and we don't have anywhere else to go," Luke said, bringing in three suitcases. "Where should I put these suitcases? They're Angie's bunch."

"Just sit it where you are," Aunt Cee-Cee said. "Until we straighten out who will be where."

"You're not staying here," Gabrielle said. "I don't know how to say that any clearer. You can go to a hotel, a motel, the Y, or a shelter. But you can't stay here. You can't."

"We can't afford a hotel. There are too many of us for the Y or the shelter. And it doesn't make sense, since we have family that has a place big enough to accommodate all of us where we can stay," Aunt Cee-Cee said.

"We let you stay with us when you needed somewhere," her uncle said when he came in.

Gabrielle looked at him, then had to look upward. "I know you didn't just say what I think I heard you say. I know you didn't." She began to stare at him. "You're not staying at my house. And you know full well why. He's not staying here," she said to Aunt Cee-Cee. "I'm telling you, this man is not staying in my house." She turned back to her uncle. "Don't force me to call you out in front of your family."

"Honey, let me handle this," Aunt Cee-Cee said to her husband. "Go get the rest of our stuff out of the vehicles."

"No, don't go get anything else out of anything. And you need to take what's in here already and haul it *right* back to your cars, trucks, SUVs, whatever," Gabrielle said.

"Mama said you were a Christian," Angie said. "What kind of a Christian are you supposed to be?"

Gabrielle clenched her teeth. "Tonight we can *definitely* call me a WIP—work in progress."

"Well, don't it say somewhere in the Bible that when we didn't have a place to stay, you opened up your home and gave us a place?" Angie said.

"What do you know about a Bible?" Luke said, laughing. "You're just parroting what Mama said when we were getting ready to come over here. I told y'all I didn't want to come here anyhow."

"Well, where are you going to go?" Laura said. "You don't have a job. You don't have a girlfriend that will let you come and stay with her. Where you gonna go? Huh?"

"I have friends," Luke said.

"You're not staying with any of your hoodlum friends," Aunt Cee-Cee said.

"None of them will let him stay with them anyway, and he knows it," Angie said. "He just wants to feel like somebody likes him." She popped her chewing gum three times successively. "What you got to eat in this house? We're hungry. Mama told us we could eat when we got over here."

"Gabrielle, please, just let us in first," Aunt Cee-Cee said. "Then we can sit down and discuss this. We don't have anywhere else to go. You know I'm telling the truth. You can't just let us sleep out on the streets or out in our cars. We have a baby and small children here. Come on, now. Let's see if we can't work something out, at least for tonight."

"Okay," Gabrielle said. "But don't bring all of your stuff in, just what you need to stay one night."

"Sure, sure," Aunt Cee-Cee said.

"Can you show me to my room?" Angie said to Gabrielle.

"Y'all are so trifling," Laura said to no one in particular. "That's why you won't have to worry about me, Gabrielle. I just need to get the okay from my two friends saying I can rent out their extra room, and I will be *out* of here."

The doorbell rang again.

"It's open!" Gabrielle yelled with frustration.

"Hey. How are you?" Zachary said as he walked in and found Gabrielle in the midst of the crowd of people. "Are you having a party or something?"

Gabrielle threw him a look that more than expressed just how much she wasn't in the mood to play. "Not tonight, Zachary. Not tonight," she said.

Chapter 45

*Produce your cause, saith the Lord; bring forth
your strong reasons, saith the King of Jacob.*

—Isaiah 41:21

Gabrielle grabbed Zachary by his arm and escorted
him to the kitchen. "Do you believe this? I don't
believe this. This can't be happening."

"What is it?"

"They were evicted. Their house was foreclosed on,
and they were put out on the street. And you know
where they decided to come? Here with me. But they
can't stay here. They just can't. I have too much going
on to have to deal with this right now." Gabrielle broke
down.

Zachary pulled her into his arms and held her. "What
else is going on?"

"Just before they all came crashing into my home, I
got a call from the woman who adopted my daughter."

"She called you? But how? I thought that was something sealed and couldn't happen unless it was an open
adoption."

Gabrielle stepped back. "The woman is well-off. She has more than enough money and the means to do whatever she wants. Her little girl is in need of a bone marrow transplant. And according to her, it looks bad. She didn't want to call me; she *had* to. My . . . her little girl is dying, and she *will* die, if they don't find her a match."

"Wow. You are having a rough time. I'm so sorry, Gabrielle. Did she tell you what it is, what the child has that's requiring her to need a bone marrow transplant?"

"No. And I didn't ask, because frankly it doesn't really matter *why* she needs it; she needs it. That's the only thing that matters: she needs it."

"You're right. So what do *you* need? What can I do to help you right now?"

Gabrielle's body slumped. "How about getting these people out of my house?"

"You want me to? Because I can go in there right now and tell all of them to leave, if you want," Zachary said.

She smiled. "It's really not your problem. I'll handle it. But thanks anyway."

"Well, as much as I hate to say this, at least you're talking to me again. I was beginning to worry you were trying to get rid of me."

Gabrielle didn't respond.

"All righty then. Well, we still have tickets to see *The Color Purple* tomorrow. What time do you want me to pick you up?"

"Oh, Zachary."

"We're still going, right?"

She looked at him. "Did you not see all of these folks in my house when you came in?"

"I saw them. Either they'll be here tomorrow or they won't. Either way, that shouldn't keep you from going to see a show you've been excited about seeing for the past month."

She shuffled her feet a few times. "You know how much I want to see it."

"Then I'll pick you up around five?"

"Ah," she said, bending her head back, looking up at the ceiling, then bringing her head back straight. "Yes. But make it five-thirty. I'm not going to allow them to steal this from me."

"And I don't mean to tell you how to handle your family, but I will tell you this. If you let them stay without a clear exit strategy agreed upon from the beginning, you're going to find yourself with a real problem," Zachary said.

"But they're family."

"And you're not responsible for their well-being."

"But aren't I my brothers, sisters, aunt, uncle, and cousins' keepers?" she teased.

"I don't think that's what that scripture is talking about. And before you say anything, I realize my sister has been at my house for a while, but I believe the two situations don't even compare. My sister wanted her own place. I talked her into staying with me. Plus, she's been a lot of help."

"I know," Gabrielle said with a whine. "And those people out there—"

"Excuse me," Angie said, "but are you planning on cooking or ordering something to eat? We're really hungry. And Mama said for you to bring her something to drink." Angie left the kitchen.

"Ground rules and an exit date," Gabrielle said. "Because they are not about to make me lose my religion."

Zachary laughed as he grabbed her and hugged her. He placed her face gently between both his hands, pulled her head slowly toward him, then kissed her on her forehead. "If you need to, now, you know you can always escape to my house."

"You'd better be careful with your invitations. I just might take you up on it."

"But I was serious. If you need to get away, or if you need some peace and quiet, my house is your house." He kissed her forehead again. "Oh, this is hard!" he said, realizing just how much he loved her, and how much he wanted to take her into his arms and literally whisk her away from all of this. "This is *really* hard."

She looked at him. "Yeah," she said, as though she knew exactly what he was talking about. "It is, isn't it?" She bit down on her bottom lip.

Chapter 46

And Ruth said, Entreat me not to leave thee, or to return from following after thee: for whither thou goest, I will go; and where thou lodgest, I will lodge: thy people shall be my people, and thy God my God.

—Ruth 1:16

Angela decided to go and visit Ransom Perdue at the nursing home and get this behind her once and for all. It had been two weeks since she'd first seen him, and she needed to quit letting her imagination get the best of her.

"Mister Perdue," she said after he came into the lobby area. The nurses had called him to let him know there was a visitor to see him. She had used her great-grandmother's name to help sway him not to turn her away as someone he didn't know.

"Yes, ma'am, little lady."

"It's good to see you again. I don't know if you remember me, but we met briefly when you visited Johnnie Mae Landris's house about two weeks ago. I was leaving when you and your grandson were coming in." She extended her hand to shake his.

He shook her hand. "Yes, I remember that face. What can I do for you?"

She sat back down. He sat down in the chair next to her. "As I told the nurse who called you, I'm Pearl Black's great-granddaughter. I know that you and she were close friends."

"That we were. Closer than most who were kin. Your great-grandmother was one of a kind. She was one who would stick by you no matter what. And it didn't matter if you were blood or not. She was like Ruth with Naomi. You don't run into folks like Pearl much anymore. She was a gentle woman who could get in your face if she needed to and get you told off without you even realizing you'd been told off until a little while later. I told her once that she could cut you and cure you with the same swipe of a blade. That's the Pearl I knew. She was a beautiful woman, just like you. I hope me saying that ain't out of order or doesn't offend you."

Angela smiled. "No, Mister Perdue, it isn't and it doesn't."

"'Cause I know folks can be accused of sexual harassment nowadays, just for what they think was a compliment. I don't mean no harm. Although, I will admit that a lot of stuff folks do nowadays and even back in my day goes a little too far. When I was coming up, it was all right to tell a pretty lady she was pretty. Now, you have to be careful. And please call me Gramps. Everybody else does. This Mister Perdue stuff messes with me. Unless, of course, I don't know you; then Mister Perdue is right appropriate."

"Okay . . . Gramps." She smiled. "My great-grandmother was the one who raised me," Angela said, "since

I was a little girl. My mother died when I was five, and Great-granny stepped right in and took care of me just like I was her own child."

"I'm sorry to hear that about your mother. And I know most times, it's the grandmothers that do the stepping in." He said it as though he was posing a question.

"My grandmother wasn't around. It's sort of a long story."

"I know about long stories. I just learned a couple of weeks ago that what I believed to be true about my own mother wasn't at all the truth. It's something how folks can take a truth and turn it into a lie."

"I remember my great-granny talking about you. She told how her mother was the midwife that delivered you. She said you had 'gifted' hands, that you could take a piece of wood and other material and make the most beautiful things out of them. I told her you were an alchemist. She liked when I used big words that she understood easily. I saw one of the boxes you made."

"The Wings of Grace box," Gramps said. "Those boxes I made all them years ago have almost made me into some kind of a legend. Is there anybody who doesn't know about them?" he joked.

"They have become somewhat famous in their own right. Great-granny had the one apparently Sarah Fleming had given to her for safekeeping. That was how we met Johnnie Mae Landris. Great-granny was so excited. She'd never met an author before. She was so impressed that a 'real live' author had come to visit her at her house."

"Mrs. Landris is an author?"

"Yes, sir. Except her books still carry the name she used when she first started out being published. I think she does that in order not to lose readers who may think the new books are by a different author other than herself. Her books are published under the name Johnnie Mae Taylor."

"Well, I'm not *real* big on readin'. But I bought one book and have kept it with me down through the years. A book I got autographed by an Ernest J. Gaines fellow."

"I bet I know which one it is. *The Autobiography of Miss Jane Pittman*."

"Yep," he said with a smile. "I came across that book and it rang so true for me. My copy is a little tattered, but I still have it. It's in a trunk here with me now."

"You were telling me about your mother and how you learned something wasn't true that you believed to be true," Angela said as she was trying to figure out how to bring up the topic of family with him. "I would love to hear about that. I mean, I heard Great-granny tell the story a few times about how you came to have the name Ransom."

"Yeah, I heard that tale when I was younger. How my mother was giving birth to me. How the midwife, Pearl's mother, had put scissors under my mother's mattress to ease the pain. How she'd motioned for them to bring her the Bible, her turning the pages and pointing to a word in the Bible, thinking that any word in the Bible had to be a good word. How she died with her finger on the word *ransom* in Matthew 20:28. Told them that was my name. It was a good story, used to make me proud to carry around the name of Ransom. But I just learned that *that* story couldn't possibly be true."

"Why not?"

"My mother that supposed to have died during childbirth didn't die. My mother was actually a colored woman named Adele Powell who had passed for white. When she learned she was pregnant, she knew it was her husband's, but she was afraid if she gave birth to me in the white community and I came out even with a tinge of blackness, her husband would think she'd done something with a colored man. So she sought out the black community when she went into labor. She lied about why she was there. The midwife delivered me—"

"In truth, she was my great-great-grandmother," Angela said when she actually thought about it.

He nodded, agreeing now that he'd thought about it in those terms. "Yeah. Anyway, she did what most colored folks did in cases like that. I guess to keep the lie from totally exploding in anyone's face, she made me up a birth past and found me a home. As a child, who's going to question that? Especially back in those days. Some of the grown folks usually know the whole truth, but there was a time when children weren't told grown folks' business. We could be seen but not heard. And if no one ever told the real story, generations of folks grew up with lies or cover-ups presented as their truths."

"Yeah." Angela opened up her purse and slowly pulled out the photo of the man standing by a young version of her great-granny. "I found this in a box that Great-granny specifically left before she died." She handed the photo to Gramps. "It must have been important or meant something special to her."

He took it and adjusted his glasses better. He smiled. "That's my old Pearl. She could be a little sassy when she wanted to be. I loved that woman, I truly did. God didn't make many like Pearl, although I've found one woman in here with a little sass at times."

"I agree," Angela said. "Do you recognize that man standing beside her? Would that happen to be you?"

He frowned. "I've never seen *this* specific photo before," he said. "You know Samuel L. Williams and I were the best of friends. Samuel always had my back. Good old Samuel."

"Great-granny married Samuel Williams."

"She did? Well, I'll be. Pearl married Samuel? I never suspected *that* would happen."

"Yeah. Samuel was my great-grandfather. They had four children."

"Well, I'll be. We all used to hang out together. The three musketeers: Samuel, Pearl, and me. We loved going to this place called Candy Land, hanging out at the Young Men's Institute, especially the library. It was one of those books at the library that gave me the idea of making those wooden carved boxes folks call Wings of Grace. I saw something like it in a book."

Angela pressed her lips together tightly. She had been mistaken. That was her great-grandfather in the photo. The man Arletha resembled was actually Samuel L. Williams. Well, at least she hadn't mentioned her suspicions to anyone else besides Brent. She at least hadn't tarnished her great-grandmother's name or memory by blabbing her thoughts to the people who knew her great-granny, like her grandmother or Johnnie Mae.

She was thankful that God had kept her from flying off the handle with what she had just now learned was an incorrect conclusion.

Chapter 47

*Lest Satan should get an advantage of us: for we
are not ignorant of his devices.*

—2 Corinthians 2:11

Pastor Landris didn't look at the check or the envelope of money when he got home Sunday night. He'd placed both along with his check from his own church in his top drawer of his nightstand and spent the rest of the night doing things with his family, Mondays were his day off. He got up and ate a nice breakfast with Johnnie Mae and the children before they went to school. Johnnie Mae also took Mondays off, most days not even writing her book, unless of course she was under a heavy deadline and it couldn't be avoided. Pastor Landris enjoyed his alone time with his wife.

That was why their marriage worked so well. They spent time together and didn't allow life to suck everything away from them being able to sow into each other's lives. They had date nights and days, when he would ask her out, then treat her the way he did when he was trying to woo her before they were married. It wasn't a matter of keeping her by doing what he'd done to get her. It was taking it to another level, and doing things with purpose, on purpose. That's what he told those in his congregation who were married. He believed if you preach it, then you should be practicing what you preach.

So, while Johnnie Mae was getting dressed for the day, he was getting his bank deposit slip ready, ensuring that he made copies of all checks, regardless of whether he would receive a W-2 or 1099 statement from a group at the end of the year or not. He kept meticulous records of every dollar he was given, no matter how large or small. It drove Stanley, his personal accountant, crazy.

"We don't need to record every single dollar someone gives you," Stanley said in the beginning when he would get Pastor Landris's weekly tally. Still, he kept on doing it.

Pastor Landris opened the envelope with his salaried check from the church and wrote that amount on the deposit slip. He then opened the check he'd received from preaching at Divine Conquerors Church. His eyebrows rose when he saw the amount. One thousand dollars was more than he was expecting for speaking there.

In fact, he hadn't spoken there for the money at all. He was genuinely trying to meet Reverend Walker halfway so they could move to a better relationship. It didn't bode well when preachers acted like the world, seemingly envious or jealous, unforgiving, and malicious in some of their actions. They were supposed to be an example to their family, to their flock, and to anyone in the world who just might be watching.

Pastor Landris recorded that amount, then opened the envelope full of cash. The first bill was a hundred-dollar bill. The next bill was a hundred, and the next one . . . the exact same thing. With each shedding, there was a hundred-dollar bill beneath it. It was like peeling an onion—each layer, though different, was pretty much the same. When he saw that from start to finish there were nothing but hundreds, he started over, this time actually counting them as though they were ones. When he finished, there were two hundred hundred-dollar bills stuffed inside that one envelope: $20,000.

"What's wrong?" Johnnie Mae asked when she walked into the bedroom fully dressed in a gorgeous black and gold velveteen jogging suit and caught him pacing.

"This," he said, waving the envelope with the money inside.

"What is it?"

He pulled the money out and handed it to her. She looked and saw one-hundred-dollar bills throughout. "How much is this?" she asked, her hand over her heart to calm it.

"Twenty thousand dollars."

"Are you sure?" she said, looking at it again. "Of course you're sure." She handed it back to him. "Where did that come from?"

He put the money back inside the envelope and threw the envelope onto the bed. "Yesterday, after I finished preaching, Reverend Walker gave it to me."

"Why? Why would he give you that much money? Although I do personally know that some preachers, the mega preachers especially, are making even more than that to speak. But not cash. They're not being paid in cash. At least, I don't believe so."

"This is a setup, Johnnie Mae. I feel it in my spirit just as sure as I'm standing here. If you're going to pay me that much money to speak, you wouldn't pay it in untraceable cash. The church wrote me a check for a thousand dollars."

"Maybe Reverend Walker didn't think it was enough," Johnnie Mae said. "You know, he recognizes you're larger than even *you* realize. Maybe when he saw that it was only a thousand dollars, he-he—" she stammered. "You're right. It doesn't make sense."

"Well, at least you were trying to give him the benefit of the doubt." Pastor Landris shook his head. "He's up to something, and it's not good. Well, I'm taking this money and giving it *right* back to him. If it's a legitimate gift from someone, as he claimed it was, then he's going to have to tell me who gave it to him. And I'm going to make certain that person knows I'm reporting every single dollar of this."

"Okay, Landris. You do what you feel you need to do," Johnnie Mae said.

"You're not going to be mad at me, are you? For standing you up on our day out."

"No," she said with a pleasant tone. She rubbed his arm with her hand. "You take care of your business. I'm with you all the way. We don't need something like this hanging over our heads. If it is on the up-and-up, at least you need to have peace about it. If somebody really is trying to set you up, then slap a little Isaiah 54:17 on them. 'No weapon that is formed against thee shall prosper.' The devil is a lie! He's already defeated, in the name of Jesus."

Pastor Landris leaned down, caressed her face, then kissed his wife. "I love you so much," he said. He kissed her again, then went and retrieved the envelope of money off the bed, smiled at her once more, winked, and left.

Chapter 48

Be not forgetful to entertain strangers: for there-
by some have entertained angels, unawares.

—Hebrews 13:2

Pastor Landris drove to the church only to learn that Reverend Walker also took off on Mondays. The secretary called Reverend Walker when Pastor Landris refused to make an appointment to see him upon his return to work. Pastor Landris insisted she get in contact with Reverend Walker somehow so he could speak with him today. He'd already called the numbers he had and left messages. He knew she would have a special way to get him.

"Reverend Walker says he will be happy to see you tomorrow at ten. So, if you'll come back then, he'll be glad to talk to you," the secretary said.

"I need you to call him back on whatever number you just reached him on and tell him that it's imperative that I speak with him now," Pastor Landris said.

"I'm sorry, Pastor Landris, but I can't do that."

Pastor Landris frowned. "You can't or you won't?"

"I can't." She instantly looked like she was about to cry. Her reaction didn't go unnoticed by him. "Reverend Walker told me not to call him back unless the church was on fire." She tried to make light of her statement by masking it with a smile.

Pastor Landris calmed down. After all, it wasn't her fault Reverend Walker was having her do this. It wasn't fair to her for him to take out his frustration on her.

Pastor Landris smiled to put her at ease. "Please tell Reverend Walker that I'll see him first thing in the morning," Pastor Landris said. "And you have a blessed day now."

"You too, Pastor. And Pastor Landris, I really enjoyed your sermon yesterday. My husband did, too. He said we might come and visit your church one of these days."

Pastor Landris put on a smile. It was hitting home why as Christians it was important to be angry and sin not. "You are certainly welcome to come and visit anytime you desire. We would be happy to have you," he said.

"Pastor Landris?" she said.

"Yes."

"Reverend Walker usually comes in around nine AM. I just thought you might like to know."

"Thank you, Sister . . . ?"

"Greer. It's Katrina Greer."

"Well, I thank you, Sister Greer. I hope I didn't *completely* ruin your day. But if I did, please accept my humblest apology." Pastor Landris placed his hand over his heart and bowed his head to her slightly.

"Oh, no," she said, smiling and shaking her head. "In fact, I'm honored I got to talk with you today. You're a powerful minister, Pastor Landris. Please continue to preach God's Word the way that you do. Don't let the devil stop you or try to take you down. You just keep on preaching the God-Heaven truth. God's got your back."

Pastor Landris nodded as he smiled at her once more. *She definitely has a way with words,* he thought. "I'll do that, Sister Greer," he said. "I'll continue preaching the *God-Heaven* truth." He then left.

Chapter 49

*She will do him good and not evil all the
days of her life.*

—Proverbs 31:12

Gabrielle and Zachary went to see *The Color Purple*
on Friday. The Broadway hit show was just as
wonderful as Gabrielle imagined it would be. She and
Zachary laughed and played around when they went to
eat afterward. Zachary truly made her happy. And the
way he lovingly looked at her when he thought she
wasn't looking told her that she did the same for him.

"Now, are you ready to tell me what spooked you?'
Zachary said. They sat in a booth in the restaurant, opting to share a deep dark chocolate brownie topped with
a large scoop of vanilla ice cream and lava-looking
chocolate sauce oozing down its sides instead of each
tackling an individual one.

"I don't know what you're talking about." Gabrielle
leaned in as she took her long-handled spoon and
scooped a bite, carefully placing it in her mouth.

"You know what I'm talking about," Zachary said as

he allowed the ice cream and chocolate mixture to melt in his mouth while refusing to take his eyes off Gabrielle.

"Zachary, I hate guessing games. I always have. That's why I don't care to play Jeopardy."

"What? You mean you don't like Jeopardy? Woman, is something wrong with you? Who doesn't like figuring out what the question is based on the answer?" he teased.

She shook her head and laughed. "You're right. What is wrong with me?" She took another bite.

"Well, at least I got you to laugh. Okay, so you don't feel like guessing what I'm talking about. Then allow me to get straight to it. Before we went to my parents' home, you and I were fine . . . great. I could feel the love growing between us."

She pulled her now-empty spoon from out of her mouth. "Is that right?"

"That's right. Even after we got there, you and I were doing great. You went to see Aunt Esther, and by the way my father says she's progressing fantastically since we came. So much so that her doctor is starting to believe prayer really *can* change things. That's what Aunt Esther told him when he asked her what happened: love and prayer."

Gabrielle tilted her head softly and looked into his eyes. "I'm so thankful that you brought me and Miss Crowe back together. I didn't really know just how *much* I needed to see her. It was like having a story told and being left to hang, unable to read the next chapter. I knew she'd been in an accident, but I didn't know if she was alive or dead. When I finally learned that she was alive, I still wanted to look in her face myself. Then her asking me to dance for her like that. My goodness!" Gabrielle quickly started fanning back her tears. She held her head back, then straight. "Thank you *so much* for doing that."

"Okay, so we agree that you going to Chicago with me was a good thing. You visiting with my aunt was also a good thing. So tell me: where did things break down?"

Gabrielle thought about the conversation she had with his mother. "I didn't realize things had broken down," she flubbed. "You and I have our lives to lead. You with your practice and emergency hospital calls, and me being named the director of the Dance Ministry and leading it the way Johnnie Mae believes I can do. You also know that I'm still doing housekeeping work at that house. There's just a lot going on these days."

"Why don't you quit working at that house?"

She pulled back. "Why? Because you think my cleaning someone else's house is beneath me?"

"No." He shook his head as he released an exasperated sigh. "Because that's a lot to be doing when you're trying to organize a ministry and do all the *other* things you do. You attend Dance Ministry meetings on Tuesday nights, Bible study on Wednesday nights, church on Sunday mornings, and church staff meetings now when they have them on a Sunday night. And that's when you aren't attending a baby christening and/or a baptism on Sunday nights. Now you're in charge of the Dance Ministry, which requires you to do administrative work as well as deciding and approving what routines will be performed. That's a lot to do in addition to going and cleaning someone else's house Monday through Friday, for what . . . eight hours a day, not counting commute time."

"Well, what about you? You have your own practice, plus you're on call if something happens that requires you to come in, like yesterday. You go to Wednesday night Bible study and Sunday morning worship service, and sometimes you've been at the hospital all day, or in many cases through the night and early into the morning."

"Okay, I see what you're trying to do. You're trying to divert the conversation away from my original question."

"I wasn't trying to do that. You were the one who said I should quit my housekeeping job as though there was some dishonor or disgrace in that kind of work."

"That was not what I was implying. But for some reason that's striking a nerve with you, which means maybe that's where some of the truth lies," Zachary said. He took her left hand. "Okay, let's try it this way. Did you tell my mother things about your life?"

"Zachary, let's just drop this, okay?"

"Yes or no. Did she get you to tell her things about your life like maybe when she corralled you into the kitchen or when she got you alone at some point? It's a yes or no question."

"Yes," Gabrielle said.

"Did my mother say something to you about your cleaning other people's houses? Yes or no."

"Yes, but—"

"You can keep the commentaries. All I want is a yes or no answer." He licked his lip, then bit down on it. "Did you tell her about what you used to do prior to being a maid . . . a housekeeper?"

"Zachary, we really need to go. You know I have folks in my house. And the way they treat people's things, it will be a miracle if I still have a house standing when I get back. You know if they don't respect their own things, they sure don't think anything about anyone else's."

"Did you tell my mother what you did before this year? Yes or no."

"Yes." She pushed the bowl with the remaining dessert toward him, pulled her hand out of his, and picked up her purse. "Can we please go now?"

He grabbed her hand again. "Gabrielle, did my mother tell you or imply that you weren't good enough for me?"

"Zachary, please, can we just go?"

"After you answer my question."

She pulled back from him. "You can't keep me here against my will."

"Gabrielle, I'm not trying to keep you anywhere against your will. All I'm trying to do is find out what happened with us after we went to Chicago, you seeing my aunt, and the sudden change in temperature between us that, ironically, seemed to have occurred the afternoon I came back and found you and my mother huddled up in an intense conversation in the living room. . . ." He fell back, then slowly rubbed his hands together.

"That's it, isn't it?" Zachary said, leaning forward. "When I came in, she was telling you that you needed to break things off with me. That's what she was telling you when I walked in that day. And you actually listened to her." He sounded disappointed.

Gabrielle moved back toward him. "Zachary, it wasn't like that. Your mother loves you. Dearly. She only wants the best for you. You know that."

"So, you agree with her." He frowned as he looked intensely, but lovingly, at her.

"What do you mean, I agree with her?"

"You agree that you're not the best for me. You agree that I don't know what I'm doing by being with you. You're questioning my judgment and my ability to know what's right for me and what's not. You think I'm irresponsible in my decision making."

"See, now you're just trying to twist things around. You're a great doctor, and you know that. All I said was that your mother wants you to have the best in life, and the best *possible* life. *I* want you to have the best possible life as well. In that respect, then yes . . . your mother and I absolutely *do* agree."

Zachary scooted toward the end and stood up. "Sure. I understand. So . . . you're ready to go home? I'll take you home then. I wouldn't want to keep you somewhere you don't want to be." He held out his hand to assist her in getting up. "Never let it be said that I had to kidnap a woman in order for her to be with me."

"Zachary—"

"Was everything to your satisfaction?" the fiery, red-haired waitress said.

"Everything was wonderful," Zachary said, having already placed the money inside the black padded folder, with a more-than-generous tip. "And now, I must escort this lovely woman home."

Chapter 50

For which I am an ambassador in bonds: that therein I may speak boldly, as I ought to speak.

—Ephesians 6:20

"When you decide what you want to do," Zachary said, standing outside Gabrielle's front door, "let me know. I don't ever want you to feel like I forced you or guilted you into doing anything you didn't want to do."

They hadn't said much on the ride home from the restaurant. Zachary was giving Gabrielle the space she wanted. Gabrielle wasn't sure of the right thing to do. She'd already fallen in love with Zachary. But did love give her the right to be selfish and possibly mess things up in his life because of some of her earlier decisions?

Talking with Zachary's mother, the housekeeper put-down wasn't what had gotten to her. She was proud of what she was able to do, even if some people had the nerve to want to look down on it. She thought about the scripture in Colossians that said whatever you do, to do it heartily, as to the Lord, and not unto men. No one could ever, in good conscience, throw her performing that type of work in her face. But her earlier days, those dancing years, someone *could* use against Zachary were they inclined. She didn't want to put him in a position of having to deal with or defend that segment of her life.

She turned to go inside the house without commenting. He touched her arm. She turned back around, and he kissed her softly on her cheek. "Bye," he said.

"Bye," she said back, feeling as though she'd just lost her best friend.

As soon as she stepped into her house, she couldn't believe her eyes. The vase with silk flowers was missing. There were clothes on the stairway banister and on the floor in the foyer. She saw what looked like a perfectly made strawberry handprint on one of her walls. She walked over to get a better look. She was mistaken. It was actually strawberry preserves.

She briskly went in search of somebody . . . anybody. When she looked in the kitchen, there were empty bottles and cans everywhere. Four pots sat on the stove. She looked in them. They were practically empty with evidence of various foods like spaghetti noodles, spaghetti sauce, Alfredo sauce, and chili. Every plate she owned seemed to be either on the counter or on the kitchen table. The stainless-steel garbage can was overflowing with trash, and scraped-out food had hardened on the floor around it.

Hearing the television blasting, Gabrielle turned and marched to the den. She was clearly on a mission now. There she found Aunt Cee-Cee lying on one end of the couch with her feet propped up on a couch pillow, and her cousin Laura on the other end, half-asleep, both of them facing the television. Two of Angie's children were with them, throwing popcorn at each other and eating the fallen kernels from off the floor. She didn't know where Angie's baby was.

"Aunt Cee-Cee!" Gabrielle said. "Aunt Cee-Cee!" Her aunt jumped as she awakened and turned in her direction. "Will you *please* turn that thing down?!"

Aunt Cee-Cee pointed the remote control at the television and turned it down. "You're home," she said as she struggled to sit up. "How was your evening?"

"My evening was fine. At least it *was* fine until I stepped back into my house. What is wrong with all of y'all?"

"What do you mean?" Laura said, stretching.

"Have you seen the kitchen and my foyer? I haven't gone any farther than those two areas. There's a strawberry handprint on my wall. The kitchen looks like a tornado swept through it. Is anybody familiar with the concept of cleaning up behind yourself or watching your children so they don't feel it's perfectly fine to throw popcorn everywhere?" Gabrielle directed the last part about the popcorn at the two children.

The children started crying.

"See, Gabrielle, you scared them," Laura said. "Come here, you two." Laura held out her arms. "Angie!" Laura yelled. "Angie!"

"What!" came a voice from near the stairs.

"Come and see about your children!"

Angie stepped into the room a minute later with the telephone stuck to her ear. "I'm on the phone," Angie said as she walked over to her children and practically snatched them up off the floor.

"Don't be so rough with them," Aunt Cee-Cee said.

"Look at this mess they're making," Angie said to her mother.

"Well, then you need to clean it up," Aunt Cee-Cee said.

"I'm busy." Angie turned to Gabrielle. "Would you mind getting this up for me?"

Gabrielle gave Angie a look that clearly questioned her sanity. "I don't *think* so," she said.

"I'm trying to find a job," Angie said in answer to Gabrielle's look. "Hold on a second," she said to the person on the line. She pressed the mute button. "Gabrielle, somebody called you a little after you left. She said to let you know she called, and that it was important."

"Who was it?"

Angie shrugged as she walked the children over to her mother. "I don't remember her name."

"You didn't write it down?" Gabrielle asked, annoyed.

"I was busy on the phone," Angie said. "Besides, I couldn't find a pen and paper. She also left a phone number."

"Why did you even answer my phone? I didn't tell anyone to answer my phone. I have an answering machine. At least that woman, whoever it was, could have left a message, and I would have been able to retrieve it," Gabrielle said.

Angie put her hand on her hip. "I answered it because I was on it. The person beeped in, and I thought the least I could do was answer it for you. The next time, I just won't bother." She unmuted, put the phone back up to her ear, and resumed her conversation.

"Aunt Cee-Cee," Gabrielle said. "You and I need to talk."

"Sure. Fine," Aunt Cee-Cee said. "But we're out of milk, eggs, cereal—"

"And toilet paper," Laura said. "Why don't I just make a list of what you need to go buy."

"What happened to all of the toilet paper? I had a brand-new nine-roll pack in the linen closet."

"Do you have any idea how many people are living here now?" Laura said. "I used a roll all by myself. And I hope you know that they make the rolls smaller than they used to. These companies are doing anything they can to make money these days."

"Aunt Cee-Cee, we need to talk now," Gabrielle said through clenched teeth.

"I'll go write out the grocery list," Laura said as she stood up and left.

"Okay. What do you want to talk about?"

"I've tried to be understanding. I've tried to put myself in your shoes. I've tried to do what a good Christian ought to do. But as Christians, God has not called us to be tramped on the way you and your family are doing here with me. I'd like all of you to leave my house."

"And we plan on leaving. Just as soon as we get back on our feet," Aunt Cee-Cee said.

"No. I'd like for you to leave before the weekend is over."

Aunt Cee-Cee chuckled. "You mean by this *coming* Sunday?"

"Yes, I mean by Sunday."

Aunt Cee-Cee bent down her head and looked up. "This Sunday coming up? This Sunday?"

"This Sunday coming up," Gabrielle said.

"If we leave this Sunday, then how are we all going to go to church with you? You see, I figured out why things are going so much better for you than us. The only thing I can see you do differently from us is that you go to church on a regular basis. So, I told everybody here that we're going down to the same church

where you go, and we're going to get whatever it is
you've gotten from being there. I figure if we go this
Sunday, God will turn things around in our lives before
the next Sunday. We could likely be back on our feet in
a few weeks, and in a few weeks be out of here." Aunt
Cee-Cee scooped up a handful of popcorn out of the
bag and popped it in her mouth. "Do you think your
church might give us a donation or something to help
us get into a home?"

Gabrielle threw up her hands and stomped out of the
room. She couldn't take any more. She went up to her
room. Both Jesse and Luke were in there wallowing on
her bed as Jesse ate spaghetti and they both watched
television. "Please get out of my room," she said so
calmly it almost scared her.

"The show is not off yet," Luke said. "And all the
other TVs are taken."

"And I'm not finished with my food yet," Jesse said,
picking his teeth.

"I *said,* get out of my room."

"You are so selfish," Luke said after clicking off the
television with the remote control. He threw the remote back onto the bed as he walked past her and
glared.

Jesse picked up his plate off the bed and followed
his older brother. "We're out of drinks," he said to
Gabrielle as he walked past her. "Mama said we don't
have any money to buy anything, so we needed to tell
you whatever we were out of so you can get it."

Gabrielle didn't say a word. As soon as Jesse cleared
the doorway, she closed her bedroom door. She went
and got her Bible, turned to Ephesians chapter six, and
began reading at verse ten. When she sat down on the
bed, she saw spaghetti sauce all over her just-cleaned

bedspread. Tears started making their way down her face.

"Lord, I know you told me to be strong in You and in the power of Your might. I'm trying, Lord. I have put on the whole armor of God. I'm trying so hard to stand against the wiles of the devil. I know that we're not wrestling against flesh and blood. All that's going on right now in my life is merely the devil going to and fro seeing who he can devour. We're wrestling against principalities and the rulers of the darkness of this world, against spiritual wickedness in high places. Lord, it's getting hard. . . . You see how hard it's been for me just these past few days. But you have instructed us to stand.

"To stand with our loins girdled with truth, having on the breastplate of righteousness, our feet shod with the preparation of the gospel of peace. But above all, Lord, we have been told to take the shield of faith so that we're able to quench all of the fiery darts hurled at us from the wicked one. To take the helmet of salvation and the sword of the Spirit, which is the Word of God, and to use it. I'm praying, Lord . . . praying without ceasing. I know You see what I'm dealing with today. Please direct me in what is the right thing to do and what is Your divine will. In Jesus' precious name I pray. Amen."

Chapter 51

Or else how can one enter into a strong man's house, and spoil his goods, except he first bind the strong man? and then he will spoil his house.

—Matthew 12:29

After Gabrielle finished praying, her phone rang. Before she could pick it up, it stopped ringing. At first she thought whoever had called had changed their mind and hung up. Then she felt a pull to go check her phone anyway. When she looked, she saw the phone was registering that it was in use. She picked it up and pressed the talk button.

"I need you to get off the phone," Gabrielle said in a quiet, calm voice.

"But I'm on it," Angie said.

"I know that you're on it. And I need you to get off . . . my phone."

"You are *so* stingy with your stuff," Angie said to Gabrielle. "Listen, Trey," Angie said to the person on the other end, "I'll hit you back later. My cousin is tripping."

Gabrielle stayed on the line to ensure Angie had hung up. After she was sure, she clicked the phone off. The phone immediately started to ring. The caller ID didn't register a name or a phone number. Thinking it was most likely Trey calling right back, Gabrielle promptly answered it.

"Hello," Gabrielle said at the same time the person on the other end was also saying hello. "Hello," she said again. "Who are you calling to speak with?"

"You were the one who called here," a male voice replied.

"Clarence? Is that you?" Gabrielle asked.

"Gabrielle?" Clarence said.

"Yes."

"I just hung up from calling you," Clarence said. "Some woman answered and said you were busy and you weren't able to come to the phone. She didn't ask who I was or anything. She just clicked me off without even saying good-bye."

"Okay. I get what likely happened. It's happened before where I've answered an incoming call while I was already on the phone. If you don't hang up just right, it's like both numbers are still connected, and they ring back at both places simultaneously when you finally hang up from the other call. It doesn't happen every time, but it *does* happen."

"Who answered your phone a few minutes ago?" Clarence asked.

"One of my houseguests."

"Visiting?"

"Nope. Crashers, actually. They have nowhere else to go, so they decided to come and live with me," Gabrielle said. "I'm sorry, Lord. I'm sorry. That was wrong of me."

"No, you just told it like it is. But I thought you were

a lot smarter than that. You do know that after they take root, it's going to be almost impossible to uproot them from your place, don't you? Well, all I can say is: you're a better person than me."

"It wasn't like anyone *asked* me. It's my aunt and her family. And I'm talking about the *whole* family, including three grandchildren."

"Wait a minute, you mean they didn't ask you? They just showed up at your door?"

"You got it."

"Oh, girl, don't let anybody just do that to you. No one has a right to disrespect you in that way. And if you think this is something a Christian is supposed to lay down and take, you must not have read or paid attention to the scripture where Jesus turned over a few moneychangers' tables. Because they were pretty much taking advantage of the people. Thieves, that's what Jesus basically called them. And I don't think anybody can be more Christian than Christ. Sure, we are told to love, we're told to forgive, but we're not told to become doormats. Now, that's *my* interpretation of the scriptures *I've* read."

"I was trying to talk to Aunt Cee-Cee, and she was telling me they plan to go to church with me on Sunday. And then they'll likely be out of here in a few weeks," Gabrielle said.

"I understand you want people to go to church. But please tell me you didn't fall for that line. Please tell me you didn't."

"Of course I didn't fall for it. It's just hard knowing you have somewhere to live and they don't, and you won't open your door up for them," Gabrielle said. "It's hard."

"Let me see if I can't break this down for you. Earlier this year, you were about to lose your house the same way they have lost theirs. I'm not saying to do unto others as they have done unto you, but based on what you told me when you and I first met: they put you out with nowhere to go when you were eighteen. Eighteen. Am I right?"

"Yes, but—"

"Just a minute. Stay with me, now. Had you been put out of your house, as it were, could *you* have gone over *there* to live with *them* the way *they* have now done to *you?*"

"But, Clarence, as a Christian—"

"But Clarence nothing. Just answer my question. Yes or no?"

"What is it with y'all and these yes or no questions?" Gabrielle said, thinking back to her earlier conversation with Zachary.

"Yes . . . or no?"

"No. But I want to do what God would have me to do."

"Do you think they will be out of your house in two weeks?"

"No."

"Three? Four? Six weeks?"

"Honestly?" Gabrielle said. "I believe a year from now they'll likely all still be here unless something major happens."

"Will that be okay with you?"

"No." Her voice cracked.

"Then why put yourself through all of this?" Clarence asked.

Gabrielle heard the phone line open. "Are you still on here?" Angie asked, smacking on something. "How much longer are you going to be on the phone? I need to make a call."

"Please hang up the phone," Gabrielle said calmly.

When Angie didn't hang up, she said again, "Please . . . hang . . . up . . . my phone. *Now*." She heard the line close.

"Again," Clarence said. "Why would you put yourself through this, knowing that it's not going to end anytime soon?" Gabrielle didn't answer him; she only sighed. "Gabrielle, when people are trying to get themselves together and do better, that's one thing. When people are just trying to use you or get over on you, it's up to you to draw a line. You can't allow the devil to use others to stronghold you. I'm telling you now."

"So you think I should put them out now," Gabrielle said.

"I can't tell you what you're supposed to do. I *can* give you wisdom from my perspective. I can tell you what God is saying to me on the matter. But ultimately, you have to hear the Lord for yourself. You know what God has been telling you. You know, Gabrielle. Sometimes we think we're helping people when it's possible we're merely getting in God's way. Who's to say that God isn't using this situation to get your family's attention so that they can hear *Him?*"

"You're right, Clarence. But you called here, and I'm sure you didn't call to talk to me about my family or my troubles."

"Yeah, but it's okay. That's what friends are for. We're told to bear one another's burdens. I called to see if you'd like to rehearse tomorrow for my grandfather's birthday celebration. We don't have a lot of time to get together. After we see what we're looking to do, you can practice at home on your own time."

"Tomorrow? Yeah, sure."

"Well, I *was* thinking about coming to your house, but now that I hear about what you're dealing with, I think it would be great, for both of us, if you just come over here."

"Yeah, we do need to get together. I can't wait to see what song you've chosen."

"Oh, I believe you're going to love it. I'll play it when you get here. I bought a copy of the song for you so you'll have it for your own rehearsals," Clarence said. "So, tomorrow, around what time?"

"Noonish is good for me."

"Then noonish it is. I'll see you then."

As soon as Gabrielle hung up and placed the phone back in its base, it rang one time. When she looked at the number on the caller ID, she could tell by the name that it was for Angie.

She couldn't do anything but shake her head.

Chapter 52

*The glory of young men is their strength: and the
beauty of old men is the gray head.*

—Proverbs 20:29

Johnnie Mae walked in on Angela and Gramps as
they sat in the activity room.

"Well, hello," Johnnie Mae said to Angela, since she
was most surprised to see her there.

Angela stood up and greeted Johnnie Mae with a
hug and a kiss even though they had seen each other at
work at church earlier.

"I came by to see my mother," Johnnie Mae said. "If
you had told me you were coming this way, we could
have come together."

"I wasn't sure I was coming until the last minute,"
Angela said.

"Hello there, blessed woman of God," Gramps said.

Johnnie Mae realized that with her preoccupation in
trying to figure out why Angela might have been there,
she had failed to acknowledge Gramps.

"Gramps, I'm so sorry. I guess you thought I was

completely trying to ignore you." Johnnie Mae hugged him. She looked down and noticed the photograph he held in his hand. "Who is that a picture of?"

Gramps handed it to her. "That beautiful, feisty woman is Pearl during her younger years," Gramps said.

Johnnie Mae took it and looked at it. "I remember seeing this." She glanced at Angela, hoping she might shed a little more light on what was going on. But the more she thought about it, it did make sense. Ransom knew Angela's great-grandmother, and not only had Angela been close to Pearl, but Pearl had raised her. Of course she would want to talk to the person who knew her great-grandmother back in the day. He could fill her in on things while she filled him in on the Pearl she'd grown up knowing.

"And do you know who that fine fellow is standing beside her?" Gramps said.

"He looks like you," Johnnie Mae said. "But that can't be you, can it?"

"I had this friend named Sam, Samuel L. Williams—"

"That's my great-grandfather," Angela interjected.

"I got a photo almost identical to that one," Gramps said, nodding his head in the direction of the picture. "It's funny how people tend to save the same things. That proves how close Pearl and I were. Angel was telling me that Pearl had this photo in a cigar box. I got one similar to it in my room, inside my Wings of Grace box. You two care to see it? It's a little different."

"Sure," both Johnnie Mae and Angela said. Angela was at least thankful to know there were two photos around of her great-grandfather with her great-granny.

"All right," Gramps said, slowly standing to his feet. Johnnie Mae turned, still holding the photo, trying to decide who she should give it back to. She decided on Angela, since it was hers. Gramps would have enough to occupy himself with.

He found the picture rather quickly. "This little box has really come in handy. The things that are most important to me can be found right in here. Amazing how we can reduce our lives to fit ever so neatly into a box. Birth records, important papers, copies of your will if you have one, captured images in time that hold memories even when your own mind no longer can." He handed the photo to Johnnie Mae first.

Johnnie Mae looked at it, smiled, then handed it over to Angela.

"My great-grandfather is a lot more animated in this photo. In the one Great-granny had, he looks so stiff—like he didn't know quite what to expect. Here, he's playful. I like your photo, Gramps."

Gramps started to chuckle. "I'm sorry, but that's not your great-grandfather in that photo. The man in that photo as well as your photo is me. Sam and I did look somewhat alike, so I can understand you mistaking him for me. But that's a photo of me and Pearl, not Pearl and Sam."

Angela looked at the photo again and allowed her legs to ease her down slowly onto the tan leather recliner.

Chapter 53

*I behaved myself as though he had been my
friend or brother: I bowed down heavily, as one
that mourneth for his mother.*

—Psalm 35:14

"Angela, are you sure you're okay?" Johnnie Mae
said as she handed Angela a cup of water she'd
gone out and gotten for her. "Angel?"

Angela took a sip of the water. "I'm okay," she said.
"I'm okay." Then turning back to Gramps, she asked,
"Are you certain this is you?"

"Of course I'm certain."

"But earlier you said it was your friend, Sam. When
we were in the lobby area, you said something about
this being Samuel." Angela looked from the photo to
Gramps.

"Actually, I was trying to say that I had a friend
named Sam who *took* that photo. He'd borrowed the
camera from another friend who had one, which was
rare to have back in my day. Sam took that picture."
Gramps laughed. "We didn't know how to take no pic-

ture. He must have given Pearl one and me another. I didn't know she had that one; she probably didn't know I had this one. These are the earliest known photos of me, before pictures ever became the norm." He scratched his head, then rubbed his chin.

"Come to think of it," Gramps said, "my daughter asked if I had any pictures of me when I was young. I didn't even think about that photo when she asked. She wanted to use them for my birthday celebration." He smiled. "She told you about my birthday party when we were at your house," he said to Johnnie Mae. "And Angela . . . Angel, you certainly are welcome to come if you like. It's going to be Saturday, November seventh, at Pastor Landris's church, from what my daughter told me the other day."

"Yeah," Johnnie Mae said. "Pastor Landris and I are definitely going to be there. In fact, your family has asked him to say a few inspirational words, nothing long, since it sounds like it's going to encompass lots of people saying all kinds of wonderful things about you and your life."

"I told my daughter to keep things short and simple. But she ain't paying me much attention. I think she's trying to go all out."

Angela hadn't said a word. She was staring at the photo Gramps had allowed them to see.

"I suppose you're thinking about your great-grand-mother right about now," Gramps said when he noticed Angela was preoccupied with his picture. "If you like, you're welcome to take that picture and get a copy of it. I'd like to keep the original, though. You understand. It's all I got left of me and Pearl." He smiled upon saying Pearl's name. "That woman know she cared about me. She was truly one in a million."

Angela was polarized when it came to what to do at

this point. Should she tell him what she suspected to be true and see what light he might be able to shed on it? Should she do it right now, since the perfect opening had presented itself? Or should she wait until Johnnie Mae left and discuss it alone? Should she talk to Arletha first? Maybe she should ask Johnnie Mae to step out of the room and ask her advice on the matter.

God, I need You to tell me what to do. Please . . . just tell me what to do. Please.

Chapter 54

God is in the midst of her; she shall not be moved: God shall help her, and that right early.

—Psalm 46:5

"Well, I hate to cut this short, but I really need to go see my mother," Johnnie Mae said. "I saw the two of you when I was passing by, and I thought I should stop and say hello."

"I'm so glad you did," Gramps said. "You definitely are a ray of sunshine. But I guess you can't help but to be since you're born of the Son." He snickered. "Get it?" He chuckled some more. "S-o-n instead of s-u-n? A ray of S-o-n-shine like the s-u-n that shines."

Johnnie Mae smiled. "I get it." She stood up. "Gramps, it's always good seeing you. And I *will* see *you* again. If not here, then with bells on at your birthday party."

"I'll be looking for you."

"Just save me a dance," Johnnie Mae said. "And Angel, I'll see *you* tomorrow at work," she said to Angela. She then left, closing the door behind her.

Angela cleared her throat. "Mister Perdue . . . I mean, Gramps, are you certain that the man in this photo is you? You're sure?"

"Oh, there ain't no doubt about it. I remember when we took it back in 1943. I'd just come back to town. The only ones who knew I was still there was Pearl and Sam. It's a long story you may or may not have heard before. But Pearl had been hiding me out because there were still some people who wanted to do me harm. I was trying to find Sarah and my daughter. Pearl was trying to help me, to fill me in on everything she knew. That picture there"—he indicated with his head—"was taken a couple of weeks before I took off again. I never went back. I should have. I regret it. But after I left, I never went back."

Gramps sat back in the straight-back chair. "Most folks thought I'd merely run off the first time I disappeared, or worse: gotten lynched. Only a handful of folk knew the real truth. And only two knew the whole truth, and that was your great-grandparents, Pearl and Sam—true friends 'til the end. Although I admit, I *was* surprised, but glad to hear they married. It proves life goes on, no matter what bad we have to overcome."

Angela took a deep breath and exhaled slowly. "Mister Perdue . . . Gramps, I don't know exactly how to say this, other than to just come right out and say it. But I have reasons to believe that you might possibly be my great-grandfather."

He tilted his head upward and stared into her face. "What you say?"

She opened her purse and pulled out a photo she had brought with her of a younger Arletha. She got up and handed the picture to him.

"That's my grandmother. Her name is Arletha. I might be wrong, and if I am, then at least it's just between you and me, and you can straighten me out about it. But I believe Arletha is your daughter. The photo Great-granny had in that box is a photo of you. You and Arletha look so much alike it's chilling. It's almost like you spit her out. And I didn't just come here with a half-baked theory. My grandmother was born January 28, 1944. When I count back nine months from that date, it puts her conception around April of 1943, although it's possible she was born premature, which would make that date later."

"I left Asheville April twenty-ninth," he said, staring hard now at the photo of Arletha. "She looks just like my second son. They could pass for twins," Gramps said.

"So you don't think I'm crazy or merely reaching here?"

"No. I believe"—he started wiping at his eyes—"I believe you have given me a gift I was never expecting in my life. I don't know how much of God's goodness I can take in one year. First, I finally find my oldest daughter, Memory. After all of these years, I *never* thought that would happen. And now, it looks like I have one more daughter I never even knew had been created." He was crying now.

Angela hugged him. "I didn't know how to bring this up to you. I prayed for God to lead me to do the right thing." She sat back down, allowing him to quietly process this.

"So, she"—he shook the photo of Arletha—"doesn't know anything about this?" he finally said. "Not even it remotely being a possibility?"

"No. I thought it best to talk to you first. If you weren't anywhere near Great-granny during that time, there's no way what I was thinking was even possible."

"When did you suspect this?" Gramps reached inside his pocket and took out his handkerchief. "My goodness. My, my, my." He looked up at the ceiling. "Whew!"

"The day I met you at Johnnie Mae's house. Looking in your face was like looking into my grandmother's face. I did some research, found that picture, thought it was you. I even asked my husband . . . Oh! My husband!" Angela said, springing up. "I need to call him and get him to pick up our children. My husband's name is Brent." She took out her cell phone. "We have two little boys: Brent the Second and Shaun."

"Boy, oh boy, my family is certainly growing by leaps and bounds. First Memory and all of them, now Arletha and all of you. When can I meet Arletha? I got to see her."

"I need to figure out how to tell her this. Arletha is not your normal family girl," Angela said. "That's a story I'll tell you about later. But it took me a while to find her, and then to get her to admit that she and *I* were even related. I don't know how she'll react to the news of you. But knowing her, it could be bad. You never know."

"I want to see her. I want to meet her as soon as you can arrange it. I have to. Then I need to tell my other children. My daughter, Zenobia, is probably going to flip. At first she had no sisters, and now she has two." Gramps stood up to keep his legs from stiffening up. "You just arrange for us to meet. I'll take care of the rest. This ain't exactly your row to hoe. I'm her father. It's my job and my responsibility to tell her."

"Thank you," Angela said as she called Brent on her cell phone about getting the children. After she hung up with him, she tried to think of the best way to bring Arletha and Gramps together so the two of them could talk.

She called Arletha. "Grand, I need to come by your house. I'll be there in a little while. Oh, and Grand, I'm not going to be alone. I'm bringing someone with me."

"Who?" Arletha asked. "Who are you bringing?"

"It's a surprise."

"You know I don't like surprises. I told you that."

"Grand, please. I promise you're going to love this. I'll see you in a little while."

"Angela, you can come, but I don't feel like company tonight."

"Bye, Grand. I'll see you in a little bit." Angela clicked off her cell phone so her grandmother wouldn't be able to argue with her. "Okay, now, if I can get you out of here, I'll take you to meet Arletha." She tick-tocked her head, slightly satisfied with herself, then smiled.

Chapter 55

For now will I break his yoke from off thee, and
will burst thy bonds in sunder.

—Nahum 1:13

Gramps tried explaining things to the director after the head nurse told him she couldn't allow him to leave. It didn't matter that he was a grown man old enough to be her great-grandfather or that he was capable of coming and going as he pleased. He couldn't leave.

"Mrs. Underwood, while I'm sure she is a decent and honorable woman, is not on your approved list of people authorized to sign you out," the director said to Gramps.

"You're telling me that I'm almost two weeks away from turning a hundred and I can't leave this place without someone else's permission?"

"Mister Perdue, it's for your own safety and protection as well as ours," the director said. "What if something happens to you? Then we're the ones responsible."

"What do you think? This sweet young lady here, who is young enough to *also* be my great-granddaughter, is going to kidnap me or run off with me?"

"I know you think you're making a joke, but sir, do you know how many young women manipulate older men for their money or their insurance if they have any?" The director sighed. "The data would astound you."

"Johnnie Mae Landris!" Angela said. "She can vouch for me. She *was* here visiting her mother. We belong to the same church . . . her husband is my pastor. I'm her assistant. Can you ask her about me? She'll tell you I'm who I say I am and vouch that I'm not a threat or a danger to Mister Perdue."

"I'm curious what the urgency is for you to take him? What's your angle? From what you've told me, you've never stepped foot in our establishment before. And the first time you come, you want to take one of our residents off with you? And you think that's okay." The director shook her head. "Someone who is authorized to sign him out will need to come down here and do it in person. Not tell us over the phone, because who can really say who's on the other end. Gramps, if someone from your approved list comes in and signs you out," the director said, "you can go. Otherwise, you can't leave with her."

Gramps shuffled away as Angela walked beside him. "Can you believe this? Do you know how humiliating this is for me? I'm a grown man, and it's like I'm locked up or some baby that has to have a parent sign me out."

"Mister Perdue—"

"I told you to call me Gramps."

"Gramps, I can see where they're coming from. I *could* be someone shady trying to take advantage of you. I know your family would have a fit on them if they let you wander out of here, either by yourself or with someone they don't know. So can you call your daughter and have her come sign you out?"

"I don't want Zenobia to come. I'm not ready to tell her what's going on. Not yet. I want to talk with Arletha first. Then Zenobia and I will have this discussion. If Zenobia comes, she'll ask fifty million questions. And if I tell her, she'll want to go," Gramps said as they walked back to his room. "I don't suspect from what you've told me about Arletha that she'll fancy both of us showing up on her doorstep. No, it's better if we don't let Zenobia know anything is going on."

They reached his room and went in. "I will tell you who we *can* call, though—my grandson, Clarence. Clarence won't push to ask a lot of questions if I tell him not to. And he won't tell his mother anything if I ask him not to. Now, Knowledge, that's my other grandson, is his mother's son. Knowledge don't trust nobody, not nobody. I'm sure he would grill you, and *then* call his mother and blab everything to her no matter what I ask of him. Let me find Clarence's number here and we can call him to come sign me out. He'll do it, no questions asked."

Gramps flipped to the back of his Bible and found Clarence's phone number. Angela dialed the number and gave her cell phone to Gramps so he could do all the talking.

Chapter 56

For the vision is yet for an appointed time, but at the end it shall speak, and not lie: though it tarry, wait for it: because it will surely come, it will not tarry.

—Habakkuk 2:3

"Where have you been?" Brent asked as soon as Angela stepped inside the house from the garage. "You called me three hours ago to go pick up the children. I was worried about you." He gave her a quick kiss, more like a peck, on her lips.

"I called you and told you I was all right and that I would be home soon," Angela said. "Where are the kids?"

"In the kitchen eating. They were hungry. I had to fix them *something*."

"Let me guess: beanie weenies."

"They love my beanie weenies, and it's all I know how to cook that they really like." Brent followed her as she hurried into the kitchen.

"Hi, guys!" she said, putting her purse on the counter.

She gave Brent the Second, sitting at the table, and then Shaun, sitting in his high chair, each a big hug and a kiss.

"Mommy!" Brent the Second said with fanfare. "Daddy fixed our favorite."

"I see," Angela said, rubbing Shaun's head as he chased a weenie with his hand.

"I want some more," Brent the Second said, holding up his plate in the air.

"I want some more what?" Angela said, walking over to him and picking up his plate as she continued to stand beside him.

"I want some more beanie weenies *now*," he said with a giggle. She tapped him on his nose. "I want some more *please*," he said with even more giggles.

She got him more, sneaking a forkful off his plate for herself.

"So are you going to tell me what's going on?" Brent said to his wife.

She kissed the children again, then walked out of the kitchen with Brent in tow.

Flopping down on the den sofa, she grabbed one of the decorative pillows and hugged it. "I went to visit Ransom Perdue, or Gramps, as he likes being called. And although it took some doing, it turns out I was right, Brent." She looked into his eyes. "Gramps admitted, not that he knew it before now, that he *is* Arletha's real father."

"You're kidding," Brent said, nestling up to his wife.

"No, I'm not. So I tried to arrange a meeting between the two of them, and you know how Arletha can be."

"I don't think I like where this is going," Brent said, hugging her even more.

"Before we even left to go visit her, we had to battle a nurse and the director of the nursing home trying to get Gramps a 'furlough' just so he could leave with me." Angela chuckled. "The director, Miss Frigid, was not hearing that at all."

"Miss Frigid? Is that her real name?"

Angela looked at him and smirked as she shook her head. "No, silly. You know I was just being funny and descriptive at the same time. I don't recall her name. Gramps and I were too busy trying to figure out how to get him out of there."

"I hope you didn't sneak that man out of that nursing home," Brent said.

"Of course I didn't. How would something like that look on the nightly news? Breaking news: Woman kidnaps elderly man from a nursing home. Details as they develop." She imitated the way a news reporter might say it.

"So, were you not able to get him out?"

"Yeah, we got him out, by calling his grandson, Clarence. He's the guy that sang 'I Trust You' when Pastor Landris preached at Divine Conquerors Church."

"Yeah, I remember him."

"Well, that's Gramps's grandson. And apparently he and Gramps are cool enough that Gramps could just ask him to come sign him out without having to explain to him why or what he was up to. I get the impression that Clarence and Gramps are in cahoots quite a lot. Gramps may be old—which, by the way, we're going to his one hundredth year birthday party November seventh at six PM, so don't schedule anything for that night."

"How do you know I haven't already scheduled anything?"

"If you have, cancel it. This is my great-grand-father's birthday party." She grinned. "We're not missing this for *anything*." She did the Cabbage Patch dance.

"Bossy, aren't you?" he said, leaning in close as though he was going to kiss her. "You know, I like it when you're bossy."

She hit at him. "Behave," she said. "Anyway, Gramps may be old, but he still has a lot of fire in his belly. That's how I want to be when I get old. Still getting around and enjoying life. Maybe not as fast as I used to, but living life like I don't really have a care in the world. Any other man who had just learned he had a child he didn't know about may have tried to back away from it. But not Gramps. He embraced it so fast he almost knocked me out of the way trying to get to his daughter. And do you know what Arletha did?"

"What?"

"She wouldn't come to the door and let me in. I called her and told her I was coming over. I suppose the mistake I made was telling her I was bringing someone with me."

"Oh, now, let's see. We're talking about the same woman who looked you dead in your face and told you flat out that she wasn't your grandmother. The same woman who came to your wedding, watched you get married knowing how much it would have meant to you if she had been standing beside you, yet she never said a word. The same woman who, even after she admitted she was your grandmother, didn't want you to refer to her as such and asked if the two of you could start off your new relationship being friends. The same woman who, after about a year, finally consented to you calling her Grand. *That* Arletha?" Brent said.

"The one and only. You would think I would have known she would react that way, but call me naive. I just thought she'd grown in that area. How was I to know if I told her that I was coming to visit and bringing someone with me that she would revert to her old ways and not even come to the door for me?"

Brent squeezed Angela. Angela wondered how he always knew exactly what she needed from him when she needed it without her ever having to ask.

"I called Arletha on my cell phone. At first she wouldn't answer. Of course, I got worried, had a flashback of the last time she didn't come to the door and we found her lying on the floor almost dead. I was beating on the door and calling for her. I'm sure Gramps thinks I'm certifiable now. He probably doesn't want to be kin to either one of us after this episode." She snuggled up closer to Brent. She loved the smell of his cologne, Obsession, the same brand Pastor Landris wore.

"When I called her again after that, she must have remembered that I don't have a problem with calling the police and having her door busted down, so she answered the phone. Before I could say anything, she blurted out, 'I'm fine. I'm not answering the door. So go home to your family and take whomever you have out there with you.' *Bam!* She hung up. Well, you know me."

"Persistent to a fault," Brent said. "But in a good way," he quickly added before she could give him her evil eye.

"Anyway, I decided I would call her back and just blurt out something to make her answer the door."

"And what exactly did you think you were going to say over the phone?"

"Brent, you know Arletha. I was going to say, 'Your father is standing out here with me.' Or 'It's your father. Now open the door so we can talk.' Just put it out there and make her listen from there. Telling her Ransom Perdue was out there wouldn't have made her open it. I had to say something dramatic to get her attention. But she didn't give me another chance. She refused to answer the phone again." Angela heard Shaun crying. She jumped up and ran into the kitchen.

Shaun's empty bowl of beanie weenies was turned over on the floor. "Oh, little man, it's okay. Don't cry. Mommy has it." She picked him up out of his high chair. "Look at you—you're a mess. Let's go upstairs and get you into the tub."

"Me too?" Brent the Second said, holding up his plate to show he was finished.

"Yes, you too."

"What?" Brent said with his arms wide open. "You're just going to leave a brother hanging? I think you need to quit reading Johnnie Mae's books. You're starting to tell your stories the same way she writes hers. I, for one, despise cliffhangers."

"Okay, Brent," she said as she carried one child in her arms and marched the other one alongside her up the stairs. "Gramps didn't get to see, meet, or talk to Arletha. I took him back to the nursing home, and he and I are going to come up with another strategy later." She stopped, smiled, and looked at Brent.

"The end," Angela said with a laugh at her own cleverness as she continued to the bathroom to run bathwater for her two beanie-weenie-sauce-encrusted sons.

Chapter 57

*The wicked have laid a snare for me: yet I erred
not from thy precepts.*

—Psalm 119:110

Pastor Landris had gone by Reverend Walker's office
the next day as agreed upon before going in to work
at the church. But when he got there, Mrs. Greer told
him Reverend Walker was not there. He'd had a family
emergency and had been called away out of town. He
had asked that they reschedule their appointment upon
his return, but Reverend Walker couldn't say exactly
when that would be. As it turned out, he was gone for
five days. His oldest son by his first wife had had a
heart attack. They weren't sure whether he was going
to make it at first. But by the grace of God, he pulled
through.

After Reverend Walker returned, he had such a
backlog that he tried to put Pastor Landris off for another week. Pastor Landris wasn't having any of that.
He wanted to know what was going on with that cash

money he'd received. He couldn't put it in the bank, because if he did, it would trigger paperwork to alert the government, including the IRS, of its existence. Banks were required to report deposits of ten thousand dollars or more. And even though it was cash and he could have broken it up to deposit it, he was sure there was something in place to track folks who tried to game the system this way as well. Besides, he wasn't trying to sneak and do anything. He'd done nothing wrong.

Since he didn't know where the money had come from, he wasn't about to deposit it into his account. But that meant he'd had to put it somewhere in his house. He'd never kept that much cash in his house before. He was thankful they had a wall safe, so he had put it there until he could speak with Reverend Walker about it.

He now had a firm appointment. But when Pastor Landris walked into Reverend Walker's office, he didn't like what he saw.

"What is he doing here?" Pastor Landris asked.

Reverend Walker got to his feet. "You remember Mister Threadgill, don't you?" he said.

"Yeah," Pastor Landris said as he first shook Reverend Walker's hand, then cautiously shook William Threadgill's.

"Oh, please, call me William," he said to Pastor Landris, and looked at Reverend Walker as though those instructions were for him as well. "We're all family here. We're all brothers in the Lord. Although I'm not a preacher like the two of you, we're still a part of the same family."

"Please, Pastor Landris," Reverend Walker said as he sat back down in his overstuffed burgundy leather chair, "have a seat."

"I thought you and I were scheduled to meet. I've been trying to get with you for more than a week now. I can wait outside with your secretary until the two of you are finished up."

"I apologize for not being able to meet with you until now," Reverend Walker said. "You know how demanding our lives can be as ministers of the gospel. And whether people believe it or not, we still have families and the things that come along with that."

Pastor Landris remained standing, although Mr. Threadgill had sat back down in his chair, across the desk from Reverend Walker. "How is your son doing?" Pastor Landris asked Reverend Walker. "Your secretary told me he'd had a heart attack."

"Thank you for asking," Reverend Walker said, softly tapping together the matching fingers of each hand. "He's doing much better. He's just forty-five and had a heart attack. The doctor said it was his pack-a-day smoking and what he's been eating for most of his life that caused it. I've tried to tell him that his body is the temple of God, but I suppose some folks think they're untouchable and that things like this only happen to other folks. He certainly got his wake-up call, as we all at some point tend to get. I pray he'll make the necessary changes his doctor is prescribing." Reverend Walker laced his fingers together as he leaned forward.

"As for Mister Threadgill, I invited him, knowing you were going to be here. So if you would . . . please, have a seat." Reverend Walker smiled and sat back up straight.

"With all due respect to this being your office," Pastor Landris said, "I've told Mister Threadgill here that I'm not interested in anything he is proposing or cares to discuss. And I don't appreciate you trying to set me up when I've been trying to get with you on another matter. So, I'll just wait outside your office until you two are finished." Pastor Landris turned around to leave.

"Pastor Landris," Reverend Walker said, "Mister Threadgill is here because of the money you received: the twenty thousand dollars *cash* presently in your possession."

Pastor Landris stopped dead in his tracks. He turned around slowly.

"So . . . if you will, Pastor Landris," Reverend Walker said, "please come and have a seat."

Pastor Landris came back toward Reverend Walker's desk. "There's no need for me to have a seat. It appears you've answered my question." Pastor Landris took out the envelope of money from inside his coat pocket and dropped it on the desk in front of William Threadgill. "I'm not interested in receiving anything from you or your elected official for any reason. And if you think I'm for sale or that our church is, then you have another *think* coming. Count it. It's all there."

Mr. Threadgill picked up the envelope, smiled, then put it back on the desk without counting it. "Impressive, Pastor Landris. I'm impressed. You've actually had this money for over a week and you weren't tempted to use *any* of it?"

"I assure you, Mister Threadgill, had Reverend Walker here been candid with where it had come from in the first place, it never would have left this office *in* my possession. I don't play this kind of game. So whatever the two of you are cooking up or have cooked up, you can leave me out of it." He nodded. "Good day to you both."

"Pastor Landris, before you make another hasty decision," Mr. Threadgill said, "you might want to take a look at these." He handed Pastor Landris a large, gold-colored envelope.

"There's nothing in there I care to see," Pastor Landris said.

"Oh, I don't know about that," Mr. Threadgill said as he pulled out several eight-by-ten glossy photos. "Even if you're not interested, I'm certain the Feds or, at the very least, the media and your congregation might be." He laid out the photos on Reverend Walker's desk.

Pastor Landris glanced at the top photo. "What is this?" Pastor Landris said, picking up the picture of himself with Reverend Walker handing him the stuffed envelope of cash. He looked at the next picture; it was of him putting the envelope inside his suit jacket. The other photo was of the three of them talking, which appeared to be in a conspiratory manner and had to have been taken when they were outside the office when Mr. Threadgill first approached him.

"What does it look like?" Mr. Threadgill said.

"I know what it *looks* like." Pastor Landris turned to Reverend Walker. "That whole afternoon was a setup? You weren't trying to reset any buttons between us, as you said; you were trying to get me here so you could produce these pictures to try to blackmail me. The two of you acting as though you'd never really met before. Then getting me back here in your office so you could give me that envelope, making it appear like I was taking a bribe or something while someone else was hiding away, snapping away."

Mr. Threadgill put the photos back inside the envelope. "Pastor Landris, what I'm asking of the two of you is not anything other preachers aren't doing or haven't done before. And all I'm asking is for you to hear the whole plan out. Think about it, pray about it if you feel led to do that, and if you still can't find a way to say yes to it, then . . . I can't be responsible for what becomes of these photos."

"But I'm innocent of what these pictures are portraying and you both know it, no matter *how* you might try to twist your unfounded lies," Pastor Landris said to both men.

Mr. Threadgill scratched his head. "True. But most things are perception, and I can promise you that this looks like something may have been going on. Even if you're able to prove otherwise, think of the public relations hit your name and your church will take while you defend it. And then there will always be those who, no matter what you're able to do, will believe that the rich and famous, once again, have merely manipulated the system to get off the hook. Why put yourself, your family, and your congregation through all of that when it's not necessary and all you really have to do is cooperate."

"Pastor Landris," Reverend Walker began, "what they want really doesn't require much from us. It's what we do most of the time anyway. Tell people what we think God is telling us to do, and convince them it's in their best interest to go along with it. That's it. I don't know why you want to make things so difficult, a mountain out of a molehill."

"Reverend Walker, if you feel okay in doing this, then that's on you. But I'm still not interested, and I'm going to pray for you . . . for both of you." He looked at them both, alternating his gaze between them.

"I tell you what," Mr. Threadgill said. "This is a lot to process in a short amount of time. Why don't you think about it, and we'll talk later. In the meantime"— Mr. Threadgill picked up the envelope with the photos and the envelope with the $20,000 and held them both out to Pastor Landris—"you can hang on to these. And believe me, there are plenty more Benjamins where *those* came from. *Plen*-ty. That was merely your down payment."

Pastor Landris looked at him, then at Reverend Walker. "Thank you, but I believe this concludes my involvement with *either* of you." He then turned and left Mr. Threadgill holding both envelopes and Reverend Walker holding a look of disdain on his face.

Chapter 58

But mine enemies are lively, and they are strong:
and they that hate me wrongfully are multiplied.

—Psalm 38:19

Pastor Landris went home even madder than he was when he walked out of Reverend Walker's office. He had called Sherry and told her to cancel any appointments he had for the day. Instead of going to the church to work, he'd opted to go back home. It didn't take long for Johnnie Mae to discover he wasn't at work and become worried about him.

Johnnie Mae knew he'd had an appointment with Reverend Walker. She also knew something must have gone terribly wrong if Landris had decided not to come to work and hadn't bothered to call her to tell her what was going on. She told Angela she was going to go home for a little while as well. That only raised suspicion with anyone in the know that something was wrong, for both of them to be away from the church.

Those on staff also knew not to gossip or speculate about what might be going on. They just decided to pray that whatever was happening, God would step into the midst of the situation and take care and control of it.

When Johnnie Mae walked into their bedroom, she found her husband on his knees in front of their bed in prayer. On the bed was a large white envelope with the words *Personal and Private* written on it. She didn't say anything as her husband continued to pray out loud, at times, even in the Spirit. She just quietly went and kneeled down beside him. He opened his eyes and looked at her. She began to pray along with him. He went back to his prayer.

When he'd prayed ten minutes more, Pastor Landris wound it down, ending with his customary, "In Jesus' name, Amen."

He got up, sat on the bed, and pulled her up—holding her gently in his arms. "What are you doing here?" he said.

"What I'm supposed to be doing, being by your side," Johnnie Mae said.

"How did you know to come here?"

"I suppose that's what happens when you pray. God dispatches His angels, and they begin working on your behalf. I suppose one of your angels, or perhaps it was the Holy Spirit, directed me to come home."

He hugged her tighter, gently squeezing her before kissing the top of her hair.

"Talk to me," Johnnie Mae said. "What's wrong? What's going on?"

Pastor Landris let go of her. "It was a setup. Reverend Walker and this man named William Threadgill set the whole thing up."

"Is this about that money you wanted to talk to Reverend Walker about?"

"Yes. And when I walked in Reverend Walker's office, there was Mister Threadgill. It turns out he's the source of that twenty thousand dollars I received. It was bribe money or a way for him to blackmail me. I don't know how I would label what the two of them are up to. And quite frankly, I'm not trying to find out. I told both of them I wanted no part of their scheme or any of their plans."

Johnnie Mae shook her head. "It's sad what's happening these days with preachers and elected officials. Businessmen and preachers making side deals that benefit them, all in the name of the Lord. It's sad. I don't know whether it's arrogance or if these preachers don't actually believe God is going to do anything about their wrongdoing."

"Well, I think many of them may have done something at one point and gotten away with it. They believe either God doesn't really care about that or that God isn't going to do anything, so they try to get, while the getting is good." He leaned his head back, then straightened it. "And believe it or not, what's even sadder is that some of them may actually believe what they're doing is right. You know—the end justifies the means. They get the money, help out some of the poor along the way; they did something good with it, so that makes what they've done okay. I don't know. But I know I'm not interested in getting tangled up with anything that even *remotely* gives the *appearance* of evil. I'm not doing it. Not if I can help it."

"Okay, so you told them you weren't interested, and then what happened?" Johnnie Mae took her husband's hand and weaved her fingers between his.

He looked at her, raised the hand that was now one with hers, and softly kissed her hand. "You know me all too well, don't you?"

"I know there's more to this than you've told me so

far. So what are they trying to do to force you into this? Because I know you gave him that money back."

He smiled, kissing her hand once more. "They have photos of me seemingly taking the money. If I don't agree to play along, they plan to put those photos out there and, most likely, team up together to say I knowingly took a bribe. Forget the fact that I've not put the money in our bank account."

"Thank God you listened to the Holy Spirit," Johnnie Mae said. "Anybody else would have deposited that cash if not spent some of it until they learned differently."

"Yeah, I thank God for ordering my steps. If I had deposited that cash and then given it back, they would likely have said I'd backed out of a deal I'd originally cut with them. I'm sure the two of them, or however many of them there are, are putting their heads together right now prepared to lie and say I took the cash and got cold feet, which is why I gave it back after keeping it for a little over a week," Pastor Landris said. "Of course, you and I know I would have given it back the following day had I been able to meet with Reverend Walker. But he was off work. And after that, he went out of town—"

"Landris, you don't have to explain any of this to me."

He smiled. "I suppose I'm rehearsing what I might have to say to the Feds or to someone later when they claim my story doesn't ring true."

"Well, God knows the truth. And He's the one who really counts."

"Yeah, but I don't want my name dragged through the mud. I don't want people believing wrong things about me," Pastor Landris said.

Johnnie Mae laughed. "Landris, people already drag

your name through the mud. They're going to talk about you no matter what. All the good you're doing and folks are already saying hateful things about you, about both of us. Well, they talked about Jesus."

"You're right. Remember in Matthew the eleventh chapter around the eleventh through the nineteenth verses when Jesus was addressing how they talked about John the Baptist as well as Himself?"

"Is that where Jesus was talking about how folks were calling Him a winebibber?"

"Yeah. People had been talking about John the Baptist, saying John came neither eating or drinking because he lived out in the wilderness and ate locust and honey. The people were saying that John had a devil. Then the Son of man came eating and drinking and the people were saying, 'Behold a man gluttonous, and a winebibber, a friend of publicans and sinners.' But then Jesus said that wisdom is justified of her children. *Justified* here meant vindicated. Those who followed John during his time and teaching and Jesus—their children, so to speak, or disciples as we know them—their decision to listen to this prophet called John and the Messiah named Jesus proved to be well founded. They talked about John and Jesus. Thank you for reminding me of that. I try so hard to walk in a godly way. And when people go out of their way to set you up just to bring you down for their own glorification, I confess, it deeply troubles me."

"I know," Johnnie Mae said. "But so far, you've done the right thing. You've prayed about it. Now you just need to listen to how the Spirit of God is leading you and walk therein."

Pastor Landris gave his wife a quick kiss on her lips. "God must really love me," he said. "Blessing me with someone like you." His eyes danced as he spoke. "Oh,

I have *got* to be God's favorite, I don't care what any-body else says." He smiled.

Johnnie Mae shook her head. "I'm sorry to burst your bubble. But I'm God's favorite. Look how He blessed me with you, our beautiful children, and the knowledge that no matter what we're going through, God is right there with us. To know that even though the storm may be tossing the ship to and fro and it may look like we're going to perish, Jesus is onboard. Jesus, Who can speak to the winds and the waves and say, 'Peace, be still.' Jesus, calling what He desires no mat-ter what things may look like. Teaching us not to focus on or talk about the problem, but to call forth that which we desire, to call those things that be not as though they were."

"All right now, you're speaking the Word up in this place. Peace, be still," Pastor Landris said. He picked up the envelope off the bed and stood up. "Peace, be still." He kissed Johnnie Mae again. "Have I told you that I love you lately?" he asked.

She shook her head. "Not since"—she looked up at the ceiling as though the answer were written there—"six o'clock this morning." She glanced at her watch. "It's almost eleven now."

He bit down on his lips. "You'd better be glad I'm still on the clock. Otherwise—"

"Okay, Pastor. Let's keep it holy, now."

"Always," Pastor Landris said. "Always. Look, the bride of my affections, I have something I need to take care of." Pastor Landris waved in the air the envelope he'd received many years ago from Reverend Paul "Poppa" Knight with strict instruction to use if neces-sary. An envelope that contained enough information inside of it to totally shut Reverend Walker down, if he needed to. "Pray for me," Pastor Landris said.

"Let the Lord order your steps," Johnnie Mae said to the man she knew who, like David in the Bible, was a man after God's own heart, as he strolled out of the bedroom.

Pastor Landris turned back to look at her. "Always," he said, blowing her a kiss. "Always."

Chapter 59

And let us not be weary in well doing: for in due season we shall reap, if we faint not.

—Galatians 6:9

Angela and Gramps got Clarence to sign him out of the nursing home once more, the Saturday after their failed attempt to see Arletha on Thursday. Angela had tried calling Arletha on Friday to talk some sense into her. But Arletha was refusing to answer the phone—punishment to Angela for trying to carry out a stunt like bringing someone to her home when they hadn't fully discussed it first. Arletha had called Angela at home and left a message on her answering machine, letting her know that she had indeed heard her phone ringing and that she wasn't answering it on purpose.

Angela knew Arletha could be stubborn when she wanted to be. But she also knew she would never leave her *and* the children to stand outside and not open her door if the children were with her. So she decided to get Gramps, have him sit out in the car until she could talk to her grandmother, and she would work some plan to bring the two of them together, at least to talk.

Angela had Brent the Second stand where Arletha could see him and know she had the children with her. She rang the doorbell that she'd finally talked Arletha into having installed, since knocking wasn't always loud enough for her to hear when she was in certain rooms. After Angela rang the doorbell again, she peeked inside to make sure, if Arletha was spying her out, she would also see Shaun in her arms. Shaun had Arletha wrapped around his little finger. Shaun waved as his mother instructed him to do.

Arletha opened the door with a grin.

"I'm sorry. Okay?" Angela said. "I know how you are, and it was wrong of me to have tried bringing someone to your house to see you without us discussing it first or at least giving you more information."

"Hey, Great-granny," Brent the Second said. "Give me five."

Arletha gently slapped his awaiting palm with her hand. "All right!" they said in unison—something the two of them liked to do. She hugged him, then kissed him on his forehead.

"Hi there, Shaun," Arletha said. He immediately reached for her. "Look at you. You missed Great-grand, didn't you? Give me some sugar." She took him. He puckered up in an overexaggerated way and pressed his little lips hard against her cheek while the two of them made their usual "Mmmm-muh!" sound together.

"Grand, you're not going to speak to me?" Angela said.

"Did I not speak to you? Oh, I'm sorry," Arletha said, barely looking at her.

"I'm sorry. I don't know what else to say. I had good intentions," Angela said after she closed the door and began to trail behind Arletha, who was carrying Shaun and holding on to Brent the Second's hand as they headed for the kitchen.

"Who wants chocolate milk?" Arletha asked.

"Me," Brent the Second said, raising his hand in the air and waving it frantically.

"Grand, are you listening to me?" Angela said.

"Of course. You were wrong, and I agree." Arletha took down the plastic, cartoon-laced cups she'd bought especially for them. The one for Shaun had the extra piece to help him with learning to drink from a cup without spilling liquid everywhere. "You've been acting strangely these past two weeks. When I ask you what's going on, you don't want to tell me. Well, the other day, I didn't want you just stopping by and bringing someone, a surprise or not, to my home without me knowing what was going on. It's as simple as that."

"Okay, I was trying to surprise you. That backfired royally. I confess, I thought I was doing something that you would be happy about later, but clearly I miscalculated. I brought Ransom Perdue here. And I felt bad having that ninety-nine-year-old man standing out there while I beat on your door only for you to pretend you weren't in here."

"You had Ransom Perdue with you?" Arletha tilted her head slightly to the side. "He was here in Birmingham?"

"Yes."

"Well, why didn't you tell me that? Wasn't he an old friend of Mother's?" Arletha said, referring to her mother, Pearl. "She wrote something about him in that journal—" Arletha stopped for a second. "Is that why you wanted that journal? You were trying to locate him, and you did. Then you brought him by here, and I had the poor man standing outside. I'm so sorry," she said. "But you should have told me you were bringing an old friend of my mother's over here. I would have let you in even if I didn't want to be bothered with company. How old did you say he is? Ninety-nine?"

"In fact, he'll be turning one hundred on November fourth, with a birthday party being held for him by his family on November the seventh. He's invited all of us to come—me, Brent, the boys . . . and you. His whole family is going to be there," Angela said, trying to figure out how to go about this whole thing now. "It's going to be here in Birmingham . . . at my church."

"Oh, I don't really care about his family. But I still would have liked to have met him. So, he's in Birmingham. Well, maybe you can arrange to bring him over again one day soon."

"He's in my car right now."

"What?" Arletha said, shoving a hand in her waist. "You left a one-hundred-year-old man out in the car by himself? What are you thinking?"

"Grand, he's a grown man."

"Yeah, but you have to treat older people, especially when they get up to that age, like they're children. What if he has Alzheimer's and he's wandered off? You know his family will blame you. Go out there and get that man. And I pray that he's still out there, and that he's all right." Arletha started fanning herself with her hand. "Goodness gracious, you young folk just don't think things through. What on earth were you thinking? Leaving an elderly man that you hardly know out in a car by himself."

Angela smiled as she hurried outside to her car. "We're all set," she said to Gramps with a big grin when she reached him.

"So . . . what all did you tell her?"

"Just your name and that you were sitting out here in my car."

"All right. I'll take it from here." He stood up straight and started up the porch.

Chapter 60

And the people said unto Joshua, The Lord our
God will we serve, and his voice will we obey.

—Joshua 24:24

Sunday morning Gabrielle arose to heavy bass almost shaking her room with hardcore hip-hop music. She scrambled out of bed, threw on her robe, and ran to find the source of the sound.

"Hey, Cousin! What it is?" Jesse said as soon as she burst through the door of the room where he was staying.

"Turn that mess off!" she yelled.

"I'll turn it down," he said, pointing a remote control toward the massive stereo system with four-foot, black speakers flanking each side.

"Turn it off!" she yelled again. He complied. "What is wrong with you?" she asked in a quieter voice.

"I just bought it last night, and I was trying it out. My bad. I suppose I should have thought about what time it was. But when you've been out partying all night and you haven't slept and you're already up, I guess you don't think straight. I'll wait until everybody is up and try it out later."

She smelled bacon coming from the kitchen. She left Jesse and followed her nose.

"Good morning," Aunt Cee-Cee said. "I see you're up and at 'em bright and early."

"That's because Jesse thought it was a great idea to try to see if he can't demolish the house merely using sound waves. Didn't you just hear all that noise blasting?" Gabrielle said.

"Oh, Jesse just bought that thing last night. He didn't mean any harm. It's a three-thousand-dollar system, and he wanted to try it out to make sure everything is working right with it."

"Three thousand dollars?" Gabrielle said.

"Yeah."

"Did he buy the thing hot?" Gabrielle asked, trying to find out if it was stolen, thereby making him, and possibly her, an accessory to a crime.

"Heavens, no. Jesse knows I don't play that. Sure everybody likes buying something cheap, but karma will come back and bite you. You likely call it reaping what you sow. You buy something stolen, and someone will steal your stuff and sell it to someone else cheap. Trust me: that's not a great feeling at all. No, Jesse paid cold hard cash for that mammoth of a thing. I'll have to go see it, now that he's put it together."

"Wait a minute," Gabrielle held her hand up as she sat down at the kitchen table. "You're telling me that he actually had three thousand dollars, and *that's* what he chose to do with it? *That?*"

"Yeah," Aunt Cee-Cee said nonchalantly as she took out a large pan of golden-brown biscuits and placed the pan next to the stove without using anything to keep it from burning the counter.

"Will you please put that pan on that cooling plate so it won't scorch my counter," Gabrielle said, veering slightly from the subject at hand. Her aunt picked up the pan and placed it on the cooling apparatus. Gabrielle continued. "Back to Jesse and his stereo. You knew about this purchase prior to him making it?"

"Of course. Jesse tells me everything. He's been saving up for that stereo for a year now."

"I'm sorry," Gabrielle said, "but maybe I'm missing something somewhere. You all have been evicted out of your home and it's okay with you if Jesse throws three thousand dollars away on a stereo system that, by the way, he technically has nowhere to put or plug into, other than from the kindness and generosity of others."

Aunt Cee-Cee carefully poured the eighteen whipped-up eggs into the frying pan of bacon drippings. She turned to Gabrielle as she stirred the scrambled eggs in the pan to keep them from scorching. "I see nothing wrong with him taking his own money and using it for whatever he wants to. It's *his* money." She turned the eye off after the eggs were done and walked toward the entranceway. "Kids, breakfast is ready!" she yelled.

"I'm through now. You can use the kitchen if you want to fix your breakfast," Aunt Cee-Cee said. "But there are no more eggs, bacon, sausage, or biscuits left. There *is* a box of cereal still in the cabinet. None of us really like that kind, anyway. When you come home from church, can you stop and pick up a few more things for me?"

"What do you mean when I come home from church?" Gabrielle said. "I thought all of you were going to church with me today."

"Kids! Luke, Laura, Jesse, Angie! I'm not going to call you again! Your food's getting cold!" She turned back to Gabrielle. "We're not going to make it today.

As you know, Jesse and Luke went out last night, as did Laura. They all came back pretty early this morning. Had to wake me up, calling me on my prepaid phone, using up my minutes, since you won't give us a key to your house so we can come and go as we please. Of course, Angie has her children, and if I'd agreed to keep them, *she* would have been out."

"So, none of you are going to church today?"

"No, but I promise you that we're going to go next Sunday. You just need to remind us Saturday night so we'll be ready."

Gabrielle nodded slowly as she pressed her lips tightly. "Okay. Let me see if I can't put this in the best Christian way possible. Hold up, because I don't want to get it wrong." She got the Bible she kept in the kitchen and turned the pages. "Just so you won't accuse me of saying it wrong or being wrong, this is coming from Joshua 24:15. And it says, 'And if it seem evil unto you to serve the Lord, choose you this day whom ye will serve; whether the gods which your fathers served that were on the other side of the flood, or the gods of the Amorites, in whose land ye dwell: but as for me and my house, we will serve the Lord.' You can disregard the reference to the Euphrates, which is what the other side of the flood was. And you can disregard the allusion to the Amorites, which in this scripture was referring to the people who occupied the land where the children of Israel were at the time. But the part that says to choose you this day whom you will serve is relevant to our conversation, as is the part about 'as for me and my house.' You see, I realize you don't respect me, but this is still *my* house."

"That's all folks say Christians tend to do," Aunt Cee-Cee said. "They will take scripture out of the

Bible and just use them all Willy Neely however it suits their purpose at the time. If I can disregard the Amotites . . . Amorites or whatever you called them, and if I can overlook the reference to the flood, then I can disregard that statement about *my house*."

"Good try, but the 'my house' part stands. Because the Word of God is saying to me right now that anybody living in *my* house, whether invited or not, will be at church or will not be living here." Gabrielle folded her arms.

"I told you, Gabrielle. We'll go next Sunday. Aren't you supposed to be doing things to win us over to Christ? Aren't you supposed to be showing love and compassion and not attitude and threats? How are you supposed to get us to want to even visit your church if all we hear from you is you complaining about your stuff and things, and what we're using up, messing up, or eating up? God is still working on me. At least, He's gotten my attention, that's for sure. Now, you just need to be a bit more patient. Maybe you should pray for more patience while you're at church today."

"And maybe you should go to church today and pray for somewhere for you and your family to live," Gabrielle said. "Because come Saturday, all of you will be out of *this* house, or at least on your way out. I think that's being more than understanding and compassionate. Six more days; I'm giving you six more days to find another place to live. And if that doesn't work for you, then you're more than welcome to leave today."

Angie walked into the kitchen with all three of her children. "Ma, I don't feel good," she whined. "Can you keep the children for me today while I go back to bed?"

Aunt Cee-Cee went over and felt Angie's head.

"Well, at least you don't have a fever. I sure hope you're not getting that swine flu or H1N1, whatever they call it."

Angie handed her mother the baby and sat the other two at the table. She turned to leave, then turned back around. "Oh, Gabrielle. Some dude called you yesterday and some lady. The lady called twice, in fact. She said it was important. She said she'd left you a message already the second time, but she hadn't heard back from you yet."

"Did you happen to get their names?" Gabrielle said.

"I told you the last time that I don't have a pen and paper so I can't write anything down. Besides, I'm not your personal secretary. It's not my job to take messages. They ought to call back. That's what my friends do when they call. They call until they get me. I think the guy's name was Zebedee or Mallory, something like that."

"Zachary?" Gabrielle said.

"Yeah, that's it. Zachary. Come to think of it, I think he called twice, too. And the woman might have been the same one that called you the other day. Don't even try and ask me her name because I told her you weren't here. When she kept talking, she should have known I wasn't listening because I quickly clicked back to my call." Angie walked over to the stove and looked at the food. "Ma, can you fix me a plate and bring it up to me?"

"Sure, baby," Aunt Cee-Cee said, holding on to all three children.

"Oh, and Trey is coming over later so be sure and send him right up to my room when he gets here," Angie added.

"That's not going to happen," Gabrielle said.

"*Why* is she always tripping?!" Angie said about Gabrielle. "Will you *please* tell her that I'm grown, and she can't tell me what to do?" Angie said to her mother.

"Angie, I don't want your friends *at* my house or *in* my house. There will be no fornication or anything remotely resembling that going on, not up in here. So you need to call *Trey* back and tell him not to even bother coming to *this* address. Not *here*."

"I thought you were going to church anyway. You won't even be here for anything to bother you," Angie said.

The phone started ringing. Angie went to answer it. Gabrielle was closer and snatched it up before Angie got to it. She looked at Angie as though she was questioning her sanity for real this time.

"Hello, this is Jessica Noble. May I *please* speak with Gabrielle? *Please.*"

Gabrielle heard the panicked urgency in her voice. "This is she," Gabrielle said.

"Thank God you answered. I've been trying to call you for the last three days. I've left you several messages. The doctors have things set up for your blood test to see if you're a good match," Jessica said. "But we need to hurry. My daughter is getting worse with each passing day."

"Tell me when and where. Hold on; let me get something to write on." She pulled paper from a notepad held with a magnet on the side of her refrigerator. Jessica then gave her all the details she would need in order to go forward.

"I'm going to say a special prayer for her while I'm at church today. She's going to be all right. I just know she is. This is going to work. I believe that."

"Thank you. I certainly believe in the power of

prayer. And Gabrielle, thank you for everything you're doing. I know you aren't obligated to do any of this. And this definitely wasn't what you signed up for. I appreciate your heart when it comes to this."

"I choose to believe God has already worked this all out. We're just going to have to trust Him and move in the way He's directing us to go. That's all we can do."

When Gabrielle hung up, she looked at the digital clock on the stove. She only had an hour left to get ready and make it to church on time. *Where* did *the time go?*

Chapter 61

*And he said unto me, Son of man, can these
bones live? And I answered, O Lord God, thou
knowest.*

—Ezekiel 37:3

"How did it go?" Brent asked Angela after they
got the sleeping boys in the house. She was at
her grandmother's house for more than five hours.

"Okay. You should have been there."

"I wanted to be there. You told me you didn't think I
should go," Brent said.

"I know, I know. But how was I supposed to know
what would happen?"

"I'm all ears," Brent said as they sat down on the
couch. He shifted his body slightly to angle more toward her.

She grabbed his ears gently and tugged on them. "I
love your ears."

"Just tell me what happened. You're such a tease."

"No, I'm just in love with my wonderful, handsome
husband," Angela said.

"I think you need to stay on message," Brent said.

"Okay, okay." She told him how Arletha insisted she go and get Ransom from the car. "That was actually a relief because I didn't have to convince her to let him in. Gramps came in"—she giggled—"isn't it something that everybody already calls him Gramps and now it turns out he really is my great-gramps."

"So, Arletha and he agree that he's really her father?"

"Just let me tell this my way."

Brent picked up her feet, slipped off her flats, and began massaging her feet.

"See, now, you're wrong," Angela said. "You know how much I love when you do that."

He smiled. "Okay, so Ransom goes in the house, and then what?"

"Grand is playing with the boys in the kitchen. I walk inside just in front of Gramps. Grand is giving the boys a sandwich and she sees me walk in and she's about to ask if we'd like something to eat. When she sees Gramps, nothing comes out of her mouth. Dead silence. In fact, she's standing there with her mouth wide-open. Seeing her hit Gramps so hard, she and he both had to sit down. It was as if somebody had punched him in his stomach. He sat across from her and they literally stared at each other." Angela closed her eyes when Brent started rotating her toes. She rotated her head as though her head and toes were connected.

"Brent, I'm telling you," Angela continued with opened eyes, "I *thought* that they resembled each other. But when you have the two of them together in the same room, it's like their features are reflecting off of each other. And they have some identical mannerisms. Gramps didn't have to tell her why he was there. She knew who he was. Then he pulled out that photo of himself and handed it to her. She started crying when she realized that the man in the picture standing next to her mother was actually Ransom Perdue and not Samuel L. Williams, as she'd first believed as well. Maybe if she had stayed around instead of running away when she was sixteen, she might have figured out Samuel Williams wasn't her real daddy. Maybe Great-granny would have told her the truth. Who can say?"

"Wow, you're right. That must have been something to witness."

"And then Gramps told her how it might have happened that he was her father, not the man she'd grown up believing was. Gramps had been falsely imprisoned for ten years. When he was released, he came back to Asheville to find Sarah and his daughter. Now, here's where I possibly had some information that I hadn't even thought about that would affect Grand. I stopped Gramps's storytelling to inform Grand that Memory was the daughter he'd come back to find. 'Memory?' Grand said with this eerie, puzzled look on her face. He then told Grand how he'd finally gotten to meet this daughter only a few weeks ago, for the first time in her whole seventy-five years of life."

"So that means Arletha and this Memory person are half-sisters," Brent said.

"That's correct. I believe it was a woman named Memory who told my cousin Gayle . . . you remember Gayle? She came in early and helped out with our wedding. I think Memory told Gayle she'd met a woman named Arletha in Birmingham after Gayle mentioned she was searching for someone by that name."

"Wait, wait, wait," Brent said. "My head is swimming. You're going too fast."

"I thought you said I take too long to tell a story,"

Angela said, slipping her feet out of his lap and back onto the floor. She then grabbed his feet, pulled off his shoes, and began to return the favor.

"So what you're saying is that Arletha and Memory know each other," Brent said.

"Yeah, and it turns out to have been a *total* shock to Arletha's system. In fact, I thought she was going to pass out right there on the spot when she heard it. We had to move from the kitchen to the den because she needed to lie back on the couch a minute to get herself right."

"I bet."

"No, you don't know all of it. It turns out Arletha and Memory actually lived together for a while when Memory was hiding out, or something like that. Can you imagine learning that someone you thought was a stranger, and by some lining up of the stars, you had rented out a room in your house to her, turns out to be your half-sister? I can't imagine how Grand felt."

"Well, that means they already know each other, so that has to be a good thing. Right? Now Ransom will only have to tell Memory that Arletha is her sister," Brent said.

"You would think, right? Only, Grand admitted that she and Memory didn't part ways on the best of terms. In fact, I believe it was pretty bad, *pretty* bad."

"How bad? Did she say?"

"Bad enough that she drove the elderly woman to church—our church, in fact—and dropped her off at the front door, telling her not to ever darken her door again."

"Whoa, that's pretty rough."

"Yeah. Grand admitted as much. And now Gramps is planning on telling Memory about Arletha. I suggested he call Memory then, but Arletha thought not.

They're all going to be here for his birthday celebration. It should be an interesting birthday, that's for sure." She picked his feet up from her lap and placed them back on the floor.

"You're finished?" Brent asked with a frown.

"Yes, I'm finished. I was only planning to rub your feet for a little while."

"No, not 'are you finished rubbing my feet.' Are you finished with the story? You were talking about Ransom telling her how he happened to be her father. Remember?"

"Oh, yeah. I got a little off track when I was telling you about Memory and Arletha knowing each other. Okay, Gramps had returned home after being on a chain gang for ten years. When he got back, Pearl told him he needed to lay low because Sarah's half-brother, Heath, was still out to get him. Heath just happens to be the father of that monster I've told you about named Montgomery Powell the Second. You remember, I told you how he almost caused Pastor Landris to lose his religion; at least that's what Johnnie Mae told me since I wasn't there that time. When Montgomery raised his hand to her and was about to hit her."

Brent nodded. "Yeah, yeah, yeah. I remember you telling me about that."

"Anyway, Great-granny talked him into making a show of leaving town for anybody who knew he'd come back. Then he sneaked back in town and hid out with Great-granny, who told him about everything that had happened, which included facts that only three people knew at the time—that his daughter hadn't died, the way everybody had been led to believe. They faked her death, placed her with a woman named Mamie Patterson, and she was safe. But they didn't know whether Sarah was alive or dead. Not after Heath took over when her father died and had Sarah declared insane and put her away."

"Man, no wonder you were over there so long. This is like a soap opera or some kind of a miniseries."

"Oh, it was interesting, for sure. Gramps said he left at the end of April 1943. He had no doubt, sitting there looking in her face, that the child originally named Arletha Jane Black was his daughter. But he never knew Pearl was carrying his child. After he left, he didn't come back. And she had no way of getting in touch with him, even if she'd wanted to. Which, knowing her—for his safety—she wouldn't have done. Early on, he was never in one place long enough for anyone to get in touch with him."

"So he probably didn't know about the man Pearl married and who Arletha grew up believing was her father."

"Gramps gave his thoughts on that. He, Pearl, and Samuel Williams were all the best of friends. He believes when Great-granny learned she was pregnant, especially at her age, which was thirty-nine at the time, and especially since she didn't even believe she could carry another child . . . Okay, side note. It appears Great-granny had been married when she was twenty-two to a man who was extremely abusive. His last abusive act caused her to lose the baby she was carrying, and the injury sustained was said to prevent her from ever conceiving any children. Gramps believes Samuel, also Great-granny's friend, must have plotted with her to keep anyone from knowing who the real father was. He threw the out-of-wedlock pregnancy suspicions onto himself, then later married her to seal the deal. Knowing now that she could conceive children, she and Samuel had three together."

"And no one was ever the wiser," Brent said, yawning.

"You tired?"

He yawned again. "A little bit." He stretched.

"Well, let's see if we can't catch a little nap before the boys wake up."

He grabbed her and let her lay on his chest as he lay back on the couch.

"Brent," Angela said.

"Huh?"

"I love you."

He hugged her tightly. "I love you more."

Chapter 62

Recompense to no man evil for evil. Provide things honest in the sight of all men.

—Romans 12:17

"I'm sorry, Pastor Landris, but I don't show you as having an appointment, and Reverend Walker gave me strict instructions that he not be interrupted or disturbed," Mrs. Greer said as she stood in front of the door to physically keep Pastor Landris from going through it when she saw he was not going to stop from her verbal order.

"Well, Mrs. Greer, don't you worry. I will tell Reverend Walker that you more than gallantly carried out your orders. And that I pushed my way right past you." He gently touched her shoulder. She moved to the side. He opened the door and walked in.

"I'm sorry to just barge in like this," Pastor Landris said.

"I tried to stop him, Reverend Walker," Mrs. Greer said softly and rather unconvincingly.

Reverend Walker stood up. "It's fine, Sister Greer. It's fine." She left. "Pastor Landris, I didn't expect to see you again so soon. Had I known you would be coming back, I would have told Sister Greer that my 'do not disturb' instructions didn't apply to you." He bent his head toward Pastor Landris, then raised it back up. "Please, please, have a seat."

"That won't be necessary," Pastor Landris said. "I don't plan on staying long."

"So"—he clapped his hands—"you've reconsidered our offer? Is that why you're here?"

"No. Actually, I came by to bring you this." Pastor Landris softly laid the large white envelope he'd taken out of the safe onto Reverend Walker's desk.

"What is this?" Reverend Walker asked, picking it up and examining it closer.

"Something from your past you might recognize. Actually, it was something given to me from a mutual friend. Poppa Knight gave that to me before he passed on. He thought I should have it in case I ever needed it."

"I don't understand."

Pastor Landris sat down, since it was taking Reverend Walker so long to open it and look inside. He watched as Reverend Walker took out the papers and flipped through the stapled document.

"Where did you get this?" Anger surrounded Reverend Walker's voice.

"I told you: Poppa Knight."

"I don't believe you. How did you get something that isn't supposed to even exist anymore? How?"

"I told you: Poppa Knight gave it to me."

"Why would he give you something like this?" Reverend Walker shook his head as he scanned familiar pages and words telling of incidents he thought were long-ago buried with his friend and confidant, Paul "Poppa" Knight. "So what did he do, leave this for you after he died?"

"No, actually he asked me to come to his home and gave it to me back in 2004."

Reverend Walker put the information back inside of the envelope and dropped it with a thud onto his desk. "You actually expect me to believe you've had this all this time and you've never used it?"

"No offence, but I really don't care whether you believe it or not. The truth is he gave it to me, and I've had it for a little over five years now."

"Okay, so what do you want in return for this and your silence? You want me to let this deal drop you're being pressured into doing?"

"I've already weighed in on the fact that I'm not doing it, and all of your and Mister Threadgill's blackmail and bribery efforts mean nothing to me. No weapon formed against me will prosper. *No* weapon." Pastor Landris stood up. "I just came by to give you that. That's it." Pastor Landris started for the door.

Reverend Walked jumped to his feet. "Pastor Landris, do you honestly think I believe you're just bringing that to give to me and you don't want anything in return?"

"That package is yours to do with *as* and *however* you please." He nodded.

Reverend Walker laughed nervously. "Yeah. You probably have other copies just waiting to slam me with, the first chance you think I need to be taken down."

Pastor Landris turned and faced Reverend Walker. "There are no other copies. I've had that long enough to have used it had I wanted to do you harm. If I was ever going to use it for my benefit, it would be now that you and your thug buddies are trying to blackmail, bribe, or muscle me into something I've clearly said I'm not going to do. Waiting to take someone down the first chance you get is apparently something you think about. And that way of thinking says more about *you* than it does about *me*. Or maybe it *does* say more about me than it does about you. Who knows?"

"So what are you planning on doing now?" Reverend Walker said, taking a few more nonthreatening steps toward Pastor Landris.

"I plan to pray for you and hope that you repent, for one, and two, stop being so judgmental when it comes to others. What's inside that envelope makes it abundantly clear that you, of all people, should *never* criticize anyone who was once a sinner and is now trying to give service to the Lord. If what's reported in that envelope is anywhere close to being true—robbery, rape, possibly murder—you, Reverend Walker, have no place or room to speak against or judge anyone else about their past sins. I completely understand why everyone condemning the woman caught in the act of adultery walked away when Jesus said, 'He who is without sin, let him cast the first stone.' Everyone was likely thinking about their individual sins . . . some of which having dire consequences."

"So now you're being judgmental against me? You're doing to me what you claim I've done to others. You're trying to judge me. You're no better than I am," Reverend Walker said with a deep laugh and a bit of disgust.

Pastor Landris chuckled slightly. "You are right about one thing: I have no place to judge anyone, and I have not done that. I don't know what God will do in anyone's life that may later cause them to be the best advocate out there for the Kingdom. Peter denied

Jesus, and look what he did later in his life. Paul perse-
cuted Christians, and look what happened: two-thirds
of the New Testament was written by Paul or influ-
enced from the work he did for the Kingdom of God
after his conversion." Pastor Landris paused.

"I don't judge others mostly because I realize that
God is not through with any of us yet," Pastor Landris
continued. "None of us are perfect. But I am being *per-
fected* daily; therefore I forgive you even if you haven't
asked. And I don't need that envelope"—he nodded toward Reverend Walker's cluttered desk—"or what's in it
to fight my battle. I'll let God handle you, Mister
Threadgill, and anyone else who dares to unfairly and
unjustly come after or against me. Now, if you insist
upon going against God by coming after me when I'm
walking in His will, then the only thing I can do for
you is to pray that God will be merciful to you in His
vengeance on my behalf. But I refuse to render evil for
evil. Although—between me and you—I wouldn't
want to be in your shoes right about now for all the
money in the world."

"Pastor Landris . . ." Reverend Walker took a few
more steps toward him.

Pastor Landris nodded his good-bye and walked out
the door. He tipped his head toward the secretary who
sat smiling and typing away. "You have a blessed day,
now, Sister Greer, you hear," he said as he strolled past
her.

"Thank you. I will, Pastor Landris." She smiled. "I
most certainly will."

Chapter 63

*As snow in summer, and as rain in harvest, so
honor is not seemly for a fool.*

—Proverbs 26:1

Gabrielle came home after church to hustling and bustling as her uninvited houseguests were loading up their various vehicles with the things they had brought into her house a few days earlier. Aunt Cee-Cee was sitting on the couch in the den.

"My husband has found us another place to stay," Aunt Cee-Cee said. "Since you were adamant about him not staying here, he found a place where we can all live together. I suppose his timing was perfect, since you were insisting we get out anyway. I'm just glad we didn't waste the day going to church with you, although I still plan to visit your church someday. I'd like to see for myself what all the hoopla is about."

"I'm glad things worked out for all of you," Gabrielle said. "I really am."

Aunt Cee-Cee smiled at Gabrielle, which only made Gabrielle suspicious of where this conversation might be going. The aunt she knew would not be acting so calmly and agreeably after being asked to leave in the way she'd been that morning, a new place to live or not.

"Gabrielle," Aunt Cee-Cee said. "When we were moving to come here, I found this letter addressed to you. I'd forgotten about it, actually. You see, it came for you and I had mistakenly put it up, forgetting to give it to you. Then when I did remember, you'd already moved out of our house. I wanted to give it to you even though it is about nine years late being delivered and to apologize for the honest confusion." She handed Gabrielle a large white envelope.

It was from The Juilliard School of Dance dated the January she was set to graduate from high school. "Why is it opened?" Gabrielle said, noting the envelope's condition.

"Well, yeah. You see, when it first arrived, I did open it up to see what it was. After that, I put it up, and like I said, I didn't think about it anymore until after you'd left."

"But if it came while I was still living at your house, why didn't you give it to me then? It was clearly addressed to me. Not to the parents or guardian of Gabrielle Booker. It was addressed to me. Why didn't you give it to me in January when it first came?"

"Because you were giving me so much trouble and I was upset with you," Aunt Cee-Cee said in a huff.

"How was I giving you trouble?"

"Accusing my husband of trying to come on to you when clearly you were the one at fault, tempting him and everything."

"I never came on to him. He was the one coming into my bedroom. I told you about it and you did nothing. Then he did it again, and you still did nothing. The third time I came to you, hoping you would protect me, and instead you went to him, and he came and told me I had to be out of the only place I had to live after I graduated high school and turned eighteen. I turned eighteen May thirtieth."

Aunt Cee-Cee's nose flared slightly at Gabrielle's words. "See, that's exactly what I'm talking about. If you had kept more low-key around Dennis, then maybe he wouldn't have been at a weak moment and thereby tempted. What do you expect to happen with men when you're bouncing around all perky, laughing and giggling and being silly? It wasn't his fault."

Gabrielle nodded. "Okay. Blame the child for what some grown man did that was wrong and inappropriate. Aunt Cee-Cee, if I had walked around him half-naked, which I never did, he still shouldn't have ever acted that way with me. I was a child. And even if I had come on to him, which again I did not, he was the adult who was supposed to act like an adult and know better than to try to get with a minor. Forget the fact that I was under your guardianship and he was like a father figure to me. He was wrong, and you were wrong for upholding him and not protecting me."

Aunt Cee-Cee's eyes became slightly misty. "Maybe you're right. Maybe I didn't handle that situation quite the way I should have. And I hope you don't hold any of the past things that have happened against me."

Gabrielle's antennae immediately went up again. "So what are you *not* telling me?"

"What do you mean?"

"I think there's more to this story and this"—she shook the envelope—"that you haven't told me yet. We may as well get this all out in the open. Oh, I didn't tell you who I saw earlier this month, did I? You'll never guess, not in a million years. Guess who I saw that I haven't seen in ten years. Guess."

"Miss Crowe," Aunt Cee-Cee said.

Gabrielle pulled back, shocked Aunt Cee-Cee had actually guessed, and guessed correctly. "Now *how* in the world would you happen to know that?"

"Because I received a letter that I'm sure could have only been initiated by Esther Crowe. I thought the woman was dead, but I can see clearly that she's not."

"I'm listening," Gabrielle said. "I can tell this is going to be good."

Aunt Cee-Cee released a loud sigh, her shoulders heaving up, then down. "When you received that letter there"—she shook her head as she looked down at the envelope, then back at Gabrielle—"it indicated that your entire tuition had been paid in full. Well, when I knew you weren't going to attend their institution, it took some doing, but I was able to convince them to refund the money to you."

"How could you do that?"

Aunt Cee-Cee held her head up in defiance. "It took a little doing, I won't lie. After letting them know you wouldn't be able to attend, it helped that Miss Crowe had been in that accident, because even though she was the one who'd paid for everything, she wasn't easily accessible for them to get in touch with to return the money to her."

"What an awful thing to say. I don't understand you. I never have."

Aunt Cee-Cee shrugged. "If you walked in my shoes, maybe you would. But in any event, through a bit of manipulation and somewhat unscrupulous activities, I was able to get them to issue you a refund. And I suppose that would have been the end of things, except Miss Crowe is *not* dead, and apparently when you went to see her, she found out you never attended the school. When she, or whomever she got to do it, checked on the money she'd paid, they learned it had already been refunded. And I suppose their investigation led them back to you, which actually has led them back to me, since I was the one who signed your name on the refund check."

Gabrielle sat there speechless. She found it hard to believe what she was hearing.

"Well, say something. I deserve whatever horrible things you choose to say to me. Now, I'm sort of under investigation that might turn out to be criminally bad for me."

"Oh, you think?" Gabrielle said as she stood and began to pace like a caged lioness.

"I know I have no right to ask this, but will you please talk with Miss Crowe and get her to drop this? I'll pay back the money; somehow I'll find a way to get it and pay her back every dime plus interest. I just need you to reason with her. Let her know that I didn't mean to harm anyone. We just needed the money at the time. It's been hard. Trying to raise my own four children and then taking on you."

"Yeah, right. Me, the trouble-making child. Me, the child who brought in a monthly check to you without having much of it actually spent on me. Me, the child who was the maid of the family. And to think: you put me down, and then I grow up in life and people are *still* trying to put me down. But you know what, Aunt Cee-Cee, I forgive you. For all that you did to me as a child, for bringing down my self-esteem, for breaking my spirit, for treating me like I was nothing, for never showing me any love or respect, I forgive you. I forgive you, not to let you off any hook, but I forgive you so I can go on with my life without having to carry around the baggage of what you did or didn't do *to* or *for* me."

Aunt Cee-Cee smiled. "Thank you. Oh." She clapped

her hands together and looked upward. "Thank you so much, Gabrielle. I knew you would not hold any of this against me. And I promise you, I'm going to do better. Starting right now, I'm going to do better. And will you please tell Miss Crowe that I'm glad she's doing okay, and that she's not going to regret dropping this investigation against me."

Gabrielle tilted her head slightly. "I'm sorry. But I have no intentions of telling Miss Crowe anything."

"But I thought you said you forgive me."

"I do. But forgiveness doesn't mean you may not have to pay for your wrongdoing. It means I'm no longer your jailer trying to make sure you pay. Forgiveness doesn't mean you're going to get away with things you may have done. It just means the person who was wronged is no longer holding hate or malice in her heart against you," Gabrielle said. "In fact, I'm going to still pray for you. And I hope that no matter what happens, God will use it to help you come to Him and be drawn nearer to Him."

"So, you're not going to help me out of this?"

"No. After forgiving you, there's nothing more left for *me* to do."

"You can tell the authorities, or whoever asks, that you signed that check. Or if they ask you to testify that you didn't sign it, you can just refuse to say anything one way or the other. You could do *that*." Aunt Cee-Cee sighed. "Gabrielle, we're still family."

"You mean you want me to lie?" Gabrielle said with an exaggerated frown.

"See, that's why you used to get on my nerves. I tell you what, your day is coming. I remember hearing a preacher say once, when I went to church, that it rains on the just and the unjust. Gabrielle Booker . . . Gabrielle Mercedes . . . whatever you want to call yourself these days, you're going to get yours. Someday, you're going to get yours!"

"Aunt Cee-Cee, you are right. It does rain on the just and the unjust. Rain can be a good thing, which means good things come to bad people. And rain can be a bad thing, if you're flooded out, which means bad things can happen to good people. But the difference, when you give your heart and soul to the Lord, is that whatever is happening in your life—good or bad—you're not going through it alone. But I have a Savior, and His name is Jesus. And I would love for you to know Him the way that I do."

Aunt Cee-Cee stood up. "If you're not going to help me, then I don't want to hear this junk. I don't care about hearing anything about Jesus or your Lord and Savior. We need a thousand dollars in order to move into this place your uncle found for us. Can you loan me that so we can get out of here?"

Gabrielle laughed. "Whether I can or not, let me be honest with you. I'm not. And the reason is not because I'm mad at you, or I haven't forgiven you, or that I'm trying to make you pay for something from the past. It's not even because I know, like the money I've already loaned you, I'll probably never see it again. It's because God is not leading me to do any such thing. And not to sound insensitive, but if you really need money, I think you should talk to Jesse about taking that wonderful new stereo system he just bought back to the store for a refund. Then all of you need to pray to God for some wisdom, because some of the things you're repeatedly doing are never going to lead you back on the right track."

"All I asked you for was to borrow some money. If you're not going to do that, then frankly, you can keep your unsolicited advice to yourself." Aunt Cee-Cee started to walk away. "One day, when you need us, I can only hope that I treat you a lot better than you've treated us these past several days. Good-bye, Gabrielle. You won't have us to be kicking around any longer. Me and mine are out of *your* place. And just so you'll know: none of us liked being here anyway! It's too restrictive."

Gabrielle watched as they vacated her premises, thankful that only a few of her own possessions had managed to somehow make their way along with them.

Chapter 64

A word fitly spoken is like apples of gold in pictures of silver.

—Proverbs 25:11

After they were all gone, Gabrielle's doorbell rang. When she opened the door, Zachary stood before her.

"Hi," Zachary said.

"Hi."

"I'm sorry for coming by without calling first," he said. "I promise I won't stay long since you've made it abundantly clear that you want some space between us."

"It's okay, you can come in." Gabrielle opened the door so he could walk through. She closed the door and spun around to catch him looking around.

"It looks like a cyclone hit."

"Yeah, my houseguests just vacated the premises about an hour ago. My maid will be here later to clean up. You know I have my own personal maid, don't you?" she said, speaking of herself. "She's really good, too." She led Zachary to the kitchen. "I was about to make myself something to eat. I didn't eat breakfast before I left for church. Then I came home to total chaos, and now this German shepherd . . . this pit bull inside of my stomach is growling and letting me know I need to eat something."

"Would you like to go and get something? I haven't eaten yet myself. In fact, I wanted to ask you out to dinner today, but I realize something different is going on between us, and you likely would have said no," Zachary said. "I called you yesterday. Twice, in fact. You never returned either of my calls."

"Yeah. I just got the messages this morning. My cousin liked talking on my phone, but she didn't believe it was her job to take down or relay, in a timely manner, any messages from people who were calling for me on *my* phone. A phone that, incidentally, I rarely heard ring because she had her ear glued to it night and day."

"Oh, see. Now that's why people shouldn't jump to conclusions without getting the full facts first. I was thinking you hadn't called me back because you were letting me know you really weren't interested in anything more with me." Zachary stepped over to her and grabbed both of her hands. "Is there a chance we can move forward with *us?*"

"Zachary, I don't want to do anything to hurt you . . . ever. And I don't want anything from my past life to mess up your future life later on. It would kill me if, instead of being a blessing to you, I became a curse to both you and your career."

"Those sound like words straight from Leslie Morgan's lips. Gabrielle, I want you to know that I'm not giving up on us. You might think you're going to walk away from me, but I'm telling you: I'm not letting the best thing that ever happened to me—after being saved, of course—get away from me without a fight." Zachary pulled her over toward the kitchen table and, while still holding both her hands, he sat down, pulling her along with him.

"I have things in my own past that could hurt me. What am I supposed to do? Run away from myself? No, I realize that all of us have something we're not proud of or that we know was a mistake. We can't change our past, but the decisions we make now *will* impact our future. I am making the decision now to pursue you with every fiber in my body. Because years from now, I want my future to include you. I want us to be together . . . raising our own children to know and to love God just as much, if not more than, us. I want us to grow old together . . . more in love, even than we are now."

"You love me?" Gabrielle asked. She looked up, her eyes meeting his straight on.

He took a deep breath. "Gabrielle Mercedes, I love you so much that I can't even think about a world . . . my world without you in it. I love you so much that I'm here now letting you know I'm not planning on going anywhere. Even if you tell me you've made up your mind, I want you to know that you are worth fighting for and that if I go, I'm not going away easily. I don't care what you did in your past. I don't care that you clean or have cleaned other people's houses. I don't even care that you've had a child and that you gave her up for adoption. Honestly, I admire you even more for doing that. You were thinking about that little girl and her future. All of these things are part of your past. What I *do* care about is that I've found you now, and that you love the Lord. I want to live my present and plan a future with you. And even though you have offended me greatly—"

"How have I offended you?"

"By telling me I don't know what or who's best for me. Or that I apparently make really bad decisions."

"When did I do or say that?" Gabrielle asked with a frown.

"When you listened to my mother tell you that you should walk away from me, as though I don't know what's good for me. I found you, Gabrielle. Do you hear what I'm trying to tell you? I found *you*." He touched her face. "And Proverbs 18:22 says, 'Whoso findeth a wife findeth a good thing, and obtaineth favor of the Lord.' Gabrielle, I believe you are my wife. At least, that's the Word I hear from the Lord. We can play this courting game, but you and I both know there's something strong between us. I want God's favor in my life. And regardless of *your* past or *mine,* God has the final word. You want more time? Fine. I'm willing to step back and give you that time. But if you think I'm giving up on you completely or planning on not being there when you need or are looking for me, then you're sadly mistaken, sadly mistaken."

Gabrielle raised her hand slowly and touched the left side of his face. "I'd be a fool to walk away from you. And I've already done enough foolish things in my life. I want to walk in the steps just as God is ordaining them for me."

"So what's your heart telling you, Gabrielle? What do you hear the Holy Spirit saying to you right now?"

"To not let the devil talk me into walking away from the gift God has prepared for me. I'm hearing God say to let His Word be true and to let every word contrary to God's Word be a lie. My past *is* my past. And your past is your past. But God doesn't deal in time the way we do. And all that counts to Him is now. I hear God saying, faith is now."

"Girl, you'd better stop this." Zachary grinned. "Or else you're going to cause me to get down on one knee right here, right now, and ask you for your hand in marriage."

Gabrielle laughed. "Zachary, we'll proceed with our courtship as we originally agreed. I really do want to get to know you better. The *you* that's inside of *here*." She placed her hand lovingly on his chest. "I can't say whether later you and I will agree that we're really supposed to be together. But I'm going to trust God. I trust God, therefore I can trust Him to take care of whatever comes my way. And that includes the good and the bad. And speaking of good and bad, I'm scheduled to take a blood test to see if I'm a good match for my . . . for the little girl I gave up for adoption."

"When are you scheduled to do that?"

"I'm calling tomorrow to set up a time. We're doing things in a more secretive way. You know, because of the unique nature surrounding all of this. They won't use my name, just assign me a special number. We're trying to respect the adoption process we agreed on. I just pray I'm a match, because I want to do whatever I can to help her."

"Well, there are generally six HLA markers. . . ." Zachary noticed the frown come across her face when he said HLA. "HLA is histocompatability antigens. They will take your blood and hers to compare HLA markers. That's how they determine how great of a match you are. The more markers that match, the more likely the transplanted bone marrow will take without causing a severe immune reaction. When people want to be donors, they generally do a cheek swab initially to work up the numbers, then they perform a more in-depth blood test to match markers. Since they know you're her birth mother and that you likely have *some* matches, they don't need to do a swab. That's why you're doing the blood test at this point."

"Plus, her mother said, they're running out of time." Gabrielle wiped away a tear from her eye. "I just want her to be all right. That's all I want. And whatever I have to do to help her, I'm going to do it."

"And if it turns out you're not a good match?" Zachary said. "What are you prepared to do then?"

"What do you mean?"

"I mean, if you're not a match, are you going to talk to her birth father to see if he's willing to step up? Although, in truth, a sibling is generally an even greater match for other siblings. If he has other children, it's possible one of them may be a match, even a perfect match, if neither of you are."

"Well, I'm not going to ask for any more trouble than one day brings to me. One day at a time. And today, all that is before me is *me* being a match. I pray so much that I am. And if I am, I'll gladly give the bone marrow without deliberation or hesitation. She'll get well, and things will go back to normal. She'll grow up in her loving home, I'll keep working at improving my life, and everything will be right with the world again." Gabrielle made a face as though she knew in her heart this was a lot to hope for.

"Well, let's pray," Zachary said. He held her hands as he prayed for the health of the little girl in need of a bone marrow transplant as well as the many others they didn't know by name. He prayed for his aunt Esther, his family, Gabrielle's family, and for peace and joy to multiply between the two of them and all those they cared about. He prayed for Pastor Landris, his family, their church family, and all elected officials.

"Now," he said after he finished his prayer, "how about some dinner?"

"Can I have a rain check?" she said. "You saw this house when you came in. It's going to take me the rest of the day, and then some, just to get it straight. I really don't understand how folks can not respect other people's property that they work so hard to get. I'm not worshipping my things, mind you. But I thank God for what I have, and I appreciate what He's blessed me with. I want to be a good steward of what God has placed in my care." She shook her head. "I just don't get it."

"I'll tell you what. I'll go and pick us up something to eat. Then I'll help you clean up."

"Careful there, Doctor Z. It looks like I may have already become a bad influence on you."

"What? You think I don't know how to clean a house? I know how to clean. I'm not above getting down and dirty. You show me to your mop, and it's going to be on." He grinned.

Gabrielle started laughing. "See, that proves you're a fake. Who even uses a mop anymore?"

"Oops, my bad," he said with a laugh. "So, are we back? Are you and I back together again?" He held out his hand as one waiting for another to give him five or accept an invitation for the next dance.

"We're back," she said, quietly slapping her hand into his.

He held on to her hand, then carefully . . . and lovingly . . . brought it up to his mouth and placed a soft and gentle kiss on it. Then quietly, he exhaled.

Chapter 65

If a man beget a hundred children, and live many years, so that the days of his years be many, and his soul be not filled with good, and also that he have no burial; I say, that an untimely birth is better than he.

—Ecclesiastes 6:3

Ransom Perdue was officially turning one hundred years old on Wednesday, November the fourth. Memory flew in from Asheville, North Carolina, on Tuesday so she would be in town for his actual birthday. The rest of Memory's family would be arriving on Saturday, as was most of the family coming in for the party. Her being there alone worked out well because Memory was able to spend time with her father and sister Zenobia. Zenobia had called Memory shortly after her father told her about yet another sister. Only this daughter he'd never even known existed.

"Are there any *more* sisters or brothers we need to know about?" Zenobia had asked her father when he'd informed her about Arletha. She hadn't been teasing, either, when she'd asked.

"None that I know of," Gramps had said. "But then again, I was a little floored myself when I learned about Arletha."

Memory had not been prepared to hear her newly discovered father tell her of his latest birth announcement. She knew he had two other children besides Zenobia from his only marriage. Zenobia had been excited about having a new sister, an older sister at that. Although, she had confessed to her sister, she would have liked it more had they grown up together. So when Zenobia had called and told Memory that their father wanted to talk to her about something, the last thing she expected to hear was that he'd just learned he'd fathered yet *another* child, another daughter, who it turns out was younger than Memory, yet older than his other children.

Memory couldn't help but wonder why something like this would come out now. Most folks come forward when a person dies and they feel there's an inheritance to be claimed. Maybe this was yet a ploy constructed by Montgomery Powell the Second in his attempt to try to take some of Sarah's properties away from her. Maybe Montgomery had learned that Ransom Perdue was alive and that she and he had connected after all these years. Maybe he was setting Ransom up to ask for something to give to this daughter . . . something Montgomery wanted to get *his* hands on. It wouldn't be beneath him to use a real or even fictitious sibling or family member to get what he wanted.

Of course, Memory didn't share her initial thoughts with her father. She just listened and let him tell her his version of things. How he hadn't known the child even existed, as though it was important that Memory understand he *was* never, and never *would have been,* a deadbeat father—ever. In her case, she understood that none of the things that happened was his fault. With this new daughter, he started out by letting Memory know that he'd never even been told she existed. And his finding out now was totally an act of God, revealing the truth no matter how long it may have been coming.

He told Memory how he'd met her and been convinced beyond any doubt that she was indeed his child—no DNA test would be necessary. In truth, it would have been an insult to both of them had either one requested one be performed.

Memory told her father she looked forward to meeting this new sister at his birthday celebration, along with her other two brothers she had yet to meet.

"Well, here's the funny thing," Gramps said. "From all she done told me since we talked, you and she have already met. She said you two already know each other."

Memory was puzzled about that. She thought about her various travels around the country when she was running from her shady life's dealings before she put away childish things and got her life together by giving her life to the Lord. Was this someone she had crossed or wronged in her life? Was her sister someone she would have to ask for forgiveness for something she'd done? And if so, would her sister forgive her?

"Who is she? What's her name?" Memory asked.

"Arletha Black. That was her birth name. She said you knew her as Arletha Brown. Says the two of you actually lived together for a spell when you lived here in Birmingham. Small world, ain't it?" He chuckled.

Memory tried to laugh back, but she couldn't. "Arletha Brown? My sister is Arletha Brown? Are you sure this isn't some trick? Because I hope you know that Montgomery Powell and his crew will stop at nothing to try to bring us down."

"Memory, there is no doubt that Arletha is my daughter. The truth is the light. And the truth always comes to light. No matter how well folks think a thing is hidden, the truth is gonna make its way to the light one way or another. Arletha is mine, just like you're mine, and Zenobia is mine. You're all sisters, all of you. You and Arletha are sisters just like you and Zenobia are. You had no problem accepting Zenobia, nor she with you. Now, when you come for my birthday, I'll get to introduce the two of you as blood."

When Memory hung up, she stared at the phone. She thought about how Arletha had treated her when she'd stayed with her. How she had been so judgmental. How she had threatened to turn her in to some guy who was looking for her. How she'd taken her to the church—Followers of Jesus Faith Worship Center, in fact—and dumped her off at the front door without even a second thought, merely because she was trying to live right and Arletha disagreed with her choice of churches.

That Arletha was now her sister!

Chapter 66

But the mercy of the Lord is from everlasting to everlasting upon them that fear him, and his righteousness unto children's children.

—Psalm 103:17

Ransom Perdue was celebrating his one hundredth birthday with almost as much fanfare as he'd had the previous year. The year when a few newspapers and media outlets interviewed him as he stood in a long line to cast his vote for the first African-American president of the United States of America back on November 4, 2008—a day he never thought he would live to see. But he did, and he had.

There was a small write-up about his birthday in the major newspaper as well as a major spread in *The Birmingham Times*—the largest black newspaper in the Southeast. Zenobia had shown the clippings to him and told him of her plans to have them matted and framed. Gramps just laughed at all the hoopla they were going through over him.

"All I've done is lived. It hasn't always been easy, but I woke up every day not knowing what that day held, but open to whatever God allowed to happen. Some of it was good; some was not so good. But through it all, God has been faithful, and He's brought me from a mighty long way," Gramps said. "I know, no doubt, how I got over."

Melissa Peeples had done a spectacular job. She and her husband were there with their three children, which included her husband's oldest daughter, Aaliyah. Marcus Peeples just beamed when he saw how his wife had pulled everything together, transforming, yet again, the church's banquet hall into a place of dreams. There was sheer white chiffon material decorating the ceiling with shimmers of silver and the most calming sea of blue. How Melissa could envision things like this and bring them into a manifested state always left Marcus in sheer awe. He walked around with his chest stuck out as he watched every person who came in the door gaze upward and then spin around joyfully, trying, with fail, to take in every beautiful thing.

There was a long table up front for the immediate family. Memory had yet to speak to Arletha. It hadn't been from a lack of trying. Memory had gotten Arletha's phone number from Zenobia when she'd called and put her father on the phone as he broke the news of Arletha's new family line.

Memory couldn't bring herself to call Arletha during those first few days. She was still trying to process it. And when she did finally decide to call, the phone merely rang. She then thought she'd do the right thing and leave a message on Arletha's answering machine. When she lived with Arletha, she didn't have an answering machine, but she thought surely after all this time Arletha would have gotten one by now. She knew Arletha didn't like talking on the phone. In fact, Arletha seemed to like people even less than Memory did. When Memory first met Arletha and decided to rent a room from her, Arletha being antisocial and anti-friendly had worked to be a perfect cover for her.

But Memory had changed. She was hoping now that she and Arletha were more than just two people whose paths happened to have crossed (unpleasantly at several points in their time together), that Arletha was no longer the same person she'd known previously. Memory just couldn't see anything that would ever cause Arletha to change.

And there was her dilemma in trying to connect with Arletha in earnest. Still, she was determined to try . . . for her father's sake, she would try. She would put aside her own feelings and differences with Arletha, smile, and make it work for whatever encounter they might have, especially during their father's birthday celebration.

So when Memory and Arletha came face-to-face in the banquet hall, Memory braced herself for some type of backhanded insult. Words that would prove how much holier and better Arletha was than anyone else, especially a wretched soul like Memory.

"Memory," Arletha said, walking toward her former house tenant.

"Arletha," Memory said with a smile.

Arletha walked right up to Memory and hugged her. Memory was taken back. "God is so good," Arletha said. She looked Memory up and down. "You look wonderful." She hugged Memory again. "I'm so happy to see you again."

The hug felt genuine. Memory was a little off balanced now. She hadn't expected what appeared to be a sincere greeting.

"Listen," Arletha said. "There's something I need to say to you. Something I should have said to you a long time ago. Something past time should have been done."

Memory dropped her smile. She knew what likely was next. *Judgment. Correction. Rebuke.* "Okay." She steadied herself for Arletha's verbal attack.

"I'm sorry," Arletha said. "I was wrong. I have asked God to forgive me for the way I was toward you and so many. I thought I was *so* saved because I thought I *lived* so right and that I *did* everything so right. But I was lacking what I really needed: a true relationship with God, and love for others. What I did to you was wrong, and there's no excuse or explaining it away. And I'm not just *saying* this to you. I've learned even more, how life can change just overnight. One minute, we just happen to know each other from a brief moment in time. The next minute, we learn that we're real sisters. I'm saying this because I truly mean it. I only pray that you'll accept my apology. Please forgive me."

Memory looked at her, and before she knew anything or could stop herself, she found herself crying and tightly embracing Arletha. "Of course I forgive you. And I love you. I don't know what has happened, but it appears God has touched both of our hearts. Neither of us are the same as when we first met. It's never too late with God. He's God!"

"Ooh, Sister. Now, don't be starting nothing up in here!" Arletha said. "You're going to make me come out of these cute little J.Reneé shoes my granddaughter bought me. That child just fusses over me, I tell you what. She took me on vacation last week. Said she wanted to do something special for me. We had the nicest time on a seven-day cruise. I was a little concerned about the weather and all that water, but it was great."

"That must have been where you were when I tried to call you," Memory said.

"You called me? My granddaughter's been trying to get me to get voice mail. She even gave me an answering machine. I told her if I ain't there, whoever wants me can call back until they get me. I don't have time for all these newfangled contraptions. They're just a burden with unnecessary stress. If you call me and I'm on the phone, you'll get a busy signal. If you want to talk to me, then call me until I answer. Getting me is on you."

"You keep talking about a granddaughter."

"*I* have a granddaughter. And that girl is just like me: stubborn to a fault, although I like to call what we do persevering. She was determined to make me admit that I was actually her grandmother. Well, I was, but I was still trying to run away from my life."

"Like me," Memory said.

"You know, you're right. Just like you. I guess that proves we really are sisters." Arletha laughed.

"So what's your granddaughter's name?"

"Angela Gabriel Underwood," Arletha said. "In fact, it was she who figured out that Ransom Perdue was my father. It's certainly been a toll on my heart these last few years. First a granddaughter finds me, now my father. A lot of changes going on. A lot."

"Well, you know what they say: the only thing we can count on is change."

"That's for sure," Arletha said. "And I'm learning that all change ain't bad."

Gramps strutted up in his black tux, white shirt with matching cane and top hat. "Ain't this here a beautiful sight for these eyes. I'm glad to see you two getting along so wonderfully. Will y'all look at this place? Ooh-wee, this sure does look good! Make an old man feel like a million bucks. Feel like maybe my living really ain't been in vain."

"Hey, Gramps," Clarence said, weaving his way to give his grandfather a hug.

"That's one of those bear hugs there," Gramps said, patting him on the back.

"Yeah. It's about to get started. I have to get ready. But I wanted to come and give you a hug before everything really gets crazy around here and I really *can't* get to you."

"I haven't seen your daddy. Is he still gonna be here?" Gramps asked Clarence. "Your mama said she invited him. I told her it didn't bother me, but I ain't seen him yet. Of course, we know how he loves to make an entrance whenever he comes into a place. Always the showman. But you know how I like being, and for things to start, on time."

"I know how you are about time," Clarence said. He touched the pocket watch his grandfather had given him a few months ago. "And no, my father's not going to be here after all. You know . . . not after everything that happened yesterday."

"What happened yesterday?"

"Maybe I should tell you later," Clarence said. "I don't want to ruin your party."

"Whatever you got to tell me about your daddy, I promise you, it ain't gonna affect my celebratory mood in the least. So, what happened with your daddy?"

Clarence wanted to kick himself for having brought

it up. He just thought his grandfather had heard. "He's been arrested. Something to do with an elected official and some bribery scheme they were cooking up. He's in some hot water, for sure. One of the men involved tried to implicate Pastor Landris, but Pastor Landris came right out and told the truth about what he knew. The church secretary backed up Pastor Landris's story. Daddy then stepped it up and confessed that Pastor Landris really had nothing to do with it. I don't know what's going to happen now. But you know Isis is a lawyer, and she's good. If anybody can get him out of the mess he's apparently in, my brother's wife can."

"Well, he'd better be talking to the Lord and asking for His help. 'Cause folks is going to prison left and right these days. I keep telling folks they need to do right. They get in these positions and get greedy. God has a way of bringing you down to earth in a hurry. You know if God kicked Satan out of Heaven, these mortal folks here better stop trying to play God like He don't mean what He say about wolves in sheep's clothing."

"Okay, Gramps." Clarence smiled. "I'm leaving. Got something special for you."

"Just having my family all here is special enough. God has truly blessed me."

The celebration began fifteen minutes later. There were more than two hundred fifty people there. Various folks spoke, no more than two minutes each, about Gramps and how he'd impacted their lives. Several times Gramps blurted out, "That's right, y'all, give me my flowers while I can smell 'em. Whatever you got to say to me, say it while I can hear you." Gramps had everyone laughing.

Pastor Landris was asked to speak words of inspiration for about ten minutes. He stood, promising not to be long but desiring to carry out the family's desires.

"Briefly, I'd like to speak to you from John the first chapter beginning at the third through the fifth verse. 'All things were made by him; and without him was not any thing made that was made. In him was life; and the life was the light of men. And the light shineth in darkness; and the darkness comprehended it not.' Tonight, we have assembled here to celebrate Mister Ransom Perdue's one hundredth birthday. And I'm sure if you were to ask Mister Perdue, he would be the first to tell you that every day has not been easy. He would likely tell you that there were days when he wanted to throw in the towel and just walk away. But he didn't. And tonight, he's surrounded by a family that loves and appreciates him greatly." Pastor Landris stood behind the lectern at the family table.

"In the scripture I just read, it talks about how all things were made by God. In the scriptures that precede this, it talks on how in the beginning was the Word. And the Word was with God. And the Word was God. The word *Word* is capitalized in that first scripture because this Word is what we call a proper noun. You see *this* Word, which is logos, became flesh. And *most* of us know Him as Jesus. I say most, because I realize not everybody *knows* Jesus. Oh, some know *about* Jesus. Some of you may have heard others speak *of* Jesus or *on* Jesus. But you see, there is a *difference* in your life when you have met Jesus . . . had an encounter with Him. I'm talking about when you *really* know Jesus.

"If you don't believe what I'm saying, then ask Saul who, after meeting Jesus on the road to Damascus, later became a truly changed man named Paul. You see, there is a difference in knowing *of* someone, *about* someone, and in knowing *them*, which can only come from a one-on-one relationship *with* them. I'm talking about spending time getting to know them."

"Amen," people were saying at various intervals.

"I want to encourage you not to just say you know Jesus as you still walk around in darkness," Pastor Landris continued. "I've said this before, and I'll say it again tonight. Light and darkness cannot occupy the same place at the same time. If there is light, then there can be no darkness. Jesus is the true Light. You've heard people say, 'The truth is the light.' But let me tell you that in the fourteenth chapter of John in the sixth verse, Jesus declared, 'I am the way, the truth, and the life.' From this scripture, we can see that Jesus, Who is the truth, exhibits the ultimate characterization of the Truth is the Light. If you have ever had a conversation with Mister Perdue, he will boldly tell you that he never could or would have made it if it had not been for the Lord on His side.

"When men wanted to take him out, the Lord sent angels to make a way of escape for him. That's what God will do for you. It's a great accomplishment to reach the age Mister Perdue has reached. And I just want to go on record, Brother Perdue, by saying that according to the scriptures we're looking for another twenty more years out of you."

The audience laughed as folks looked from one to the other, nodding.

"Don't laugh. The scriptures tell us we can have between seventy and one hundred twenty years. I'd like to conclude with Psalm 103, verses one through five. 'Bless the Lord, O my soul: and all that is within me, bless his holy name. Bless the Lord, O my soul, and forget not all his benefits: who forgiveth all thine iniquities, who healeth all thy diseases; who redeemeth thy life from destruction; who crowneth thee with loving-kindness and tender mercies; who satisfieth thy mouth with good things; so that thy youth is renewed like the eagle's.' Thy youth is renewed. Thy *youth* is renewed like the eagle's." Pastor Landris smiled and shook his head.

"We all need to bless the Lord. We all need to stand on His Word. And when you gaze upon this blessed man of God"—Pastor Landris pointed his hand toward Gramps—"I want you to see for yourself that when God says something and you believe it, and you act on it, then it *will* come to pass. It may not come when or how you wanted it, but it *will* come. Mister Perdue told me he has stood on these words in Psalm 103. And just look how far God has brought him. We have not, because we ask not." Pastor Landris nodded.

"It's like ABCDEFG," Pastor Landris said. "Ask, Believe, Confess, Do, Expect, and have Faith. Then after it has manifested, you can go to G: Give thanks unto the Lord, for He is good and His mercy endures forever. And I suppose that now brings me to the letter H. Happy birthday, Ransom Perdue. And may you have many, many more. Thank you." Pastor Landris took his seat to a generous applause.

Clarence stepped onto the stage that had been prepared so everyone would be able to see no matter where they were sitting. Gabrielle stood there frozen—like a statue, in a position with her hands raised toward Heaven. She was wearing a blue chiffon dance outfit that matched the décor of the room. The music began to play. Most there knew the song from the first few beats of hearing it. Marvin Sapp's "Never Would Have Made It."

Clarence sang his heart out, and Gabrielle danced (despite knowing now that she wasn't a perfect bone marrow match for the eight-year-old little girl) as though she'd grown wings. The two, whom most would have written off as the chief sinners among them all, brought that whole hall of more than two hundred fifty people to their feet in a thunderous, glorious praise to the Lord. They truly blessed God and blessed the people with the gift God had blessed them with.

After they finished, Pastor Landris was asked by Gramps to extend an invitation for anyone who was there who might desire to be saved or rededicate their lives to God.

"Come if you'd like to make Jesus the Lord of your life," Pastor Landris said. "All you have to do is come forward, confess your sins by saying, 'Lord, I'm a sinner.' That's it. You don't have to run down every sin you've ever committed. Just say, 'I'm a sinner.' Tell God that you believe Jesus died on the cross for your sins and that God raised Him from the dead. Ask Jesus to come into your heart. And according to the Bible, you shall be saved. Anyone who desires to come, please come now. Won't you come?"

Gramps stood to his feet and began to sing, "Never would've made it." One person got up and came forward, then another, and another. And by the time he finished singing, eighteen people from his family, including a son, Andrew, and Arletha had come forth.

Gramps wiped tears from his eyes as he said, "I couldn't have asked for a better gift than knowing some of you who came forward today are going to meet me on the other side. When this is all over with on *this* side, I want all of you here tonight to meet me in Heaven, where we'll see Jesus . . . face-to-face. I thank You, Lord. For You have been good to me. You've brought me from a mighty long way, a mighty long way. And I never could have made it had it not been for You. You." He pointed upward. "You, Lord. I thank

You. Come on, everybody. I've got my ticket." He waved his hand.

People came and hugged Gramps. He continued to praise God as he wept. "God is good. Ain't He good?" he said as he hugged each person. He then hugged each of his children, which now included Memory and Arletha. "Oh, yes! God is *good!*" he said.

Don't miss the newest novel in Vanessa Griggs's
Blessed Trinity series

The Other Side of Divine

In stores August 2013

Prologue

And take the helmet of salvation, and the sword of the Spirit, which is the word of God.

—Ephesians 6:17

When I tell you how beautiful, you're not going to believe *just* how much so. In fact, beautiful doesn't even *begin* to describe it or give it justice.

I'm sorry. Please forgive me. I'm getting ahead of myself here. I hate when someone starts in the middle of a conversation as though you've taken part in what was apparently going on in their heads before they began to speak and you have no *earthly* idea *what* they're jabbering on and on about.

To those who don't know me, my name is Esther Crowe. Those who know and love me best call me Esther, Aunt Esther, or Miss Crowe. A few folks even call me Zion from my days when I had a dance group called the Daughters of Zion many forgotten years ago. The miss part of Miss Crowe is actually a *miss* statement. There I go again: my attempt at a little humor and playing on words. I love words. For anyone who may have missed it, I was playing on the word *mis-statement*.

I was born Esther Morgan, no middle name. I married into the last name of Crowe. My husband died young (much too young) early into our marriage, from complications of an illness called lupus, to be exact. I don't like talking much about it. Suffice it to say, I never remarried; I never got around to finding anyone special enough to fill his space.

Then there was that terrible automobile accident that pretty near claimed my life here on earth. I was spared, although barely. For ten years, it was as if I didn't really exist. But then my nephew, Dr. Zachary Wayne Morgan, stepped into that Chicago nursing facility, bringing with him someone near and dear to my heart: my dear, sweet Gabrielle Mercedes Booker all the way from Birmingham, Alabama and all grown up now.

Gabrielle dropped the last name of Booker and goes by Gabrielle Mercedes. That poor child has indeed lived a hard life. That wretched woman who was given charge over the almost four-year-old at the time was actually the cause of Gabrielle (eight years old when I first met her) and I becoming acquainted. I was out in the community on a summer jog and Aunt Cee-Cee (Mrs. Cecelia Murphy) was out there treating that sweet child like she thought her name was Cinderella (before the glass slippers). I laugh sometimes because Gabrielle has told me on more than one occasion that I was like her very own fairy godmother.

I suppose it's true what some folks say: What Satan meant for bad, God will use it for good.

I figured out a way to get that precious little girl some joy into her life while she endured being treated even worse than a redheaded stepchild. At least I'd like to believe I brought some good into that child's life. But Gabrielle could dance, oh my *goodness*, she could dance! The first time my eyes fell on her running around picking up after those four other children like she was their hired help, I saw the greatness in her. I often described her movements as like the seeds on the feathers of dandelions being carried in the wind: Graceful with a capital *G*. I saw the greatness in her future.

Gabrielle's aunt Cee-Cee tried to say I believed Gabrielle was the child I never had. She even said jokingly (or so she claimed after she didn't get the response she'd apparently hoped for) that I could have Gabrielle outright, for the right price, of course. If I could have gotten Gabrielle without the insult of seeming to buy her, I would have taken that child in a heartbeat, in a *heartbeat*. After I learned how badly Aunt Cee-Cee had done Gabrielle after my automobile accident—taking the money I'd paid for Gabrielle to attend Juilliard, then throwing her out on the streets with nowhere to go . . .

I don't even like thinking about that. Why couldn't I have been here? I wanted so much to see the look on her face when she received the information about Juilliard. But to think: That wretched woman took that money, stole it is what she did. . . . Well, needless to say, Cecelia Murphy's day of reckoning is coming. And you can believe *that*. Those that live by the sword shall die by the sword.

I didn't think of Gabrielle as the child I never had. What folks have to understand is none of us *truly* own anything or anybody here on earth. Everything belongs to God. Psalm 24:1 provides the title and the deed. "The earth is the Lord's, and the fullness thereof; the world, and they that dwell therein." My father used to say, "If folks think they own it, then let them die and see just what they *really* own. You brought nothing into this world and for certain, you'll take nothing when you leave, not even these earth suits we fondly call our bodies."

I miss my father. Our parents taught us that if we saw someone in need, especially a child, we should try to do what we could to help. That's how things were back in my day. Yeah, I'm close to sixty years old, short by almost two years. Nowadays, if you say something to a child, not only might the child cuss you out, but nine times out of ten, when the parents find out, one or both of them will hunt you down and cuss you out.

Yes, I meant cuss and not curse. Having been a schoolteacher, I know the difference between the two words. Cussing is a whole other word and a whole other level than cursing. High-society folks, who make their subjects and verbs agree, curse. Folks who want to get you good and told cuss.

But back to what I was saying. I don't want to get off on that because that's a whole story in itself. I was in this horrific automobile accident. Everybody, including me, believed my life as I'd known it was over. Then Gabrielle stepped into my room and danced me back on my journey to recovery. There was such an anointing in my room that day, oh my goodness! I felt the glory of the Lord sitting . . . the weight of His glory on me. There's nothing like the glory of God to lift you up.

Yes, God raised me right up off of that sick bed. I heard Him speak to me just as clear as you hear me speaking now. "There is more that I require of thee. Get up, Esther! There's too much still left for you to do."

So I girded myself up. I began putting on the whole armor of God. I held up my sword, I'm talking about the Word of God, and I was ready to get back on the battlefield.

If God has ever told you to do anything, please know that God equips those He calls. He raised me up off that deathbed, and in a little less than a year's time, my speech has become ninety-five percent clear again. My dance returned, not so much in my legs and feet as in my heart. There's something glorious to be said about dancing from the heart.

People come up and say, "Esther, how are you doing?" And I say, "I'm still kicking, just not as high."

After God got me back on my feet, He told me I had to go help Gabrielle one more time. That there was a huge battle coming, and I needed to be there to assist. All I needed was one Word from the Lord. Over the objections of my family (mostly from my sister-in-law Leslie Morgan, also Zachary's mother), I packed my bags and told Zachary what time to pick me up from the airport. These new flying rules are horrible. I feel like Rip Van Winkle with everything that changed while I was out. What's all this taking off your shoes and folks with purple plastic gloves patting all over you? I'm almost an old woman. What exactly do they think I'm going to do?

There I go again: another subject for another time.

In mid-November 2010, I left Chicago and arrived in what had been my hometown for a few years. When you obey God, things fall into place even if to us it doesn't appear that's what it's doing. God knows what He's doing. *I* thought I was coming to Birmingham, Alabama, to help Gabrielle plan a wedding she and Zachary were taking much too long to move on. There was also that little unfinished legal matter between me and Mrs. Cecelia aka Cee-Cee Murphy, better known now as "the defendant."

So after a beautiful Christmas with Zachary and Gabrielle (not to leave out my biggest surprise of all, little Jasmine Noble, who can dance just as wonderfully as her mother Gabrielle), who would have guessed that at the beginning of 2011, all Hell would break loose. No, I did not cuss here. When I say Hell, I mean Hell in every biblical sense of the word with the devil, his imps, and the fire and brimstone. Well, all of Hell broke loose. It's definitely what you would call the *other* side of divine.

God knows in advance of spiritual warfare when prayer warriors are needed to be called to arms and in place. God sent me to Birmingham (the home of U.S. Steel that helped give Birmingham its nickname The Magic City because of how fast the city grew, although some say it was because of the smog that caused the city to seemingly disappear then "magically" appear again), for such a time as this and . . .

You know what? Instead of me telling you everything, why don't I just let you see for yourself?

Chapter 1

The light of the body is the eye: if therefore thine eye be single, thy whole body shall be full of light.

—Matthew 6:22

"All right, Jasmine, spell energetic," fifty-eight-year-old Esther Crowe said as she and soon-to-be-ten-year-old Jasmine Noble sat on the couch in the den wearing their matching red Minnie Mouse shirts.

Jasmine smiled as she correctly spelled the word without even the slightest hesitation. Her brownish/black hair was pulled up into a cute little ponytail, her hair having grown tremendously in the thirteen months since her successful bone marrow transplant. Jasmine giggled. "Okay, Miss C," Jasmine said, calling her by the special name she'd given Miss Crowe as she'd done with Zachary, in calling him Dr. Z, and Gabrielle, whom she'd once called Miss G before calling her Mama. "Now it's your turn."

Miss Crowe placed her hand on her chest. "My

turn? How did I end up getting a turn? I'm not the one who has a spelling test tomorrow."

"Are you ready? Because this is going to be a long and tricky one that *always* seems to mess me up."

Miss Crowe nodded. She'd been a middle school teacher many years ago and there was nothing that put a smile on her face more than watching a child with an uncontained hunger for learning. "Hit me with your best shot, Miss Jazz."

Jasmine giggled again. "Okay, your word is Mississippi."

"Mississippi?"

Jasmine grinned and tilted her head to the side. "Yep. Mississippi."

A big smile spread across Miss Crowe's face. She repeated the word again, and then began. "Mississippi. M-i-crooked letter-crooked letter-i-crooked letter-crooked letter-i-humpback-humpback-i."

Jasmine was cracking up with laughter as she tossed her head back, falling back onto the sofa. "What?"

"You said Mississippi so I spelled Mississippi," Miss Crowe said. "Have you never heard it spelled that way before?"

Jasmine rolled onto the floor, kneeling as she giggled madly. "I most certainly have not. Crooked letter crooked letter, humpback humpback-i?"

Miss Crowe was laughing now as well. "Yes. Crooked letter-crooked letter"—she drew the letter S in the air with her index finger twice—"humpback-humpback"—she then drew two letter P's—"i," she said while cocking her head to one side and folding her arms like a rapper who'd just successfully delivered a rap.

Jasmine got up and sat back on the couch next to Miss Crowe. "That was *too* funny."

"Well, that's some of the things we did in the old

days to help people learn to spell difficult words. The next time you have a need to spell Mississippi, you can sing that song in your mind, and you'll get it right every time, no problem."

Gabrielle Mercedes walked into the den. "Hey, you two. How are you feeling, Jasmine?"

Jasmine ran to Gabrielle's opened arms and hugged her. "Mama!"

Gabrielle smiled. There was nothing like hearing those words, especially after all they'd been through in the span of just a little over a year.

There was Jasmine's lifesaving bone marrow transplant at the end of December 2009. Then Jasmine's adoptive mother Jessica Noble died of cancer on March 30, 2010, which of all days was also Jasmine's birthday.

Jessica had desperately wanted to tell Jasmine that she *was* adopted. Sadly, she ended up taking her last breath before getting a chance. And as if that wasn't enough, in May of that same year, Gabrielle finally told Jasmine she'd been adopted by the Nobles before Jasmine learned in July, in the most horrific way, that Gabrielle was not merely a friend of the family as she'd been led to believe, but instead, her birth mother. "The mother who didn't want her and had given her away," as she overheard it carelessly blurted out from the mouth of the beautiful Paris Simmons-Holyfield.

Yes, it had been a journey all right, all coming to a climax November 2010 with the court's final approval of Gabrielle's adoption of Jasmine just as Gabrielle's beloved Miss Esther Crowe waltzed back into her life, vowing not to leave until she'd physically witnessed wedding vows exchanged between her very own nephew and the one some liked to call "the daughter she never had."

And now, it was a new year, 2011—a new season in every sense of the word. Engaged and come June 11, 2011, Gabrielle was set to wed the most amazing man: Dr. Zachary Wayne Morgan. For once, things were finally coming together . . . finally starting to look up.

Gabrielle strolled over to the couch and gave Miss Crowe a hug. "How did things go with the two of you today?"

"I told you that Jasmine and I would be fine. This baby is never a problem."

"I keep telling you I'm *not* a baby!" Jasmine said vehemently but with total respect toward an adult in her tone.

Miss Crowe pulled Jasmine over to her and hugged her. "I know, baby. I know. You're not a baby. Got it!"

"You just did it again!" Jasmine laughed and hugged Miss Crowe back.

"Sorry, baby. I know you're growing up into a big girl." Miss Crowe rocked her several times before letting her go. "But you'll always be my baby. Just like Gabrielle will always be my baby." Miss Crowe slowly shook her head. "It's amazing. I first met Gabrielle when she was around eight years old. And the first time I met you was when you were just a little past eight. That's something, isn't it?"

"Actually, I was nine and a half when we first met," Jasmine said.

Gabrielle placed her hand on Jasmine's head. "Close enough. That would be considered a little past eight."

Jasmine grinned. "Me and Miss C had a great time today."

"Miss C and *I* had a great time today," Miss Crowe corrected.

Jasmine rolled her head in a circular motion. "Well, whichever way, we had a great time today." Jasmine looked at Gabrielle. "She helped me with all of my spelling words, so I'm ready to ace my test tomorrow."

"So you're feeling well enough to go to school tomorrow?" Gabrielle asked. "Because if you don't—"

"I'm fine," Jasmine said. "Now ask me how to spell Mississippi."

"Mississippi? Was that one of your words?" Gabrielle asked. "I don't recall seeing that one on your list."

"No. But go on. Ask me how to spell it."

"Okay," Gabrielle said as she glanced at Miss Crowe, who was also grinning like she'd eaten Tweety the bird. "Jasmine, please spell Mississippi."

Jasmine promptly spelled it the way Miss Crowe had shown her. She flopped down on the couch and giggled hard.

Gabrielle placed her hand on top of Jasmine's head. "That was good. I've heard people do that before. So I see you're learning all kinds of tricks from one of the best teachers around." Gabrielle glanced Miss Crowe's way and winked. "Well, I'm going upstairs to change."

"Dinner's ready. Miss C and I cooked," Jasmine said.

"Is that right? Well, I see you two have been quite busy today."

"May we eat in the dining room?" Jasmine said with her hands in a prayer mode. "Please, please, please."

"Sure," Gabrielle said. "Why have a dining room if we're not going to use it?"

"Yay! I'll set the table." Jasmine ran toward the dining room.

"Being around her is making me so much younger," Miss Crowe said. "I'll be back to my twenties at this rate. But she's such a precious and such a beautiful child, inside and out."

"Thanks. And I concur. She really is, although I can't take much credit for the terrific little girl she's become. Her adoptive parents laid a wonderful foundation with her. I'm merely maintaining and building on that."

"Now don't cut your contribution short. Jasmine has a lot of your genes running around inside of her. That child reminds me so much of you," Miss Crowe said, shaking her head. "Especially when it comes to dancing. I've nicknamed her Happy Feet after that penguin in that movie." Miss Crowe did a few tap dancing steps.

"Well, I'm going to go and change into something more comfortable so we can have dinner in the dining room. I appreciate you so much for keeping Jasmine today. She wanted to go to school, but that shot she received yesterday caused her to have a fever. And I knew, even if I *had* let her go to school as she was begging for me to do, they would have sent her right back home. Besides, I don't want to take any chances, not when it comes to her health." Gabrielle shook her head.

"You don't have to explain anything to me. I've told you that I'm here to help out in any way that I can," Miss Crowe said. "It didn't make sense for you to take off work when I'm at your disposal."

"But I don't want to be imposing upon you, either."

Miss Crowe waved Gabrielle's comment away. "Child, please. I was laid up for over ten years. I've gotten all the rest one old woman needs for at least the next ten years. I'm ready to be useful again. And being here with the two of you is the best medicine any doctor could prescribe."

"I don't know why you keep calling yourself old. You're not old," Gabrielle said.

"I know late fifties isn't considered old these days,

but believe me: I really am getting close to being a senior citizen—there's no two ways about that. And in case you didn't know, you can get an AARP card at fifty. But being here, surrounded by you and Jasmine, makes me feel young again. You can't buy what the three of us generate. We're three true dancers from the heart."

"I'll be back in a few. I'm going to put on my Minnie Mouse shirt so then we can be the three *Mouse*keteers." Gabrielle went upstairs.

Five minutes later, the doorbell rang. "I got it!" Miss Crowe yelled, mainly for Gabrielle's benefit. She quickly made her way to the door and cracked it open about the size of her small framed body. "Yes?"

"Good evening, miss," the older gentleman with a small patch of white, off centered in the top of his black hair, said. "I'm sorry. I'm looking for a Ms. Gabrielle Mercedes. Is this the right house?" He looked down at the index card that trembled slightly in his hand.

"That depends," Miss Crowe said. "Who are you?"

The man smiled. "My name is Benjamin. But everybody calls me Bennie."

"Bennie?" Miss Crowe said with a frown.

"Yes, ma'am."

"And might you possess a last name you'd care to disclose while you're passing out your first name?" Miss Crowe gave the dressed-down gentleman (wearing light brown pants and a crisp long-sleeved white shirt, incidentally with no coat, even though it was the dead of winter) a slow, methodical once-over just in case she might need to give a police description later.

Bennie flashed a full grin, showing that he wasn't missing any of his teeth as far as his grin extended. "Yes, ma'am, I most certainly do. It's—"

"Booker," Gabrielle said as she stepped up behind Miss Crowe and opened the door wider. She looked him dead in his eyes. "Hello"—she took a long hard swallow, one that could be heard as it went down— "Daddy."